FRAGMENTED *BODIES*

RONNIE BROWN

CRANTHORPE
MILLNER
PUBLISHERS

First published by Cranthorpe Millner Publishers (2025)

ISBN 978-1-80378-253-9 (Paperback)

www.cranthorpemillner.com

Cranthorpe Millner Publishers

Printed and bound by CPI Group (UK) Ltd
Croydon, CR0 4YY

For Roddy and Jane Gordon and the music.

'I believe cats to be spirits come to earth.
A cat, I'm sure, could walk on a cloud without coming through…'

Jules Verne

'After all, what's a life anyway…?'

E.B. White

Chapter 1

'Where is tomorrow? In another world.'
- Night Thoughts, Edward Young

They loaded the white van; Mo and Byron were ready. They went for breakfast at Bettys Café, the tea rooms in Harrogate, where they made a fuss of the waitress and complimented the staff. They needed to be noticed.

The very notion of the Imperial Suite caused Byron to rail against Imperial figures and their statues. (Byron had been reading a scholarly book on the British Empire.) The Café Imperial location was indeed grand. Traces of the British Empire's presence were everywhere in England, informally and otherwise, from the Commonwealth to cricket, Westminster to Harrogate. Nowhere was it more apparent than in the press and recent politics. Its opulence was revealed in a café in Harrogate.

A short discussion about cricket and empire was interrupted by breakfast. With a mouthful of food Mo switched from Harrogate and cricket to The Imperial Hotel Delhi, the stuff of romance and detective fiction, a symbol of murder, looting, English exceptionalism and white supremacy. Mo had been there.

"Still relevant today," Mo remarked savouring the Swiss

breakfast Rösti. In Mo's opinion, it was superlative, well in keeping with their new status. Mo's ambitions leaned towards a career in academe.

The Gruyere and cream with pan-fried grated potatoes, poached egg, mushrooms, dry-cured bacon and tomato was 'mouth wateringly' good.

Byron's English breakfast couldn't compare with the comfortable continuity of the greasy spoon the NAAFI had served up, though both had their merits. One word sufficed: awesome, the coarsely grated potatoes, the cheese adding a touch of difference to Mo's Rösti.

The waitress accepted the 'handsome gratuity', as Mo called it, with a smile. They were noticed. Alibi-related memory would help their case; their regular visits meant they didn't fall into the once-seen stranger category.

The hit was twenty-five minutes away.

During their next visit to Harrogate, when they had time to kill, it was to be eggs Benedict. Despite the tattoos and Mo's nose ring, the waitress thought they were lovely. In the van parked across the common the rifle was wrapped up. The genteel aspect worked well; the waitress would remember them.

Byron drove. "Mo, after all the years of killing – faceless victims, some innocents, some scum – now someone I feel I know."

"A minor celeb, that's all, a scribbler and wit. Are you getting wet feet?"

Byron thought about it, about permissible victims. They were always 'one of them', never 'one of us'. How different was an individual victim to the faceless victims of war, a person rather than a statistic? "This is an academic – one of us."

Mo nodded but remained silent. Byron spoke again.

"He seems vulnerable. He's a comrade, an individual. I feel I know him."

Only then did Mo respond. "Max was an individual, and a child."

They drove into Otley. The quarry's situation in the middle of a terrace meant it would be difficult to enter the place without the neighbours seeing them. Their instructions insisted on a straight kill. Sensory deprivation, religious humiliation and plain old torture were out in this case, though some, a minority, took licence. This hit didn't have a religion.

Both were obedient soldiers, most of the time, both were good at their jobs, and both were well practised with their own version of doubling. Reverting back to 'normal' was not an issue for them. As Mo put it, "It's us or them!"

The lights at the Black Horse crossing showed red. "Yes, it's our just world, Byron."

Byron wasn't sure what was meant by that. Was there a hint of sarcasm in the word *just*?

They moved off along the A659 and pulled into the car park behind the Cross Pipes pub. They waited in position. Mo hadn't quite given in to the one-shot-no-torture brief – not even torment.

Jim had authorised the hit, but Jim was a fool who got himself killed. A fierce academic curiosity bothered Byron about Jim's demise. Mo seemed less concerned. Jim was gone, another statistic. It was a job; it paid well. That the target seemed so important to the client made Mo laugh. He was a nonentity, a bit writer, and the money was good.

Byron wanted to disagree with the first part. Mo's comment comparing him to Paris Hilton was unfair. Although he did appear to crave notoriety, there was some substance there.

His early success as a writer encouraged the media with their Dr Death slant. He was toxic; toxic this and toxic that – the very use of the word was toxic. "*The Parable of the Poisoned Arrow* or *Poison for Arrows*," Byron said, deeming both to be relevant. "The media aimed such at their perceived audience preference and aimed to satisfy their prurience. Why on Earth do they caricature assassins and academics?" No answer came from Mo.

Byron, following politicians and Penny, answered, "It's character assassination." Byron saw the hit as a person who had risen from nothing to something, then shrugged it off. Edith Stein's work on empathy came to mind. Empathy hurts, and there was no room for such. We must check to see if his book is in the university library."

Mo muttered something about confusion and rhetorical questions then clammed up.

Both missed *The Tableaux Twins* book launch at Headingly Bookfest due to a job. His talk was reported widely, the press hounds baying for a bone. He gave them it, the whole skeleton and the marrow. How accurate their reportage, was questionable. A colleague informed Byron the talk was sensitive and tasteful. The upbeat moments were more to do with the publication history, the plot, plus his own incidental moment, the point of no turning back. Byron was a discerning reader; Mo suffered a tortured mind.

A bullet from a high-powered rifle in the right place could mean a slow death. Alternatively, it might offer a chance to live. Could that be classed as torment? Bleeding-out can take five minutes or more. It would be foolhardy to interrogate him on his back doorstep, so one shot it was. The kill meant leaving the facts of Jim's death as an unknown. Their debates on the matter were heated and endless.

Mo finally spoke. There's an element of risk. I recall a moment in Afghanistan when you said we eliminate possibility."

"Correct. We could plan further."

They had done several dry runs, but much depended on how busy the car park was. Chance was always going to be an issue, and they'd worked hard to eliminate possibilities. They checked the car park on several consecutive mornings. Their recce was rigorous. Early mornings on weekdays a few cars were left, and for an hour or so the designated space was free. The space was near to the exit. Others would do, though a speedy exit might be necessary. They deduced that early morning was it; that was their window.

A car had pulled out as they entered the car park and now it was empty. Usually, two or three cars were behind the pub and not a soul around. "It's all in the prep," Byron said, denying their good luck.

Their intelligence, or as Mo called it snooping, told them the hit was inside quite a lot. He was also out for long hours during the day. His patterns appeared random, his progress through life the same. His randomness confused them. Marksmanship was one thing, field craft another.

"He always uses the back door," Mo had confirmed. If he chose this route now, their position offered a view of the target, which was excellent. Byron was not assured by Mo's assertion, however. Their target was a man of contradictions.

The car park was quiet. They parked as planned — as far away from the house as possible — the back door of the van left ajar. A discussion on rifles followed. Mo positioned the rifle, Byron's old Arctic series rifle resting it on a sandbag just inside the door. "She's up there with the best, Byron." Mo patted the stock lovingly. "Made in Britain."

"The SPx-80 is bloody good too," Byron added, then settled down.

They waited. One shot should suffice. The rifle was stashed in a black polythene sheet, then put back under the painting and decorating materials. If disturbed, there was access to the front of the van through the rear. The rest, they would have to improvise. What's a kill without risk? The prey (they avoided using a name for academic reasons) was a man of interest. That had to put that aside. For Byron, it was better he was a stranger. Byron thought deeply. *We are strangers.*

They were aware of the changes in society, one where strangers abound. Mo, drawing on academic texts, painted the world as a 'sea of strangers'. Neither wished to be a media event; rather to earn good money and remain incognito. Anonymity was good. They sought no publicity but were happy, however, to play on media effect as a camouflage; to make the killings appear unplanned or the work of crazy vigilantes.

They had a clear view of the back door across a small

lawn raised about seven or eight feet above the car park. A silver-grey cat had positioned itself on the window ledge, enjoying the morning sun. A shiver of anxiety showed on Byron's face as the cat stretched and looked across to the van. Their target was in the kitchen and in Mo's sights. Then Penny moved. Unlocking the back door, the target stepped out to savour a bright nippy November morning which promised showers. Mo focused.

Byron urged, "Take the shot, now!"

The sun had burned the damp mist away. It was quiet. They heard his mobile ring as he opened the door. He turned back in the half-open doorway to pick it up.

Mo lowered the rifle. "Shit." Mo focused again. Lining up the sights, Mo aimed at the kitchen window above the sink, preparing to shift immediately to the back door if he reappeared. Their reconnaissance proved accurate. He was aimless. He disappeared from sight, then reappeared.

Mo wasn't aimless. The shot was possible through the window, the target bobbing around with his phone to his ear. That would be demanding, a challenge. The open door implied he was coming back. It had to be one shot, and it had to hit the target. Suppositions were the victim's territory. The philosophy of supposition would fill in their evenings, the disagreements heated.

"Not long to wait now, Byron." Mo held the rifle steady, then focused the sights on the cat for a second and leered. The cat stirred as if aware of an unwanted presence. Cats can sense death. Arching its back, and hissing, it jumped down onto the lawn out of sight.

A moment of anxiety occurred for Byron then the cold

tremor passed. The association with cats, darkness, and death should have suited them symbolically, but no, cats were aloof and unsettling. Dogs were hateful, cats demonic. Their aloofness was disconcerting and, for Byron, their presence frightening.

A battered green car pulled into the car park. The car was directly below the line of fire. A stocky-built man climbed out, followed by a beanpole of a man. They both stretched. The beanpole reached in the back and lifted out an old, brown leather suitcase, the kind one can only buy in retro shops, tan-brown leather, a period piece, and well cared for. He seemed to be looking straight at them. He stared momentarily at the van; he shielded his eyes from the sun.

Inside, Mo rested the rifle on a sandbag. Without a word, the beanpole placed the old suitcase down and began to walk the thirty or so yards in a straight line towards the van. Byron was issuing orders to Mo at machinegun rate. "Abort, Abort." The rifle was withdrawn, the van doors closed abruptly, and Byron was behind the driving seat in a second. Neither could fathom out why he was walking toward the van in the direct line of fire, taking his time, yet to them, eating up the ground with his stride.

The stocky figure stood still and was staring toward them. The taller one stopped. That second's pause gave them time to get moving. He couldn't have seen them; the sun was behind the van and in his eyes. The shorter one's hand was reaching into what looked like an old naval-issue bag.

The silver-grey cat leaped down from the lawn through the railings into the car park and snarled; his back arched, his ears flattened, and his tail was erect. Byron shivered violently.

The cat moved across the car park towards the van, then stopped still and shook himself as if shaking off a raindrop. As the van drove away at pace, Mo caught a glimpse of the beanpole who turned to see the cat. Did he see them? The cat may have done them a favour.

They turned right past the pub and into Otley town centre. No one followed.

Byron dropped Mo off at work five minutes away. Nothing was said. They shifted everything into their work van. Byron drove away to ditch the stolen van. The back lane off Pool Road was quiet, Knotford Nook deserted. They might leave it there for a day and see if any notices appeared. It could be useful. Travellers used the land by the roadside, and wagons were often randomly parked there.

The disappointment of the failed hit and the adrenalin rush dissipated. Deflation, disappointment and questions remained. What the fuck happened? Could some fine-tuning have resolved it? Plenty of time to work things out. *Success is failure turned inside out.* Coincidence was also at work. The random lifesaver mocked them; it had no reason.

Who were the two men? Did one of them smell danger? Byron concluded that it was best not to connect the dots.

Chapter 2

The anonymous postcard dropped through the letterbox a week before. The nameless sender had read Penny's *Tableaux* book. That was obvious from the unnamed sender's comments. Direct references to the Ophelia and Chatterton postcards sent by the Burns' to Penny were unmentioned, though implicit in the text: '*The world before us is a postcard…*' in brackets, the author's name, Mary Pearson. Following this strange quote, 'We are not that far away. A postcard from elsewhere. A painting and a poem'. A few words of verse followed: '*Midst skulls and coffins, epitaphs and worms.*' This sent Penny scurrying to the Internet. A book order followed.

Penny wanted to communicate with the card sender. He'd quoted the latter poem previously in his book; a verse dedicated to the graveyard tree, the yew.

No name, no address. The second card made mention of Margaret Attwood's poem *Postcards*. It spoke to Penny of mischief and showed a knowledge of verse. It sent him on a trail to read postcard poems and fret about the author of the messages. He discerned an element of sniping in the cards, yet they didn't seem petty in nature. There was rhythm, line and imagery.

His scholastic nature desired to know the author; the author wished to remain anonymous. He teased himself and concentrated on the text. Surely the author is a 'scriptor', a producer? It was for him to explain the meaning. This one knew their stuff. He thought, *this one is educated*. But the card said we. He thought of the real meaning of dual authorship and the many meanings a passage can have.

The writer appeared to be saying something important. A warning? Hello? Or was he, the reader, assigning meaning? He put them down, suppressing a laugh. Postcards are pleasant. He tried to recall the last time a letter had dropped through his door. In a few words, a postcard can advertise, say 'wish you were here', offer warmth. But from where? From whom? Wish you were where? Was it co-authored?

Did the writer want to avoid judgement? He tried to avoid making a connection between anonymity and abusive behaviour. A book reviewer had made snide comments about the *Tableaux* book and left no signature. Penny suspected a person from his past, a grudge, and tried to put a name to the writer. He was familiar with the negative trait in academe: the scornful, the inferiority feeling, old rivalries, jealousy and envy.

Was the sender simply impish, responding to his own puckish sense of humour? Was the sender of a nasty nature, shadowy, hiding in the crowd? There was no hint of toxicity, only slanted references. The sender was articulate and, in his opinion, hooded. Perhaps the sender just didn't want to let people know who they were? That put a cap on that. They had access to personal stuff also; personal information on the Internet was readily available.

Was it Lance? Doxing was more likely his kind of game. He wondered why Lance hadn't dipped into revenge porn… yet. He'd read that some had multiple victims. On reflection, his own sex life offered no chance. From the top down, partial lies abounded. He allowed himself a what-if moment. Deepfake technology would be more Lance's thing. Perish the thought.

He replied through his blog. Two can play. He posted one verse, doggerel: 'The Bone Orchard'. He made it up on the spur of the moment and regretted it instantly. It was now out there in the public domain. It belonged to them, the public. 'Carved epitaphs, dark refrains, headstones battered by the rain… lost songs and lyrics undiscovered, in the graveyard of lost songs and lovers'. Graveyard doggerel.

He pondered about copycats. Had the senders read *The Tableaux Twins*? Anxiety crept in. He fretted further over his knee-jerk reaction, his poor ability with verse, the ambiguity of the bone orchard. Then he closed his laptop and picked up the paper, the crossword only half completed, and went downstairs. He stuck his crossword pencil (it allowed him to make errors or mistakes and erase them) behind his ear in memory of times past: market traders and older folk. He stopped short at licking the lead point. He had forgone the crossword to make a 'fuck-it' list – places he didn't want to visit, things he definitely didn't want to do. (Bahrain, watching cricket.)

His scholastic side was bothering him. He desired to write more freely, to reconstruct the past differently, resolve the problems of the past, in the present, in writing. Imagine history with a feelgood ending? Not really.

If he were going to celebrate heroes and villains, he would create them himself, fashioned from those who might recognise themselves, not some fucking caped crusader from Eton, Roedean School or both. Artoria or Arthur, 'twas all the same. He loved *Marvel* and *DC Comics*. He just didn't like public or independent schools. Writing was important to him, not only in terms of his academic pride but myth-busting also. Not averse to creating myths himself, his own backstory read like a creation myth – dual authorship. Snipers are usually fairly stable in terms of emotions.

"Anybody home?" The door was open. In Penny's mind the greeting contained a hint of the sardonic.

"Come in, Dove, kettle's boiled."

Dove had clocked the number of the van. Periwinkle turned back and collected his Gladstone bag from the boot. With his brown leather suitcase in one hand, bag in the other, he followed Dove. The cat brushed against his leg. He bent down and stroked it.

Dove turned and grunted, "What was that about?"

"Tell you when we get inside." Periwinkle gave a guess-what glance as they walked up the steps the few yards to Ronnie's. As they did, they heard the kettle whistling. Dove was still clutching the gun in his bag. He heard Penny chanting:

"Think you're so criminal… I'm the bad guy…" He stopped singing. Three cups stood ready as they entered the back kitchen. Dove eyed Penny: he signalled to Periwinkle to say something. Penny indicated the cups and went into the living room. Both his friends looked concerned.

Penny looked quizzical, sat down with his cuppa, stretched his legs and looked from one to the other. "What?"

The silver-grey cat had moved to the windowsill and was staring in, his head moving sideways and upwards as the three men spoke.

This looks serious.

Chapter 3

Mo and Byron deliberated. They went back over their notes. His public face gave them some idea of his movements; his blog was helpful as a profile. He often left the house about 10:30 a.m. They needed to rethink the hit. If the tall man had seen them, then the alarm bell will have been sounded. They could now put a name to the visitors: Dove and Periwinkle, private investigators, and friends to Penny.

Their surveillance indicated he was in his study early morning, probably working on his writing, or his blog, which he appeared to enjoy for its reverse chronology (sometimes), and much earlier if he was researching (sometimes). The conclusion to the plot begins the story: random, chaotic, lucky. They aimed to change the latter.

A new world had emerged for Penny; one of digital audio files and public appearances. His occasional podcast revealed the quirky, the macabre. His take on current events, both sardonic and challenging, were aired alongside amateurish songwriting, mostly verse — as he saw it, doggerel. *The Figurative Doggerel Spot* was an intended feature in a column, also never realised. It was to be a departure from the literal and prose. He made notes about the pathetic ballad *Mary's*

Ghost. He had a different pathetic in mind.

Mo and Byron, the real snipers, agreed that pathetic ballads were better for country music, a genre they had little time for. Indeed, they had little time for genre and its organising principles. As new academics, register was the buzzword. Too many impurities in genre.

During their surveillance, private information had leaked onto the Web courtesy of the anonymous Wedjet. They read it but chose to ignore it. Not that shallow, Byron concluded that it was bitter.

Wedjet was to play a part.

Penny's excuse for his verses was that they were for posterity, not the usual warts-and-all defence, which he found pitiful. Yet they were warts and all in their 'painting'. He wasn't sure of his own voice, which sounded fine in his head, not on the air. His blog allowed him a safety valve and a space to air his opinions on anything. In the media he found a suitable replacement for academia, his humour, his opinions, of which there were many, along with anecdotes from his back catalogue: politics, police and past reminiscences.

His satire, *Breakfast Means Breakfast* on Brexit, mingled his love of bad puns with parody. Many of his anecdotes had a sort of illusory untruth effect (Penny's take) — that is, folk didn't really know whether to believe them or not! Many of the tales sounded fictional. His colour-coding blog was a winner.

Was it true? He counted the hits daily. Despite a growing

number, he would be overcome with doubt. His earlier experiences in Carshalton with the twins and later with the Loftus werewolf helped him question the truth of everything. The victims' bodies still haunted his dreams. He was scared to follow that all the way. He toyed with the truth himself, as did others. Ah, the colour-coding story.

How many people had questioned the story of a man, Browne, who went to the doctors' in the 1970s. It was his first ever visit to a contemporary-style surgery. Browne had never visited anyone but a family doctor, a small surgery with a fish tank. He swore one of the fish had a plaster. Daunted, he entered the large new reception. He gave his name to the receptionist. She handed him a black tag with a number on it. He looked bewildered. "What do I do with this?" he enquired politely.

"You take the black tag around the corner and sit on a blue chair, and wait for a blue light to see Dr Green, Mr Browne."

Browne felt better, though decided to follow it through. The result was a rash of anecdotes about the worst doctor he'd ever come across: the bad Doctor Green. The rash was incurable. The listeners couldn't wait. Anything that satirised waiting for an appointment fed the Covid years' listeners. (He was careful to protect his beloved NHS at the same time.)

Underneath, he aimed for a serious point, but not always. Bloggers joined in. His anecdotes were popular. The blog was his platform – nine-and-three-quarters – a place with no barriers.

Mo and Byron listened. They recognised that underneath

the erudite passages, academic wit and emotion, he was often groping for words, unsure of himself. His statement that he was born with imposter syndrome struck a chord. They both enjoyed the cut and thrust and understood his problem. They had some sympathy though they saw it as a class thing.

He was enjoying himself. And he hoped he was imparting something educational. Sometimes was a key in everything. He was a self-appointed 'sometimer', definitely not a 'sometimey'.

Penny's art history talks were in danger of threatening mainstream television (or so he thought). No one offered him a slot. A bonus was a long message from Tammy. He treasured it and the fond memories of their meeting. He called her – same number. An email relationship began. He followed her research. Her first success in her viva voce inspired him to do a blog on her work. She loved it, and he began to love her messages. That her viva was on her fortieth birthday was the greatest present of all. She sailed through. She would treasure his *Tableaux Twins* book and saw *Dark Arts* to be 'food for thought', a comment he took to be deliberately ambiguous. He'd followed her work unknown to her, a form of academic stalking.

Tammy could see that Penny's involvement with the twins accounted for some of his earlier behaviour, his absence that day at the Tate. She decided to meet him again. It was to be a resounding moment.

His lunchtime talk at Tate Britain on his pet subject, representations of suicide, went well. Inevitably he was drawn into a discussion on the *Tableaux* publication and the nature of his writing in *Dark Arts: Fact and Fiction*. Tammy was there. To his statement that he was a writer of fiction, though fact meant something (he too could be ambiguous), she asked a question: "Do authors of fiction ever fall in love with one of their characters?" She added to it two more.

Penny thought hard about that and decided he loved them all but tried not to judge them. Then he thought of a cop out. "In a way it's a love/hate relationship." In truth he thought the book to be part fiction, part fact. The publisher encouraged some gap filling.

"How much of your writing is autofiction? What are you trying to avoid? "

He stumbled over the words. To the latter a lawsuit would have been the honest answer. To the former: "*The Tableaux Twins* wasn't a memoir, more an attempt to get inside the characters and plot." Then he wandered, dreaming of his own fiction. "The characters, Peter and Annabelle apart," he replied, "are hybrids, imaginative hybrids, I'd like to think. That included me. I asked the publisher if they would leave out the usual rider and say that if anyone thinks they recognise themselves in the story, seek help or hand yourself in to the nearest police station."

He tried again. "I see myself in several characters, myself apart. It's like looking in the mirror and seeing either your mum or dad. Tammy recognised his circularity, cause effect and nothingness. He was still suffering. His book signing at a major bookstore was an opportunity she missed due to a prior engagement — an interview. His panel events were hilarious, his take on famous artists heretical. His favourite rogue Gaugin was on the hit list as usual; a man used to luxury, deeply commercial and thinking only of selling… He echoed Pissarro's words, a man he respected. And, in keeping with honest academics, gave him a footnote. This was followed by a comment about selling and the price of the book.

What was nice for Tammy, with some reservations, was that this was a new man, a more relaxed person than the man she met at her talk. He was beginning to enjoy life, and he wanted to share that. She wasn't totally convinced he was there yet. He did keep looking over his shoulder, so to speak. He tried to qualify his thinking.

"It depends on the mood; it depends on change. As for the love aspect, the twins' story is both a fiction and a fact. I began to feel sympathy for Peter, and a strong desire for his wayward sister. Love? No. I hope I've managed to answer your questions." He avoided the cheesy answers about love, desire and want.

At the end he looked for her. She was gone. He hummed a Tom Wait's song as he packed up.

Often at night, he awoke in a sweat. The fact that Peter and Annabelle's images were trapped in a story now, held prisoner in publication, eased some of the trauma. The autofiction question troubled him. She was clever. When he wrote, could he avoid it? It was rhetorical. A certain amount of such felt liberating. Better, he thought, to make things up.

Then there was the van in the car park, the one that drove off quickly when Periwinkle decided to investigate.

Chapter 4

Tearing the legs off garden spiders was fun for a week or so. A dress rehearsal. Seven-year-old Byron caught bluebottles and practised tying their legs to a piece of cotton, the other end of the thread to a drawing pin. This required dexterity. Watching them fly in circles and buzz frantically was fun. That too became boring. School was tedious, classes stupid, bluebottles squished. That's what was told to the squaddies in the forces. They were prepared to put aside any questions, indeed it would've been risky to interrupt, and it kept them amused. Whether it was true or not didn't matter. Byron had clearly read up on psychopathy. One clever squaddie thought Byron too self-aware to be 'barmy'. Better to make things up?

Byron's stories detailed a graduation to ill treatment of animals. A self-confessed psycho? School was easy, top results followed. By the age of thirteen, the apprentice slaughterer detailed advanced methods of killing. Byron was highly intelligent.

The abuse continued, a Scots terrier from down the road blinded and left wandering. Other animals suffered too. Disgust, mingled with hate for animals and humans alike, flourished in the mind of a child, grew and expanded unhindered by parents and teachers. It was a CV that sounded fraudulent, a misrepresentation, but in the dry climate of Afghanistan and cold winters, the stories were never arid and, like the local food, spicy.

That is what was told to colleagues in the army. Byron's actions in the field reinforced the story. No one questioned it. It was going to be some years before the truth of Byron's background was uncovered.

Byron's ability to 'mentalise' was extraordinary; it was caring that appeared absent. At nine, an anti-intellectual, never realising it was simply another form of intellectualism, young Byron claimed to be a rare breed even among the many with personal disorders, a supreme manipulator, one able to throw shade over the misdemeanours. A headteacher thought young Byron was not just rare, but the rarest of the rare. And he meant it as a complement.

Quoted film tastes leaned towards *Misery*, though secretly *Brief Encounter* was a favourite. Is that bad taste? Prisoners were kept in dreams presented and rewritten, for Byron an intervention into history which was exciting and heart-warming.

The grown-up Byron listened to a podcast.

Raz'd from the book of Fame or more provoking,
Perchance some hackney hunger-bitten Scribbler
Insults thy memory and blots thy tomb
With long flat narrative, or duller rhymes…

That the author used it as a critique of his own writing

was typical. He was quite engaging and the quote teasing. He trawled the depths for snippets and his poetic references were many.

He thanked the anonymous postcards sender. He invited more. Interesting or not, he was their next victim. And they didn't mess up. Penny was a dead man.

Byron met Mo when they served in the army. Byron's reminiscences charted a 'progress' from cats to human killing. Mo's story was one of torture, a neighbour's pet cat tormented horribly and left to die. Crushing, combing, castration, de-nailing, disfiguring and mutilation all added to a growing CV that could have been very different. Teaming up with Mo had some sense of truth and inevitability, a later location being the prison educational wing where both studied Literature.

The squaddies and inmates who listened to tales of torture weren't sure of anything. They feared them both. A lack of empathy with others began to bind them together and helped them understand each other's feelings. Both detested animals and people, though Byron was less concerned about torture. A born sniper, Byron was clever enough to see other perspectives and deploy them. Both found people amusing or, more accurately, dense. Byron deemed Mo to be narcissistic and cruel. Mo teased Byron for being 'borderline'.

They had met before on a different playing field where level has no meaning. Missing out on the Beef War and along the way Tony Blair, they were in Helmand province,

Afghanistan – The Resolute Support Mission. Detainees were sport to both.

Both ended their careers with a pension and a dishonourable discharge. Both ended up in prison with a record that spoke of a catalogue of unspeakable violence on and off the field of battle, though some not proven: the killing of children who worked the poppy fields of Afghanistan, the beating and torture of detainees never substantiated. Two offences were proven, Byron guilty of cruelty, though the case for cruel bravery was argued; Mo mistreated a prisoner.

Mo heard a quote from Pascal's *Thoughts* and looked it up. Mo was a hunter, a sadist, a soldier who wanted something, but no one was sure what it was. Mo was the 'glory and the scum'. Mo was thinking scum. Six years in prison followed. Legally disallowed from purchasing a firearm, they turned to education. Dismissal with disgrace and confinement certainly bumped up their résumé. They were the bad guys. They still managed lighter sentences than they deserved.

In prison they made a play of not knowing each other, then teamed up soon after they settled in, became model inmates, and attended classes in everything. They excelled in literature. They learnt from each other. Their critical skills and the Covid pandemic earned them an early release. Mo's superstitious nature saw their coming together as a sign, and the two slowly but surely began to form an alliance, one based on a shared cruelty, a love of killing, and a loathing for those around them in prison, a hatred that they cloaked with some finesse. A meaningful relationship. They both attended a painting and decorating course and showed a flair for the work.

The trade itself would be very useful to them in civvy street. Their legal representation had been first-class, and the sentences reduced with every chance of a probationary period. They both gained a first degree in their time inside and were looking at master's courses when the time came for release. They were watching television and laughing noisily at an ad for Help for Heroes when news of their release came through. Byron was testing out their grasp of newly acquired linguistic skills, the old trooper expletives thrown in for good measure. "Heroes my arse, victims you mean. Fuck, that's a linguistic shift if ever there was one."

"What is a hero?" Mo cackled and affected a limp, whistling, dragging a leg across the floor while playing an imaginary flute.

"You're an animal, Mo. To think you studied the Romantic poets for three years."

Mo was quick to reply. "I'm a fucking hero! Look at me. I killed more of the enemy than the Spitfire, more than the Dambusters. And I came out unscathed! Then again, the latter didn't kill the enemy, did they?"

Who the enemy were was debatable. Byron despised everyone, including Mo. They were yet to form their true partnership, one based on expedience and market prospects outside. They were organised, clever and capable of social intercourse – to a point. Byron and Mo were narcissistic, conniving and glib. Both knew how to play the system. They were also ruthless murderers, and on their way to freedom with a business plan. Two business plans in truth, one was a painting and decorating business, the other assassination. Price Matching? Price undercutting? They went for high, matching and undercutting made redundant for justification… You want the best?

Byron left the prison in late August access. A month after, Mo followed. Both went straight into an access course which focused on literature. It would provide the would-be assassins a cover, though there was a genuine interest, particularly in the Graveyard Poets, one that yearned to re-establish their meaning for the twenty-first century. Neither needed an access course, but it looked good.

On successful completion of their courses, they applied to do a Masters' degree as mature applicants. They stunned the differing selection committees with their knowledge and grasp of literature, and especially their keen interest in poetry. The Prisoner's Education Trust and other bodies of a liberal nature funded them; the universities saw their inclusion as a plus in widening participation. Indeed, it was. Both had graduated with first-class honours inside.

Filtering wasn't a help. Offenders committing crimes of violence or otherwise have to declare their guilt – covering up is illegal. In this instance, the Rehabilitation of Offenders Act worked for them, nevertheless. The benevolent gods of widening participation and desire for revenue meant they were going to get a place anyway.

By agreement, they chose differing universities in the same city and moved in together. Leeds was convenient. Leeds was the thirty-second safest metropolitan district in England when placed in order of the theft crime rate. The district fared better in terms of violent crime – twenty-ninth. Byron reminded Mo there were only thirty-six. They aimed to change all that.

On the side, they bought a van and did some painting and decorating. It allowed them access to homes. It was an ideal front for their genuine business. It supplemented the small grants and made them look good. Testimony to their bipolarity helped their case. It works wonders in the new age of enlightenment. That they faked it was by the by. Munchausen's syndrome might have been a better diagnosis, but still an error. Mo had read misdiagnosis by Depression and Bipolar Support Alliance was rife. Easy – circular insanity, manic depression then bipolarity. Outside they threw off the burden of illness; threw away the antipsychotics and went to work.

Prison had served them well. Mo was a fast worker. Byron did the finishing, the big picture and the detail. Frustrated by the paint work and enthralled by the killing, they relished the intellectual demands of university life. Disposing of Ronnie Penny 'as they wished' was a welcome contract. They so wanted to enjoy it. Two separate clients had commissioned the killing. The first had offered a reasonable sum '… to dispose of in whatever way, Ronnie Penny'. Dove and Periwinkle could follow as a separate contract '… if they wished'. How casual was that? The stocky man in the car park they could now put a face to, and the beanpole.

They were less concerned about Dove and his lanky comrade Periwinkle. The notion of a conflict between ex-SAS and their seafaring sister the SBS would be a test of their skills. On land they would certainly have an advantage. Killing Penny was going to be fun and profitable. They would have done it for free. They owed him. The science of revenge is complicated, for them it was just desserts. They wanted to make it last and enjoy it – a dessert, a sweet, a pudding, depending on where you come from. Dessert might require a fork or a knife. Both knew how to use them.

On the quiet, Byron did enjoy his talks and would miss them. Sometimes the job threw up moral aspects. They were easy to reconcile. Their time serving queen and country taught them how to disengage, both from battle and bloodshed. They laughed together about collateral damage and surgical strikes and were in tears with servicing a target. They had no wish to sanitise their language or blame others. Displacement was for cowards; killing was an individual thing. Neither wished to share blame with the other. Mo referred to the Catholic Church's moral disengagement, Byron referred to the 'Bobo Doll' experiments and offered a skewed take on an academic study by Bandura that they lived in shit and 'gross violence and adapted'. That finished the conversation.

The message to them via post box was clear and arrived before Jim's unfortunate demise by an assassin. Details of Jim's demise in the woods at Handale were unclear. The very thought of a cat mauling them caused Byron nausea, and acute anxiety. A musky smell would invade the senses, and a queasiness which Byron understood was the smell of a big cat, the scent of fear.

If anything happens to me, dispose of Penny! It must be Jim.

The second client was anonymous, the fee a bonus. To them two contracts smacked of an offer, the assassins equivalent of buy-one-get-one-free. No trades union could achieve such.

The big cat issue worried them and wasn't clear. It increased by leaps and bounds their mutual fear and hatred for the feline species. To boot, they both found the story of Jim's death flawed. They would relish questioning Penny under some duress. Who had actually done the job?

Cats died quite regularly over the weeks of their preparation. One has to keep one's hand in. This was going to be enjoyable.

The second brief simply wanted his removal. It was the basic wage for the job. Thank you, Tony Blair. The contractor was anonymous. That it fell into their hands was an odd coincidence; on completion, the money paid to them in full via a box number. Yet, they were curious who the second offer was from. Payment for doing what one loves negated the curiosity. And they did like their job. How many people can boast that?

Their academic studies were going well. Both were scoring good grades. Prison had given them what the army and civvy street couldn't. Both took good advantage of it. Both enjoyed the cut and thrust of academia. Outside of that they did their reconnaissance on their target, Penny. Troublesome as he was, their incentive to destroy the man strengthened as their enquiries revealed that Penny was a popular figure, well liked, barring some old colleagues who were envious of his success and his ability to bounce back. That made it all the better. Torture, Mo argued, should definitely be a part of the job. Fuelled by hatred, they formed a stronger bond, neither suffering low self-esteem, neither were lonely or insecure. They hated.

On the side, Byron found Penny interesting.

Mo learnt from Byron, who offered a less destructive profile. Jealously guarding the past, Mo offered a precis from which a more covert person emerged, one more able to fly under the radar, more comfortable in the shadows. Mo's characteristics were different, defiant, oppositional, but channelled often into classroom questions, which the teachers thought intriguing. When caught misbehaving, Mo's ability to feign regret and disguise the disregard for others, was worthy of a scholarship to RADA. When a bullying classmate, Max Smith, was flattened and kicked in the balls, it was Max who received the ticking off for bullying. Charm won out, plain old lying charm. Peer pressure meant nothing. Comrades accepted the story, and in the field the certifiable characteristics were borne out. Both were legend. One or two bright sparks assumed legend a keyword. Could they be that bad? Wisely, they chose not to question.

Neither appeared to get a sexual kick from torture or killing and, as yet, neither read up on it in medical journals, otherwise throttled pigeons might have abounded. It just came naturally. Their zoo sadism was hidden from parents and teachers alike. The way forward was the military, though the police force had some attraction. Better to travel, commit crimes overseas. Both joined up.

Chapter 5

Penny believed he could smell emotional impairment; it surrounded him as a child and while growing up. He could detect it on people's breaths; he could recognise it from a distance. It was the soldiers from the 'accursed Island of Ten Devils' as he described it to Periwinkle. To Periwinkle, that sounded fair enough.

Penny then admitted he might have to set aside his childish animosity towards Hart; he might need him in the battle and there was a fight brewing.

He missed Lilian. The healer's death had left him empty. Her voice had kept him from making silly mistakes, her vitality and wisdom had guided him through the twins' gallery of horrors. She had died the night he was walking the road to Handale Wood outside Loftus, the same night Jim died. Sixth sense convinced him she had led him off the path and saved his life. In a more rational moment, he wondered if intuition led him astray. Six months or more had passed when he found out about her death.

He refused to build a resistance to the bad feelings and the deep shame he felt at not being in touch. He decided to maintain contact with her ghost. Avoiding the spiritualist church, he would speak to her every so often to assuage the guilt. He held her voice in his head. In life, Lillian had given comfort to others. Daily he thought of Lilian and her healing. He didn't even know how she died. Guilt to him was a Catholic thing. He felt the need to embrace it. It was good practice for what was to come.

He would never know the truth. It was so complex. Sudden death gives rise to contradictory narratives. His old self had witnessed a punch-up at a funeral of a suicide. The expression 'I knew him better than you' was bandied around before the fisticuffs. Superiority was in the red corner and dismissive in the blue.

He contacted her son, with no luck. He assumed that she gave out too much and when it was her turn, there was no energy to heal the infection, repair the wounds or to grow new tissue. Her energy kept others alive. Her budget had run dry. His self-narratives kept him awake. She was with him in his mind constantly. Why that night? Someone who lived to give meaning to life may have left behind chaos. Not Lillian.

Selfish thoughts abounded alongside remorse. She wouldn't be around in person to help when he needed it. He missed her for good, and good old self-centredness. The latter only helped to exacerbate the regret. He would wake in the night bathed in perspiration, the dreams of deprivation; dreams of confusion and errors of judgement on his part plagued him.

In the morning, he would wake singing. A man of contradiction, he baffled folk. The dreams flowed. The interrupted sleep was beginning to tell on him in terms of his inability to analyse the dreams and their manifest content, which he decided was counterproductive. Spadework was better, dream work abandoned.

More frustrating was the fact he couldn't locate exactly where the smell came from. It was aggravating. It was like hearing a bothersome noise, an alarm, a beeping, or several signals at once; the washing machine telling him the cycle over; in tandem, the microwave or some other annoying gadget, of which there were many, and not being able to pin it down. It was, he sensed around the corner. The odour was there, strong and problematic; for him it was a sickly smell, one of rank psychosis. Accompanying it, he suspected, was his lifelong companion – trouble – and it was not in the shape of a board game.

In the university, as in life, it had surrounded him too. His life's destiny was to be with the impaired; 'loonies' as he had called them before his own education and issues led him to a more correct use of language. He still preferred fruitcakes. Then there were many malingerers. That took in everyone, his comrades Dove and Periwinkle apart, and a small group of others. In his newfound (or forced) retirement, he would choose his company carefully.

Small incidents signalled a shift in his demeanour and learning. In the supermarket car park, an irate lady had slammed the door of her four-wheel drive then bawled at her young child, "Get the fucking bags out the back where I fucking throwed them."

Penny felt it his duty to correct her. "It should be where I've fucking thrown them!" He said it firmly and politely. The response was unkind. He sloped away. A lesson learned. Learnt?

The weather too was signing to him, shifting rapidly throughout the day, affecting his behaviour. After a day's research in the library, one where he was sidetracked into seeking out gender inclusive language, he went back to research further the theme of Dark Art with the view to a follow-up. He wondered if people liked being referred to by an acronym. He examined the torturous work of a moulting deer *Rui* by Ed Schaap. He recalled Brownleigh: an animal skinned and in shocking pain. He caught the X bus back; he made a list. He thought of Memling, Bosch, Brueghel, Goya and Fuseli, and read Max Porter's *The Death of Francis Bacon* for the umpteenth time, a tiny *Iliad*, Porter's journey over seven paintings, a reimagining in verse. There was a mischievous element to it. He wondered what Bacon would think of the inclusive language.

Looking forward to a shower and some food, he turned up the cobbles and headed home. Outside his back door a large silver-grey cat sat waiting for him. He tried to stroke it. It rolled over and bit him on the thumb, then for good measure, scratched his wrist. For days he was feverish and went to see the practice nurse.

"That's what cats do," was the unsympathetic comment.

The cat, he thought, was a tom. He needed to learn from the cat. Why on earth did it bite him? What did he do? He felt some contrition about telling the nurse he might want to change the spelling of practice.

He discarded very quickly the idea that he too might have

nine lives. When he returned from the doctors' a day or so after the bite, silver-grey was waiting on the step and rubbed against him. Unfathomable, smart, magical, he couldn't help admiring the beast. Silver Grey's jaw was the biggest Penny had seen in a cat. When he yawned, his small face almost disappeared. He didn't want to check his or her gender for fear he would get 'clawked' again. He took pride in deploying local dialect but questioned using the masculine, not for any sense of specificity but designated for all cats. He enjoyed the debate with himself on the gender neutral, then the refusal to give the cat a voice. He read up on it. Naming 'it' gave him power, payback for bloody scratching and biting.

Picasso's allegory *Cat Catching a Bird*, and the absolute power of holding off the moment of death for the bird, brought to mind the slow death of Max. It also spoke of war and personal events. The cat's eyes were emerald and highly transparent, bright green jewels from the Cleopatra mine. If female, it was Cleopatra. Silver Grey would do. He called it Silver Grey for a while. It appeared to respond, so he shortened it to Silver. It signified his trust in 'him'. His choice of name had nothing to do with Jeff Beck or Motorhead. Penny's dislike of all songs with Silver in the title disbarred such. Hey-ho. Should he follow Eliot and give it three different names?

The cat was there every day on his step or curled up on his lawn. It looked well fed too. He left food for it despite its plump condition and his bandaged thumb. It ate everything and settled back to sleep under a bush. He felt its presence at night. He peeped out to see if it was there. The colour was an effective disguise, yet he knew it was there watching, waiting.

"I must stop assisting people and cats." He vowed he would leave behind his philological self. It would be difficult, for it came naturally to the pedagogue. Correcting people's spelling and email errors had to stop. Language changed. If people decide that 'we done this' and 'we done that' was proper English, then so be it. He reflected on his own errors and mistakes borne of his upbringing, and his own mispronunciations.

That struggle apart, his retreat from academia was going well. Since his Loftus case, his uncanny ability to be in the wrong place at the right time or the right place at the wrong time (or should that be the wrong place at the wrong… the permutations all seemed to fit), he had stayed out of mischief. It didn't suit him and was out of the ordinary. It didn't bode well.

He needn't have fretted.

Today, a bright day in late November, something had changed. He knew it was November, though dates weren't so important now. After his retirement he threw away years of desk diaries with scrawled appointments and disappointments. During Covid the clock and the calendar lost their control.

His new addition was a notebook which he filled with ideas; his promise to himself to keep only a pocket diary to put his runs in. Empty pages were no longer a victory. He did feel fitter. His notebooks were filling with ideas. What to do with them was bothering him.

The baggage retained in the old desk diaries was slow to burn. He watched them turn to grey ash. Years of toil fluttered like glowing pixies dancing in the smoke, then flitted up the chimney. His instincts, be they in part a product of years of oppositional politics (his term), were correct. The warning feeling was just that and nothing else. An alarm bell rang inside. The silver-grey cat greeted him every morning on his doorstep. He even stroked it. Silver it was, mercury, a messenger. What it was trying to impart he didn't have a clue.

He watched a robin settle on a spade handle, taking control and establishing for itself a prime position for seeking out bugs and worms. While admiring its pluck, the robin's earthbound cheek, he decided that there was something important about the whole thing; something to do with imagination, thought, loftiness of spirit. He must stop reading Jung.

He mused. Here he was, a successful author of a book on the Tableaux twins and creator of his alter ego, a new Penny, perhaps a bad Penny, an art historical sleuth; his closest friends the apparently straightforward Dove and enigmatic Periwinkle, private detectives. Musing apart, the trauma of the Tableaux Case threw darkness where there was light, caused sleepless nights, checking under the bed, Brownleigh crawling eerie thoughts, the dead returning, the ghastly statuary and, overall, a feeling it was still happening. He tried to see it as therapy, exorcise the demons. He read from Thomas Gray's *Elegy Written in a Country Churchyard* as it seemed pertinent to the latter. He read the words aloud.

'Ev'n from the tomb the voice of Nature cries,
Ev'n in our ashes live their wonted fires'.

A new phase in his life was beginning and the robin would help him. He dreamed he spoke with Jung and asked him who was allowed into his bedroom. Damn it, the cat would be important too. The crank calls and messages had to stop. His fandom responded to his 'barmyness' in kind. Today, when he finished working in the library, he would ring his friends Dove and Periwinkle. He would tell them that the robin was back. Robins didn't live very long, so he couldn't be sure it was the same one he'd seen in the garden last year.

Not much else to report. He also felt he needed help of the kind only Dove and the unfathomable Periwinkle could provide. They could smell a rat at a distance and, if need be, dispose of it.

Kids generally adored bugs and animals. Young Penny dreamed day and night, his visual capacity working overtime, seeing in his sleep. At six years old wandering aimlessly, he was cut off in a field of spiders, well, that's what he told his pals, caught in a giant spider's web. He was forever the storyteller, playing with the truth. His backstory was elaborate and subject to variation. He entitled it: *As true as I'm riding this bike*. He tried using back narrative instead of backstory. It didn't feel right.

As a child he didn't understand spiders, the symbolic importance of the eternal weaver, its creativity and killing power. The multiple webs seemed to tie the field together, their visibility and delicacy highlighted by heavy dewfall, tiny discrete spheres of glass which stood out across the tall blades of tufted grass and rat's tails covering the common. Grandiose narratives were common to all, and mythology and fact indiscernible. It was much later when he discovered

Courbet's statement: 'Let us be true even if we are ugly' that he tried to change.

To the seven-year-old, millions of brightly coloured brown, green and black scurrying arachnids was mind-numbing. The dew-laden webs held him in a trance. He was rooted to the spot in the middle of the 'forever' field, which seemed expansive, when in fact it was the size of a small building plot. The Yorkshire fog grass seemed to extend forever, the view like looking down a microscope, like Durer's botanical drawings and paintings. He turned slowly each way, shuddered, then ran. He saw one giant spider and fled. *Aragog* it wasn't. As an adult, it dawned on him that it was the imagined cage formed by the webs that frightened him, not the darting creatures.

The weaver's webs of illusion were a constant reminder of interconnectedness. Just as the writer meshes the loose ideas together, so the spider spins. Spiders are okay. As adulthood came about, he began to detect a web, one that was his own, one that brought him back to his field of spiders time and time again. He decided it was an omen. He voiced it on his blog. He recited Whitman's *A Noiseless Patient Spider* and its filament and Emily Dickinson's *Cobwebs*. He thought deeply about *'the spider as artist.'*

In true Penny flibbertigibbet fashion, he chattered, leaping here and there and on, to Mary Howitt's *The Spider and the Fly*. *'For who goes up your winding stair can ne'er come down again.'*

One of the postcards said the web closes in. He immediately switched to *The Mock Turtle's Song* and parody. When that didn't resolve the uncomfortable feeling, he put down the poetry and returned to childhood. Free child ego state was never far away. He returned in his mind to unfettered childhood: spontaneity, and as usual recklessness.

In his mind, he was back fishing for minnows, fetching home jam jars of tadpoles, newts, and a caddis fly; catching butterflies to let them go; roaming the local 'Woody Pond'; climbing trees, and playing street games – Kingy, Chasey, hide-and-seek, footy, skipping with the lasses – that was his childhood outside the house. He took two leeches home one day attached to his left leg. Dad, who had been watching far too many old movies, wanted to burn them off with a cigarette. Mam simply removed them by pushing the mouth sideways and flicking them away. Penny quickly gathered them up and took them back to the beck in a jar.

He invited his listeners to participate. He talked games, sweets, and spiders. He openly portrayed his past, a child who worried, was anxious at school, frightened of dreams and wanted to be the leader of a gang. The replies were wonderful. The skipping rhymes and poems of the street rang out interrupted by the rag 'n' bone man, or the noise from the works. The lasses skipped on. They even sent in skipping rhymes: 'Jenny, Jenny, touch the ground, Jenny, Jenny turn around'.

School was the downside, that and indoors. He recalled his mam crying and rushing outside to bring in the bedsheets splattered with inkblot smudges of soot that had to be rewashed. 'Soot from the works blackened the sheets, rained dilute acid onto the streets', he sang.

He was ill for a while the year after the spiders. He recovered much to the surprise of the doctor and his mam.

In bed he both blamed and thanked the spiders. On the window ledge stood two bottles, one of Abidec and the other Minidex, the medicine to aid his recovery. Next to them was a spoon. He hated that spoon. He couldn't recall which was which medicine. One was vile and brown-coloured, the other vile and green-coloured. Yeuky was appropriate. For health and distancing reasons, he was in the single bed for his recuperation. On a weekend, hearing his friends play footy or tag below in the street was mental agony. That was as close as Penny came to understanding torture. Mam was too busy with three younger siblings. That offset the agony of isolation. He could read and draw.

During that month, his poetic and artistic nature surfaced; the poetry crude in its structure, the drawing unusual, following a line without taking his pencil off the paper. His ability to create pathways out of problems, and his sense of not being lonely when he was alone, came about. He invented continuous line drawing.

The flowered wallpaper on the bedroom wall was company for him. Little faces appeared in it that could've frightened him, but he took to them and spoke with them. When he went to art college years later, he learnt about metamorphoses. He recalled the tiny imps in the shapeshifting flowers on the bedroom wall. He loved *The Chipmunks* film and the first *Shrek* especially. He emphasised with Shrek: he was cranky, dangerous, though not aggressive. All this detracted from his suspicions that he was being targeted.

And he was…

Chapter 6

The proposed day of the hit changed. Mo was edgy. "Look here, Byron. The café's closed. I'm not doing it today. We always have a nice breakfast at Bettys Café in Harrogate before a job. It's unlucky."

Byron was well aware of Mo's superstitious bent. "We could wait a day or so." The job had no time limit, only it had to be 'clean and professional'. Then, with the abandoned hit in mind, "Come to think of it, it didn't help last time!" And as an afterthought, "There wasn't a Bettys in that outpost, Loftus."

The professionalism they guaranteed. They were meticulous, their success rate 100%. Yet they both wanted to know more about Jim's demise.

"Sod clean and tidy," Mo had argued.

Byron paused watching the video *Zero Degrees*. Watching the fragmented conversations of the dance, the dead body on the train, dancing bodies, fragmented bodies twisting turning together, Gormley's white foam dummies, witnesses, no solos, always duets, Byron thought deeply of dual identity, the nature of the body. The boxing ring came to mind: power, race, class, dualism; humiliation, death and a journey. Now that was a fight. The boxing match, their first real encounter.

They proceeded to beat the shit out of each other until the referee called the match off. Ding dong was an understatement. A commentator swore that they might have been carrying knives or guns in the ring. Another more insightful comment written up in the army newsletter was that if one had been carrying a knife and the other aware of it, the other would've carried a gun. Their reputation was established.

They met in the twenty-foot inner width of the boxing ring, a microcosm of the world arena that was their daily field of animosity. A commentator remarked that ill-will was in their blood and, as blood spurted, both refused to lie down. They fought to their own rules; that is, the rule of no rules, or would it be that they believed the so-called rules didn't apply? A hush uncommon to any sport dominated the minute interlude. At the finish no one clapped. The pugilists didn't notice.

Afghanistan was outside for the second time in their lives. The year was 2013 and withdrawal was a reality, their army careers over and prison beckoning. The ringside audience of hardened soldiers remained silent as they battered one another mercilessly. The result was a draw, though Byron thought otherwise.

Their colleagues saw malice, revenge and a firm belief in themselves that married them together. That also made them a duo to be feared. Both had started businesses on coming out the army. Both had failed. The responsibility for their failure was the government, the system, the people. Though there may well have been some element of truth there, the absence of self-doubt ruled, their inability to achieve never questioned. Blame was economics, blame was politics; their loathing of humankind fuelled further by their distrust of people in general. Self-absorption is like that. They were supreme manipulators and played the game in life and prison to perfection. To say that they weren't self-aware, however, would be an error. Tea and cake, yes, academia, yes, and a passion for killing. Yet Byron was changing. Switching the video back on to watch the contortions, testing the uncoordinated body, the dummies and friendship disappearing into fragments. The experience was familiar.

Chapter 7

Dove and Periwinkle's business had slowed. Dove joked about the fact that they had cleaned up the city of London and there was nothing left to solve. Jobs trickled in and were enough to keep the sleuths going. Meanwhile, they kept fit, and Periwinkle took occasional trips to catch up with his mum or Saida.

Dove took to his boat for timeout. Life was fine. Periwinkle spent time in France. They both wondered if their comrade, Penny, was staying out of mischief. It seemed so, and yet so unlikely. His middle name was trouble, with a capital T. With little to do, Dove had called as Penny was poised pen in hand above the cryptic crossword.

Penny checked the number, put down his pen and answered, "Sam Spade, you old git. How are you?"

"Good. We are not doing much and thought a trip to West Yorkshire might resolve our combined midlife crises. Is tomorrow good?"

"Great."

"OK. See you tomorrow."

"Cool."

Penny looked in the fridge and the freezer. He then took

a huge travelling bag and went shopping, twice. The cat was nowhere. Silver had taken up her/his position upstairs, soaking up the first rays of the sun in Penny's bedroom. He yawned as the door closed and his face disappeared.

Outside, a watcher trembled as the cat appeared staring from the window.

In a dark corner of the prison library, Byron came across the Graveyard Poets. A love affair began. Added to an inherent mean spirit was a dangerous capacity for academic thought. Once outside, it would be put to good use.

In the process of their prison education, they moved from random petty criminality and violent assault to homicide as a business. They would, they decided, specialise in removals. Inside, they kept themselves from local issues, putting aside their desires to cut a few throats. They worked assiduously on their business plan.

They found a niche market where their skills, intelligence and desires could come together: as a front, a painting and decorating business. They wore no stockings over their heads nor masks, yet they played a masquerade. Conscience was always on the back burner. Both could affect some moral sense if necessary. Tutors inside and out of prison were blinded by their sincerity and scholastic prowess. Avoiding the situation of morphing into caricatures, they contemplated the nature of their work, meanwhile avoiding any actions that might tell. They were clever. Assuming they were a caricature would be an error.

Bearing in mind the boxing match, they brought a conceptual machine gun to a knife fight, and free from prison they bulldozed lesser intellectuals in seminars. They were careful to do so with some humour, well-rehearsed of course, and aimed at disarming their opponents and tutors. Occasionally Mo would set fire to small animals or maim a local cat. They did a postmortem on the failed hit while watching TV. The advert for sustainable cocoa and ethical tea raised a laugh.

They eyed the brief; they studied the photograph of Penny. The garage in Bradford they rented under a false name had a supply of bogus numberplates purchased at fifteen quid a shot. Stealing the van had been simple, the best place to steal one was from a hire company overnight. Time was not a premium, of course. Everything had to go to plan. Renting and changing plates was an option. Mo had spotted a stationary van parked up for several days in Keighley quite close to Feather Bank. That too was a possibility.

"The order from Jim does indicate as soon as. It can wait a day. He's not around to check!" Mo's superstitions would add a day or so to Penny's life. So what? They hoped he enjoyed his last day. Not really.

They spent some time at the garage checking their arsenal and making sure everything was in pristine working order. Then they stowed the rifle and ammunition in a hidden compartment in their own van. Bullets were always traceable, that they knew. They were also available from past warzones and former colleagues. That made it difficult for forensics.

On the way back, they skirted the road at the side of Keighley Railway Station and up to Feather Bank. The van was there. They then drove to Otley to make a start on the decorating job, a large house on the way towards Pool. They parked where anyone passing could see their own van.

They looked back on the failed hit. Plans had been laid out on the kitchen table. Some of the ideas were exceedingly dodgy, and some were fun. They couldn't afford a drone yet. Byron remarked that a drone was something to do with music, and the bagpipes, which were also scary.

Byron had reprimanded Mo. Angler's cars had been targeted by thieves along the lane behind Knotford Nook. That made the chance of surveillance greater. Mo had worked things out while running miles. The runs helped clear the mind.

Taking a bike sounded daft, but not so. Whoever rode back could call at Stephen Smith's for sandwiches, chat to the staff about the job (painting and decorating), then leave the bike in their own van. It meant keeping the parking space. Also, a means to nip out if needed. All jobs have snags. If the Keighley van were okay, they would change plates just in case.

"Actually, Mo, it's the most ragged planning we've done to date. What can go wrong?" The method wasn't important. As Byron wisecracked, "Neither was it 'academic'."

"Let's not get into semantics," was the reply. "We could kill his cat too, the fucking horrible silver-grey thing that sits outside." The injurious sense of humour and the cheating, a ploy only to test one's intelligence against great odds, was par for the course. Maybe they were becoming caricatures.

Their upward vanity would never require a makeover, rather their view of themselves distorted the image in the mirror. They knew that.

The Otley address wasn't too far, and they could travel up there in the morning. Mo had argued for a simple accidental death, a past field of study for the couple whose time in prison allowed them to learn from others, discuss method of killing and the all-important preparation and techniques of collecting data on the 'hit'. That was their methodology. As with paintwork, the prepping was all important.

The evening previous, the painters and decorators found the van parked up. Within no time they were inside and had it started. "Luck seems to be with us, Mo." The van also had access front to back. The van itself might have been twocked and ditched by whoever. Byron opted to follow in the car with a small arsenal in the back. In Bradford, they changed the numberplates, stowed the bike in the back. Luck stayed with them all the way. "Luck," Byron asserted, "is a quality."

They drove to Otley and found the Cross Pipes car park empty. Parking diagonally opposite Penny's place at the back corner, they locked up, leaving everything there. Mo stuck a note on the back stating no tools left in van overnight. It was then after closing time and all was quiet. Bettys opened at nine o'clock in the morning and that was that. Everything was going their way. The homeowners had opted to go away for several days while they decorated.

The only remaining issue was getting to the van in the morning. A change of plan ensued.

"This is not the time for empiricism," Mo chided.

A furious debate on rationalism followed, and before

Mo could get onto Kantian theories Byron stopped the conversation dead. They drove out the car park separately, parking the van at the back of a nearby supermarket, removing everything in the quiet of a misty October Otley night. The damp clung to them, and they were glad to get back to Burley. They wrapped the gun in dark polythene and secreted it in their own work van.

Choosing an Arctic Series sniper rifle for its precision and portability rather than Mo's preferred L115A3 for its range (the bullets didn't deflect easily), Byron was prepared to take the shot from a distance. They tossed a coin. Mo won. The only suitable spot was a rooftop in the middle of town. Mo won out again. "The car park will do. I'll take the shot, then we go."

Forget torture, think of the money. Their van outside the house proudly displayed its logo – Decorated Painters and Decorators – in green and gold and some odd font Mo had chosen that spoke of Victorian shop signs. A medallion that meant nothing to most adorned the side. Rebel Painters was Byron's choice, a tribute to *Rebel Writers*.

In the morning, it meant ferrying back and forth. They would move the rifle into the other van, then drive back to the car park. Not the best planning, but exciting. Byron could feel the adrenalin already, the risk, the hit and then then coming down, the anti-climax as they went back to wallpapering. The eventuality of Dove and Periwinkle arriving was part of the quality of luck, or non-luck depending how one looks at it. But they did arrive, and the job was fucked. Chaos versus order, misfortune versus luck.

Next time.

The thought of killing Penny had crossed Lance's mind. Inside he had plenty of time to stew. His stay in H.M. Prison Oakwood had been beneficial. He had interfered with Penny's emails from inside, where he had updated his computer skills and several others. He believed he had changed, and so did the parole board. Underneath, he was still the peevish, immature, spiteful, malicious sourpuss who had attended Penny's classes. He didn't wish anyone goodbye the night before, leaving early in the morning with £46 in his pocket.

"Category C indeed," he snorted once he was free of the prison gates. His ego felt it was an insult. He ignored the fact that the categorisation gave him scope for a more liberal lifestyle inside. It could've been worse. Wakefield, the Monster Mansion, sounded frightening. Reality check required. He needed to get to work. The actuality of the outcomes of his enmity escaped him. He was small time, a dabbler, petty and full of acrimony.

Revenge was foremost in his mind; he was the avenger, his understanding of equity skewed. He didn't plan anything, he was no pseudo-commander, just angry and hurt.

The subject of his loathing was drinking tea with Dove and Periwinkle. He was silent. Periwinkle explained about the white van. As he spoke, he was more and more convinced there was a high-powered rifle aimed towards Penny's back door. Dove had the van number. He rang Freeman as Periwinkle briefed Penny. Freeman called back within minutes.

"We've put a trace out for the van and notified traffic to keep an eye out around the town."

They knew it would be clean. The van was parked out of view of the main road. The back lane from Knotford Nook was the site of traveller caravans, a parked van or a wagon a common sight. Freeman promised to call back when she'd checked things out further. She trusted Periwinkle's instincts on the perceived gun incident. She was prepared to follow it up. It would seem fanciful or deluded if it hadn't been Dove and Periwinkle. This was not whimsy. Best not to disregard Periwinkle's battle instincts, his situational awareness. It was sad in some respects that he should need to carry such with him. He should choose his friends more carefully. Periwinkle had heard it all before.

Periwinkle was keen to know if any hits had occurred in the Leeds area of late, professional or otherwise. He was to get quite a surprise.

Lance was heading to Leeds. He took no notice of the morning, the bright sun casting a halo around a tall beech tree, the fresh wintry breeze. He caught a bus to Wolverhampton railway station and bought a single ticket to Leeds.

Penny changed the subject. "Do you keep in touch with

Saida?"

Periwinkle acknowledged the question with a shy grin that said yes.

"She always asks after you. She's back in Bradford. She appears to enjoy police work."

They had left out much of the details of Jim's death. Raed was aware they had omitted to come clean. Closer to reality, and with hindsight, Penny wasn't quite sure what he knew. He hadn't a clue who emailed him that night in Loftus. Having wiped it, it remained undetected.

Furthermore, he had snippets of information from the schoolyard, which he had never disclosed. At the time much seemed relevant, then irrelevant. With a clearer mind and afterthought, they took on quite a different nuance. The kids had known stuff. He knew in his heart that the killers of Max were contracted by Jim. He did of course theorise to the point of exasperation that there could be a link to Jim Trout in the present situation. Dove warned him not to let personal issues get in the way.

His follow-up to the postcard quotations brought about more graveyard poetry. He returned to his final notes in Loftus. His own knowledge of the poets extended to a diversion in the British Library while researching something totally unrelated. The compact list included Gray's *An Elegy Written in a Country Churchyard*, Edward Young's *Night Thoughts*, Blair's *The Grave*, and Parnell's *A Night-Piece on Death*. He suspected there was much more to the poetry than simple morbidity. Furthermore, revisionists would be out there correcting the slanted view with another, thus deconstructing his own morbid fascinations. Why the Graveyard Poets? Lilian always said he should follow his intuitive self, his dreams, phantasmagoria, however outlandish. He pondered. How far should this go? Should he learn more about them? Self-control was important in study, impulse to be put aside. He ignored it. He began to study in order to respond to the cards, forgetting that his actions might be chancy.

'While some affect the sun, and some the shade'… Blair's opening lines attracted him. There was no doubt which the killer or killers of Max affected. Unable to detect his shadows, he sensed it. His opponents' covert nature meant an ability to hide in the gloom. They moved in the dark, be it daytime or not. His macabre reverie over, he studied closely his comrades. "Is it linked to Jim do you think?" Before anyone could answer: "So what do we do?" He chuckled as he envisaged a crumpled wanted poster.

"It's no laughing matter, Ronnie-boy." Dove had been looking forward to a few days walking along the Chevin, drinking good beer and swopping spit with anyone who wished to. How Jim met his demise didn't bother him. He deserved it. Payback from the grave, revenge, and retaliation.

Lance was in Leeds. He searched online to find a reasonable place to stay. Inner city was his target.

SpareRoom had several hits around Burley. He didn't want to share. Sharing leads to hurt. He weighed up the cost – a double room £395 a month. The allotments were nearby; it was fairly quiet. He took it. He paid a deposit and made a fuss of the room.

"I'll be doing quite a lot of work from home." The leaser went through house rules. He would indeed respect the privacy of his housemates. (There was nobody else.) He would certainly keep his belongings out of the communal area… blah blah. His own privacy was sacrosanct, others' were not. As soon as she left him in his tiny flat in Burley, he switched on his laptop and checked his emails. Time to go to work.

Chapter 8

Though aware of Lance's hacking of one of his accounts, Penny was still careless. Periwinkle and he had undertaken a profile of the man's traits and tendencies while they were in Loftus. That Lance hadn't turned to cybercrime, or used his skills as a white hat where he could make a fortune, or espionage working for Government, or the church, refracted not on his technical skills, which were without question, but on his purpose, and motives. He was small-minded, angry and distrustful. His people skills were low. Penny could have helped him with that. Penny wondered if he hacked other people's emails, or if his phishing was for him only. The list of what Lance could've been, grew. An IT security manager was favourite.

Their amateurish conclusion wasn't as bad as the police strategy with black drivers: he wasn't to be harassed for his makeup. Lance suffered from emotional issues and a malicious streak. Even ransomware would have provided him money. He didn't seem financially motivated, he didn't want to be popular, he didn't get any fun out of it, and he wasn't politically or religiously inclined. Lance had difficulty accessing 'adult'. He might have been an 'hacktivist'. Instead, he was a creep.

For a moment, Penny was a behind-the-desk profiler, a football fan turned pundit. Weren't they all? Lance's crime scene was the Internet and profiling reductive. Lance was an attacker. He probably saw himself as a cyber-warrior. To Periwinkle he was an educated script-kid, overqualified and underachieving.

Penny's understanding of dysfunction was personal, his desire to help thwarted by his own personality. So much for profiling.

They concluded. The emails revealed nothing. His disregard for the law hampered his progress in life, and his disregard for that was down to the fact he blamed Penny for everything.

Dove made the point of saying that had Penny blown his cover on his hacking, he would still be banged up. "You should have called the police."

Penny ignored it. "Also, good you've kept in touch with Lucy Freeman."

"Freeman's been good to us in terms of business." Dove had confidence in her.

"That's fine. I don't want Hart involved." Penny wrinkled his nose and sniffed as he said it. The cat rose, stretched and stared in the window at him.

Periwinkle sat weighing up his assessment of the car park incident. "I can't be totally sure of what I saw. There was the instinctual sense of danger. I saw the back door ajar on the van. I was convinced I saw the reflection of a rifle sighting."

Dove sensed a threat too. "It's like an electric current that runs between." He nodded curtly and added, "And it's silly to ignore it, precarious, at times fatal."

Penny recalled Lilian's advice: trust your instincts. These guys had the instincts of a cat. Silver looked in the window once more, then disappeared, disapproval written all over his face.

Profiling over, the three men were walking through Danefield on their way up to the Chevin. Bright slats of sunlight ribbed the path through the tall pines; nothing stirred barring the racket of a clumsy pigeon taking off. No one spoke. Penny was recycling old information from the schoolyard at Loftus. He had laid aside theory for spade work, though he would argue the spade work often preceded the theory. He did have an idea or two!

Penny broke the silence. "My guess is Jim left instructions to finish what he couldn't. Worse still, my intuition tells me it's the torturer. Or is that plural? I would like to get my hands on them. What on earth do we say to Freeman?" As he mulled it over, Dove's mobile buzzed.

"Dove here. Talk of the devil. How's things, Lucy?"

Penny noted the first name terms.

Dove explained to Freeman what he thought they had seen. Freeman asked to speak to Penny. Penny said hiya and listened. He offered his analysis, with Dove gesturing to keep it short. He mentioned the Jim connection as guesswork. He thought of mentioning Lance too, then abandoned it. He assumed Lance was still in the nick. Penny received Freeman's news with mixed feelings.

"Penny," she complained, "we've got cases of murder piling up here. What is of interest is that several professional hits have occurred of late." She stopped, then said, "Put Dove back on, please."

Penny lost the rest of Freeman's brief as they climbed from Chevin Forest and its criss-crossed pathways to the muddy track and headed toward the Chevin top, a product of glacial landslip. Dove was deep in conversation. Below, impatient Himalayan Balsam was reaching up, exploding and spreading. Above on the ridge, the massed old wood of the bare bilberry plants, picked clean by small hands and busy beaks, looked bigger than their fifty centimetres. (Penny congratulated himself on his improving metric grasp.)

While Dove chatted, Penny mentioned the fungi and fossils to Periwinkle who took out his notepad and fountain pen to make an entry on Chicken of the Woods.

"We should gather some one day and try it, Periwinkle." Its rubbery texture and sulphur colour had put him off. "It's quite destructive to the pines it thrives on." He watched Periwinkle as he spoke, so like a tree among trees, moving with the wind, standing still, stretching, then leaf-like. He was his own camouflage. When he wasn't a tree, he took on an animal sensibility moving like a cat, weightless, graceful, coordinated and, above all, focused. The list went on. He stared as Periwinkle peeled his right foot from the ground. He looked straight ahead. Balanced, delicate, and deadly.

Penny stared at the ground. His footing faltered; his breathing faltered. He straightened up and looked ahead. Did he want to look ahead? He wasn't sure. He wasn't sure he was prepared enough. He simply wasn't sure. The ground beckoned.

Dove finished the call. "She's coming round tomorrow to catch up."

Dove, Periwinkle and Freeman had been sharing information. Their own sources were valuable, and Freeman traded readily.

At the top they sat down to take in the view. Penny spoke. "Are we going to get them first?"

Dove gave the stock meme response. "What do you mean, *we*?"

Penny discerned a new vigour in Dove's manner. He had left his cuppa and biscuit untouched. On the summit, Periwinkle was texting with an enquiring eye on his mobile.

Dove then sat still and waited. "Freeman thinks you should come back to London with us." Dove knew that would draw a negative. It did. Penny had some work to do.

"This isn't a one-off, Penny. If this is what we think it is, these guys are pros. Well, sort of."

Periwinkle's phone beeped. He studied the text, the long fingers of his free hand placed below his mouth, lower jaw pushed forward in consternation, brows knitted. He then clicked off his phone and sat back. Dove and Penny continued talking. Periwinkle would feed back when he was ready. Whatever had come through caused him to look concerned. He was searching through his contacts and sent a message.

Byron and Mo deliberated on the aborted mission. "Perhaps 'we' should have taken the shot through the window, Mo?"

Before a heated academic discussion took place on nosism –
the authorial and editorial 'we' – Byron moved the discussion
on. Their new academic self could get in the way. "We, and I
mean we, have to get the job done. If his mates are sticking
around, we have to be careful. They're not easy pickings. And
they are a bonus. Together, however, we have an issue."

"Correct! We wait?"

"Alternatively, a small gas leak that ignites might dispose
of all three."

"And a row of cottages?"

"We did worse in the army."

"This is not Helmand province. It's Otley, a market town
in West Yorkshire! Let's do our prep again; let's allow three or
four days for surveillance. They may be off back to London by
then. I'm sure they sussed us. It's the same gut reaction that
we developed in the zone." They were right in one respect:
it was the same innate intelligence they possessed; uncanny,
sharpened by battle, with an instinct for more than survival.
Byron responded with a line from a Loudon Wainwright
song *Our Own War* about survivors.

They had some difficulty in explaining why the beanpole
focused on the back of the van. Did he catch a reflection? It
was unlikely that a member of the public would suss out the
possibility of a high-powered rifle.

"Mo, there is no such thing as unlikely." They finished
planning. "Mo, it's risky. A simple spot check could uncover
an armoury among our brushes, paints and paraphernalia."

"Right, far too dodgy. We could pick him up as he leaves
the library, take him to the garage?"

The next day, they regretted their procrastinations. His

blog had informed them he would be going to Headingley to interview an author of some interesting ekphrasis, poetry reflecting artworks, his personal *Iliad*. He didn't say when. Writing in the voice of the artists, the work had an evocative nature Penny liked. He prepared to do a follow up blog on the nature of ekphrasis. He ditched his own *Ode to a Kashmir Rug* which was half-written. The poet's work was far wittier and sophisticated.

Mo and Byron waited. Mo went running. They alternated between keeping a watch and completing the Otley decorating job, which meant long hours. Penny's cavalier actions defied their assumptions, and with time they began to wonder if the visitors had seen anything at all.

"It could be a trap, Mo."

"I don't feel any hairs on the back of *my* neck standing up." Mo's voice was taunting.

"Neither do I," Byron agreed. "Still, better keep an eye out." They parked further away and walked.

Mo slipped out the van and reconnoitred. "Nothing, all clear and clean."

Byron looked. The green car was still parked up.

Penny left by the back door. He was slouching along and singing a Chris Rea song – *Fool if You Think it's Over* – his song for Brexit. What would the press do next when that ran out? He thought of the dead cats Freeman had mentioned. How about snakes? That should keep people aware for a while. Yes, snakes were it. He looked it up – ophidiophobia was the extreme. They came up through the toilet, they disappeared from captivity, and they appeared in parks, gardens and even high streets. Factual or not, the fear was real. The fear factor: a boa constrictor wrapped around a lamppost, an anaconda in the shower.

He mused. The government could welcome one or two diversions. 'Deadcatting' was becoming popular in politics. Snaking seemed appropriate?

Dove and Periwinkle thought him foolish to go to work in the university library or to do interviews in leafy Headingley.

"It's best I carry on doing my research," he confirmed, and went for the bus.

Periwinkle messaged Saida in Bradford. Precisely at 10:30 the doorbell rang. Dove answered it.

Freeman listened carefully to Periwinkle's take on the car park incident. They needed to catch up on other issues, but she was curious. She wanted to stitch together a spate of killings, some of which she was convinced were related. Freeman's comment that the reports of dead animals were causing as much concern as the human toll was fair enough brought back the pitiful memory of the burnt dog in Loftus. Periwinkle mentioned the incidental as appropriate, the fisherman's bycatch, the real target was Max, the dog just happened to be caught in the net. But he wasn't fully convinced. The dead animals preceded killings. There was a link, but what the hell was it? The bycatch theory fizzled out.

On the car park incident, Dove confirmed he felt

something. Neither he nor Periwinkle proffered any gap-filling ideas, the bare bones only. Penny, they were convinced, was the target. The list of people who desired retribution, for whatever, was no doubt lengthy, but would-be assassins?

Penny had showed them the weird messages and postcards referring to the Tableaux Case which were manifold, but revealed no threats, rather a perverse fandom. His reputation had grown – opportunities, free meals, and an offer to advertise a funeral parlour. He decided to steer clear of advertising – it could ruin his anarchic take on many things. His close-to defamatory statements about the bus services and other things competed with government populism, though as he remarked, some punters didn't seem to understand what it meant, and thus confused populist with popular.

The downside, people recognised him in the street. He recorded his contribution to a Leeds-based podcast on the uncanny and unusual; he visited an independent bookshop in his home area and gave a talk. In between he researched, he wrote, and he spent a lot of time on the phone. Who did he speak to? All and sundry, and Tammy.

Freeman asked for her contact address and phone number. Dove called Penny who felt a sense of déjà vu; uncomfortable. Was it wise to court Tammy at this juncture? Was there any point in floating that to Penny?

Dove made a cup of tea and brought a plate of biscuits. Freeman nattered. Penny had absent-mindedly left the biscuits on the plate in the kitchen the day before.

"Your mate Penny is a likeable person with a horrid knack of seeking out bother. He's also rash at times." Freeman hit the nail.

"He doesn't seek it," Dove said as the kettle whistled its boiling call, "it seeks him."

"True. What I want to tell you is strictly off the record." She didn't have to assert herself. Dove and Periwinkle nodded the go ahead. Dove put down one of his red notebooks and listened.

On the way to lunch and in a playful mood, Mo and Byron were discussing *Assassins Creed*. Their own solutions to destroying evil dominated the chit-chat, though their concept of evil – moral and natural – was slanted and included fauna. Had Penny sussed them? Penny was tricky.

Byron followed the man himself when Penny finished his interview, followed by a thorough check in the library where he was hard at work. His blog informed them he was writing the beginnings of a new story, a kids' book about a strange character called Mad Magonie or was it Mud? He acted as if nothing were wrong in the world. It didn't figure why he was so unconcerned. Natural suspicion ruled; two military minds said *watch out*. Byron listened to an excerpt of Magonie.

Mad, as he was called, had green hair and hopped everywhere. To Byron he seemed like Penny, an innocent, unaware of the world at large, yet capable of framing that world and its guilt; a contradictory figure, who Mo remarked cancelled out each tick box. Magonie was his childlike creation. With innocence can come suffering. Byron recalled the suffering heroes from Greek poetry.

"Stay your blade from the flesh of an innocent," Byron mocked Mo.

Mo replied, "Killers with principles? Bollocks."

Byron digressed. "A dagger would've done the job." Byron's romantic persona resisted calling it a hidden blade. "Mo, how about poisoning him and his friends? We have to adopt Israeli tactics. Forget all implications. Destroy the whole of his environment."

This was a part of the planning where they allowed themselves to roam free. Their associations gave rise to melodrama and for them, fun.

"Let's leave out hypnosis," Mo jested. "As for Israel, we may get ourselves into a debate about political correctness. Better to say Mossad."

"You do realise you could get thrown out of the Labour Party for saying such?"

Fuck off seemed the only suitable answer. Mo stayed schtum; Byron continued. Lunch finished; they got back to painting.

"Got it! Give them a day or two and keep watch, then unleash everything. How about using a drone; hawks, wasps and predators?" Byron stopped painting and thought.

Mo started to clean the brushes and wrap them in clingfilm.

After work, they parked up three or four doors down and went into the flat in Burley. The mundane took over.

Coincidence is a strange thing, synchronicity too. Lance was still mulling over strangling Penny when he bumped into Byron and Mo. Lance was staying just three doors away. They passed him as they walked the few yards from the van to the flat. He handed Mo a leaflet and smiled his business smile. Mo thought it amateurish and slick. But, there and then, they connected. The thin young man, who was quite good-looking though somewhat gauche, in their opinion, wandered off, leaflets in hand and up a garden path.

Mo was about to throw it away. Byron asked to read it. It was computer stuff, websites designed, laptops repaired – as Mo said, blah, blah, blah.

Byron had recognised something in Lance that spoke of prison and a past, not to mention an aura that spoke of malevolence and callowness. "Let's keep it. He could be very useful to us. Let's suss him out." At the bottom in small print, it boasted: 'If it's computer related, leave it to Lance'. Byron liked the semiotic name too but had other ideas in mind for Lance that might not involve linguistics. "Let's leave it a day or so, then get in touch." Keeping tabs on Penny's emails and diary via a laptop might be very handy and neither were that adept. Laptops were great for looking up stuff and as a writing tool. "Lance, if that's his real name, looks shifty to me, Mo."

Mo looked back. "That's an insight, a fine example of the well-honed instincts of a killer and a constant criminal. You are so right!"

Byron raised both middle fingers and wagged them up and down for good measure.

Mo's impression of a recent prime minister was good. "*Digitus Impudicus*. Tut, tut."

Byron was quick to quote the Crime and Disorder Act on anti-social behaviour. Touché. Irrelevant or not, it felt right to respond. Back in the boxing ring, the gloves were on and for a moment the relationship appeared strained.

Chapter 9

Lucy Freeman balanced her mug on the arm of the well-worn chair. "We've had several killings this last year. They have the hallmark of professional hits. One was a particularly frightening drive-by shooting outside a nightclub. One shot only and unhurried."

She looked around the room. "The target was a door attendant who died in the arms of a student working part-time. He has no connections that suggest a contract, gang related, drugs or otherwise, nor anything that would merit such. Drive-by shootings often leave the victim alive and badly wounded. This was one shot from a car. The bystanders were students. The shooter was accurate. Nobody else suffered."

"You're implying a professional?" Dove looked interested.

"Two pros, a driver and a shooter. I'm not ruling out luck. The methods of our recent killings vary though the rifle predominated. There is something about these hits that has a pattern. Dare I say they are mission-oriented, and the perps comfort killers, though I can't rule out psychological and monetary gain. Profit is at the root. Sorry, I'm guessing.

"The drive-by shooting took place in the evening, the rest in the morning, mid to late morning. They clearly have a soldierly precision about them. I can explain that further if you wish. There's no evidence left, and if you'll forgive me describing it so, some of the killings have a poetic note, as in justice meted out, be it from a perverse point of view."

Freeman watched Periwinkle put his hands together as if praying. Perhaps he was signalling their unity, a force, one not to be fucked with.

Freeman continued. "The method has a bearing on the victim and their principles – religious, political, philosophical, or whatever." Her brow wrinkled as she explained. "For example, an errant priest was crucified." Dove startled at the reference. For a moment there was a shared hush.

Freeman hadn't been party to the investigations into Max's disappearance and subsequent demise though she was aware of the torture and killing of young Max.

Periwinkle asked the obvious question. "Is there a connection to Loftus?"

Freeman shrugged.

They stepped outside. He showed Freeman the position of the van and indicated where they were. He didn't require chalk. Freeman stood and eyed the surrounds.

"I'm not sure why a shooting, though guns and rifles do shape identity, and vice versa. Vice versa might be the case here. We're dealing with a sniper. I've got a constable on it looking through army records for retired snipers. A shot in the dark, really. Forgive the pun." She thought of the symbolism of the rifle, its power and authority. "'Getting shot hurts'." That, she reminded them, was a quote from Ronald Reagan. What do guns mean? Patriarchy came to mind.

She continued. "This isn't America. The carrying of

guns is illegal. The literal truth is that it would be swift and quite simply payback or pay out." She wondered why the sharpshooter didn't take the shot that day. Their arrival must've have been at the exact moment.

Dove chipped in. "At the same time, it could be someone back down the line, something to do with the Tableaux Case?" Then he doubted himself. "The twins will get their moment of 'fame'. I'll go with Penny's theory and Jim as the source. Money is involved, it's a paid hit, and before we discuss symbols, we need a reality check." He clearly had Penny in mind.

Freeman concurred. Why Penny was wandering about worried her. He seemed regardless of his plight.

Freeman gave Dove and Periwinkle everything she had on the killings and their hallmark. She chose not to mention that Lance was out. She also omitted to include her close colleague Hart in the conversation. However, she admitted she was going to have to liaise with others. That meant Hart and Saida.

Freeman, Periwinkle concluded, was indeed a wise woman.

Dove picked up his red notebook and looked to Freeman. "You think the killings are hawkish!"

"There is evidence of strategic and tactical planning at work. To date, there has been no witnesses, implying an ability or training to camouflage or conceal oneself. There is no evidence except a corpse and usually a bullet, one bullet. Forensics have found very little. Their estimations indicate that the rifle is a high-precision model; the focus being on head shots rather than chest which points to a skilled sniper. The bullets are from military sources and therefore untraceable. That too could imply a connection with the armed forces. Finally, we think that two people are involved. You already know these facts about snipers and their work."

"What about torture?" Periwinkle asked the question.

"Sorry?"

"Have there been any instances of tortured victims in recent months? Were any of the victims tortured?"

Freeman looked at her notepad. "Actually yes, three cases over the last two years or so. All the victims were dead however."

Dove stirred. "Let's hear it."

"The three cases were horrific. Fortunately for the victim, time was a premium, and in one instance, the pain of adding salt and hot pepper to open wounds cut short by a knife. That too wasn't pretty, as the dead man bled out from below."

"Were all three victims men?" Periwinkle queried.

"Yes." Freeman looked at him. "Is that important?"

"It could be."

Dove looked puzzled. "What about the crucifixion, the errant priest Freeman?"

"A suspected paedophile. We think he was dead when they nailed him to his own church cross. He'd had his anus penetrated, or should I say he was impaled before his crucifixion. The implement was metal. Horrible, whatever the man had done…"

This invoked or connoted a moral aspect, though unjust, if that isn't a contradiction. *Poetic*, thought Periwinkle, yet bad poetry.

"Have to add that rectal injuries of this kind are uncommon." Freeman cocked her head and thought. "There was a case in Streatham where a man had a knife inserted by a vengeful wanderer who he'd barred from the pub. His friends held the man over the bar. They simply left the pub, and no one spoke out."

"What else?" Dove enquired.

"One or two were by electrocution. The other torture, as one colleague described, was 'a Saudi killing'; the bones smashed with stones. You see a connection, then?" Freeman's voice was terse, her face fixed in a frown. "We didn't connect the shootings and their clean methodology, if you forgive the term, and the barbaric nature of the torturer."

"Not surprising." Dove spoke first. "Money is involved."

"Fair point. So, it's a contract?" Freeman meant it as a question.

Neither answered.

"One more thing, Freeman, was there any sexual torture?" Periwinkle looked as if Dove had taken the words from his mouth.

"One might consider the anal case as such, otherwise, not directly. One of our cases involved a castration. We assumed them to be revenge killings. We may have to think again. You see a connection?" Freeman's thoughts wandered. What is revenge for the hired killer? What is a reward? All the psychological bullshit on punishers fails in this case. The customer might seek revenge. The concept of avenging 'angels' had some credence. Vengeance as a warning to others of specific actions might also be a point. That they should be judge and jury of acceptable conduct is also an issue. Lack of emotional attachment could rule out revenge. As for reward, that was monetary, and an aspect of the kill. Revenge could be against everyone or anyone."

A sudden rattling on the window indicated a heavy rainfall. Silver took refuge under the bushes. Freeman finished the briefing. "I'm due back in the office shortly, lads. Be good if Penny could come in and talk."

Outside, Mo watched Freeman leave and began the nine miles run back to Burley where Byron was reading, a spider chart spread out on the coffee table.

A few doors down, Lance was picking up on his first well-paid job of work, and in a short break had checked Penny's emails.

He felt lucky.

Lance was leafleting the Burley area, advertising anything computer oriented. His website work apart, he was prepared to proof or edit work, or ghost essay write for students, be it art history, social history or any of the humanities. He spent more than his budget. He wanted the leaflets to be good.

Byron recognised him. He entered the front gate with leaflets in hand. Picking two leaflets off the floor and about to bin them, the 'anything computer-oriented' caught the eye. The art history chimed too. Lance was about to walk away when the downstairs door opened.

"How good are you with computers?"

"Very good." He reached in his bag to bring examples of

his work.

Byron stopped him with the next question. "Where did you study history?"

"Art history. It was here in Leeds. An MA."

"Leeds Uni?"

"No. The Met, as it was called before it was rebranded in 2014."

Byron took the chance. "So, you might know Dr Penny?"

The reaction was similar to the result obtained by pouring boiling water onto phosphorus or thallium. Lance frothed. Immediately he turned from his saccharin sales pitch to acid. His face twisted in rage. Byron was pleasantly surprised.

"Him," was all Lance said. Byron didn't need to prod. "I've just done fucking time because of him." He blurted it out and couldn't help himself. "Sorry." He turned to walk away, realising he had screwed up badly. He had let his front slip. He felt daft as he realised pushing buttons wasn't the aim of the customer. For the graveyard folk, it was a breakthrough.

"Hang on," Byron said getting hold of his arm while looking at his name card. "We might be able to give you some work. Not highly paid initially, but with a bonus at the end."

Lance turned back. "Work? A bonus? What kind of work?" He was both pleased and concerned. His froth at the mention of Penny had connected, though he wasn't sure what or why it had achieved a result. Lance's near-pathological hatred for Penny had struck a chord. He realised too he might learn from their foot-in-the door methodology.

Looking at his business card, Byron spoke. "I'll speak with my business partner first, then get back to you, Lance." The following week, they established email contact with Lance.

For another week or so they milked his hatred for Penny. On realising his loathing was chronic, they assessed he was totally on their side. They invited him for a drink. Byron broached the subject of tracking Penny. Lance could either say yes or no, though they had an insight into his personality, borne of their own social disease and splintered egos that told them he would comply and collude. Three clever folks, three against one.

They discerned a loss of wholeness in Lance, a meeting of poetic and artistic and the talented, yet a fractured self, one lost in the postmodern world.

Byron related to the work of Annette Messager which spoke of such. Her work was profound, jarring and repellent. A fragment of a fragment. Bodies everywhere become fragmented, both physically and mentally, wholeness a dream. Byron critically assessed their own selves. They moved in another world, one that threatened others' wholeness and made them anxious. Briefly, the reflection caused a moment of doubt, then it was over. Lance also understood the concept, but unwisely put it aside.

These were not three 'headcases', as Dove would have said, nor were they three 'ghosts of the weed garden', as R.D. Laing described a chronic case; they were three highly intelligent selves with a sense of self lost in the existentially dead spectre – two hired assassins, and an active Internet ghost.

The wine they were drinking wasn't cheap and was effective. It was followed by lager. Mo took satisfaction in the fact that the truly dead were paying the bill. Lost connections and differing calibrations were at play between them. Impoverishment in a way, yet a coming together of three beings, capable of logical and academic thought whose irrational selves were either maligned by society or worshipped; dark personalities that attract media attention, too much attention.

Byron raised the subject. "Have you ever hacked anyone's email account?"

Lance was wary. He didn't want to go back inside.

Mo cut in. "Let me phrase it another way! Is it quite easy to hack into email?"

Lance relaxed. He supped his drink, a rather nice lager, and saw his fridge with two or three waiting for him when money came in. He savoured its spicy bitterness. "Of course it's easy!" He puffed up. "It does of course require some Linux and social engineering skills, apart from the general computing skills, cryptography and so on. Nothing beyond me. Why?"

"Do explain." Mo took out a notepad. Lance was still cautious. He ran the list of skills past them. They appeared immersed, intrigued.

"Do you have anyone in mind?" Lance was keen to know what the intended hit had done to them. Lance questioned himself. Had the world cheated him out of his dues? If it was Penny, which he suspected it was, plain old-fashioned requital were his motives. Laertes and Hamlet came to mind, then Harry Potter. Revenge, tragedy. A cycle of retaliation?

He was haunted by Penny. He had yet to ascertain what he was paying back. He was sure it was Penny. Why? The potential customers declined to say who. He disconnected. Please let it be Penny. Payment for hacking a site he already hacked did have some credence. If pinned down, he would be unable to define why he wanted retribution. He was in the Web, one of self-perpetuating hatred. In the realm of the psychology of haters he was an amateur. Mo and Byron had captured the market.

Lance felt some discomfort. Byron offered him another drink.

Chapter 10

Penny, the proposed kill, was walking the Meanwood Valley Trail. He stopped to watch wasps emerging from an old tree trunk. They exited from a small hole in the stump and buzzed around him. They didn't appear angry. He left them to it. It was, after all, their territory. He wondered what Hart was up to. He wondered if he had learnt the values of sharing and listening. Wasps signalled power and action. They were telling him something. Act now, Penny! Don't dawdle.

He had tried to discipline his day. During his scheduled break he wrote two texts (one can only work for so long on academic stuff) – one to an old colleague now at Leeds Beckett University and another to a pal at Leeds University itself. He deleted them without sending. His caution was a wise one.

Lance had consented to tapping into Penny's email. They had offered to pay him. Hooked on hatred, Lance fell for the plot. It was a gift. The gift, however, is complex – sometimes free, and sometimes pure, without an agenda. What would victory mean for him? Would he ever remove the threat that Penny posed, one he really couldn't pin down? Was it imagined? Just what the fuck had Penny done to him? Try as he might, he couldn't shake off the notion that Penny threatened him. Engulfed in his own insecurity, he checked Penny's mail. What was he up to?

Lance should have completed his master's degree. The gift is itself loaded and problematic. Yet Lance wasn't blind to the danger he was getting into. His splintered self and internal arguments weighed the odds continuously.

He realised that payment involved a contractual element. That worried him. He didn't want to work with anyone, and these guys caused him some anxiety, at one point an adrenal buzz, then the drone of an angry wasp.

Later that day, back at home Penny opened his laptop. He sent messages to the two universities on another site set up by Periwinkle. It was Lance free. The answers came back to him the next day. It was a result, and a surprising one. He couldn't wait to speak to Dove and Periwinkle.

In a way, it was a shame Lance hadn't picked it up, a shame for him! It might have saved a life.

Learning from the cat, Penny chose patience and decided to wait until the end of the day's work. He couldn't wait to finish but took care with the work on his 'out speak' talk. It occurred to him that cats had been useful in the past. He would buy Silver a treat on the way home. His thumb was healing quite well, the scratch almost gone. What was the cat saying to him? A treat would help, one of those yummy biscuits or some catnip crackers.

Silver dived into the carrier bag as Penny placed it down

to open the door and tore open the catnip crackers bag, scattering them everywhere. He was oblivious. He rolled in them before devouring the lot. A line for cats. Silver was hooked. Penny picked up the ravaged packet and went inside. Dove had prepared food, a navy dish quite obviously as it consisted mainly of gravy. (Or was that a sauce that had dumplings floating in it?) It tasted damn good. Homemade bread rounded it off. One had to soak the bread in the gravy to capture the origins and flavours of this Northern treat. He dived in too.

Periwinkle had been to a gym in Bradford. He'd popped in to see Saida. All was well, though she was looking around her for a change. He had recently reported she was enjoying her job. Penny chose not to ask what changed. He brought to mind his own shift in appreciation of his profession, his dalliance in getting out, even when a good deal was on the table. Periwinkle's ability to keep quiet about all matters meant he was not telling all.

Penny waited his moment. Dove had poured a beer. Periwinkle had rediscovered ginger beer. He held the spicy liquid up to the light and took a sip. Penny so wanted to taste the gingery liquid; its aroma and spiciness invaded the small living room. A bottle of Timothy Taylors' beer won out. He spun out the story of his hunch. "Well, not even a hunch really, more a vision." Playing it down, he kept the best bit for last. "I contacted the universities yesterday."

Dove opened his palms and cocked his head.

Penny continued regardless. "I had a dream in Loftus, and segments of poetry and visions of the uncanny unfolded." Beginning to sound ecclesiastical, or unhinged in Dove's opinion, he moved on. "I mentioned the Graveyard Poets, a loose group really, if a group at all." He omitted to mention the postcards which, to him anyway, were evidence rather than supposition. Periwinkle was engaged. He noted Dove was beginning to tire. Undeterred, Penny continued. "I decided to follow up my thoughts, to see if anyone was teaching about Blair and Young. Spiritual unrest was a key."

Before he could turn his discovery into a full-blown lecture, Dove opened another beer. He interrupted, "Where's this going?" He held his beer up to signify he wanted to chill.

"I'm coming to that." Penny was enjoying the moment. "I contacted the two universities to see if anyone is teaching the subject anywhere. It turns out that there are postgraduate students in Leeds studying the very same, among other aspects, leading towards the gothic." He paused. "There are three students studying in the field, two at master's level, and one at doctoral level! Now, this is the crunch: The first two are partners and connected."

"Connected?" Dove put his beer down.

Penny had him snared. He grinned, the smirk that annoyed so many people. "I was privy to information that I didn't expect." He brought the postcards into the frame. "The postcards were the clincher. Written by an academic or two, they referred to the poets. The references were highbrow. So, I decided to chase up researchers in the field. Both students on the Masters' degrees are ex-forces. Furthermore, both have a past".

"Don't we all?" Dove's rejoinder brought him back to earth.

Penny tried an enigmatic face and failed. He was rolling

around in the catnip crackers of information. "I don't know where the suspects live, but it is together. My contact is subject to some law of privacy." He raised an index finger and wagged it. "Normally, I would get a fair breakdown of their past: Joe Smith went to such and such a school, did four A levels and lives in Headingley. No detailed information given, just the bare bones, lads, the bare bones."

Dove was now curious. Periwinkle looked at him as if reading ahead. Dove asked him, "And what do you think they are up to?"

"I don't know. My idea is to let them know we know of them and see what happens. Perhaps also let Freeman know. First, I thought you might be able to find out more from your sources, by stealth or otherwise?"

"We can." Dove thought it worthwhile. "If you have their names, and it is their real names, we can soon track what regiment they were in and disclose their records, if they are ex-forces."

"I do have their names. Surnames are Byron and Wright."

"Do you have their first names?" Dove was showing signs of impatience as he wrote down the information.

The grin became even wider. "I do!" He paused as long as he could. It tumbled out. "Alice and Maureen! Alice Byron and Maureen Wright!"

Silence ensued.

"Let's not get carried away here." Dove was clearly sceptical. "Two women, ex-forces, who are, by all intents and purposes, assassins and dangerous opponents. Shit." He shuffled on his seat as he spoke. "Two black widows, spies, or two Mata Haris. They've probably been watching *Kill Bill*." Joking apart, he looked concerned.

Penny added to what he perceived as Dove's doubts. "It's the result of guesswork." Then he said, "Army records are online. You have access to the nooks and crannies of MoD. That is before we notify anyone else, if not for their sake." He was certain he'd made a breakthrough. He hid it well and complimented himself on his capacity to do so. Dove would disagree. He was strutting his stuff.

Penny saw the spider's field, the webs binding together. Dove detected he wasn't telling all. They had reached an insightful moment, the point of no return. It was going to get shitty.

Periwinkle spoke quietly. He didn't seem so happy. "I could call in a favour or two. If these women are our assassins, they are dangerous opponents. Don't dismiss them out of hand or take them lightly. And, if you are right, they are responsible for the torture and killing of a child." He added as an afterthought, "Two queens of the Amazon."

Penny didn't really know much about Dove and virtually nothing about Periwinkle. He himself wasn't quite the open book he made out to be. Dove and Periwinkle had him sussed.

"If it means a problem to you, leave it Periwinkle." Penny finished with a cheap psychological retort.

Periwinkle looked grave. "What we have so far is surmise. We assumed you were the target for a hit. I can find out who these characters are and their backgrounds. We could dispose of them if need be. We assume also that they are contract killers. If so, who contracted them?" Dove and Penny nodded their agreement. Dove shifted on his chair, then took a sip of his beer. Periwinkle didn't look so happy.

"If Jim is behind it, we have to bear in mind that he was 'attached' to Secret Intelligence Services – let's use that term for now. That means Government. Jim was a free agent and worked around the world doing the dirty work. If there is a contract, we have another hurdle to clear." So much of Penny's speak was in inverted commas.

Was it inaccurate? Was it unacceptable? Was it a quote? Reference to something academic? Periwinkle wondered.

Both men knew what was coming. Penny now realised the locus of Periwinkle's discomfit: not the two women, the contract.

"The contract is open to all eliminators and passed on and fulfilled by someone else if they fail. We can remove the current killers; the contract will remain." Periwinkle looked at Dove as if to say please pick up where I leave off.

Dove assumed the mantle. "We need to discern exactly who issued the contract. That is going to be exceedingly difficult. We could interrogate the two women. If they are military, they will be able to combat interrogation, to a point. Torture isn't our thing. It would seem it is theirs - if your feelings are correct." He took a long sip of his beer.

Penny looked flummoxed. "So, what do you suggest Dove?"

"Firstly, we suss them out if they are who you think. Secondly, if we can unsettle them that will be to our advantage. That might sound stupid but there is a rationale to it. Your idea of blowing their cover makes sense. It might cause them to go on the rampage. Are they guilty?"

Penny couldn't think what the rationale was.

Dove explained. "Could they be innocent? On the one hand, if we disrupt their cosy lifestyle and interrupt their studies they will suffer. On the other, antagonism can give us quite an advantage - if they bite. We need to find out where the contract is coming from." He stopped there. Penny had the distinct feeling he had more to say, and it wasn't good. He had always known they had moved in a darker world than his own. This was it – welcome to my world.

Then he revealed his plan. "I'm going to give a combined group talk to the masters' students on my little book on Dark Art and *The Tableaux Twins*. It's not so much the subject matter as my methodology they're interested in. At least one of them will be there."

Dove and Periwinkle eyed one another. Both thought he'd cast aside his yet unpublished work on Oldman, and undercover work. Yet here he was going undercover again. Discovery could mean death. Penny never seemed anxious about such matters.

Down the road, Lance was thinking that he didn't like the painters and decorators. In fact, he despised them. They were creepy. That placed them way down, or up, the ladder of unpleasantness to Lance himself. Such is the pecking order of inhumanity. The causes and the need to find out why they were like that was strong, his own curiosity aroused, time running out. He was getting legitimate work and enjoying it. He suspected their motives were evil. He couldn't discern what the hell it was, just a dark feeling, something beyond his own pettiness. He felt threatened. His tendency to knock people down perhaps to build himself up was under threat.

He was learning.

He was also holding a losing hand, two aces and two eights. His time in prison had taught him quite a few card games. At night in dreams hooded crows tapped on the window. He often awoke in a cold sweat. He changed and got back into bed, checking doors and windows before he laid wide awake. Dark was knocking on his door. He didn't like it. He had studied signification under the best. He dreamt of empty graves, a black thrush singing. It didn't represent inner peace.

Chapter 11

The 'best' was having issues himself. He felt he was relying far too much on his friends. He too realised his place in the hierarchy was fragile. His utopian illusions needed questioning. He decided to disappear, then thought better. He'd wait and find out what Periwinkle could dig out from 'above.' Curiosity won out. He wondered how his life as an academic (retired, without inverted commas) was going to pan out. Was it worth troubling the two masters' students and decorators to see what happened? He didn't want to screw their chances up of betterment.

Periwinkle wasted no time at all. While Dove and Penny were cracking open another beer, he had contacted someone on the inside. He offered another pathway.

Penny and Dove were nattering when Periwinkle left the room, mobile in hand. He returned and sat down. "I've got you an appointment. It will have to be tomorrow, or at the latest the day after."

"An appointment?"

"I think you should go rather than me. I think it's important that they meet you."

"They?"

"The chaps in the ziggurat, one chap in particular."

Penny looked lost. "The ziggurat?"

Periwinkle smiled. "Babylon-on-Thames." Periwinkle was clearly loving the play of things.

Tempted as he was to say, 'come on, it's my job to be cryptic and confusing', Penny held back. He didn't really know Periwinkle at all. The man was a mystery. The clue began to dawn upon him. "Not the building in Vauxhall, the SIS building?" He put his beer down. "Shave off." He looked flabbergasted. Dove laughed. Penny certainly had learnt a lot at Portsmouth University – even local parlance. Periwinkle's toing and froing amused him too.

Penny couldn't wait. "I'll go tomorrow. I can take my notebooks. I'm plotting a new story."

Periwinkle took a notebook out of his waistcoat pocket and his fountain pen, wrote, then carefully put the top back on, placed it in his waistcoat, tore the page from his notebook and placed it on the table. The notebook too disappeared into his waistcoat pocket.

"Just as well it isn't at Century House," Penny said. "Is there really a tunnel through to Whitehall?"

"Penny, you will need to see Lucas Guess on the eighth floor. He will arrange for a pass to be ready for you in the reception area. Take ID with you, preferably your passport. Tell Lucas what you know about Jim in brief, and as much as you can about our two assassins. No guesswork. Oh, and give him best wishes from Mum and I." There was an emphasis on the word *brief* which Penny assumed was Periwinkle telling him not to elaborate or, if you want, waste time.

Penny was silent. He started to open his mouth. Dove

spoke for him. "Got it?"

"Yes," he stammered. "What time?"

"On the paper."

He picked up the piece of paper. The neatly written note read: Lucas Guess, Room 817. 14:30 prompt.

"No notetaking, Penny!" Periwinkle looked stern.

Penny's short-term memory, which he deemed to be failing, demanded the notebook. Odd thoughts, odd moments, they all went into the book, a brown, faux leather pocketbook he'd bought in yet another high street shop that went to the wall. He tried writing right to left like Leonardo in his notebooks so if anyone tried to read them, they would require a mirror. His left to right was bad enough. He was paranoid about losing them. He copied stuff into his laptop at home. His thoughts were never private.

Chapter 12

Byron and Wright decided to let Lance in on the deal, though only partly. His loathing of Penny was the incentive. His ability to tap into computers was another. His hatred for Penny and his petty nature was apparent. He was a genius with computers. The combination of those aspects would work for them. An errand boy.

If they could discern Penny's working patterns without dogging him, they could save time, lift him after or before his 'work' and have some entertainment. Before was ideal. It would give them time before his so-called comrades would know he was missing. They decided to give it a few days more.

Lance provided them with work schedules. However, writing is a strange business. Penny arose early. He clearly didn't write every day. Some days he wandered. Byron saw his meandering as a wanderers' fugue, no plan, no schedule no aims. Lance could only offer a vague schedule. It was enough. At the same time Lance was looking for a way of stepping away from these two characters. Yes, they were intense, intelligent, at times witty, but he feared what was under the surface. They were attractive, clever, and at times humorous, incongruous, ironic and delighting in wordplay.

Above all, transgression ruled. Despite finding it entertaining, Lance failed to find some meaning in it all. He was not a lover of the absurd, nor of nihilism, though his own disappointment rankled, took over and put the mean in meaning.

The money they paid him was good. Was it worth it? He asked himself that question over and over again. Prison had taught him something. He could sense pure evil, not in the sense of the urban art gallery he'd visited of that name, but something more, something lacking in mercy, a sense of a thrill perhaps. Thrill kill. He tried debating graffiti as art or vandalism. It didn't help. Murder as pleasure kept him awake at night. He began to question himself, put into play the critical reflection of his lessons, to question badness, to analyse his own distorted values.

On the scale of things, he was but a shoplifter up against the Ripper. He did a mental SWOT analysis; he examined his own strengths and flaws. They were minor on the scale of things, but the relative nature of evil wasn't the issue here. The threats he discerned outweighed the strengths and opportunities. Responsibility came into it. He thought of Penny. Penny was honest, that he knew, but not always. He concluded it was time to change. What were they going to do? He felt fragmented. He could see his personal flaws getting in the way. His everyday desire to hurt Penny was teaming up with a desire to hurt anyone. He knew he would have to problematise those binaries Penny had warned about. He blanked out the fact that there might be a fix for his problems, a different conversion therapy. Bad move. The pay was good. He reflected also on his personal cowardice and that hurt. He opted for plan A.

Chapter 13

The train from Leeds was ready to leave. Penny ran for it and dropped his ticket. Leaving the door open, he dived back onto the platform, turning a deaf ear to a station guard bawling at him. He picked the ticket up and leaped back on. The next train would have done. He carefully put his pass and ticket together. He made a vow to get the app which allowed him to book his next journey online and barcoded on his phone. His notebook remained at home; he felt naked without it. He fidgeted; he stared out of the window. There was a slight delay. From the window, he watched a water rat run along a log suspended over a pond and dive in. As the train was about to move off, with an apology, he saw the rat reappear, run up the log again and jump in. No one else seemed to notice it. Then the train started up.

The building was engaging, glass of varying types, triple glazed, bulletproof and made in Germany. He had chosen to carry his backpack only with water and a banana. At the door he was careful to follow protocol, and resist grinning.

Dove had cautioned him to drop any humour for a day. He showed his ID and fixed his eyes on the security man. He glimpsed around casually for cameras. The man resembled Dove in stature and was no doubt adept at the same things. He too moved with that grace; he possessed that centre of balance that Penny had tried to achieve. Security checked his bag. The man asked him to wait in the lobby. He pointed at several chairs. Penny sat and waited. It was 14:10. The next fifteen minutes caused him to sweat. It wasn't so much the trepidation, more the excitement of being in a place most people would never get access to. Clandestine came to mind and that appealed to the master spy in him.

They called him at exactly 14:27. A security guard escorted him to the lift. She said, "Floor eight. Room 817. She too looked handy in the fisticuffs department. "Left out the lift."

He muttered a thank you and entered the lift. The floor came up before he could even think. He stepped into a corridor and turned left. It was 14:29.

'Keep it simple, Ronnie-boy, keep it simple.' He knocked on the door. His hooded top felt comforting, his black jeans appropriate, his tartan shirt relaxing. The brown desert boots completed his outfit. Neither Periwinkle nor Dove had implied a dress code. Expecting a loud and authoritative 'come in', he was surprised when a young fresh-faced man opened the door.

"Doc. Penny! Please come in." The man was tall, not as tall or gangly as Periwinkle, but tall. Like Periwinkle he hardly touched the ground when he moved. He indicated a comfortable chair and took a chair himself near him, rather than behind the huge desk. The window revealed a splendid view of the Thames. "They gave me this refurbished office a few years after the IRA attacked the building in 2000." He grinned. That meant he was older than Penny first imagined. Lucas shook his hand warmly and spoke. "Have a maximum of forty-five minutes, Doc. Fill me in on Jim first and then the two ex- forces personnel."

Penny did just that, following a strict chronology, making no embellishments, tempted as he was. Lucas listened. Did he detect a wry smile when he related the story of Jim's death in the woods near Hanwood Priory? He wasn't sure. Lucas gave little away. Penny decided he had either been a pupil of Periwinkle, or he was related to him. When Penny had finished, he signalled so by spreading his hands, then bringing them close together and turning his head as if indicating another person's turn. Seminar stuff…

Lucas surprised him. "Please relate the final bit about Jim again, the episode in the wood, just as you did before."

Penny did so.

Afterwards, Lucas Guess spoke with the flair of a good therapist. "You told me the story twice word for word. I doubt there was the slightest difference in the storytelling. However, the first time you told me as a matter of fact, each word chosen carefully and the story complete. The second time you expressed emotion as you mentioned certain aspects, referring to the young boy Max and what you fictionalised, and what really happened. Fascinating. You must've been a very entertaining lecturer, Dr Penny!" He stood up and moved towards his desk. Penny eyed the ground, painfully aware of the past tense. Lucas was, to use a topical term, forensic.

"You don't have a description of the two women. We do. They are well documented and well-dodgy."

Penny looked over his specs.

Lucas responded, "Ronnie or Ron?"

"Ronnie, please." He looked at the clock. "In the time left I'll make some entries on my laptop. I doubt anything will come through immediately. If you tell me your email address, I'll send what I can via that. I hope too it's secure?"

"It is. I have two and Periwinkle set one of them up." He glimpsed at Lucas to see what effect Periwinkle's name did – nothing. Lucas started to type. A warmth crept across his face as he worked. Was it the mention of Periwinkle? Work?

Penny hadn't bothered to dig out what the connection was, but for some reason assumed that it was important. He needed to stay on the task.

Lucas finished his typing and then stood up again. It was 15:10. "I'll be in touch as soon as I join a few dots. If there's a contract floating around that's emanated from here or down the road at Thames House, I'll find out. The rest is confidential. We will block any monies involved and thus, the contract on your life." He shook Penny's hand and escorted him to the door. "Oh, and please give my love to Uncle Peri and his mum. Is he still practising those lethal martial arts?"

"Martial arts?" Penny didn't know anything about that.

Lucas grinned. "You obviously didn't know. There's so much hidden, or should I say not revealed. He's an expert, definitely. Studied in Japan. When my sister and I were teenagers, we used to call him Uncle Ninja, the killing machine. We used to joke about it. Sis reckoned he didn't need a gun. He's also very quiet. He won't tell you much. His colleague too – Dove.

They both saw a lot of action together and came through. Some talk about it, some don't. What you have are two very good comrades."

Penny took to Guess. He too moved with stealth. Penny vowed to work on that and on his core. As for Periwinkle, he had been witness to the results of his abilities. Nothing surprised him. He hadn't grinned once. He wanted to ring Dove and tell him.

"It's been good to meet you. Until next time." Lucas dismissed him. Penny, taken by the martial arts aspect, vowed to learn more about it. Ground fighting might just come in handy. He stumbled away. Yes, he was aware his two friends had been through it, but what? He was aware that Periwinkle was almost magical… like Silver. He took the stairs. He must get fitter. On the way downstairs he passed a man in his thirties who in his estimation was about to say hello and then stopped. The man turned away slightly as if he's made an error of recognition.

Penny smiled and got a smile in return. Penny was convinced he'd never seen him before. But he stored away in his pictorial brain an image. Black, head shaved, looked very fit, nice smile. His loose-fitting jacket, green shirt and grey loafers completed the picture of a man at ease and supremely fit. The baggy outfit did nothing to hide the musculature. Penny looked back to see the man clear the steps three at a time and disappear. Penny suspected he was heading to the eighth floor. The man definitely recognised him, and he was about to speak. He meant nothing to Penny. He let it go. Penny knew he had so much to catch up on; new clothes, fitness, and a move or two from Uncle Ninja. His visit helped bring back one of his popular words: the guesstimate. He couldn't fathom who the man was on the stairs, he couldn't even guess.

He left the building feeling safer. Yet something didn't jell. Lucas Guess had a reassuring manner. What he intended to do and what he could do was a complete blank to Penny. He was, however, a relative of Periwinkle's. To Penny there was no doubt that very connection had got him into Babylon to meet Guess. He had no idea what Guess was in the hierarchy. He still felt better. For better or for worse, worldliness and evil, that is the duality of Babylon.

From Vauxhall he walked to Waterloo, took the Northern Line to Leicester Square and changed to the Piccadilly Line and on to King's Cross. He had time to buy a sandwich and a newspaper in the shop. He stared up at the board. The Leeds train was ten minutes away. *Martial arts of what kind?* he wondered. He had an uncanny feeling he was mixing with two heroic figures: one the stolid and deceptive Dove, and the ethereal Periwinkle. His academic side, that so European aspect of his, wanted to know. He still felt for Europe. His other side was intrigued by Eastern Asian philosophy. Following his own take on such, he decided that it was not knowing that was important. The grey areas were the best. On the train he ate his sandwich. He stared out of the window thinking of absolutely nothing. It was the most relaxing journey, an emptying out. The newspaper remained folded in his pocket.

He passed Guess's message onto Periwinkle with a twinkle

in his eyes. "Lu… Lucas sends his love to Uncle Peri." He nearly said Lucifer. Periwinkle acknowledged it with his dimpled smile.

"Is he OK? Did he mention his mum?"

"I would say so. He is so chilled, it's hard to discern what would rattle him. I doubt much. He never mentioned his mum."

"Then she must be okay." He returned to his book he'd pulled from Penny's eclectic mix of history, weird fiction, 'faction, and fickin' detective stories'. (The last two snippets were Dove's description of his library.) The collection of books was thinning out as he felt the need to remove old baggage. A book lay on the side. *Living in the Tao* had been a present from a Lishi instructor. He loved the gentility, and yet strenuousness of the exercises. The dance-like movements enthralled him. Moreover, the poetic terminology such as Hand of the Wind appealed. He made a promise to find out what it all meant. It was all so different from his time in the ring as a teenage boxer. Pugilism versus poetry with a view to maiming the opponent. Verse could do it.

As per usual he made his own moves up. Reading the Tao book was a pleasant surprise. He had often identified with Asia and had issues with the Western ego. His reading had led to his realisation that he was horribly European. Meditation, exercise and a change of lifestyle worried him. Writing had helped. He was in touch with the trees, the air, the water, the earth, and beginning to understand the inner self. Should he start making sourdough? He made lists, endless lists, and wrote about air and such.

Should he include fire alongside water, or had he been

reading too many implausible novels about art history and secret signs? He couldn't articulate it, but if he'd asked Periwinkle, he might have taken a path of a very different nature. Periwinkle had urged him to write about his closeness with the sea, the sand. He was beginning to understand. On the beach he felt at ease. He listened to the tide retreating over the pebbles, its percussive snare a gently brushed drum rhythm over the murmuring sand. He watched the night sea, moonlit and mercurial running like liquid metal as the moon, beautiful Selina, caught the white-capped hoary beads as they shattered into tiny glasslike fragments. He liked being alone with this; time was not important. This was the beginning. This was lesson one.

The seminar group of postgrad students had read his work on the Dark Arts. It was the twins in person they desired to know more of. He stuttered into it, then relaxed. It was his story. He referred to his interview on Table Read, then asked them to introduce themselves. He was disappointed to find that Maureen was absent. Alice was very much to the fore of the group, relentless in her questions and probing, Alice, slim, wiry build, dark hair with the most piercing deep blue eyes, eyes that missed nothing.

He found her intriguing. He looked for signs of her other self but was distracted by her eagerness to find out about the twins and their assumed psychopathy. Alice was vivacious, bright. She was able to turn theories upside down, play around with them. He felt that same pull he'd felt with

Annabelle. Alice recognised it. He avoided asking her leading questions. He so wanted to discover her backstory.

"What do the twins' diaries and documents reveal that led them to the so-called artworks? And what led them to commit murder? I assume you don't mind me referring to the bodies as artworks."

"No, not at all, Alice, excellent questions." He wondered about questions, the what questions, the why questions. He wondered what led her. He wondered why. Her demeanour was pleasant, her interest academic.

Before he could answer, Ralph, another student, a young man with a long beard (ZZ to Penny) added to that. "And what is your own opinion of their statements? That is, do you accept their take uncritically?"

"In a word, no. I'll begin with Alice's question and move to analysis. That will offer time for you to critique both my analysis and deconstruct, if you like, their text." He looked around. "I must add that the book is a history in one sense, in that it takes place in the past, though the story belongs to a literary genre not unlike the pre-Romantic work of your Graveyard Poets." He looked at Alice. "Theirs was an attempt to speak to the universal, and a degree of melancholy beneath the writing, the oral statements and the work itself. You must ask yourselves why the sudden interest in the Graveyard Poets in twenty-first century Britain. What is their relevance to the here and now?"

Alice looked intrigued. Eggleston sat back with a knowing smile and his own sombre meditations. Penny resumed.

"The discs – the material on the discs was massive. I'm still working through them even after publication. My aim is to see if I could discern the moment when they decided to do the work, and the incidents, or whatever, that sent them on their final creations."

He decided to let them do the work. He gave them two handouts documenting the first sculpture, and a further one discussing the dilemma they were faced when purloined bodies ran out and killing followed. "In a way, they were graverobbers." He eyed Alice. The group read. Gasps and tuts followed. Penny scrutinised Alice. Her questions surprised him.

"Were they devoid of moral sensibility? Did they show an ethical side to their nature? I don't want to answer my own question, but was it a case of moral blindness?"

Penny's answers covered many issues. He quoted their original texts. Another handout followed. "Peter and Annabelle were totally aware of the ethical issues. Remember Annabelle was a nurse, he a dentist, familiar to biomedical ethics, values. We are thrown into a debate about art and morality — that is, if we accept the 'tableaux sculptures' as art. Autonomism separates values and art, and their writing suggests they gave themselves their own law...

They left many documents — letters — to each other during their forced separation, and I repeat *forced*. That was their own take on their schooling. Their father wished them to grow apart, his son to follow in his footsteps, his daughter to become a nurse, nursing labelled as female work. The debate hinges on woman's power and powerlessness. They both let him down. That runs as a thread through their diaries. They point the finger at me and my scholarship for the later work, the early work developed in a medical and theatrical context, one of experimentation with bodies, bodies as object of art, not objectified or degraded, in their words, rather 'given new spirit'. They had bodies at their disposal. Rightly or wrongly, they decided to work with them. To them, the bodies became symbolic.

"The twins read profusely; they studied the sculptors. There was a footnote to Edna Manley and her early frustration with the art 'world', others to predynastic work, Epstein, and of course the postmodern and spirit revival: Pocomania." He smiled. "It isn't clear whether they dabbled in such at all. In my opinion, spirit possession was for the work and not for them." That, he thought, was debatable. No one contradicted it – shame.

"In other words, they were incredibly well read. Did they examine their own preoccupations with sickness and death?" Alice prompted him.

"Indeed, and in their world the sculptures performed the exorcism. The works performed such and made links to the modern community, acting as memorials. In their own words, the works mediated between life, death and sickness for a community doomed to perpetual sickness, a postmodern condition. Their opinion, in this case."

"Objectification surely connotes some degradation?" Alice interrupted.

"Exactly, the viewer has to see that, yet the twins' own life offered a way forward, in a sense. Peter and Annabelle raised many questions of androgyny and issues of difference. One can trace their path towards interpersonal detachment through their art and their documents."

He handed them a small document from Annabelle's

diaries. He watched. They read greedily and gasped; they concurred. Annabelle showed the ingenuity of a great general, strategic planning, a capacity for abstract thought, the desired goals and results. She was a visionary in that she was aware that most plans can turn to shit (her words) and improvisation is always required. She was the decision-maker, Peter the dreamer.

A student spoke. "The stability of their writing is bewildering, as is the matter-of-fact way with which they undertook their task."

"Yes. The decision to purloin bodies was hers, the first sketches his, and he was a damn good drawer. They took their first body after their father died and even contemplated using 'Dad' for a work of art. Difficult at times to see if they were joking. The idea evolved and two young successful well-to-do adults began to work on real bodies, their ability to obtain them organised by Peter, the themes arranged jointly, following an art history, and culminating in their suicides, both in sculpture and in 'life'." He handed a small memo around. He talked a little about the centrality of the body in art. One student cleverly remarked that it was representing the body that was central; this was the body as art, and that too had a history, for example the reclaiming of the body by feminists and performance artists. Another mentioned the long history of suicide. Penny took up the latter first.

"They challenged suicide as a loss of meaning; they challenged the spiritual as a quest for meaning, and perhaps meaning itself."

Another student interrupted excitedly. "They mention Jeremy Bentham's auto-icon."

"They do. It was an influence. He's still there at UCL, a presence, but I'm told he's not voting anymore." (The old ones are still the best.) The students were familiar with the line; muted laughter followed. Penny returned to the significant memo. He indicated one of the quieter students to read a short passage. She immediately brightened up.

"The memo: 'Peter, the lecturer Penny has been on the radio again telling us where to go with our work'."

"Thanks. Well read. In one respect I felt responsible, but don't believe they meant to shift blame. Rather, they saw my role as a mentee would." He avoided his more down to earth 'wait until your father gets home' analogy. He moved on quickly, advising the group might speak after, but too late.

"Their detachment is in the subtext of the document!" The quiet student, Bettany, spoke. "The shared and the non-shared seems to play a pivotal role in their development towards their taking lives."

A barrage of questions followed. In charge of the seminar, the course tutor, Professor Eggleston, intervened. "I think we should hear Dr Penny out first. It is quite clear we are discussing one of the broader aspects of psychopathy." Eggleston remarked on the philosophy of tears and the silent language of grief in the graveyard poetry and made some links. Penny was grateful.

"Thank you, though in my reckoning the strands merge, the notion of impulsiveness is highlighted throughout Annabelle's diaries." He handed out a further sheet. "Peter shows a more detached view. The problem we have is assessing the shared environmental factors, and the fact the twins were different, but somehow merged into one." Penny dropped the academic and told them of his lived experience in the gallery, their voice as one. Peter was sociable, Annabelle less so, and both twins multidimensional.

"A short handout on Peter's first description of the sculptures will indicate some differences. I can't say too much, otherwise you won't rush out and buy the book. Suffice to say, the twins' self-awareness and critical analysis says more than many profiles will. Both shared a belief in their dominance. Read your own diaries and assess them in this light. Both were fearless. I have to paraphrase, I'm afraid, and being afraid was alien to these two. Childish problematic traits are not always an indicator; the need for stimulation was. When they crafted a snowman as children they fashioned it to look like their father. The dressing up resulted in a living picture of Dad, the beginnings of the tableaux. My reading of the twins' documents (and they are vast, as are their extended conversations) indicate no genetic influence. I'm no expert. Some socially shared aspects are apparent, environmental, if you like. One thing they shared: lack of guilt. This is apparent from childhood. Neither were dysfunctional. Peter held down a brilliant career, Annabelle too, up to a point, though her father deemed her headstrong, to his mind that is, for a woman."

They laughed. Alice shared a smile.

"Most problematic was their truthfulness, be it shocking. I found their descriptions of the preparation of bodies and the strategic planning that underpinned their 'art' *(he allowed himself an inverted comma gesture as he spoke)* to be without fault. If one was looking for detachment, then there is a contradictory warmth in their discussions of their artwork.

Twin modelling factors are problematized here. Neither had grandiose opinions of their art, more a pride in the sense of artistry. Their own findings would require analysis by experts in the field, those interested in differences between monozygotic and dizygotic. The twins were the latter. I have offered to turn over the documents for fieldwork."

He broke off. The students raised their hands for questions. Alice seemed very interested in his problems with psychopathy and art. Others chipped in, and Eggleston did a summary of which Penny was jealous. Alice asked him about his own detachment. A cute question.

"It's academic."

"And the twins?"

Penny chose not to pursue that and was relieved by Ralph who asked him if he was a twin. Laughter.

"That the twins were academic is without question, Alice, their boldness too, though that is a debatable aspect of psychopathy, the point you all seem interested in. There is a lot of questions unanswered. Their childhood was fairly 'normal'. They were well-to-do and often left to their own devices. Not unusual. When I was of an age for scrumping apples, they were planning masquerades." He jumped ahead. "A vital point in their development was on receipt of their first body. The paragraph is worth reading out. It has a clandestine nature. They wrote it when they were in their early twenties and were beginning to rebel against their strict parenting:

"'Peter, just think what we could do with bodies, real people!'

'I know, Annabelle, I've thought about it for some time'.
'Think of those statues, their musculature, their physique'.
'If only we could portray their minds'.

"In a weird sense, I can see no better choice of words. They believed with the suicides they could do that... Complex as it is, the minds of the victims echoed for them the minds of the portrayed. They had unconsciously pursued suicides before Chatterton. Ajax? Cleopatra? The letters between them suggest a gentle melancholy something akin to your eighteenth-century poets. Annabelle and Peter were prepared for death. That is of course public knowledge. Their detailed notes list all the victims, and they were victims. Their souls can rest for the believers among you."

Eggleston curtailed the barrage that followed. They finished with a couple of bottles of wine students had brought in. As per usual the important questions then followed. He tried to avoid Alice and mingle. She was still probing. Alice's charm more than matched his own, but neither were pathological liars, otherwise a career in politics might have ensued. Both had good judgement. She spotted his slanted dialogue; he spotted her discernment and her attempts to disguise her aloofness.

He finished with a large handout of comparison and contrast between the growing twins. Their own sense of detail was apparent as youngsters, their belief in their work a real thesis to wrestle with in postmodern times. He noticed Alice never took a single note. He shook several hands, including hers, a warm, steady handshake. He hoped he had disguised his interest in her. He thanked all for their investigative questions. Then he left. There was still so much more to say. The twins spoke so much about the impact of death, their mother, their father, their elder brother, and finally planned and executed their own art.

He emailed Tammy to tell her of his findings.

Alice hadn't told Mo of the talk. She was furious. Alice tried to tamp it down. "It wasn't that great, Mo. It gave me more of an insight into the man we are going to remove. Consider it as intel." She failed to mention her attraction to Penny and his interest in her.

"The tapes the twins left were most interesting. The tabloids imploded with references to Francois Villon." (Some academic on the make leaked the name of this medieval poet-villain).

Maureen said 'he' was a bloody rogue; a crim. Alice assumed it was a compliment. Did Mo mean Villon? Maybe she meant Penny.

"Mo, none of the expected traits were revealed on the tapes. They spoke with warmth of their work, their quoted statements showed sensitivity and questioned the ethics of art and sculpture, desire to please, even, and to listen to other authorities. The amorality posing as a set of malleable morals that Penny had witnessed at Carshalton was problematized. They referred back to him. That was the problem."

"Not our problem," Mo concluded, "his." She drew an imaginary pistol, aimed and fired.

Chapter 14

Dove 'persuaded' Penny to go running. He was keen to keep fit. He also wanted to pick Dove and Periwinkle's brains on the martial arts. They kept to flat ground running alongside the River Wharfe. They picked up pace past the allotments and along to the gravel pits, recently cordoned off with an otter fence, then around and back on the road through Knotford Nook. Otters, Penny understood, were fearsome predators. He watched his friends. They saw a white van parked up. They wondered if Freeman had clocked it. The numberplate was different.

Both men looked balanced, graceful, and very fit. Dove's baggy tracksuit barely seemed to flap or move as he glided along, as if he was part of the adjacent river, connected to the stream and going with it. Penny was slowly gathering what he thought was a greater understanding of his two friends' partnership. He felt on the periphery. Then he smiled to himself – that is where he belonged.

There were advantages with acquaintances and consequential strangers. These men were friends. Yes, they were hosts to his ideas, yet they had their own and were not to be ignored. He decided on the run to move to a more co-operative partnership. It would begin with a new regime. When his head cleared, he realised they were way ahead of him. As he aimed to catch them, he studied.

Periwinkle moved with the grace of a ballet dancer. Penny felt new muscles working, and aching. Yet, he couldn't emulate either of his two friends' balletic movements. When he tried, his feet hit the ground even harder, causing a slapping sound. He did as usual – he put one foot in front of the other and kept going. It was a good run. He felt fitter, less concerned about time or place. The landscape was a painting to him. He held onto that and the experience of mysteriousness, reading without supplementing the landscape, becoming one with it. He travelled through it; he stood where he wished. Withdrawal, sanctuary, flatness, imagination. He began to work on his fitness.

His new health regime, along with the blogs, was clearing his thoughts, and what remained was a more grounded self. That was how he liked to put it. His mixture of yoga and Pilates was totally his own concoction, a mash up, a veritable smorgasbord of both. Dove dubbed it 'piloga' then 'yolates'.

It worked. Penny moved with more awareness, not the cat or the river like his comrades, though he would strive to achieve more. The prospect of information from Guess concerned him. So much was stressful, so much needed eliminating. He thought of a friend who stopped reading newspapers, stopped listening to the news, thereby removing all stress factors, as he saw them. When the Covid epidemic broke, a friend of his friend called to say he couldn't visit due to the pandemic. He said, "What pandemic?" Knowledge was distress. Delusion was good.

In between their chats and rambling, Periwinkle secreted himself away or disappeared for hours. Once in a while he made calls. He tapped away on his laptop. Then he would read anything from Penny's shelves. They could hear him upstairs. At one point Penny heard him say, "Really? That bad? Oh dear." The problem with listening in and picking up a fragment meant reading between or outside the lines, and so he closed his ears.

"What is bad?"

Then Periwinkle reported back. He confirmed Byron and Wright were both drummed out the army, 'cashiered' as he put it. "But wait for it," he added, "they both appear to like killing. In one case, Wright was suspected of putting a bullet in a wounded man's head, the other inflicting pain 'close to torture' on a captured Afghan soldier. Both disregarded all codes of honour." He didn't enlarge on their activities. It was clear that Alice and Maureen showed no affinity with others and little guilt. Reading between the lines, they manifested a sociopathic dislike for humankind, animals and, he added, for each other. "Then I came across a gap, which coincides with your prison theory. The gap itself implies another issue."

Penny wondered if that had come from Lucas.

Lance was sharp enough to understand false trust and recognised the grooming process. Deceptive as the process was, he realised they'd targeted, primed, and outmanoeuvred him by educated guile a whole degree beyond him. He had trusted them. His change of interest in his willingness to help them or meet them was useless. He was isolated and vulnerable. He claimed he had some work to do. They were fit, and dangerously intelligent and tattooed. They, he concluded, had done their research well. Mo had a nose ring that he couldn't quite make his mind up about. He was the victim. A runner was the best way out.

They scared him a bit, no, scared him shitless. He'd met similar cases along the way, especially in the nick and at the university. Their hatred for animals worried him. Animals in his opinion were more ethical than humans, and never went to war with each other. Did they? Yet the very thing that scared him drew him in. Lance dived in the deep end and spied on Penny. He reported back on Penny's work routines and email content.

He felt wanted, empowered, fretful. What were they up to? The note through the door inviting him around for drinks and a chat was torn up. Lance started to pack his meagre possessions. Then he changed his mind.

Chapter 15

It was several days before Dove confirmed that Alice and her colleague and flatmate Maureen had been in prison, together, both for crimes of violence against harmless victims. He didn't proffer details. What to do next? "That doesn't make them the killers or the torturers of young Max," he said, "but, by gum, they certainly fit the profile. They are obviously quite brainy too. Let's call Freeman and brief her. A call from the law might stir the pot a bit."

All agreed. Penny suggested wheeling in Jeremy Bentham to cast a vote. Unaware of the extent of his surveillance, he would have seen another irony in the Bentham connection if aware of such. The Internet was the new panopticon, the obsession with total information and access to it, due to the threat of terrorism, was real. Penny was being watched.

"It's a gamble. We need to be careful how we approach it," Periwinkle rounded off. He was right. Dove agreed. He didn't want to fuck with their new-found careers. Well, not deliberately.

Penny assumed Dove didn't really mean what he said about being careful. The assassins, as Penny had taken to calling them, deploying new romantic language, were ex-forces. That weird notion of esprit de corps might be relevant.

Dove added to it. "Having done time or not, they have a thriving business, and it would be unfair to screw that up." Then without waiting for an answer he called Freeman.

Periwinkle sighed. "The rich build their own prisons to live in. The poor steal from them." Penny made a note of it. He added: *Where is the prison now? The cells are open, the bars are gone.*

Dove was succinct. Freeman recorded it. She thought any angle was worth pursuing. And with a policewoman's zeal she sent two 'men' out to call on them. One was a woman. The police and pronouns were an issue, as Freeman testified; policing speech was an issue. If people choose to be marginalised that is their problem. "I've asked them to suss them out, that's all, both the pronouns and the people." Talking to Dove she said, "I've asked my men to enquire if they know Penny or have any connection to him. We want to rattle the cage a little, but not reveal too much… Best not mention him directly but in some obtuse way."

Trolling came to mind. Obtuse seemed appropriate.

Byron and Mo were deep in planning their second attempt on Penny who was carrying on as if he knew nothing. They began to believe that was the case. This time there was to be no fucking about, just a shot to the head and out, then back to work and back to 'school' removing all evidence to a place in Bradford. The Cross Pipes car park was out.

They had another hit too which they decided to do

before, and several painting and decorating jobs. The removal of a woman whose only crime in her husband's eyes was to burn his dinner. Alice joked that he was eating it at the time. The punishment fitted the crime. Business was looking up.

Lance kept them informed. Penny was working on a novel which featured Headingley. Penny was planning to wander the area. He had chosen a path which led to a small secluded wooded opening. It was simple. From there he would walk to the bus stop opposite Woody's pub. This intel provided opportunities to make the kill.

Mo desired more. She still wanted to pick him up. The dark triad that governed her thoughts was at work and wished for fulfilment. They were both capable of resisting. They had read Annabelle's notions of planning and absorbed them. Lance warned them that Penny was capable of changing his plans, always favouring the random.

Byron was to take a shot from close range. They were both tooled up, knives carried by both. The job required an armoury. They would follow him separately. The cut was to be one that was fatal yet allow the victim time to die slowly. There was another knock on the door. Then a note dropped through. They waited. A car drove off and, reaching the window, Mo saw the police car. "It's the law. They—"

Byron cut in. "Relax, just checking on our new status. We're upright working citizens and students trying to better ourselves."

Mo read. The note was handwritten. It stated their names in full. It asked them to ring a Detective Freeman as soon as. They waited an hour. Byron called.

"Sorry, we were out at work when you called. Got to

make a living."

Freeman was out of the office. An administrator clocked the call. He said that Detective Freeman would get back to them. Byron tried to dig out the purpose of the house call.

The speaker didn't know or preferred not to say. "I suspect a routine call, ma'am."

Byron resisted the urge to say she was not a ma'am, said thanks then rang off. Routine Activity Theory and the notion of a target came to mind. Penny, the suitable target could be behind this. RAT it was. But was it routine? The offenders hoped that this time his capable guardians would be absent.

Freeman's staff reported in. If the couple were out, as they said, their van was parked a few doors down. Two days passed. Mo and Byron had more or less forgotten the house call. It was time to let Lance in on the plot. They had played games with Lance.

He came round; they told him. Lance bought into it with zeal. The promised pay-off was beyond his wildest dreams. All he had to do was keep track of Penny's online diary, then bugger off smartly.

This odd couple were going to finish Dr Penny off, and at that moment he revelled in it, though it didn't jell. Lance had a growing awareness of his underlying naivety. In prison, alongside the shrewd and streetwise, his confidence had waned somewhat. He questioned himself. Was he precipitating his own doom? Was he heading back to prison? The discussion over, Lance was enjoying a cold beer when the police called for the second time. The reality hadn't sunk in. He had crossed the line.

A rapping on the door indicated the return of the law.

The music within told the police they were at home. It was Beth Hart and Jo Bonamassa. As Beth Hart stretched her vocal cords to wonderful effect on the climax of, *I'd Rather Go Blind*, the caller gave what Mo described as a copper's knock. Mo had already glimpsed out the window. "It's police." Byron answered the door blocking it while Lance hovered in the kitchen. Following Mo's directions, he headed for the fire escape.

Alice opened the door to the two uniformed officers. "About to get in the shower. Can I help, officers?"

Lance was halfway down the fire escape. Thank God for risk assessment measures. He thought of probability, then headed home.

Alice beckoned them in. Mo was reading a book. Byron turned the sound off as Joe Bonamassa's vintage telecaster reverberated around the room, raw and powerful. WPC Jarrett looked around. PC Murphy did the talking.

"Just making enquiries into an incident on the morning of October twelfth." Murphy kept it vague as instructed. "Won't keep you long."

Mo put the book down and her glass.

"Could you say where you were on the morning of that day?"

Byron waited. Mo spoke first, peering over the top of her book. She chose, as near as damn it (well not quite), the truth. "We were in Otley beginning a decorating job along Pool Road. We had breakfast in Harrogate and picked up the keys and started late, around ten."

Byron interrupted. "Close to 10:15, I would say."

"Can you verify that?"

"I expect the neighbours will vouch for our presence. We aim to be fairly quiet, but some noise is inevitable."

They had left a radio playing Radio Two which to some might signal a presence. Radio Two seemed appropriate for reasons of its listeners, according to younger colleagues and critics, mostly over thirty-five and staid.'

Jarrett and Murphy turned to go. "We won't keep you. Leave you to your homework!"

Mo smiled as she made a mental note of their knowledge of their current studies and status.

"No worries. Thanks. It's an effort at times building a business and studying."

Byron, who had stayed standing, headed to the door.

Jarrett turned and asked the question: "Do either of you know Ronnie Penny?"

Mo shook her head. Then realising that all tabloid readers knew of Doctor Death, changed her mind. "Oh him, Doctor Death. No, not personally, but recall him from the papers. He sounds a character."

Byron jutted in. "He gave a seminar recently to us at the uni. He's a sound academic. I follow his blog. Seems nice."

Murphy spoke this time. "He's retired. Recently he has suffered some harassment. Nothing serious."

"Oh dear, poor guy. Harassment, you say?" No clues were forthcoming.

Murphy spoke again. "Nothing we can't resolve. Thanks for your time." At that they left. They walked as if unconcerned and got in the car. As they walked towards it a curtain twitched. Jarrett caught a glimpse of a young man three doors down, but not enough time to register his features.

Jarrett's instincts told her he was not just a bystander.

"Murph, did you notice there were three glasses on the table? Wonder who was hiding in the kitchen."

"Let's report back to Freeman."

In the flat, Mo left the window and looked at the third glass. "Do you think they noticed anything at all? "

"Not sure. Didn't seem too bright."

"Look, we both have a seminar tomorrow, Byron, so down to work. Let's see how it pans out."

The shower beckoned.

Freeman was interested in the feedback. Finally, Jarrett mentioned that someone else had been watching from behind a curtain. "Might just be a nosy neighbour. And then there's the third glass." Jarrett nodded an affirmation.

"Next time, one of you can hang out the back and watch the fire escape."

"Good work, you two. Might be worth knocking three doors down at some point in passing. Make up some excuse." That was Freeman giving an order.

"Will do, ma'am." At that, they left the station, feeling quite elated but not sure what they had done. Jarrett had an inkling it was to stir up something. If that was the case, why not do it now before they went off shift?

"We're finished, Jarrett. My missus is already struggling to see to the young 'uns at bedtime."

"Okay. I'll drop you."

The address wasn't far from Meanwood. They stopped at

a semi in Cookridge. Murphy mentioned he had his sights on moving his family to Horsforth. "Still, the schools were good in Cookridge so that was something."

Jarrett turned the car and drove back to Burley. She parked further away, walked a few streets then rapped on the door. The young man who answered had his laptop under his arm and closed the lid as she spoke. "Sorry, sir, we are making door to door enquiries about a missing person. Are you the only resident?"

Lance wasn't sure if it was the same woman he'd seen earlier. "At the moment, yes."

She fumbled in her pocket and apologised. "It's been a long day, and I've left her photo in the car. I'll come back." She took out her notebook. It was a pretty lame excuse. The young man seemed nervous. Jarrett hung on in.

He rallied. "Anything to help."

Then she asked what he feared all along. "Just for the record, can I have your name?"

He faltered. "Peirce."

"Peirce, what?"

"Lance Peirce, pronounced Purse. I'm a web designer!"

"Do you have a card? Might pass it on."

Lance's leaflets were in the hall. He chose one and handed it over.

"Thanks, Lance. Just starting up, are you?"

Lance was growing warier by the minute. "No, I started some time ago, then got myself into trouble. It's a fresh start, I guess."

The police officer nodded. "I understand." She smiled. "Thanks for being straightforward, Lance." She could check records later. "Goodnight for now, and sorry to disturb your work."

"Thank you." Lance went inside and collapsed on the old sofa. Where was he to go now? The two up the road were clearly trouble. He'd had enough. He decided to take that step back. He couldn't. He was now a confidant in a proposed killing. The glow was dimming. The problem of probability. He tried to work out the stats. He should have listened to his inner misgivings.

Penny was wrapping up for the day and heading to the pub to meet Dove. He hinted at how he might get fitter. All Dove could say was, "Do you fancy doing three rounds with me?"

"I'll buy three rounds in the pub. How about that?"

Dove didn't argue.

Periwinkle was in Bradford visiting Saida. Penny chose the junction for its beer. In his writing clobber, an old fisherman's jumper with a hole in the sleeve and brown boots (his 'muck'), he sat down, put his backpack on the floor and savoured his beer.

Dove found a seat near the door. They took a moment to sup some ale. Neither spoke. Wiping the froth off his mouth with his sleeve, Penny made to speak. He did something he'd promised not to do. "Who does Periwinkle get his information from?" And in true form another question followed: "What martial arts did he study?"

Dove took a long sup of his ale and said, "Ask him." At that, he rose and bought two more. He did say one more word: Nectar.

Penny understood that was not a code word. These moments were precious to Dove. He didn't want them marred by questions. At that moment, Penny decided that he would take a few days' break, try to give his friends a tour: Salt's Mill, the Trinity Centre in Leeds, a few walks along the river, a run out to Bolton Abbey, maybe a walk up onto Barden Fell. It is bleak and lovely, close to nothingness… and brought him to himself. The walk would take them either to Simon's Seat or The Valley of Desolation.

Lance didn't check Penny's emails that night. In fact, he did some cleansing. He wiped all evidence of his activities with Alice and Maureen from the laptop, and sat down to compose a website, a logo for a small outlet making soap and candles. The money wasn't great, but it was honest. His legitimate business was picking up. If the police came checking, he could at least prove that. He was in a knot of his own doing. Hubris and hatred had tied it. He thought of Penny and hate. He needed to let go. No, he despised hippy shit about letting go. A hint of a smile broke his worry.

Penny was careful how he broached the question. He asked after Saida and got a shy 'fine, thanks' answer. He went for the blunt approach… in a roundabout way. "Periwinkle," he said cautiously, "if it's a problem giving your old sources, I'd rather you didn't. You don't need to call in favours for me."

Periwinkle stared at him, his deep blue eyes twinkling all along. Penny continued. "I mean, if it's a problem?"

Periwinkle looked down, then up, and replied. "I realise that you know nothing about us, really. We've always appreciated your holding back your curiosity which we know is difficult for you."

Penny felt small.

"Enough to say I have relatives in high places, places I shunned myself, places I didn't want to go to. I was happier with Dove and my comrades. Having said that, I must add that our officers were on first name terms with us... that is 'the men.' If I can help, I will."

Penny felt humbled. He muttered a sorry.

Periwinkle said, "Not required."

That was that. Penny felt satisfied. He preferred the enigma that was Periwinkle. The martial arts could wait

Periwinkle added a rider. "I will tell you something else: if we start digging up top, there are going to be repercussions. The best we can do is get so far up and attempt to single out someone in the chain that can put a stop to this nonsense. Lucas is our man. He will get through to us, inevitably."

'This nonsense', as far as Penny understood, was a reference to his impending assassination. It sounded healthier than killing, and that sounded daft.

Periwinkle looked determined. "We may have to split up to do this. Jim was a mover, and he may have worked for others. His contact in the chain of things, which is the one above him, is in the Gulf of Oman. Do you fancy a holiday, Penny? You have visited the Gulf already. How's your Arabic?

If we put pressure on our two scallywags, they too will disappear and that might make it difficult to find them…

"They might go back to Maidstone and Birmingham where they came from. Both came from respectable families, which doesn't at all surprise me. We might have to scour the Far East or Brunei if we scare them off. They are familiar with both. America too is a possibility! I'm second-guessing at the moment, and that is not very professional."

Penny hoped it was the desert. He felt at home there in a way he could never put words to. He saw the desert first as a giant beach, then it came alive. It had its own persona, and he liked it; scurrying ants, evasive foxes, the wind scorpion or camel spiders, slithering snakes, scorpions, turkey-like birds and the dreaded desert locusts, deemed to be tasty by the locals. He recalled the laughing dove and its intricate nest with more than one hundred and forty twigs. He eyed his friend and smiled.

He was back in the Gulf. The Bedouin lifestyle amazed him. Across the dry Wadi a man arrived with his camel. Before too long he tethered his camel, set his tent up and had coffee on the go. Two days later, when Penny decided to go and chat, he got up and the man was gone. He heard that the late Sultan Qaboos had a small village built to encourage these itinerants to settle. The Sultan decided a royal visit was in order. He found the residents housed in tents; inside the houses the residents kept the goats. Outside, they erected their tents.

"Maidstone and Birmingham?" he said. Dove and Periwinkle sat back waiting for the anecdote with differing views on the outcome and length of his tale. He'd already started…

"I was eighteen and at art college in Birmingham. They threw me out, you know." They did and urged him on. The story was uncanny. So much of Penny's life bordered on the inexplicable. "I went to London on a Friday night to see a show, a major exhibition, on a whim… Actually, the show itself is a story worth recounting, but I'll stick to the text."

Dove whistled a thank you.

"On a whim I decided to visit two friends in Maidstone, both art students. We had a really silly and very drink-oriented weekend. Come Sunday teatime it dawned on me I had to get back. I had little money left and I set off to hitch. It was getting dark. I managed a lift from a guy who dropped me at a convenient spot near the motorway which I guess was the M25. As night came down so did a horrible damp fret. Two hours passed and nothing. I began to feel cold, quite desperate and doubted my actions. Indeed, I felt teary-eyed and worried. Out of the mist a light-coloured Mercedes appeared and stopped…

A couple in their late twenties sat in the front. The man simply said, 'Get in'. I did and thanked them and sat shivering. I glanced over my shoulder and behind me to the right was a skull. At that point, the man laughed. He introduced himself and his wife. The skull, he explained, was for an amateur dramatics production of *Hamlet* and his wife was a part of it. He, it turned out, was a doctor! He jokingly said that gave him access to Yorrick."

Periwinkle looked intrigued. Dove was fiddling with a biro.

"They proved to be excellent company. They asked where I was going. I simply replied, Birmingham. They were too. The buses ran all night then. I might just have had enough money in my pocket to do it when they dropped me. A long walk was more likely.

"We entered the Birmingham area. The man asked where I lived. I told him, Yardley Fields Road. The silence that followed was uncomfortable. I could tell I'd said something wrong. What can be wrong with an address? It was quite a nice area. Penny liked very much the old lady who owned the digs. She made amazing rice pudding.

"Finally, he spoke. 'What number?' I told him as we drove towards Yardley, thinking all the time of my luck. The crunch, my friends, was that the couple actually lived in Yardley Fields Road. They drove me to my door. They watched as I went in… a bit like the police do… Another story. It's many years ago and I never forgot their kindness. Sadly, the coincidence spooked them. I hope they're out there still."

Dove grunted and spoke. "The luck of the devil." Periwinkle mentioned something about odds, lucky stars and correspondences. He'd been reading Penny's books again.

Penny was about to start again on the exhibition anecdote when the phone rang. He picked it up and the person rang off – not immediately, after several seconds. He didn't bother to check the number.

Chapter 16

Lance couldn't avoid his neighbours Mo and Byron. While making sure he knew they would inform on him for his illicit hacking, they told him they were going to kill Penny soon. It felt both invigorating and terrifying. They could suss that. They sat and waited. He said, "Good," though he didn't sound totally convinced. The thought had crossed his own mind when angry. The anger had dissipated, and fear taken over. He was shocked at how Alice and Mo had evaluated his character. He was beginning to think self-consciously, and it worried him. "How can I help?" he stammered.

"You already have," Byron replied. "If you continue to let us know his work schedules, we can do the rest. All we ask for is your silence. You will have a generous sum of money in an account of your own choice. We can ensure it's not traceable."

Lance was about to ask how much when Mo told him. He whistled. It was beyond his dreams. What kind of upgrades could he buy for his work?

Is there a catch? he wondered. When they left, he opened his laptop and checked emails. He had felt some relief to inform them that Penny had cancelled a few appointments. In truth, his stomach was churning, bile rising in his throat. This was not like bricking someone's window. Hacking was dodgy. Being an accomplice to murder caused some consternation. He was also making connections. His hacking of Penny's emails in Loftus had caused alarm bells to ring. The two weren't simply killers, they were torturers. It had to be them. He wondered about disappearing or contacting the woman police officer, Jarret, who came round. He took a drink to steady himself. That too annoyed him. He needed it.

Freeman was impressed with Jarrett's work. She conjured up a picture of Lance as they took him away towards the end of the university fraud case. It was beyond the call of duty, as she put it dryly to Jarrett, but a grand job. Murphy had taken the piss something awful out of her over a swift lager in Woody's bar. She could manage that. And she knew he was in his own way praising her. That was Murphy. His parting shot was to refer to her as Detective Jarrett. She felt aglow at the idea. One day…

Freeman reported the news to Penny. He received it with mixed feelings. "I thought he was still banged up?"

"Not anymore! He's back in business. I suspect he was never out of it."

Penny made his mind up to send a few emails. He asked Periwinkle to check his laptop again. He hoped Lance wasn't tracking him still; well-worn platitudes came to mind. His own path had never been straight though he would be angry if anyone referred to it as crooked. It meandered and took turns. As for narrow, forget it. A few alleyways and ginnels yes, narrow, no. He hoped Lance was okay. Lance was clever. To Penny Lance's personal myopia meant he relegated distant aims and objectives; he cast aside long-term for immediate things.

In a moment of dread Lance dialled Penny's number. The same dread made him put the phone down. His tummy was loose, his head buzzing. He bottled it and cut the phone.

Freeman considered her next move. "Lance seems to have connected with our two ladies, Byron and Wright." Her eyebrows reached a climax.

Penny could only say, "Not good." It was time to act. Freeman continued, "We must aim to unsettle them now." As uncle 'Peri' said (Penny couldn't resist it) that might scatter them. Then he changed his mind. "Best to wait until Guess does his work, then nail them."

Dove grunted and offered his opinion at Freeman. "Let your lads and lasses do it. Lance will be first to crack."

Lance realised he was way out of his league. It was keeping him awake at night. Dreaming in between fits and starts of sleep was beginning to take its toll. He needed to escape.

Penny was hateful, but dying at the hands of those two didn't seem fair. Doubt was a dreadful companion. It walked with him daily and kept him awake at night. What could he do? Jobs were trickling in; a trickle could lead to a flood. He felt trapped, sutured. He took a bus to Otley and walked around. Calling in the pet shop, he saw a yellow bird in a cage. He wanted to free it. It would die out there. It was singing. The variety of its song was a musical score, warbles, whistles, intermittent percussive rattles. He stared at the sign. It stated: *Harz Roller, a canary.* It gave him an idea. Was it too late?

Chapter 17

Lucas Guess was also handy with computers. He had visited the virtual dark corners and walked the dusty roads of the Internet. His road map would have put the government to shame. Actually, one didn't need to work at that, they appeared to excel at that themselves.

It was intel versus semi-grasped factoids. He weighed up the results. He made a phone call. Then he began to compile an email. He gave, what he considered, enough information with some caution. He began to draft a letter.

To Doc Ronnie Penny

It was good to meet you. I will pull no punches here. My research and intel have amassed a bulging file on your two women. They are indeed extremely shifty if you'll forgive the expression. (He then changed shifty to nasty and deleted the rest of that sentence.) We have decided to do some surveillance on them ourselves. They need watching.

Both contracts on you have emanated from the dark periphery outside of this office, though sadly linked. Yes, there are two contracts! Jim is responsible for the first. He seems to have employed the two women before. I believe the second contract is a back-up in case of failure. He was taking no chances. He is probably responsible for both. An element of doubt exists.

I will see that they are made null and void. This will occur almost immediately. It may not help. They might decide to act and do the job as a result of this — malice might take over. We will be watching. I can assure you; Dove and Peri will be on the case also.

If you need anything please let me know. Please give my best to Uncle Peri and please inform Freeman.

LG

Penny read it twice. *Bloody hell.* His unsafe mailbox contained one message. He left it. He was at the same time scared and excited. Two contracts, both associated with Jim. Jim wasn't a man to take chances. It was time to act. He called Freeman. He had no need to mistrust Guess, be his story partial, and the element of doubt worrying. Guess didn't seem like a man with any doubts. It left too much for the reader. How did he find out? Is there another assassin? If there was, he'd kept that quiet. The whole thing bothered him. The other email was from Lance — Wedjet. It remained unopened. It was in his spam.

He gathered the troops Dove and Periwinkle. He told them of Lucas's email. Waiting for a response, nothing came. He looked at Periwinkle. "I suppose he's in a difficult position. He can no doubt authorise the freezing of funds?" He imagined his friend was also being evasive.

Periwinkle looked away. Dove spoke for both of them. "So, we're going in, then?" By going in Penny assumed he was going to kick their door down and sort them out.

"I've hinted to Freeman that Alice and Mo are suspects in

the killing and torture of Max," Penny said.

Dove looked concerned. "Did Lucas tell you that?"

"No. He said they were extremely nasty, and Jim has employed them previously. He didn't extrapolate."

Periwinkle looked at Dove. Dove looked at Periwinkle. "What did Freeman say?"

"She said leave it with me. You've done well. I don't know where you get your information from, but thanks."

Penny recalled the university and the dean. *Leave it with us. You've done well.* Then everything went back to 'normal'. His misgivings bounced onto Freeman who was already organising what Murphy called a posse to hunt down the painters and decorators, the Graveyard Poets as they were now known. Murphy suspected that came from Penny. He could look it up later as it obviously had some meaning. In a briefing Murphy took a liking to Penny. He found his patter engaging. Jarrett wasn't sure.

Lance was desperate. "Penny, Penny, Penny, pick up your email, you silly fucker." He was close to panic and close to calling again. His past wouldn't permit it. In the very moment he needed courage he couldn't muster it. Silly pride got in the way and foolish misgivings.

Penny looked for an answer.

Dove said, "Leave it with Freeman. These two are slippery

as eels and I don't think we've nailed them yet."

The eels were driving from Leeds as they spoke. Lance was in the back, his beloved laptop next to him. Freeman's men drew a blank. The flat was clean. Their books remained – a lovely collection of academic works, worth a bit too. They didn't have time to pick them up. They wouldn't need them anymore. Mo was spitting blood. Byron detracted. She'd left one very important book. At some point she was determined to go back for it.

"The bastards!" Mo was livid. "They have nothing on us yet. Our academic studies are gone. Our decorating business screwed. The contracts void, the money frozen. How the fuck did they do that? Penny isn't capable." Mo turned the van onto the motorway and put her foot down.

"Calm down. We don't need money to slaughter the fucker," Byron added. "The sensible thing is to relocate, start again. Penny will at some point be on his tod, and then we move. We have a fair amount stashed away! Even more sensible would be to leave it altogether." Byron tried to lift the mood. "It's simple enough to find new IDs." In their anger, and with the impossibility of renewing their academic careers, they weren't aware of the dark green car following them.

Lucas was true to his word. The Company, as Dove referred to them, were onto the killers. Lucas listened to the story and acted on it. He researched them. Lucas recorded his conversation with Penny though he never gave Penny the professional courtesy of telling him so. It was par for the course. Lucas had spoken with Freeman. Freeman had put out a call to watch out for them but had added the warning not to apprehend, just find out where they were going. They had emptied the garage at Bradford and loaded up. The place was empty. The gun racks and so on suggested an armoury. The garage was clean.

Freeman nodded to Jarrett, indicating they were done. Forensics would move in. "They certainly know the ropes,"

Murphy was outside the garage. He spotted something in the mud. It was a black USB flash drive, trampled into the clart. He picked it up and handed it to Freeman. "What do you think?" he asked her.

"Let's get it into work as soon as and see." Freeman raised her eyebrows and gave Murphy a congratulatory swing of the head and a wink.

Jarrett punched him in the back playfully. "Class creep."

Byron and Mo had been sitting pretty for some time. That was over. Penny was to blame. Vitriol oozed, but common sense and tactical training won out. They had serious work to do. Night was coming down. They decided to pull off the road and detour by the Peak District. No chances taken. The M1 was far too exposed. And if the police had connected, there would be a search for the van. They pulled off and changed numberplates. They checked the back. Lance was still unconscious and bleeding. They took the precaution of leaving the weapons elsewhere.

The unidentified men that had knocked on their door weren't police. They didn't look armed, but they meant business — a young black guy and another older, supple and tall. Lance's email had changed everything. Lance lay still in the back of the van, a large blanket used for covering furniture thrown over him. He had sung like the proverbial Harz Roller. Canaries don't use email. Penny never picked up.

The green car followed at some distance. The lights were enough to guide them. Then the lights went out. The green car swerved as the tyres hit something sharp. The driver controlled the skid, pulled over and bumped a tree. The other man grimaced. He took a flashlight out the back. On the road was a laptop, and some metal spiked strips. First, they took cover. "These guys are no amateurs." The back left tyre was shredded.

The laptop lay on the road next to the spikes which had only caught one tyre. That was sufficient. They phoned in. Stay put was the order. They stayed undercover for as long as they thought necessary. The driver then crawled across the road and picked up the laptop. Crawling back, he felt cold sweat down his spine. The laptop was stained. Blood? Their brief was to keep an eye on the van. That was it. They had lost them. Neither were carrying weapons.

Mo and Byron would be miles away and looking for somewhere to stay. The van would suffice, and it would be somewhere they could keep watch.

Chapter 18

Penny wondered what Lucas could tell him about the night in Handale Wood. He thought of his own fictional character Oldman, and he missed him. The more he thought about the issues he discussed with Guess, the more it bothered him. Guess had seemed amused by the recounting of those moments; the Oldman Factor, as Dove now called it, Penny left out. Dove had cautioned him to miss that detail out, well, not to ask questions. Tell the story, see what results. No gap-filling, no bullshit, no fiction.

A replacement car was on the way to pick up the men in the green car, though they were already changing the tyre. Their foxes had escaped the pack. As light began to dawn, they heard a muffled whimper, the cry of an animal hurt, a baby whimpering. The driver took the flashlight again. Fearing a trap, he circled around the bleating.

That's when he found Lance, or what remained of him. He was half in half out a roadside ditch. They called for an ambulance, immediately insisting on Emergency. They cancelled the other lift. They drove back with the ambulance at full tilt to Sheffield. Sheffield was nearest. This poor guy needed help. They, on the other hand, needed to ask some questions. Lance was incapable of speaking. Only blood and a whimpering came from his mouth before he lost consciousness totally. His laptop was in the green car. Lance's message to Penny never connected.

Lucas called his men. "Please contact Detective Freeman at Leeds Meanwood Station. Also call this mobile number and speak to Periwinkle." Used to the foibles of the department, neither questioned him. Periwinkle? Thought they'd got rid of silly codenames when the posh boys were marginalised, and the grammar schools and academies took over. The driver mumbled something about chance and the Eton rifles, the right to work, and sang a few bars of a Paul Weller song to take his mind from the sad mess they picked up on the road – Lance.

Freeman had read the contents of the flash drive picked up by Murphy. Emails from Penny, mostly. The final one was a warning from Lance. *They're going to kill you. Please call me. Lance.* His number was underneath. It was unread, unsolicited and in his spam. Death by spam.

Separately, he had typed Mareen and Alis, the misspelling signifying his fear, or haste? Lance appeared educated and could probably spell perfectly well. This was a man in terror.

Freeman closed the laptop. The poets had flown. Freeman took a call from the driver. He didn't give a name. He was at the Sheffield Hallam hospital with Lance who was in a bad way. He was lucky to be alive… or not. Lance couldn't speak. Freeman grabbed her car key and was out the door, phone tucked under her ear before the call finished.

Periwinkle also received his call. He thanked the man who appeared hesitant when he spoke Periwinkle's name.

Mo and Byron were deliberating. "We should split up, get rid of the van and find alternative transport." It wasn't a question. Mo was issuing an order.

"Yes, sir," Byron mocked, though she knew it made sense. "One of us has to kill Penny when the heat dies down. Neither of us should know where the other is. We can use the mobiles. Check in once a day, the usual code. From now on we change names too."

They had prepared for this day. Neither expected it to come from where it did and involve the hapless Penny, and so soon. "He must have friends in high places," Byron concluded.

"I doubt it. More than likely it was his cronies."

They could never understand the nature of friendship, its deep-rooted nature, loyalty, the kind of friends that walk in when others walk out. They should have read their poetry more carefully. Elizabeth Singer Rowe's *Friendships in Death: Letters from the Dead to the Living*, friendships which are '… not extinguished with the breath of life'.' It was beyond them. Friendship is immortal and the network invaluable. To dead friends.

Penny was on the old bridge in Otley staring into the water when Periwinkle phoned. The bridge must be eight hundred years old. He would check.

Recently, the river Wharfe had broken its banks and flooded the fields. The river was still running high. As he stared, two passers-by had shouted, "Don't do it!" and waved from a car. Might've been funny a few years back. In this time of fragmented identities and uncertain interpersonal relations not so. He waved anyway, avoiding the controlled arm close to the body wave, a spin-off from the royal wave but lacking its decorum. His development of such a theory was cut very short.

"Lance is critical. He wants to see you."

Penny legged home as fast as he could. Dove was waiting in the car. "Get in." They set off and, barring a couple of tailbacks, they were closing in on the hospital in under an hour. On the way Dove said, "Did you check you emails yesterday?"

"Only the secure line." He fumbled for his phone. There it was – a message from Lance, a warning. Consumed with guilt, that of the survivor, Penny fretted. Who would grieve for Lance? His mum? Penny had met her once. He wished he hadn't. "How is he?"

"Serious, though hanging in." Dove drove into the grounds of Hallam. Penny leaped out. Dove drove around, looking for space while Penny ran into the hospital.

"Where is he?" he enquired. The man on the desk eyed him. "Lance Peirce. Sorry. I'm Dr Penny." Once again that title and the assurance that goes with it worked.

"He's in a private ward."

Following the directions, he found the ward. A police officer sat outside. Penny introduced himself. "We were expecting you. I doubt he can say much. He wrote your name on a piece of paper."

Penny walked in as calmly as he could. A nurse stood to the side of the bed. Lance's bottom half was cover by a raised section and an ominous-looking sheet.

In a perverse translation of Sharia law his tongue had been removed. The offending muscular organ was found by the side of the road. The police officer on the door said, "The victim wants to see you. I doubt he has long left. He can't talk."

Lance's life was hanging by a thread. So many people exist, suspended by a mere thread, in hospitals and at home, the thread that Penny vowed he would cut when it was his turn. This was the fate of the servile courtier who had discovered regret: Lance.

Freeman was already in the room. The nurse protested. She showed her ID. Freeman was about to say, 'I warn you it's not going to be pretty.' Penny had already pulled up a chair and was sitting by the bed. His face showed no anger, no remorse, nor upset. He was looking at Lance as a teacher about to discuss an academic matter with a bright pupil.

Lance was barely alive, propped up in the bed by a frame. His right hand was mush, one of the hands that typed the last message. It looked like a bunch of overripe blackberries. He stirred and he registered recognition with watery eyes as Penny entered.

Gently Penny took hold of his left wrist and held it. "Hiya, Lance. So, what is this tutorial for? It's good to see an old student, especially of your calibre."

Lance moved as if to relax. It was clear he was in extreme pain. His eyes closed, and tears filled them. Penny guessed he could see OK. He squinted as if to open them and to say, 'bullshit.' Here was his arch enemy. He indicated his laptop with a fist and the pulp that was his right hand.

"The two men left it here," the nurse explained.

Penny wondered if Lance wanted it. He started to reach out, keeping hold of his wrist, avoiding his mangled hand. Lance managed to shake his head, a tiny movement that brought excruciating pain to him. Tears filled his eyes again. He pointed once more, this time at Penny. The effort and pain was clear. He slumped back. Lance was dying. Life-prolonging machinery and medicine was holding him from the grave.

So many of the dying remained hanging in limbo, aided and abetted by modern medicine, attached to tubes, machines and fed and changed daily. Freeman eyed Penny in apprehension and Lance with pity. She'd seen worse, though this was despicable. She simply wanted to destroy the people who did this. They, she thought, didn't qualify as human beings.

Lance moved again. He took his hand away from Penny. A paper and pencil appeared by his side, and he began to write with his left hand in a scrawl that was barely legible. He took a break. Then he wrote again, taking a further break. Penny rested his hand on Lance's wrist. Lance turned his head and tried to acknowledge him. His look signalled that it was all he could do in writing. His head went down in what Freeman read as shame.

"Don't fret, Lance. We all make errors. I'm an expert." Penny smiled and shrugged.

The extent of his injuries only became clear later. Lance had informed on them in a moment of decency, a sense of propriety Penny had looked for in vain at times, but always suspected was there. And when it came, he had missed it. He swept aside his own bad feelings and kept positive. "Can I do anything for you?"

The paper fell. Freeman picked it up handed it to Penny.

"You take it, Freeman. Give me a couple of minutes with Lance. He was one of my best students." Freeman stepped outside. Penny knew already that the paper simply named the two perps. It named one. Underneath he had started to write *sorr*—

Penny spent the next five minutes talking about the highlights of the MA course, the successes only, the high grades Lance had achieved, and his stunning versions of Seurat's images on the laptop. The nurse stood close.

Lance responded by drawing himself up an inch or so. Penny noticed a partly severed leg. How had he lasted this long? Penny eyed the nurse. "Any chance of a glass of water, please?" The nurse nipped out, relieved to be away for a minute. Penny had seen a water dispenser down the corridor.

Penny leaned over and whispered quietly into Lance's ear. "Time to let go, Lance. It's time to cut the thread, my friend." He smiled. "Your bravery will stay with us. Well done. Top marks as usual. We will see to the rest. They, Maureen and Alice, won't get away. That is a promise!"

Lance understood perfectly well what he meant. He tried to grip Penny's hand. A smile wouldn't come. He closed his eyes. Penny allowed him to hold on and relaxed. He looked at his blond hair and his young sharp features and whispered softly in Lance's ear. "Imagine a pair of scissors, Lance. Cut the thread, my friend."

Lance gave his hand one more squeeze, his jaw dropped open, and he was gone.

The nurse returned with a glass of water. She looked at Penny who was still holding Lance's wrist. He let go. Freeman and the doctor came in. Resuscitation was out of the question. The nurse looked awkward. Penny said. "He went peacefully!"

Freeman said nothing. She knew vengeance wasn't good for a law officer but fuck it, she would kill those bastards with her bare hands.

Penny felt a simple detachment, one that was going to help him over the next few weeks. Why it was at that moment he thought of Hart he couldn't tell. No doubt he would have accused him of finishing the job. In a sense he had. His mind wandered into fiction, veering away from the harshness and cruelty that is life. There is cruelty in fiction too.

"Poor Lance. A lost soul if ever there was one." For a second a chip showed in the armour, then he rose and exited the room, leaving Freeman with the laptop and the paper, and walked down through the modern building and out the door.

The hunt for Mo and Byron was on big time. Tracked by the law – Dove, Periwinkle and Penny – the noose was tightening. SIS had officially pulled out, but Lucas had been in touch to say that the Handale matter was secured. Penny had reservations about what he meant by 'secured'. He hoped for settled.

Penny thought of Saida, her common sense and ability to inspire; he thought of Tammy and her quiet confidence. He imaged the man on the stairs the day he went to Guess's office. Bloody hell, that man knew him. It was to haunt him. Who the hell was he?

It would be a good thing for them if the police were to get there first. Penny's stoicism was replaced by anger at Lance's death. He probed for some sense of decency in the poets, finding nothing to redeem them.

His visions of Max came back along with his dream, the Graveyard Poets. It wasn't a red-misted anger that took over, or a burning desire for revenge, rather an icy coldness, a deliberation, a desire to seek them out…

The two poets were heading for the grave and torment. He wanted to believe in Hell and damnation. He couldn't. No friends would call these two beyond the grave. He would help them on their way. Dove drove and Penny remained silent.

Why he should be loyal to Lance defeated Dove. He understood the sometimes-perverse nature of comradeship. To Dove, loyalty had to involve self-sacrifice and was reciprocal. Lance had sacrificed perhaps. Why so late? The irony of the unsolicited email was the sting.

As they arrived along the main road to Otley Penny spoke. "I need to complete the task."

Dove drove into the car park, and in silence they went indoors, then he opened a bottle of good Scotch. They drank a dram or two. Then Dove went to his room. Penny sat for a while, poured another and drank it straight down, then went to bed. He slept. He had no dreams. He woke with a thirst and the concept he found difficult to comprehend, that of reprisal. Old words like chivalry came to mind, yet fundamentally he wanted to see Maureen and Alice dead.

Periwinkle was in the kitchen sitting at the table when Penny went downstairs. Dove was sitting outside on the small lawn. Penny took his old brown ceramic teapot out and made tea. He couldn't manage breakfast. "I need fresh air."

The woods were sublime. The pines smelled fragrant. The trees offered help. He walked on the needles and felt their comfort. Periwinkle put it into words. "The answer is here, Penny." He picked up an acorn and handed it to Penny. "Plant it and do nothing."

Penny didn't understand. He looked for some prompt to help.

"The answer will come," Periwinkle added, "it will come."

Penny's mind was racing. He concentrated, breathing deeply, imagining himself going down a ladder slowly, five, four, three, two, one, zero! Then he saw a beautiful yellow-brown sky and his beach. He surfaced and saw Dove and Periwinkle were up ahead and Dove was studying the trees. He needed the seaside. They drove to the north coast.

The tide was retreating. The beach's glassy sheen was interrupted by several dead crustaceans. The sun shone. Periwinkle and Dove left him to his imaginings. The weekend back on the Northeast coast saw the three running miles and Periwinkle showing Penny some elementary moves in self-defence. Lesson two was about to take off.

Dove offered to show him how to shoot, which he declined. He was not fully convinced that learning to shoot was a promising idea.

The sickness that was the poets was terminal. They were incurable and vile. The smell had decreased. He had always tried to believe that no one was born evil. Their presence and their poetry followed him in his heightened state.

Byron's take on their condition would've surprised him. In her mind, it was good that was so often defeated. Evil prevailed, the country itself was divided, our security taken away, the seas around our coast poisoned with raw sewage, and chemicals. Was that good? Alice even felt a pang of anger for the decline in animal welfare, but above all she recognised that 'we' had lost our sense of being. England had contracted a life-threatening illness. Evil was winning. She considered meaning and made a list of reservations, not to be discussed with Mo.

They were never going to give up. Penny's life plan hadn't included killing or being killed. Did he have a life plan? So much seemed random, intuitive, moving from one scenario to the next. Trying to think what moves he'd made with planning defeated him. Yet it all seemed to fall into place.

In referring to the killers, he ceased to highlight the graveyard bit. It meant less words spent on what he deemed were total shite, rubbish, fit for the dump only. He thought of tipping them into a rubbish truck alive. Even that was too kind. What he realised was that they weren't about to give up. They would come for him. Looking for them would be difficult.

Dove and Periwinkle stopped and waited for him.

"I think they'll be in touch, Dove. Their whole persona and reason for living outside of the killing zone has gone. Their workaday face has gone, their academic careers have gone. All that remains is their lack of any moral fibre whatsoever and a thirst for recompense. One doesn't need a degree in psychiatry to fathom out what their path will be." He was partly right, though his thoughts disjointed. Balanced and unbalanced, he thought of his childhood field of spiders, their cohesiveness, their solitary nature and their sociability – two worlds.

Dove kept his words to a minimum. "My thoughts too. They'll be in touch. What do you want to do?"

Periwinkle intercepted Penny's retort. He pointed a finger at the sky as he spoke. "And we don't really need to look for them. They will come to us."

Was the us meant to sound comforting? Penny wasn't sure. Penny had to get his act together. It was him they were after. *What do you mean by us…* He was fitter than before. His running and exercising had made him more alert; more comfortable. He still possessed no professional skills in terms of fending off an attacker. Street fighting, or barroom brawls were different, grievances, compliance, fun even. Justice? He needed to beef up on his skills. The sea air helped. They walked the sands from Saltburn to Teesside. As the tide withdrew, they skirted the groynes, picking up pebbles and skimmed stones.

Dove reminded him, "Training starts after Saturday." Dove looked pleased.

The next day, the pals were back in Otley. Dove had the telephone book, a slimmed down thing these days. He wondered if he could tear it in half. "There's a firing range in Bradford. In fact, there's more than one. I'll check them out. Meanwhile Periwinkle can take you through some self-defence moves. You might not need a gun then."

He believed they would play games with him before the attack. That might provide time to pick up a few new skills and competencies. First, on his return to Otley from the coast, he wanted to invite his friends over and cook some food. Periwinkle liked the idea. He asked Freeman, and if she had a partner, please bring them along to the Last Supper. Second, he was preparing himself mentally for training.

He shopped for days and was in the kitchen for hours. He refused all help. The dinner was set for Saturday evening. It was still only Thursday, and he was cooking and preparing things. Freeman was okay and was bringing her partner Asma with her. They offered to bring a pudding.

"Nice thought," said Penny.

Saida was looking forward to it and she too said she

would bring something sweet. He explained the food would be 'Asian' or a hybrid of differing cuisines.

Penny had wondered about Periwinkle's disdain for guns. He divided the next day up between preparing his food and for his first training session. He was quite serious about it. He mulled over Lucas's comments about Uncle Peri.

On their return from the brief sojourn by the sea a plain postcard was waiting for Penny:

Methinks I hear a voice begin.
Ye ravens cease your croaking din…
When men my scythe and darts supply
How great a king of fears am I!
Your turn to seek the grave.

Penny looked at the postal date and location. He quoted from *Young's The Complaint: Or Night Thoughts on Life, Death and Immortality*: "As 'we fatal sisters would outspin'…" He paused. "I guess the fatal sisters will be elsewhere by now, spinning their *eternal schemes*. The game begins. I would love to respond." He looked pleased.

Penny knew William Blakes's illustrations for the book. The verse was a flop. He knew about flops also. The illustrations lived on; the poem found the grave. A graveyard poem buried. He liked Blake's theory of contraries – Lance came to mind. Blake confounded the literary and metaphor. Penny understood that. Time was running out and he was procrastinating.

Periwinkle handed Penny a huge canvas bag and pointed at the car. On a lonely spot on the moor above Bolton Abbey, Penny began his training in earnest. Penny carried the gear up and was breathing heavily. He understood that what Periwinkle was aiming to do in two weeks might normally take years. He considered himself a good learner and a fast one (barring maths and physics). Two weeks was his deadline. Byron and Mo would reappear. Two weeks might not be enough. Periwinkle insisted on one hour a day, 'from now on'.

Forty-five minutes later Penny was bone-weary, black and blue. Elbow blocks were a reflex action, eye-gouging an issue. He didn't ask whether it was jujitsu, hand-to-hand training, taekwondo, or whatever. He recognised some of it from an old-World War Two pamphlet his granddad had left lying around. Having digested it, he tried it on his brother. He'd had the opportunity to test out odds and sods in a few scrapes in the council estate. It was a strange booklet with sepia images of men in weird long woollen bathing trunks holding each other down or kicking. His own theory of coercive actions was gleaned from the estate and included the Durham farewell (or something goodbye), involving the head and the knee. One needed to assert one's identity. Turn the other cheek? Raise the right knee smartly was the saying.

Periwinkle's slant was not so much about self-defence as disabling an opponent. Holding an adversary down, gripping their ankles with his foot in his crutch was already familiar. Did it work for women? He laughed. He recalled the scary bully he tested it on as a seventeen-year-old. The boy was big and a bruiser. Penny threw him with a textbook move, grabbed his ankles and planted his boot firmly in the young man's crotch. He was unable to move. Gosh, it worked. Then the moment of victory soured. What would happen when he let go? Oh shit. What was on the next page? Run like hell.

If an assailant attacked you with a knife what could you do? Kicks, arm blocks, use of the elbow, which seemed odd to him, kneeing someone less unfamiliar, though once again not for women? He asked Dove and felt sheepish.

"It doesn't matter. It's gender neutral." He repeated it firmly. So be it.

Knee kicks and choking he'd tried once before. In the past he foolishly went into help a student in Birmingham attacked by a gang of belt-wielding youths. They were striking him across the face. Penny dived in without a thought. He picked the biggest, planting his thumbs around the windpipe while loudly warning the rest that he wouldn't let up until they stopped. Their companion-in-arms was already down on his knees and looking blue when they backed off. He collected the lad and led him away before they could rally.

He practised stances to warm up and religiously did so every day. Skipping was on the menu too. It was hard, and according to the Internet led to 'cardiovascular gain'. Ten minutes was hard graft. He loved it as a kid. He thought of Oldman skipping and the street rhymes that he chanted as a kid. Charlie Chaplin went to France… and his favourite. He substituted Jenny for Penny.

Penny, Penny turn around, Penny, Penny touch the ground…

The Saturday meal came round. Lucy Freeman arrived early with her partner Asma. Asma was a chartered accountant, and, as she added, "self-employed. Lucy," she joked, "married me in order to retire early."

If Lucy was tall, droll, and gangly, Asma was short and lithe, with a manic sense of humour that bounced off Penny and brought the two of them close to hysterics. Saida hugged everyone. She and Lucy Freeman stayed off the topic of work, though one could sense they would like time together to swop spit. Penny was as usual reading below the text. He heard Freeman say to Saida, 'give you a call tomorrow to discuss matters'.

The food: Penny had made kachumber, his favourite side dish, the red ripe small tomatoes chopped into tiny pieces alongside the shallots and chilli flakes, oil and lemon. and sprinkled fresh coriander over the top. Two different dhals were served up: moong cooked in ghee and an ordinary red lentil day-to-day dhal which folk enjoyed more than the lavish black lentil dish. On the side, two raitas, one with mint, the other with cucumber brined and squeezed out, then washed and added to goat's milk yoghurt which he preferred. He had convinced himself the goat's milk yoghurt wasn't dairy. A convenient lie. For good measure he put a sprinkle of paprika across the top. His samosas required work in terms of shape. His homemade chapattis fared better.

Asma called the samosas sambuusa, and taught them all some Kiswahili, a musical and beautiful hybrid language which Penny adored. He liked the word *sambuusa* and repeated it several times. The vegetarian filling of the samosas (sambuusa!) and pastry deserved a lyrical slant, the spicy leek and pea with ginger were 'tasty'. With a mischievous smile, Lucy mentioned he'd make a good wife to someone. His main dishes were a neck of lamb and spinach curry and his personal favourite, a fish curry and potato and cauliflower dish with some pan-roasted okra. All in all, a feast. Not quite Belshazzar's Feast.

The puddings or sweets (call them what you like depending on which end of the street you come from) were exquisite. Penny remarked that even the council estate had a posh end! Asma had made mouthwatering mandazi. For good measure she also brought along a fruit salad with a perfect lime and honey dressing. It all took hours to consume, and they did consume. Saida's selection of homemade halwa and a kheer with vermicelli with a beautiful aroma of cardamom and scattered with dried fruit was in the words of all, awesome!

The conversation was convivial with Periwinkle telling a short story about a donkey ride up a mountain. The donkey had a fixed route and try as he might to persuade the beast to go further it wouldn't. It stopped dead before the summit and turned around. Dove's salty sea-story one-liners intermingled with Lucy and Saida's witty and insightful tales of police gaffs. Asma's anecdotes of claim forms from clients were hilarious.

Penny was slaving over a hot stove. He did chip in but was completely happy cooking; serving this group of people he so wanted to keep as friends. He wondered what Hart was doing. Freeman had always been an unknown quantity and would remain partially so. He warmed to her and really felt that she was on their side.

She would prove to be indispensable.

Eventually, they took to the living room with several bottles of wine, including a Sancerre (one of Penny's favourites) and two bottles of homemade ginger beer brought along by Saida, which claimed the second 'awesome' of the evening. Beers, cider and spirits abounded and when the whisky came out Saida and Periwinkle toasted with non-alcoholic ginger beer. Asma took a small sip and pulled a face. Freeman had more than a sip of alcohol and wisely booked a cab. Everyone complimented him on his dishes. He felt he belonged. Purpose and meaning began to fill the gaps.

Asma hugged everyone on the doorstep and proclaimed, "Another foody night at ours next month!"

Lucy agreed.

Saida chipped in. "Similarly for the month after at mine."

Asma finished the conversation. "We should recover in time. It will also give Ronnie a chance to catch up on drinking." He had been quite abstemious. He longed to meet these friends again and see them all; they made a nice group. He felt he should have extended the invitation to Hart. Hart was elsewhere.

For once the dishwasher with the infernal bleeping noise signalling the end came in handy. Penny wondered if there would be an infernal bleeping noise before he died, the emphasis on the infernal. He stowed everything he could in it, washed the rest at the sink, and went to bed. Periwinkle and Dove stayed up for a while. He could hear them talking in hushed tones. He felt quite pleased with his work. The fish curry was well received and his use of pollock commended as it doesn't flake. He slept well, if not somewhat bloated.

Mo watched the guests leave.

Chapter 19

Next day he was training. He sensed and felt a differing response from his body. He did the workout with a sincerity and meaningfulness that impressed Periwinkle. There was no jokes or excuses, just a sense of purpose. He learnt to cross his wrists with the arm block. Thumb strikes to the eyes were difficult. His soft side emerged when it came to the offensive. In the boot of the car was a made-up body opponent bag. The bag hung from a tree branch and was deployed to practise kicks. If anyone had passed by and stared, neither would have noticed.

Periwinkle showed balletic grace and speed in his demonstrations of ground fighting, the idea not so much to defend as attack. Penny was slow. Periwinkle could see he had some knowledge and experience of combat from his past and wasn't frightened.

His ability to stop short of Penny's eyes, nose, throat and other body parts both amazed Penny and gave him a sense of relief. He still winced. Whether he could do it in a combat situation worried Periwinkle. It worried Penny too. His first days left him sore and aching.

"Same time tomorrow."

Dove had also arranged firearms training. That caused some trepidation. He had carried a gun around with him in London and forgotten about it. Using one was different. He felt strongly that when they attacked, they would use a knife. "I think they want to see me suffer," he remarked to Periwinkle. Periwinkle didn't respond. He too preferred the knife. Knives are cheap, knives are accessible, and knives were in the news.

The Knife Angel was touring the country. They would go and see it. Constructed from ten thousand knives, Alfie Bradley and The British Ironwork Centre's twenty-seven-foot sculpture spotlighted the increasing violence in Britain. Penny thought of the upsurge in knife crime it opposed; he contemplated the number of knives. One website stated one hundred thousand knives! Where on earth did they come from?

Periwinkle was a good teacher. Once he felt Penny had mastered something, Penny thought he would move on. Not so. Rather, he kept them going, honing the speed and finesse of each move. He also took time to show him how to use the landscape, branches, and rocks – anything to strike an opponent with, maim or kill them. Improvise, he said. The dancelike element suited Penny who loved to dance. Hitting people from behind was a problem; elbow strikes or sticks were okay. Fundamentally, Penny decided they were using jujitsu. The quantum leap was getting his head around the issue of wellbeing – not his wellbeing, that of his opponents. When he began to flag, he thought of Lance. Then they went to the seaside. The beach at Coatham was perfect for a mock battleground.

He felt exhilarated at times, exhausted at others, fitter, more flexible, and more in control. He began to understand himself more thoroughly. He realised that his so-called deceptions in the past were small beef. Hidden weapons and trickery were fast becoming a part of his life.

At the seaside, Dove declared, 'Firearms training starts after Saturday'. He looked pleased. The sea responded with a sigh and small piping birds scurried on the edge of the water.

The next day the pals were back in Otley. Dove had the telephone book, a slimmed down thing these days. "There's a firing range in Bradford. In fact, there's more than one. I'll check them out. Meanwhile Periwinkle can take you through some self-defence moves. You might not need a gun then."

Anything goes; the aim not simply to hurt one's opponent, to end their life, but to 'hurt them really bad…' as one guidebook said, '… and get away'.

The ground covered was eclectic: takedown, trapping, kicking, punching and grappling. Awareness was the core. His academic side discovered the deadly arts of Eskrima, Krav Maga and LINE, an abbreviation for destroying one's enemy in a variety of ways. Practised by US marines, Linear Infighting Neural-override Engagement was the product of a Ron. Penny looked it up. He studied. As in everything from writing to music, the art was a composite. Could he break someone's neck? He tried to think of the dean…

Periwinkle was trying to condition him to combat. Where is the enemy? Everywhere. What is the challenge? Everything. He kept going. The dance element meant balance. It would enable the struggle against another force. Penny even realised an aspect of the science of physics. Periwinkle mentioned mechanical efficiency more than once as Penny laboured. Not once did Periwinkle refer to the fact that his opponents were women. Never underestimate an opponent. Penny wasn't going to fall for some biased girls' and boys' argument, nor believe that women were less adept than their *cis*-male counterparts. Alice and Maureen were trained, they were deadly. Killing was second nature. Penny was, in their eyes, the proverbial snowflake. He was aiming to turn into a snowstorm.

He never let on to Periwinkle his studying on the side. Periwinkle watched him work and watched him ache.

If the gun and rifle issue was a problem that caused his conscience some troubled thoughts, Penny's first go on the range with a handgun wasn't. He surprised himself. He was less adept at the safety aspect. He also showed little interest in bullet calibres. A semi-automatic was his choice. He liked the term and realised its meaning. Another lesson in physics. In a light moment, he thought of the gun found in the dean's locker. How did he avoid the five-year sentence for possession? He got to use an AR-15. Dove schooled him outside of class with his own small armoury he carried with him. God knows why the police hadn't stopped him. What if they searched his car or the house? What then? Seven years or more if the firearms were intended to endanger life. Isn't that what firearms do?

The postcards kept coming from here and there. The time slipped away. Penny had an idea that if he survived the war with his opponents, he would use the cards and others for a show, an exhibition: *Penny Postcards*. Each one indicated his time for the grave was looming. The differing scripts, rapidity and number suggested the 'fatal sisters' had split up. They were from two sources. That was, at the same time, good and bad.

He was getting fitter by the day, faster and more agile, allowing his reflexes to respond to Periwinkle's varying tactics though lacking in explosiveness. He didn't want to make excuses.

Periwinkle tried hard to get him to imagine he was someone else: the enemy. Try as he might Penny couldn't cross that barrier. He was convinced that under duress he would respond. Periwinkle wasn't sure. He believed that they would attack soon whether individually or together. Periwinkle wasn't sure of that either. He had a sneaking suspicion they might split up for tactical reasons. He knew also that if it were him, one would be watching the other. Maybe not. If they chose to work together, he didn't fancy his friend's chances.

He underestimated Penny's willingness to learn and to fight back against the people who had tortured and maimed Max and dismembered Lance. Penny's control was greater than imagined. Underneath, Periwinkle detected a coldness.

Penny was putting together fragments he'd picked up over the years. The dots were joining up. When he reminded himself of Max and Lance the icy determination returned, and he moved on. Through the postcards he began to understand his perceived opponents' narcissism, their projective identification; he thought he knew their weaknesses which they perceived as strength. *Good Will Hunting* was his model. How to annoy a psychopath? Rule number one: don't let them take control.

Lance had been malicious and petty, but he didn't deserve what they meted out to him. He was going to pay them back. His payback was devoid of anger. His training was central in helping him empty out counter-productive emotions. Ten days of training went by. The coldness built up like ice on a glacier, dense, threatening. His judgments became clearer. Periwinkle called a halt. With time to ponder, he changed from training to education. (It felt more in keeping with the world and its current jargon.) Then he changed it to development. Yet he was being trained; he was learning. Could he kill someone? It was either that or be killed.

The gun thing lasted only hours. It was evident that Penny had been 'born with a gun in his hand', as the instructor put it. However, she said, he really needed to be more aware of safety when handling firearms. Her last words to her star pupil on the range indicated regret at losing him.

"Good luck with whatever you aim to do!" She had an inkling he wasn't going to be aiming at clay pigeons.

Two days went past. His body demanded to be out there training or developing; his mind was elsewhere. Then Periwinkle said, "In the car." This time Dove accompanied them. The training took a turn. Penny felt under pressure. There was two opponents: two friends. Dove showed a speed and agility that frightened him. How on earth did a man of his stature disappear in front of him and reappear behind holding him around the neck? He did. There was a consolation. He found his intuitive mind working faster, his reflexes too, and at one point he grabbed a robust-looking stick and stood balanced ready to use it. Dove showed a glimmer of a smile. Use whatever is handy.

It was a gruelling workout. Though it seemed like hours, his mobile told him it was forty minutes. He also felt they had an audience; a sense he had developed in London during his last infamous case was coming into play. Surely his comrades sensed it too. They never acknowledged it if they did. He wondered if it was part of his training. As they drove home, he broached his thoughts at an angle adjacent to where he intended to get to. Some things never change.

"What would you do if you were on the run, Dove? Where would you hide?"

Dove didn't do adjacent. "I think they'll split up, if only for a while, and go in different directions. One might keep tabs on you from a distance. They are no doubt adept at hiding." That was one question answered. One of them was watching. "As for where they would hole up is anyone's guess. What choice? Somewhere isolated or somewhere crowded. Trained personnel can survive in all kinds of terrain. And that is crucial. We have to wait. They will come back for you." He looked thoughtful. "It might be better if we did a disappearing act ourselves, camped out for a while. We too can hide." Periwinkle looked sideways, his tongue under his front teeth and nodding slowly as if thinking about it. They would wait until Penny was alone. Waiting too would be stressful for Penny. Not so for Alice and Mo. Uncertainty wasn't part of their profile, and they clearly weren't principled.

Periwinkle suggested that one of them did a disappearing act. "We have to imagine that they're tracking us."

Penny knew damn well it was a statement of fact. They were experts too, Alice and Maureen, Dove and Periwinkle. He didn't know what Maureen looked like. She could have passed him along the road. Tall, short, fat, skinny, good-looking, downright ugly? He imagined the latter, female versions of the late Rand. He hoped it wasn't Alice when it happened.

In the house Penny opened the mail, two thank-you cards and a picture postcard. The postcard had an image of *Death's Door* by William Blake, an old man stepping into a doorway, Blair's words from *The Grave* '*the keys of Hell and death*' were written on the other side. They would want him to suffer before they despatched him. It gave him time. At the end of the extract was a jumbled quotation with an addendum: '*Whistle aloud to keep (your) courage up and keep training.*'

He wished he could respond. Which one wrote it? The postcard campaign was in their favour. They knew that too. He couldn't get to them in the same way. That was the way they would play it. He would have to wait until that final confrontation to have his say. They were getting through to him. It wasn't really helping their case. His frostiness increased toward them. Waiting bred certainty. Then there was some doubt.

He mused over his growing collection of postcards. He put the new ones alongside. Other cards, more pleasant, were from Lucy, Asma and Saida thanking him for the feast 'which took several days to recover from'. He filed them too. Asma suggested a date three weeks in advance at theirs. Saida simply sent a big hug and thanks. He read them several times. He thought of Hart and began to miss him. He thought of Tammy; he thought of Dove's words previously: 'keep her out of it. Things are going to get worse'. They always did. He didn't want to keep her out of it…

Dove organised more training. They ran up the Chevin without stopping, they circled back through Danefield where the pines held the chilly air. Dove talked about the art of deception, the landscape, what could he use in the forest? The trees answered and seemed to whisper to him their support. The chill soon went. They warmed up, and the ups and downs of the outer pathway kept them working hard. All three breathed easily. Penny felt relaxed; the surrounds gave him comfort.

His running style had changed. It was less floppy. He was landing mid-sole and moving to his toes, a much better posture, though he still leaned forward and stared at the ground. He felt stronger, more centred. Dove's attention to the woodland surrounding and its density spoke more of a lesson in caution than a concern for the symbolism of the differing trees or the aesthetic elements: Jupiter and the oak, Apollo and the laurel, Attis, a god of vegetation and the lofty pine which he transformed himself into. Dove wasn't interested in symbolism at this point. Concrete issues dominated. Camouflage was great, it was useful. Alice and Maureen could no doubt hide in the open.

A light lunch followed and a discussion on what he had learned from Periwinkle. He couldn't resist showing Dove a few moves.

Dove kept his smirk hidden, tempered also by his doubts of what his friend could do against two professionals – killers. Penny could annoy them or throw them off in some way, that was for sure. If anyone could enrage an opponent, he would find a way. It might be a jibe or a throwaway aside, but it would at least stall them. It might be academic or completely cryptic, but he would find a way to piss them off. He would no doubt keep his emotions in check. The dark triad meant nothing to him. He didn't understand malevolence. His spontaneity and ability to make friends easily without manipulating them would certainly aggravate them to begin with. A smile might do it. It was the rest that bothered him.

Penny was also lucky. That might help. The Mercedes from Maidstone wouldn't be around to pick him up this time, and as for the skull… it could be anyone's. Periwinkle and he kept the Danefield run going. Penny realised it had a deeper purpose. It was a sublime landscape, one that was ideal for a sudden attack. It was ideal for cover. Hiding in plain sight, as Dove reminded him on the run, was a military thing. Snipers are the best. They can over-watch and wait until their target is visible. When and how they are coming is never clear. Concealment and the ability to distort their outline is part of the game.

'The game' was an unfortunate choice of words, but the game it was. Penny read up on that too. He looked at the ghillie suit and hood, which to Penny was like the tatters of a Morris dancer, though designed to blur the shooter in the landscape. Dove was giving him new insights into an environment he thought he knew, what was hiding in the trees. "Hide your face," Dove said, "and the rest is easy."

There was no point in turning Penny into the hunter, merely make him aware of his opponent's abilities to conceal themselves. When they attacked, they would do swiftly. His new instructors hoped it wasn't as a sniper. He just might have a chance. If it was one of them only, a better chance. Their pride and ability might lead them to underestimate their opponent, or their desire to maim first, offer time. Hope wasn't part of Dove's vocabulary, it had too many outcomes. Penny had ditched it for trust. Preparation was the way forward, not wishing. Personal response and control mattered here, not self-deception. Lesson three (or was it four?): maths.

Penny scouted the woods. Could he hide? As a child the woods offered all sorts of dens and hidey-holes. He had a craze for ninja movies some years back. At that time, he fancied his non-human status had grown. His skills in espionage and subterfuge that his university career had schooled him in were handy in dealing with the management, dean treachery and his gang particularly. How he would like to meet some of them now, though he expected they would run and hide at first sight of him. They would have to hide well. He was learning. Would he really like to give them a good hiding? Yes. As an adult he ticked himself off. He shouldn't be thinking like that. For an attosecond, and no longer, he imagined the dean across the ring from him in the red corner. A theme tune came to mind: *Gonna Fly Now.*

Ambush was important for them. Elementary spy-craft would come in handy later when he decided to tackle Lucas Guess again. Then there was his unknown colleague. He hadn't forgotten the man who smiled in recognition then retracted the smile as if mistaken. No point in telling the others that part of his plan.

Lucas knew far more than he'd given out. His colleague did too.

Periwinkle drove Dove to Menston with his pusser's bag apparent and made a fuss as they said goodbye. A car started up and turned around. Dove looked sideways at it. He went to Leeds, jumped a London train, which stopped at Doncaster, got off and picked up a car from outside the rail station. He drove off into the day, stopping only to read a short message. He headed towards York and the area around Scotch Corner, the famous White Horse. Close by was the home of the late sculptor, John Bunting, Penny had told him about. Bunting had built a chapel and studio on his acre of land. Bunting's daughter had authored a 'marvellous book' about her dad that 'everyone had to read'. He did intend to read it, that's if he ever got some prime time. Reading and drinking had been part of his purpose in visiting Penny.

He scouted around for a while then booked into a small B&B. Today he would go for a pleasant walk. Despite the wintry weather it was dry. He wanted to see the White Horse. The last sighting of his quarry had been around there. How reliable the source was, was a question unanswered. Dove took it seriously. He was cautious.

Chapter 20

It was already getting dark, and the nights cold and damp. Scudding clouds suggested a shift in the Yorkshire weather. There was expectancy in the air, one that spoke of a wet and windy spell, one that spoke for Penny of plague, and of mischief night, the restless dead and torment. The year was ending. Penny got a bit carried away with his expectancy theories. Mystic Ronnie was off on one, as Dove saw it. Dove still took note of the forewarning.

Dove remained calm. Neither Periwinkle nor Penny knew where he was. Since he took the train from Menston that day, they had heard nothing from him. The days had dragged for Penny. Freeman had reported a sighting of one of the suspects in North Yorkshire and Dove moved on. The waiting was beginning to bite.

"Fancy a run before it gets too dark, Periwinkle?" Penny was already in his tracksuit, black and yellow top for visibility and a woolly hat, not a beanie, yet pulled down in the same manner.

"Yes." He changed in no time. Similarly dressed and wrapped up, he was halfway out the door when he stopped. Silver was sitting there waiting for a stroke from Periwinkle.

Periwinkle turned and said, "Take it steadily, Ronnie. I have a quick call to make. If you go up to Danefield along the road and into the top car park and then follow our usual circuitous route slowly, I'll catch you up." He grabbed his phone and pressed a button.

Penny looked at the bin on the way out. "It's the normal bin day tomorrow. I'll put that out first. They're here first thing. There isn't much in it, mind." Bin day was always an issue for Penny. Quite often he had to check the neighbour's to see which bin went out – blue, brown, green or whatever. He wheeled the bin down below, then took off, steady away as instructed.

Outside the Junction, a few shivering yet dedicated drinkers huddled over their pints of bitter. "Meet the Swillies," he said as he wheeled into Gay Lane and upwards. One side of him so wanted to join them. He pushed along, and halfway a car passed him labouring up the hill. In Danefield the moon shone through the pines on his left and created patterns fitting for a Scandinavian textile design: bold, black, brown, overprinted on off-white with incidental splashes of colour around the branches. *OK*, he thought, a past its sell-by date design.

It felt good. He slowed to allow Periwinkle time to catch him and enjoy the fabric of the landscape. He thought of the pinewood at Carshalton and shivered. He made the car park and decided to wait. A single vehicle faced the road – a dog walker no doubt taking his or her pet for the last walk of the day. He walked the few paces to the car. He was about to jog along when a warning chill ran through him. He was obviously getting cold and needed to run. No, this was another sense, another feeling, the one he knew of danger. Periwinkle had called it precognition. He peered into the car. Nothing but an open road map on the back seat. He couldn't make out anything of the location. Looked like Ireland. He jogged back to the road. No sign of Periwinkle. It was dark. The very thought of road maps created a frisson of uncertainty. He faltered. The why, the what, and when of government. Good question. Bloody road maps…

He shook himself, turned and started running along the circling path. The cold became increasingly debilitating. He breathed heavily. The moonlight helped guide him over the rough terrain. The damp wood seemed to seep into his bones. Ignoring Periwinkle's catch-up promise, he speeded up to counter his cold sweat. He tried to remember his flight, fight or freeze lesson. Why? Good question. He ran on.

Periwinkle reached the car park. Penny had run much faster than he imagined. The cold and damp increased the pace. Periwinkle stopped also, studied the car. Then he took off. He didn't want to call out his friend's name. He padded along with barely a sound.

Penny was now racing, reciting: *And all the air a solemn stillness holds… The paths of glory lead but to the grave…* from his postcard collection.

To his relief, he saw a figure running towards him. They were steady away, as if enjoying a leisurely run. He looked comfortable; baggy tracksuit and top, beanie pulled down. Penny raised his arm to acknowledge the other runner. What happened next was so quick he never had a chance to take it in. The figure, taller than him, barely passed, then turned and followed him for a few yards. He stopped; the runner passed him. He froze. Flight was out of the question. It was a woman, tall and slender, fair hair peeking from below the beanie. Not Alice. She turned and confronted him.

He spoke. "I see you are not dressed like a barmy Morris dancer. Is your colleague hiding in the trees?" That paused her a second. He spoke again nervously, hoping to gain time. "Jill of the Green?" Penny grimaced, a twisted smile as he spoke to the tall woman with a nose ring. She said nothing.

The baggy tracksuit and beanie had fooled him. She was over six-foot tall, good-looking; not at all what he expected. Maureen? If it was, she looked incredibly agile. A knife glinted briefly in the moonlight through what resembled charcoal-drawn trees.

Penny spoke again, nervous, keen to engage her in conversation to allow himself precious time. He recited Gray again blabbering this time, "'With uncouth rhymes and shapeless sculpture deck'd.'"

The figure hesitated.

Penny blethered. "I see you have brought a knife to a gunfight. Not really in keeping, is it?" Penny judged the distance to be about three feet. He slipped his hand in his top to withdraw Dove's pistol. It wasn't there. *Shit.* He must have put it down before he left the house.

She never moved, never flinched. He stood stock still. Then she moved. He went flying. He hit the ground. As in training, he rolled away sideways to avoid the knife, a vicious-looking serrated thing. The woman was kneeling down with the knife close to his throat, but moving it downwards, then back as if deciding what to cut first.

Periwinkle stopped running. A noise through the pines told him what he feared. He veered off the track, keeping as silent as possible. If Penny's assailant heard him at all that was it. Providence and luck might prevail. No gunshot.

It was to be the knife. Penny was thinking fast. Its destination was going to be painful before she finally finished the job. Penny was still talking as he lay there, giving his critique of the Graveyard Poets using rapidly quoted lines. His mind speeded up. He forgot the lesson on physiology. Do something, it said, fight. He spoke. "It's all pseudo-religious tosh, Maureen."

The use of a first name disturbed her. She looked sideways. She never opened her mouth to speak. Silence can be frightening to some. Penny kept talking.

"Perhaps you've read the revisionist material on the topic?" His hand closed on a loose stone, which he caressed for comfort. He focused. "Surely there is no loss or bereavement for you… or me… or your colleague." The stone was cold. He wanted to touch his cheek with it.

He wondered if he had hit a nerve. Her academic side must be inquisitive. She took her time with the knife. Her other side began to press the knife into his lower abdomen and trace a line towards his groin. He could feel its sharpness, and blood running. One hand was groping along the ground, the other stopped caressing the stone and gripped it tightly.

He looked straight at her. She paused.

He continued, "Someone said it's a result of the disease of melancholy. Surely that's a simplistic answer?" With the time he had left, he was quoting one of her essays. His knowledge of the field gained in an afternoon in the British Library was limited to a few quotations. His chats with her professor at the university gave him access. Professor Eggleston allowed him a peek at the student's essays. Alice's scored an A-plus. His helpful nature and her homework might save him. A quote from the Graveyard Poets came to mind, and one she had included in her essays." "Death's odours and ghosts.'"

His voice sounded clear in the woodland. Would Periwinkle hear it? "One writer described the poetry as a disease!" He began to follow it up as she cocked her head to one side. She missed the full critique as the rock smashed into her skull with all the force he could muster from his prone position. It required moving his arm across his body. She fell sideways. Instinctively she aimed to get back on her feet. The knife fell out of her hand, the side of her head caved in, part of her lower jawbone sticking out, her teeth in a lopsided lour. One arm was twisted uncomfortably behind her back. Penny grabbed the knife from the ground by the blade, then corrected and clutched it in his right hand. Maureen's arm came from behind her back. The gun appeared as if by magic. Penny's reflex action was to dive sideways. He dropped the knife.

The gun must've been in the back of the tracksuit. As he threw himself sideways, his elbow connected hard with her right arm and the crack of a bullet resounded through the cold still of the night. He remembered saying, "Sorry, Maureen.

You just failed." He picked up and gripped the horrid-looking knife. Failure, he knew, was the one thing she would hate. It was with that thought and of young Max and Lance, he fell forward and plunged the knife into her abdomen. Then he rose and pulled the blade out. Blood spurted. She died there and then, the abdominal aorta bleeding out. Her last look was one of awe, even respect. The last words she heard were from Gray's Elegy: "'And shut the gates of mercy on mankind'." Or did she? More physiology needed. Time stopped for him, then he shook himself. Dropping the stone, he said, "Fuck mercy."

Periwinkle stood next to him.

"That was Gray's *Elegy Written in a Country Churchyard*," Penny said. "I almost felt sorry for her." Then he stood and finished with: '*When men my scythe and darts supply, how great a King of Fears am I!*' Parnell's *A Night-Piece on Death*. A fitting epitaph, don't you think?" Then he crumpled. Periwinkle supported him.

"I'm not sure the late Maureen Wright would appreciate it." Periwinkle had his phone out. Penny didn't ask how he knew her. Penny was unaware of anything around him, he was dissociating, he was in that zone between sleeping and waking. He saw Periwinkle…

Periwinkle placed his hand on Penny's shoulder. "Decision time, Penny. This is a monster you slayed. Her friend is out there." He swept the woodland with a long arm. "Two key questions: do we call the police? Do we dispose of her?"

Penny could see the benefits of the former. He had not really taken in the fact he had gouged into a woman's abdomen with a knife and ended her life, monster or not. The alternative confused him. "You mean we get rid of the body?"

"The car in the park was hers. I took a second to open the boot. Inside were some nasty weapons, plus a spade, a saw, and some industrial strength-sized bin bags… a body bag in readiness."

Penny pondered the fact Periwinkle had broken into the car, then he said, "Ringing Freeman would be silly. Let's get the bin bags."

Periwinkle said, "You stay here." It was now pitch-black and cold. Penny felt unsettled jogging up and down around a corpse, but that's what he did until Periwinkle returned. The chances of anyone skirting through Danefield at that time was zero. Periwinkle had groped in Mo's pockets and removed her car keys from her tracksuit bottom.

As a precaution they moved the body to the side of the track before Periwinkle set off. "Clean up as much as you can. Get some twigs, plants, anything, and spread what you can over the ground." He was back in no time though Penny felt he had jogged a half-marathon. He was also carrying a spade as well as the bags.

They double bagged the body as if it were asbestos and toxic. Penny could no longer see her face. The last thing he saw was the nose ring on her right nostril and the strange grimace of her broken jawbone. Then they covered the area with what they could. The blood was on the corpse and on Penny, and it was drying, its cloying smell sweet, and he wanted it off him as soon as.

"Give me your top," Periwinkle insisted, "and the gun she used." He pocketed the gun and put Penny's gore-spattered top in a separate binbag from the one containing Maureen's body. The gun and the knife went in a smaller bag. They tied the makeshift body bag. Between them they carried the late assassin to the car. Maureen's long slim body fitted with some difficulty in the boot. Periwinkle opened the door casually as if it was his. He started the car. "Getting rid of the car will be more difficult. The scrapyard on Ellar Ghyll might be most appropriate. We will see. For now, we need to get her into a bin!"

Penny pictured the stacked cars in the yard visible from the Bradford Road. He often imagined skeletons in them sitting at the wheel, drivers on their way to Hell. The M6? He blanched. "A friggin bin?" Then he shut up. The refuse collectors came first thing. "Not my bin?"

"Why not? A couple of bags over it and the men simply wheel it, attach it at the back and bob's your uncle, it goes into the crusher."

"Will she fit in? She is quite tall… was, I mean. Oh dear." Penny wanted to ask if he'd done it before. It was the best plan. On the way he suggested the outsized bins standing alongside the shops. "They're not likely to open them. They already pong with takeaway rubbish."

"The body won't smell, yet it might be apparent. What you have in that bag you have described as rubbish. It's not nice. It's either that or we call Freeman?"

The bin was outside. It was next to the larger bins belonging to the shops. They struggled to take the bag out.

They rolled the body in and covered it with two more bags. He was surprised it fitted. The body was still supple. The cold would preserve it longer. He'd read somewhere that in the process of rigor mortis bodies can move. He hoped not.

"Ditch your clothes, then scrub up. I'm going to get rid of this car." Periwinkle was off before he could protest. He bagged the clothes; put them in the bin. It was full to the top. Periwinkle forced the lid down a fraction, then left.

The night went on forever. He heard the bin cart. He froze. From the window he fixed his eyes on his bin. Next door's was close by. The huge overflowing bin from the chip shop stunk of fat. A glass of wine stood next to him. The glass was still full. The refuse collector wheeled next door's bin to the truck. The man opened it briefly. He attached it to the back on the hydraulic arm. Did up-to-date bin lorries carry spy cameras to spot infringements?

There was a clatter of metal as the bin locked, then lifted, disposing of its contents into the compacter, 'the crusher', as Penny called it. It tipped in. Colin, his next-door neighbour, had been putting scrap metal or old paint tins in the bin again. He was petrified. His turn. The man lugged the bin, which was heavy, but seemed light as he took it with one hand and stopped to say 'hi' to someone on the way to work. Then he hooked it up and, with a judder, the contents disappeared.

Chapter 21

He woke in a cell. The flashbacks were in flow: the twins' description of their first tableaux, the body, their plans to create a sculpture, one that might be public. The surgical knife hovered in the air; a cutting tool so sharp it alone scared him. He had one in an old tobacco tin on his desk, a dark blue band and a light blue over it, a remnant of past times, his granddad and his pipe and war horse tobacco, the scalpel, a Swann Morton scalpel. Now and then he took it out and examined it. Be silly to draw one's finger along it. The twins' drawings that showed the model for David were those of a skilled surgeon. He saw the knife go in, the flesh of the arm removed, the penis. As he awoke, he screamed, "Maureen."

Lucy Freeman was standing next to him. What was a nightmare and what was real he couldn't discern. He blinked around him as if unaware of his location. Horn and ivory meshed. Which gate was it?

He shouted out something about the bin collection. He awoke fully soaked in sweat. He thought it was blood and tried to wipe it off. The clarity of the vision was filmic, its length epic; the moment of waking, the hypnogogic moment, living in the dream. How long are dreams?

He was wearing a loose tracksuit bottom and a long-sleeved T-shirt, which he couldn't recall changing into. He tried to collect his thoughts. Go back… What happened? It was the most vivid and detailed bad dream ever. He tried to think. As he woke, his mind was racing through a vivid catalogue of art history's paintings of mutilated bodies: Géricault's studies of severed heads, Michal Na'aman's schematic images of eyes isolated from the body, Bosch's images of humans devoured and excreted in the *Garden of Earthly Delights*, *Goya's mutilated body of a man impaled on the branches of a tree* and, finally, Picasso's *The Weeping Woman, an image of grief.* The pain that emanated from the last image caused him to yell. He saw Maureen.

Freeman spoke. "You've been asleep for half a day. You've been calling out, mumbling, and at one point shouted so loud it awoke the sergeant on duty." He missed out on the irony as Lucy Freeman sat down next to him.

It came back in detail. He then spilled it out. Freeman didn't need to ask. He remembered the stone, the knife, the body. The scalpel in the dream. He remembered reciting Parnell, or was it Grey? He remembered the gun in Maureen's hand. He remembered picking up her knife. That was real. He remembered that he hesitated. What did Periwinkle do? The memory of the short fight came back, the gunshot, the knife in Maureen's abdomen, her last look, a questioning stare. All his academic grasp of memory and the processing of emotions came into play yet vanished as soon as they came to the fore. The ordeal in the woods was over. So was someone's life. She might have been a killer, a torturer as well, but she was someone's daughter. A sense of déjà vu occurred as he cast his mind back to Jim's death. All that was missing was a wobbly camera shot of woodland, *Snow White* in daytime, *Hansel and Gretel* at night.

Penny was in a fugue state. He wanted to be elsewhere and someone else. In the cell he had immediately gone to sleep, blacked out. He mentioned the dustbins several times.

The recall was more traumatic than the event. The image as Penny had discovered was more disquieting, the bin bag scenario a dream, the blood-stained wood real, the sylvan terror returned as the woods began to speak. There was no empty wine bottle, no glass, no dead body in the bin, and no infringements, just a police cell. He wasn't sure what day it was. If ever there was a case where he wanted to revise history, this was it.

Periwinkle contacted Dove. He had located Byron, though she had given him the slip. She had been into a small shop near Kilburn when he spotted her. He had been correct that she wouldn't be too far away. Yorkshire is a vast open county. He was lucky. Just off the A1 he had found a barn that showed recent signs of life. A fresh trace along the ground told Dove enough. Someone had used the place recently. Car tracks led up to the field. It was possible that the van he had tracked was inside, their painting and decorating vehicle, their hearse. He had a description provided by Freeman right down to a minor scratch on the right side above the back wheel arch. The plates might be different, but he could check inside and see for himself. After circling for a while he entered the barn.

On the back of the van a notice declaring *no tools left overnight*. Change 'tools' to guns. He checked and the scratch was there. Bingo! He went back to the car and waited. On the way he scouted the area, a ragged patch of land, completely untilled, rusting and rotting wheels and blades, some covered by the long grass on the periphery. An old tractor stood by falling apart with flat tyres, a once magnificent beast no doubt, now left to decay. He went back into the barn, a huge space with dozens of places to hide.

Disturbed, she would be on guard. He was waiting. *Alice, where art thou…*

He was now convinced she was in the barn. It was set more or less in the middle of the field, the skeletons of dead machinery around. The barn's situation was ideal for her purpose. A sniper of her quality could've picked him off if she wished. He went back in.

A noise in the corner made him turn. He thought after that it was the vagus nerve she'd struck, and often wondered why she didn't kill him. The heart rate is slowed, blood pressure drops, and one faints. He was out only seconds and was aware of the van roaring past him and out the field. He felt dizzy and silly, faint. His neck felt as if it had been twisted around. The van revved up and disappeared down the road. He wobbled and sat down on a bale. Then he smiled. His sloppy approach had been 'rewarded'. Moral maxims came to mind, then silly rhymes mingled: *Girls and boys come out to play… we live to fight another day…*

He was impressed by her skills, disappointed with his own search procedures. Whatever she did, it was effective. The question arose of why Alice didn't finish the job. That was a thorny one. A warning? A moment of pity? The list goes on. He ruminated. Nothing came.

He thought of *Star Trek*'s late science officer and laughed. He was tired. He waited a while then set off again, this time with more caution. He had ignored a fundamental rule and paid for it. It could have been worse. Beneath his critical assessment of his failure he had a sneaking admiration for Alice Byron. It wouldn't happen again. Would he do the same for her? Would he get the chance?

Freeman had taken Penny to the police station. Penny was beginning to shiver. He had no injuries to speak of barring a fine cut on his thigh and a knife groove on his abdomen. A police photographer took pictures, then a nurse bandaged it. Physically he was unscathed. A bruise or two appeared on his back where he hit the ground. Freeman decided to have them photographed anyway. Penny then went to sleep. She suspected a temporary fugue state, disassociation, loss of memory. It would return with a vengeance. His weird screams about the bin cart were unfathomable.

Nightmares, Freeman understood, wake people up. Penny was living a bad dream. Unsettled and fearful, he called out and there was no doubt from his calls it wasn't a threat rehearsal. Or was it? He'd killed another human being, a torturer.

The time taken gathering the statements was tedious, a time of circling, a time of revisiting a moment. It seemed on the face of things he had made a conscious decision to fly against the compelling mental death system, to disassociate himself, or the way we are meant to feel – perhaps taught to feel – after traumatic experiences. He laid it aside. He appeared a matter of fact. It was evident to Freeman and Jarrett that he was blocking his emotions.

It was more than that. He was dismantling boundaries, bringing Maureen back to life, then questioning himself for doing so. He was beginning to rewrite history. In his short time in the cells he did just that. The story took place over a hundred years before. The location, Dublin. Freeman listened.

The boundaries between life and death were at that juncture breaking down. How was he to show grief? How was he to show emotion? By what means could he counter his feelings of guilt? The very questions he had posed about the 'poets' themselves whose emotions were questionable now applied to him. He was having difficulty in showing remorse. He refused to follow what he deemed their path, the road to psychopathy and employ mimicry, a skill both Mo and Byron had to the nth degree, and which hid their true nature. It was an emptiness that refracted on his splintered self, and on his shame.

Periwinkle had demonstrated a more positive emptiness in combat. It was that he strived for, to see beyond and through his illusions. Periwinkle recounted what he heard. They recorded it. He left nothing out. Freeman asked one of the traffic police to drop Periwinkle in Otley.

Penny told his side of the story; with his usual sense of detail went over it twice. He added nothing. The car containing the bin bags, the road map and a spade was in the police pound waiting for the forensic team. The road map was to help them further down the line.

It was the bin bags that sparked his dream; it was the bin bags that promoted his interventions into the discourses of history, dream work and displacement. He began in his head to draft a story, one that would interfere in and change history. The bin bags were the nodal point for his associations, the rest was like Maureen, history.

Freeman cautioned him, at the same time supplying him with the language of the courtroom, thus preparing him for a self-defence plea where the assailant ends up worse off than the intended victim. Worse off meaning dead. Brown bread.

Her actions implied that a court case was inevitable. She followed the interview procedure to the letter, both identifying herself and Jarrett. He heard the 1967 Criminal Law Act mentioned several times, reasonable force too. Felonies and misdemeanours were mentioned.

Penny had one comment: "I expect if there is a court case it will be crowdfunded."

Freeman understood the fact that Penny saw humour in the situation. At the same time she thought it reckless. The pending case didn't appear to bother him. The digging into his past did. She presumed his own guilt was at play, his 'inner torment' as writers of fiction liked to call it. Psychologists referred to such. It was not fair.

He answered each question with a faraway look on his face that told Freeman he was thinking, and very deeply. Above all, he was being honest. "Can I have my laptop brought in, please? Need to write."

Freeman saw no reason to prevent this, but other things were more important. They weren't about to let him go. She authorised it. The laptop arrived.

The questions were endless. Each one had a logical answer, though he didn't seem too sure as he responded.

What were the grounds for believing she was going to kill you? Did you try to reason with the assailant? Could you have retreated? Could you have prevented it? Did you have any feelings of revenge? And most telling. Did you plan this in any way?

His answers were straightforward. "Her intention was to kill me. Her approach indicated she probably wanted to maim me first." He described her running the knife down his body. He touched his bandaged thigh and then the hairline cut on his abdomen as he spoke. In his mind he knew she could've easily done it. She hesitated. More questions followed.

"How did you discern this? Think about it. At what moment did you realise she was intent on killing you?"

"When she pulled the knife out, a vicious-looking brassy thing. She wanted to cut me first and make me suffer. She seemed to contemplate for a split second...

"I have to say that I acted instinctively." He wasn't sure instinctively was the right word to use. Impulsive? No. "At no point did I want to kill her. I suppose force was necessary. After I struck her with the stone she went for the gun. Of course, all joggers carry firearms these days. It's part of the kit." He apologised for his slanted humour and chose not to mention Dove's pistol. "I was naïve enough to believe that was it when the stone hit her skull. It was most frightening when she pulled the gun from behind her back, her face destroyed yet determined to finish the job."

Further images came to mind, among them a Picasso-like self-portrait by Francis Bacon, the jaw dislocated, the animalism, the energy, the game without reason. Penny mumbled. to do. That was true. He found them intriguing, worked out, *Welcome to the slaughterhouse.* The fragmented images continued. *We are never whole. The images that visit haunt us, dismemberment, castration and mutilation.*

Forensics had confirmed that someone had fired the gun once only. They would find the bullet.

"So, you felt that what you did was reasonably necessary?"

"Sadly, yes. I was talking. I can't recall the words. I didn't consciously select where to stick the knife in, I simply fell and lunged with it. It could've been anywhere. My first aim was to make her think, offer me time. The words were poetry, words from the grave."

Freeman looked confused.

"Freeman." He spoke as a tutor. "She was an academic. Her interests lay in the Graveyard Poets, an apt choice of study. I quoted them. She definitely recognised the passages. It gave me a second or two." In truth he thought it was crazy, but it worked. So did Freeman.

He felt another surge of shame and guilt. His head went down. Was the act of plunging a knife into someone's abdomen necessary, sufficient, reasonable? Her name was Maureen – a *someone*. He spoke of Jim and the similarities to the incident in the woods at Handale, avoiding saying what he really knew – the final cut. As a tear rose, he added, "I did what I did to protect myself. If the final act was vile, it was on the spur of the moment. I didn't think of anything. She brought the gun out just when I thought I had disabled her. I will question my final act again and again. The first move was in self-defence. The second, sheer desperation – not panic, but fear. I didn't feel any anger, and notions of revenge were furthest from my mind." Penny had no intention of letting himself off the hook.

Freeman and Jarrett, on the other hand, were trying to decide whether to let him go after processing. He certainly wasn't a threat to the public in the way the judiciary posed it, though some might think so. To add to that, his safety was also important. Pending enquiries and a postmortem, Freeman thought it wise to keep him in. There was another out there who desired his death. Freeman spoke with Periwinkle. He agreed.

She decided not to give Penny any options. "You're staying in custody."

He never argued.

A court would decide bail, prosecutions could rebut self-defence. Lots of ifs and buts. The evidence would hinge on the necessity of reasonable force; the burden of proof was with them. Penny was thankful Hart was elsewhere, though he had a nasty suspicion he would be along to oversee things. That Mo and Byron were the perpetrators of heinous crimes and torture might come to the fore. Was it admissible in court?

Jarrett asked the next question, well, two questions: "First question, Doc— Penny. Were you in any way trained to defend yourself in this way or in any way at all? It's a yes or a no."

Penny was silent. He thought of Prime Minister's question time. Bluster wasn't going to work. Jarrett posed the second question. "Think carefully before you answer. Were you expecting an attack from this person? Take your time and answer whenever and in whatever order."

Penny smiled inwardly at her intelligence. Freeman didn't look too bothered. Then he answered. "May I take the second question first, please?"

"Of course."

He stared at the recorder as if waiting for it to speak. Jarrett reminded him, "Everything is being taped."

"Officer Jarrett," he replied, "I have been receiving messages from the deceased and her associate threatening me." Jarrett urged him to continue. "The cards are filed away."

Freeman looked concerned. Jarrett suggested he included their names – Alice and Maureen.

"In effect, my earlier actions, which led you to check them out, caused them some grief, interrupted the flow of their lives to the extent that they took revenge on Lance. And though, not proven, I suspect them of torturing that poor boy in Loftus." He wished he hadn't said that. "The answer is yes! I was expecting an attack. When and where it would come was a daily nightmare, a daymare, and whether it would be one or both of the hired killers. It never entered my head that night. I wasn't prepared for it, if that's what you're asking." He couldn't mention the forgotten gun.

A long statement on Jim followed. Maureen, Freeman informed him, was the torturer. "Someone up there sent a file. It makes for gory reading. Alice's role is uncertain."

They briefed Penny. Was the file hearsay? Penny's theory

was it had come from a seventh-floor office in London, from a ghost. Guess? They didn't know.

The gaping holes worried Freeman. Why wasn't he telling the whole story? He was definitely safer remanded in custody. Keeping him was no legal problem and he didn't appear to be concerned by his confinement. Keeping it from the press another. It would of course require a statement or confession which wasn't forthcoming from either the deceased or her partner-in-crime and academia. Whether Byron would do so, was unlikely. Jarrett egged Penny on.

"So, you were scared? Shall we say in fear of your life?"

"Yes." Penny wasn't going to elaborate.

She pursued her line of thought. "Did you think of revenge for the suspected torture and killing of Lance and Max?"

"Yes. No."

"Which one is it?"

"Jarrett," he eyeballed her with some annoyance, "have you ever had a person known to you castrated, tortured, murdered? I hope not. The notion of revenge creeps in and then out. It is a safety valve. At the time everything happened so damn quickly I had no time to think of anything!" He slumped back. "I did not plan revenge, if that's what you imply. It entered my head not once, but several times before the event, and just as quickly left, leaving me feeling foolish. Best left for vigilante movies."

Jarrett exchanged looks with Freeman. Her eyebrows knitted together. What was going through her mind was obvious to Penny. He didn't seem to care. He looked at her and said, "There is still another out there who will want my death even more. I feel sorry for Mo. I feel sorry for Byron, per se. I use per se with reference to their condition and the fact I killed one of them. In no way did I plan to execute either of them." He pondered. He clearly had no intention of deceiving Freeman and Jarrett. In their opinion there was a delusional aspect to his statements. He was struggling to come to terms with his actions. His next statement required more analysis.

"Their narcissism I can cope with, their Machiavellian nature I can understand, their psychopathy I know; together they form a double triangle, a six-sided star, trinity, or separate. In this case their behaviour implies an inverted model, one linked to death rather than to life. They're fucking with the symbols." That last bit they partially understood. An academic like Byron would appreciate the reference. Jarrett had forgotten the questions. She wondered if he was prevaricating.

The first question was clearly bothering him. "Your first question, Officer Jarrett. I was concerned by the messages. I did a few lessons in self-defence, though their usefulness in the situation and in the time I had is questionable. I did ten classes in all."

"Can you verify the nature of them?"

"Yes. My tutor was Periwinkle! It was something I'd wanted to do. It increased my general fitness, a concern for me constantly. It gave me some self-confidence." He looked directly at Jarrett. It was clear to him that Jarrett wasn't sure self-confidence was an issue for him. He answered her unspoken question.

"It may surprise you, but self-confidence was lacking when it comes to warding off knives and guns!"

Freeman gave another tight-lipped smile.

"I had no other experience of real self-*defence* apart from a cursory reading of my granddad's military manual which he kept from his time in the forces. I was about twelve at the time. It was a jujitsu guide aimed at defence rather than attack. I'm not sure that I could simply attack anyone without some provocation, and defending oneself is very different to attacking someone, that is mentally or physically." He thought back to the pub in London with Dove. He stopped there.

They had come to a dead halt. He hoped Dove had removed his personal armoury as they were bound to search the house. There was always a flaw. He wondered if they were going to bail him under Section 25 of The Criminal Justice Act. He signed a statement. A young officer cautioned him. Jarrett remained. Freeman left to do the paperwork.

Penny threw a question at Jarrett. "I expect it will be all over the papers, Jarrett? That will no doubt flush out the other."

"If we hushed up the case, would it offer any advantages?"

No answer was required. Jarrett reminded him that it wasn't yet public. Freeman had put a press release on hold with a stern warning about leakages. She thanked Penny for his honesty.

As she picked up her papers she said, "You can call me Olivia."

"Nice name, from the olive tree."

Freeman called Dove. Dove updated her on Alice. She also called Hart. Hart kept it to himself.

Chapter 22

Undaunted, but wary, Dove had tracked down Byron. As he expected, she moved on and did so with some aplomb. She was heading west, the coast. Freeman was right, Penny was safer where he was, though Alice might just be leaving the country. Bail seemed expensive.

In an extraordinary twist, Penny pre-empted the offer and refused it. He didn't ask who had offered to put up the money and didn't want to know. They considered prestigious lawyers and barristers. He took that lightly too. "As long as it's not Braverman, Cameron and Starmer."

Dove soldiered on. He recalled the visits to Tate Modern with Penny lecturing him as they went round. He dozed in the car. A vivid dream took over the disturbed sleep. The back bedroom window was wide open; he was staring out on a funeral cortege carrying a coffin borne by what resembled The Four Horsemen of the Apocalypse. *Horseless, they slowly marched past.* He thought he knew their faces: death, destruction, pestilence and famine. One was a woman. His emotions and memories swirled in a complex interplay of recall and forget, his mind twisted and turned as the cortege carried the coffin around the car park out the back of the Cross Pipes where he and Periwinkle first 'encountered' the assassins.

The drawn images were in cartoon form darkened by a Kollwitz charcoal monochrome, a white abyss around the coffin. William Kentridge's fabulous black charcoal 1990s animations came to mind, dark and at times ghostly, with the bite of Kathe Kollwitz. A reviewer once said the ghosts of the past always haunt the present. *Maureen.* Visiting galleries with Penny could be a nightmare. The lectures were entertaining but were they necessary? *Well*, he thought, *I wouldn't have known about Penny's three Ks: Kentridge, Kollwitz or Kandinsky.*

There was a large hole in the car park ready to take the coffin, a black hole, the bottom of a mine. He peered in. A sense of falling. Then the coffin opened, and death stared him in the face. Mo stood to the side. She was smiling, her jaw shattered, Alice a shadow in the background, waiting. In the coffin was Penny.

Chapter 23

Murphy exchanged pleasantries about the weather. He said it was cold. Actually, he said, "It's chucking filly." Though sunny, the wind had dropped. "You have a visitor."

Penny was expecting a move to a holding cell. He didn't know the procedures. He was also expecting Periwinkle or Dove. It was neither.

"Dr Penny, I presume!"

He was about to say it was a lovely day for a walk, then a big breakfast when Tammy entered. He had seen her only twice, that night at the conference, then at the Tate talk, though that memory never left him, the dark copper sheen of her straight hair, her green eyes, and yes, the patchwork duffel bag, which he assumed they had searched for a cake with a file in it. He had been frightened to pursue further his email relationship. The bravado was lacking beyond the message, the emotion gone, the tone of her voice missing. He wasn't sure why she was here.

"Hiya, Ronnie. I'm in Leeds and wanted to see you." The use of his first name took him by surprise. Murphy stepped outside with a wink.

Penny pushed the thought of any food to the back of

his mind. The morning walk gushed out in the absence of anything else he could say. "Let's go for a walk along the old railway line. It once ran from Menston to Otley. The line was a lifeline until the mad doctor took his axe to it."

Tammy listened head cocked and savoured the description, making no comment about mad doctors. Not this time. He recognised the stance from his own affectations.

He could point out a holly hedge growing at the back of a modern house that fronted onto the golf course, one he planted with differing holly bushes. "Ilex, you know, male and female. I didn't buy enough. There was one gap. There always is." He could point at the spot where there was one bush short. The hedge would be three or four-foot high now. He'd help plant it for friends. Those moments now seemed precious. Small things growing. "Can you see where the gap was?"

Another hundred yards or so along the old line he would pause. A holly bush was growing wild beside the once busy track. "I took a cutting from that which was not much bigger than the bought plants and I dug it into the gap!"

At that moment he was outside in the fresh air with Tammy. She sat and listened.

Had she been sent to eke out information from him?

He wondered what gaps he'd left for Freeman, Jarrett (Olivia to him), and whether a prosecution would follow. It was to be sure one of those grey areas. He remembered reading Melvyn Bragg's *The Maid of Buttermere*. Its protagonist, the duplicitous John Hatfield, was hanged for his crimes. The public, the common masses, adored him, and in secret many of the gentry admired and copied him. He didn't want to be Hatfield, who he despised for his duplicity. He wouldn't hang, that was for sure. Gaol didn't bother him. What he did he was responsible for, his own actions, and he dwelt on the situation that had led him to slaughter someone, a fellow human being. He checked himself. Tammy was here. She sat, duffel bag beside her, and listened.

"How's the research?" He realised he'd hogged the conversation. Then he wondered if he'd spoken at all.

"It's complete. The viva was the most exhilarating and terrifying thing I've ever done."

"So, you're Dr Sutherland. Brilliant." He so wanted to hug her. The cell crowded in on him. Though it was his home at the moment, it wasn't the place he wanted to meet her. His eyes were misty. She allowed him to gather his savvy. They chattered much in the same way they did when they met, the important nothings. Murphy looked in apologetically. Tammy picked up the patch duffel bag to leave.

"See you again."

His eyes filled. After a second, his intuitive self-surfaced. He jumped up and hugged her. The wave was the same, the smile, there was no apparent self-consciousness about their location, a police cell in Leeds, his new home.

Before Murphy locked the cell door he said, "Hugging is allowed at the beginning too, but only a second, three visits a week, one hour maximum." He smiled. 'The force' as Murphy called it (he was a *Darth Vader* fan) were getting to like this strange man remanded in custody. He should really be in a secure wing elsewhere. Someone up top was pulling strings, someone in the higher echelons. No one was arguing. Up there they helped at times. At other times they escaped due punishment. As for the secure wing for Penny, many would agree.

Periwinkle called too, though separately. They ran over his statement. Periwinkle told him about Dove's encounter with Alice. He was treated to a lesson of nursery rhymes and Greek playwrights. Penny found Periwinkle's sneaking admiration for Alice strange at first, then recalled the seminar. Alice was talented. It was too easy to treat both the poets as caricatures, lacking substance. Periwinkle was cautious about his statement. He asked him to repeat a couple of sections, particularly those questions he fielded from Jarrett. "She's sharp," Penny concluded.

Periwinkle reassured him. "There's nothing much you said that can incriminate you. It's fortunate you knocked the gun away, is it not? It's for the CPS to decide if a prosecution is in order." Periwinkle ran through the evidence. "Is there enough evidence to prosecute? Is it in the public interest? It is clear you committed the act, that you are guilty of a crime in self-defence. The European Convention on Human Rights still applies. The CPS must examine the police evidence, then decide if the force used was reasonable, that is, given the consequences."

He reported back Dove's thoughts. Separate or not, Dove and Periwinkle's conversations were seamless, dovetailed. Dove, as always, put his tuppence worth in. Periwinkle dropped a tone. "They don't want Charles Bronson, the harmonica man, roaming the streets of Leeds or Bradford. In other words, vigilantes. Penny," Periwinkle assured him, "you are not a vigilante, merely a harmonica player."

"There is another Charles Bronson," Penny reminded

him.

"That's more or less what Freeman said, with rather more subtlety." Periwinkle summarised. The law felt that if the victim of an attack has done 'honestly and instinctively' what they think is necessary, they are deemed to have acted lawfully. Periwinkle was pleased Penny had used the word instinctively in his statement. The worrying factor was he wanted punishment. Maybe the law thought that too. Proportional representation for politics and proportional punishment for wrongdoing, second degree or not. Community orders were out and unpaid work he was used to.

At that moment, Penny knew there would be a case, and someone would take it against him. He knew also that the prosecution would have to rebut self-defence. Murder was a crime. In a way he wanted it. His reciprocal nature meant whichever way it went he could pay back.

Periwinkle said, "Is it in the public interest to publicise the death? Nothing has made the newspapers as yet."

His other visitor's reasons for a visit were even more of a surprise than Tammy. Hart was already heading to Leeds. The police network was like a spider's web ready to catch the fly. Who was the fly in this case?

Richard Hart, expert on murder and self-defence cases (so he said) was on his way. Saida too had picked up the news and passed on her best wishes. She knew also that it wouldn't be long before a leak occurred. She understood perfectly why Freeman would keep it under wraps. They desperately needed to catch Mo's partner and question her. By now Byron would know all was not well. No one in their right mind would argue the case for mercy or clemency for the torturer. Lance's death was evidence of their warped nature.

Images abounded in Penny's head. Periwinkle reminded him of the exhibitions. More than ever before, the images operated to relieve his angst, then as a revenge, bring it back: hopelessness and loss in Otto Dix, the physically crippled and disabled; the release in images of Pissarro's peasant paintings swamped by Kollwitz and Kentridge again, polemical politics and peasant war. A vicious circle of degenerate art, anarchy and political reality. He made lists of his own degenerate art exhibition, one which would have shocked and offended the connoisseur. Gauguin, his usual suspect, featured.

If they could get Alice to talk that would do it. They had to catch her first. They had to take her alive. How she would react to the news of her partner's killing was an unknown. Her records didn't reveal compassion as a part of her make-up, unlike her propensity for cruelty. Yet she let Dove off the hook…

The case was full of holes. Penny put it aside for the rest of his imaginary walk along the railway line with Tammy. Did he mean virtual walk? He hadn't asked why she was in Leeds. She did say she would see him again. He continued their walk.

They turned left and cut through a small clump of bushes and up to the top where they had a view across the valley. From there they walked back across the field to the Chevin pub and back down. The wind began to rustle the trees as they descended, the light blocked by moving clouds which caused the temperature to fall. Tammy offered to cook when they got in. He opened his laptop. Lesson number four was taking shape, aimed at reducing pain and distress, blocking pain signals.

Alice Byron was already alert to Mo's demise, death or capture. Their system was to call in every day with a simple message. No call came. She abandoned the van after leaving the old barn and moved off on foot. She considered her encounter with Dove. She was lucky. He was momentarily distracted by the noise; a convenient rat foraging the old barn. Good on the rat. Maybe animals did have their uses.

If Mo had come to grief, the hunt would be on for her. She ditched her mobile, replacing it with another ready for such moments. She wondered if Penny had triumphed against her comrade and fellow painter and decorator poet. No, that was silly. So much of Penny remained hidden beneath his apparent and somewhat deceptive transparency. He was honest, that was clear, he cared for people, that too was clear. In her opinion, a lot was hidden. Alice was very astute.

She travelled at night. She turned south. Her first instinct was to get out of the country. Her second was to kill Penny, then get out of the country, Spain via Eire. She recited poems as she walked inland. It helped her reflect, it was a known stress reducer, though Alice wasn't prone to such. Perhaps, she thought, it was my cosy upbringing. Her reasoned self said it best to leave Penny alone, yet the challenge was there. She had met him on her own ground. A transition was in order. She used her own psychology, and though nostalgia was alien to her, she looked back on her days at Maidstone Grammar School for Girls. It was as the textbooks stated: a 'coping mechanism'. It wasn't needed. She did wonder where Mo had been to school in Birmingham, Mo's accent posh 'Brummie'. She never thought to ask.

Her pack was heavy, the air cold. She felt happy. She recalled her time in the army, and then a van Gogh quote came to mind, one quoted by Penny: 'The night is more alive and more richly coloured than the day'. She walked. She recited the Graveyard Poets – Blair, Young, Parnell – and chided herself when words ran out.

The night was hers and sublime. Her confidence doubled as if a revelation had taken place since Mo's demise. Dawn would be soon. She started to seek a place to rest… perchance…

The hunt was nationwide. Dove was back. He called into Meanwood to see Penny. He stopped to brief Freeman on his surveillance. On the way out he saw Hart. Hart didn't see him as he was pulling his car off the Otley road across the busy lanes. Dove's opinion was that Byron was heading for a port somewhere, Liverpool was his guess.

The visitor was Hart. Penny wasn't sure he wanted him in his cell. He put down the laptop and stared at him. A constable Penny hadn't met let him in and said, "One hour," then carefully, "Sir."

Hart was always serious, but he looked grim.

"What's the good news, Hart?"

Hart smiled. "There isn't any. I'm here to help." Irony again. He sat down on the bed.

"I've read the case notes over and over. Any prosecution case is going to have difficulty, not least with their lack of funding and serious budget cuts to CPS. And there is the underlying issues of Jim's posthumous involvement, not to mention the links to quasi-governmental offices. Moreover, we intend to disclose every snippet of information we can, whether admissible or not, that is *everything* – texts, documents, Lance's messages, postcards, and everything we can about Jim and his contract, though that is difficult. We will need permission and evidence from certain people who have a knack of fading away to grey. You have a contact, I hear, in the upper echelons?" He didn't wait for a reply. He didn't expect one. "I've seen the postcards. They are now in Freeman's possession."

Penny looked sad. Hart continued. "Disclosure is everything." He paused. "The mass of evidence will work in our favour, electronic mostly. Do you know how much a mobile phone can store? Maureen's gives nothing away, but Lance's does."

Penny shook his head. To whom did Lance speak ?

"And do you know how many cases collapse due to disclosure or lack of it?"

Penny didn't.

"Too many. The Crown Prosecution Service is there not solely to gain a prosecution; they are there to assess the evidence and the financial aspects. My argument will be that the evidence negates guilt. They will see that the evidence is favourable to you, the defendant." He stopped.

"Hang on a minute. We? Our? Your argument?" Baffled by Hart's intervention Penny looked around the cell for inspiration.

"Fundamentally, I'm offering my services as a solicitor advocate." Hart didn't mention his reasons. Penny had an idea it went back to Loftus and torture. Hart explained. He was studying again, criminal law. His 'natural' role would be working for the prosecution service. Yet here he was offering a defence.

"Penny, you were in imminent danger. We can prove that. Our evidence from Lance's laptop is robust. That you acted in the first instance to defend yourself is a given. The issue of the knife may cause a ripple but nothing we can't get around. What do you say?"

"What's the second prize?"

Sweeping aside his sarcasm, Hart moved on. "On the issue of self-defence and preparedness, your arrest was as a suspect of serious criminal violation. You weren't carrying anything offensive."

Penny tried not to look guilty. Indeed, he hadn't been carrying Dove's pistol.

"The weapon you used was that of the attacker. You had no time to mull over a course of action or the niceties of it. That it was a woman may unsettle some. Disclosure comes in. We give them everything: their army records, their prison records, and their link to Jim. Oh, one final thing, I'll have a barrister in court as a helper."

"Are the Crown Prosecution Service likely to go ahead?"

"I don't know." Hart shrugged his shoulders.

Penny was thinking. So far, he had refused help. That Hart was qualified to represent him was stinging. No, it was hilarious. Penny eyed him. Hart wasn't laughing. That he appeared to have read all the information was even more interesting. Who was behind it? "Do you know when my case is in court?"

"That is not the key question."

Penny waited.

"I'll aim to put it in plain terms and as succinctly as possible. The issue revolves around reasonable force."

Penny nodded.

"Was it necessary? Excessive? Instinctive? Was it a result of training? Did you act lawfully, in other words?"

Penny linked his fingers and sat up.

"Bear in mind it's not for you to prove anything. You're innocent until proven otherwise. The prosecution has to prove that. The assailant isn't here to answer for herself. No family have come forward. No witnesses exist. Postmortem has one crucial aspect, the neurological damage, a blow from a piece of rock which takes time to discern. Forensics assure me that was not the cause of death." He waited. Penny kept quiet.

"To the point: the case is going to attract public interest. The CPS may want to take the case to court to resolve certain issues. Or they may decide that the probable verdict is 'not guilty'. Therefore, the case should never enter a courtroom! Public interest is a central issue. Your intent, another." He sat back then said, "If you think a plea of manslaughter is possible, don't bother. It isn't."

"I know some of the law. I am guilty of killing another person who I had no intention of killing, though I despised what they did."

"That's another thorny issue, the subject of young Max,

and of Jim, and his demise in the woods, the torture, the death of Max. If we had a clear link to that we'd be home free."

Penny was taken aback by Hart's grasp of the law and his forensic approach; one he'd witnessed in him as a police officer. He was still a police officer. He agreed with Hart that Jim's demise wasn't that clear.

"I could plead insane."

"I'm sure you'd be convincing. You'd have to fool a forensic psychiatrist and undergo a few other tests that would indicate cunning maybe, and several other issues, but not insanity." Hart tried not to smile and failed. He looked around the cell, the books, the laptop and a large pink file. "You seem to be at home."

"Got what I need for the moment. No chance of a large poster of Raquel Welch. is there?"

With a shake of his head and a supressed smile Hart left. Before he signalled the duty constable, he said, "I leave it to you, but don't take too long. The CPS will want this dealt with. When it hits the headlines, anything is possible. That too will prejudice a fair ruling."

The weight on Penny felt bone crushing. He thought of refusing to enter a plea. That would be insane. He was guilty of killing someone in order to protect himself from murder. No visitation of God could account for such a move. He was far from mute. The old ordeal of *peine forte et dure* had begun already in earnest. Such was the weight of words. He was crushed. He opened his laptop and began to write. Punishment it is, and strong and hard.

The dilemma remained. In Penny's estimation it was worse. At times he wanted to be guilty. Hart submitted everything alongside Freeman and Jarret's interviews and Penny's statement. The flaws were apparent. The knife issue: Penny's admittance that he 'plunged' it into the woman without thinking. Under oath he would have to face questions about that.

What did you think of before you stabbed her to death? Was she unconscious? Surely the injury sustained to the victim's jaw would imply she was concussed or unconscious?

Validate – they had factual proof of her injury, but not that she was unconscious. He admitted his role truthfully and in detail.

Confirm – they couldn't remove the element of doubt, which could work either way.

Corroborate – they really had no witnesses, though they had lots of testimonies to suggest that Penny's toxic nature was a reality. It appeared that he wasn't as popular as he imagined.

Substantiate – they had nothing to offer to reinforce a verdict of murder or his intentions, and nothing to sustain the argument. Or did they?

Verify – line up the details from statements, forensic evidence and pathology with the facts (and guesses).

Finally, authenticate – that is through expert opinion, legal or official documents the genuine nature of the crime.

Several aspects worried Penny. His belief in experts was critical. If medical, too many of them we were lab rats, though handwriting would be a fun one. If police, we were guilty. That brought about an '*oh shit*' moment: which handwriting should he use?

Did you plan to execute the victim?

Periwinkle had submitted a declaration of facts. Did it imply he wasn't going to be in court? Penny wondered. The law, plus the burden of proof, lay with the prosecution; the evidence was fragile. Penny wished they would just go to court and get it over with.

There was yet another figure to step into the breach, one they knew nothing of, one who could make it or break it. Two in truth, and one had mixed motives. Testimonies ranged from old colleagues to his counsellor therapist Jeanine. He didn't want to see any of them. Hart queried what he'd done to upset her, then realised it was a foregone conclusion. The scales of justice kept tipping back and forth. To Penny they looked unbalanced, weighed down by his past.

Chapter 24

In a small garage in Shipley, Alice Byron's final task before
decamping was polishing a rifle. She checked the inventory
of their personal armoury which, barring a brassy knife
and a handgun, were all present and correct. It included a
handsome pair of fragmentation grenades courtesy of the
US Army, rifles, and Mo's L115A3, a souvenir of Afghanistan.
Byron toyed with the detachable sound suppressor, then put
it aside and fondled her 1980s arctic sniper, a bolt action with
an eight hundred-metre range. She checked the telescopic
sights – spot on. She preferred variable magnification to fixed
as it offered more range and flexibility. Penny and his silver
cat… From a distance… She hummed as she cleaned and
prepared everything for battle, then wrapped everything in
thick oilcloth and polythene.

She closed the cleaning kit and admired the sniper rifle.
It was hers; it had served her well. She fondled her modified
x16 pistol-great for close quarters. She put it aside, checked
vests. She wrapped them too. She missed the .50 GS, which
Mo had nursed and taken. Its firepower was unmatched, its
damage output the highest per round of any handgun she'd
used.

She kept up to date. A magazine told her that the Russian Lobaev arms sniper rifle had a firing distance of up to two miles. It was a dream come true. Imagine, two miles… Phew. The advert boasted it was a 'game changer.' It was indeed. In between her preparations she recited lines from the war poets, and war poems, the first module of her degree. She chose the words of Carol Ann Duffy, a sister in arms: 'Poetry gargling its own blood.' And for her companion, Anna Gordon Keown's *Reported Missing*: 'My thought shall never be that you are dead'. Mo had screwed up in some way. Their fight in the ring came to mind and her victory which was a draw, no one was prepared to cast a vote. Happy days. Fragments of Isaac Rosenberg's *Break of Day in the Trenches* followed: 'Bonds to the whims of murder'…

She recited snippets as she packed the weapons in their various cases. She was meticulous, battle-scarred and ready. Was it wise? She swallowed the excessive pride, and concentrated. The well-read analyst that refuted dark triads had plenty of evidence to support thoughts about the future. All the bollocks about fire starters, cruelty to animals, bed-wetting… Rubbish. She ticked one box only; and her pathological hatred was for cats. That and dunking biscuits. She laughed. If anything, the triad detracted the learned in their quest for simple reasons. It wasn't wise to follow up the now redundant contract. Wisdom, she recalled, was a very bad comedian, a toady, and unfunny. *Time to think*, Alice. She allowed herself a diversion, made a cuppa on the primus and, about to dunk a biscuit, censored the move. Tut-tut! The hunt was nationwide. She watched Dove call into Meanwood to see Penny.

Certain animals and insects were cool. In the Gulf they'd watched snakes and scorpions wandering, locusts, and camels. Contrast them to goldfish in bowls, pets dressed with frills, strange fluffy dogs, and frightening and abhorrent cats. She could sense the presence of a cat. The very thought of a feline jumping on her knee and snuggling down made her nauseous. People and pets. She returned to think about guns. The silver cat haunted her. It was a strange beast. The day of the aborted assassination the cat had sensed something, something that told Alice of its uncanny nature. She shivered.

She packed what she needed, then buried the rest in a derelict part of what had once been a water treatment site. There were signs of redevelopment to come, but things were on hold. Dressed in streetwear, she bought provisions and loaded up her new car. Before she left, she cropped her hair and dyed it blonde, its original mousey colour and length replaced by a short spikey cut. Her tattoos would have to stay covered. In a broken mirror in the garage, she admired herself. A new woman. A crack in the mirror ran down her jaw.

She gazed fondly at the weaponry before storing it away. What a rifle won't do, a scatter grenade might complete. Yorkshire was a suitable place to hide out from the law. She had more or less forgotten Mo, barring a slight curiosity about what school she went to.

Dying didn't worry Alice, falling into police hands did, if only for reasons of failure. Fear of such was not in the equation. They had failed to kill Penny so far, and they (not she) had learned from it. They had gone. She wouldn't make the errors her late acquaintance had. Mo had learned the ultimate lesson. She never was as good. There was a little business to finish off. Her sources of intel had dried up, she was on her own and that suited. Alone in the field of battle, *The Remnants of an Army.*

Alice watched the police officer, Freeman, enter Penny's cottage several times, leaving with a laptop and odds and sods and a brown envelope, stopping to feed the vile-looking grey cat. On one occasion she brought a dog with her, a wire-haired thing which sat outside. The cat disappeared indoors. Penny was in protective custody. Why? Mo was dead.

A scatter grenade into the police station would be a gem of a way to finish the job and offer a few bonus points. The money was frozen, the deal was off. Better to skedaddle and move on. The idea had credence, there was money in accounts abroad. She called a contact. Would he be prepared to accompany her on a boat trip as man and wife? Passports arranged, money in the bank, job done. What then? Keeping the wounds green came to mind. Against all her principles, and an unfathomable hatred for Penny, she decided to wait. Think about killing the wire-haired terrier from two miles away, then disappearing. She buried everything she had planned to take with her and drove away with nothing.

Chapter 25

"Hart, a solicitor advocate? Well, bugger me." Dove couldn't get his head around it. "More like devil's advocate. Mind you, his knowledge of the law is amazing, his stomach for the police work not suitable. Has he left the force?"

"I don't think so."

Dove stared at Penny waiting for an opinion.

True to form Penny meandered. "It was a shock." He continued, "And on that score, I'm writing again. I take your point, though he is the devil, I know. His inherent honesty might get in the way. However, his grasp of the case is juridical. Both he and Freeman are on my side."

"Does he think the case will be brought to court?"

"Interesting point, Dove. I hope it will be. There is, as usual, things happening behind the scenes to which I have no access, no power over. I went to sleep last night mulling over my meeting with Lucas Guess, Periwinkle's nephew. I sensed his presence. In tandem with that, I felt the presence of Maureen's partner, Alice, fade."

"Alice is exceedingly good at her job." Dove looked over his shoulder as he spoke. "Several times now I've been close. Each time she evaporates. She's not only clever, she's also capable of advanced thinking. She is smart enough to say the job is redundant, the money gone, so let's move on. Another reading would suggest she is malevolent enough to want to finish the job for the sake of her own pride, and then move on. If she does, she will have to reveal herself. Freeman has a notion she will. Our mutual friend Freeman has an itch to scratch. She would like to meet her one-to-one."

"Freeman?" Penny tried to imagine the string bean of a police officer in unarmed combat. He could; it was Periwinkle, Uncle Ninja in drag. His own combative skills in the field seemed pallid. Tall and wiry Freeman could probably kick ass. "What is Periwinkle up to?"

"I wondered if you'd ask." To Penny, his tone implied he was going to skirt around the answer. "He's in London working on something. He sends his regards and says to keep your chin up. The cavalry is on the way."

It wasn't quite an untruth. It still said lots if you're Penny, nothing if your glass is half empty. He left it at that. He decided not to read between the lines.

Hart made several visits, then said he would be away for a number of days in London. He too was holding back on information, the very thing that Penny disliked about the man, his inability to share. In this case, Hart knew what he was doing. Penny didn't.

Byron watched Hart drive away. She turned the car back towards Horsforth and drove out of town. Penny was there at Meanwood. His friend Dove had called also. The tall one, Periwinkle, was absent. She turned the car and took another direction north. The Great North Road.

Periiwinkle left his nephew's office feeling optimistic. His meeting had been short. Lucas informed him that the case had brought into play an aristocratic knave of trumps, the suicide king and the queen, well, a queen's counsel, a barrister and others. The cryptic element caused him to laugh. Legal interest in the case was gathering.

Hart had submitted on request (or demand, depending how you see it) most of his evidence, though he'd held some back just in case. An invitation to 'parley' with the elites seemed unusual, though it could be a request. An order? Only too familiar with the fickle finger, he wanted to see how it would pan out. His barrister friend-cum-tutor advised he did what they said. She wanted to remain anonymous.

The Penny case was a minefield. Hart was standing on one. What would happen when he made his move? Life was like that around Penny.

Freeman ushered in his next guest. This time he hugged Tammy. Her duffel bag was gone. She was wearing a smart pleated grey skirt and white simple blouse; her face was flushed and spoke of personal victories.

"Well, Dr Penny, I'm afraid we can't celebrate the occasion yet, but hope that will be the case soon."

"Go on then. Don't keep me in suspense." Underneath he was dreading it. She looked like she'd been to a wedding, her own.

Tammy, taking a leaf out of his book, saw his agony and waited just a second. "You're looking at the new senior lecturer in art history about to replace that dreadful Dr Penny." She held back. "Actually, the panel said you were a hard act to follow."

He felt good, in fact great. He leaped to his feet and Freeman wagged her finger outside. "One hug only," then turned her back and took out her mobile.

"I start immediately. Fortunately, my predecessor left adequate documents, enough for me to slot in, though some are unreadable and some unmentionable."

"Where are you staying?"

"I'll have to find digs in the meantime. The pleasure of finding a small place of my own will have to wait."

"Stay at mine, and before you decide, you can feed Silver."

"Silver?"

"He's not my cat, he adopted me. It seems unfair that Freeman's men should have to pop by. Dove calls in now and then."

"Are you sure?"

"My books are there, as you will see. The back bedroom is empty. If you check the filing cabinets in the main bedroom, on the left there are dozens of related files. Freeman has a key and the neighbours each have one. Just let Colin next door know."

Tammy accepted. "For now. I'll look around later." They spent the next half an hour talking shop. He forgot his situation totally.

Freeman and Tammy left together. Freeman gave her the keys and said, "If you find any weapons in there let me know."

Tammy hoped she was joking. Freeman's face said that was so. Freeman was also relieved as she too had her suspicions. Despatching a man to Otley every day was a drain on the workforce. The officers themselves were queueing for the job of feeding Silver. Silver was in his element. One officer reported that a blonde woman had walked along the bottom of the yard and Silver had rushed at her, claws bared. She fled. Barring that, all was quiet.

Silver was unimpressed by Penny's absence, though he missed him and the tall man Periwinkle. He would bite Penny again the next time he saw him, for sure.

Chapter 26

Hart's invite to the Old Bailey came as a surprise. His past experiences of Penny balanced surprise with the concluding thought that anything can occur. He had often stood outside the hallowed halls and dreamed. All reported crimes are submitted for review, and examination of the evidence to the CPS unless he, that is the law, decided not to report such to the proper authorities for a full review and public interest test. Threshold tests didn't seem to apply. Bail wasn't an issue here, though he did muse over the fact whether Penny might pose a threat or bail risk to himself.

Penny, or the mere mention of him, could cause havoc in an empty room. This room wasn't going to be empty. Neither was a courtroom. The time was flying past. He was nervous about his advocacy. He consoled himself with the fact he knew Penny better than most, he thought.

He dressed smart, a suit and tie, changed the tie several times and opted for a grey with his blue shirt and dark suit. The hall mirror confirmed he was suitably attired. He put another tie in the car.

Hart thought about his client. Penny didn't appear bothered by his location. He didn't appear to be showing signs of trauma. Hart believed there was no doubt Penny showed remorse, first regret and then remorse. It was clearly something he never wanted to witness again. Hart could read below that and see Penny's empathy, even for Jim. It showed in his statements. Hart reminded him he couldn't bring Jim or Maureen back and he couldn't resolve her death.

Hart set off from Leeds early. He didn't know who he was to meet. He was clueless as to the agenda. It was best not to ponder. It was to discuss 'the Penny Case.' That was enough. Inevitably a suspicion crept into the corners of his mind and spread. The prosecution service was efficient, organised, and their conviction rates were high. One reason was that cases never got to court that were to cost money and fail with a verdict of not guilty. The CPS aimed to gather all the information. They were there to advise not to investigate, to deliver justice. Interesting word. Justice for who?

A woman died. The background was prescient to him. How much would be admissible or presentable in a court? He wasn't yet sure. Could they include Jim's 'attachment' to government? Could they prove his farming out of killing to Mo and Alice? Would Lance's laptop be the key? He pulled over to clear his head. He had plenty of time.

The questions kept coming. He would need to admit that government officials misled him in the Loftus case. Most frightening was the question of whether Penny was capable of planning such a heinous crime. His own suspicions, partly a response to Penny's elusive nature, led him to believe at one point he had played a role in the death of the twins. Along with that, he knew more about Jim's death than he let on.

Hart kicked himself. He must learn to be more

philosophical, if that was the right expression. Step one: one at a time. He tried to clear his unarticulated thoughts and concentrate on the task ahead. Problems, purposes, and possible solutions rushed through. No concrete answers.

Hart drove to the outskirts of London and parked up. He checked carefully he had everything he needed. He caught a tube to St Paul's. Both a firm advocate of London's Emission Zoning and Ultra Low Emission zones, he Googled it on his phone to see what the impact of the latter had been. It was huge. Now that was something he had no qualms about as an advocate. He bit his lip and removed any doubts from his mind. A deep breath relieves the congestion.

Freeman considered moving Penny to a PC unit until things blew over. As long as Alice Byron was out there that might be a lifetime. Penny's lifetime was the deadline. Spending twenty-three hours a day in a jail cell wasn't good for anyone. He was taken out the back and allowed an hour in the company of an officer. Penny was itching to go for a run. He overruled or scratched his itch by bringing back the memory of his last run. He found he was sleeping better, apart from those nights when Mo visited his dreams. Freeman guessed he had other reasons to be home. A cat? A cat minder even?

The hole, as Murphy called his cell, was okay; Penny was beginning to feel and see outside, the landscape, the sea, the gallery of life, its people, its problems. His identity was out there and under threat. One aspect of such remained, the monastic fragment of himself pouring over his manuscripts, scribbling his notes, safeguarded from a killer by the law. He assumed that the police were more interested in getting him into court. The evidence weighed against that. They had no problem with his behaviour. Behind his back they worried about his mental state. That was normal.

Alternatively, he wondered if they transferred him to prison protective custody it would be the same. Jarrett (Olivia that is) said it was horrid, Murphy concurred. "Let's get the case over and see," Murphy concluded. He failed to mention that intel assumed Byron was still in the area and the implications were that she would be planning to make a move very soon.

The Old Bailey as a meeting place was extraordinary. The referral or hearing, whatever it was to be, could have taken place in Leeds Crown Court. Denied the oak-lined courtrooms, solicitor advocate Hart was issued a visitor's tag and directed to the newer 1970s extension. The floggings, the pressings, had gone. None would have made Penny talk, well, anything could make him talk, but not sense — never. Down the road, the Magpie and the Stump still remained. He paused and thought of a cold beer. He felt at home.

Hart directed himself to his task. Were they going to assign the case to the Old Bailey? A twinge of nervousness followed as he headed for the south block. He checked his watch. The meeting with CPS was for 12:00. It was 11:50.

The room was a small modern box with one desk and several chairs spaced out in a seminar circle. No hierarchy, then. Circle time. He hesitated. As he did, a stout man entered the room followed by three others – two women and, lagging behind, a further younger man in casual clothes. The rest too were in the casual clothes of the professional, high-powered. Hart was the only one formally dressed. The portly man wore a tailored blazer at odds with his green polo shirt, the women slacks and blouses. Circus time.

The introductions were formal. Barbara Hope-Langdon, the QC, spoke first. She introduced herself and stated her position. If a case were to go to court against Penny, she or a close colleague would preside. A prosecution barrister renowned as 'lethal' was next – Roger R. Nesbitt – the man with the blazer, smart, efficient, decisive, scary, overweight. The first two sat down. Hart introduced himself as a practising police officer and solicitor advocate. He sat. He could see the barrister already wanted him to answer a question. He thought he might know what it was.

Next came a quietly spoken woman who introduced everyone and was also a barrister, one of the few experts employed in central casework on complex and difficult cases. Based in the Crown Prosecution service in York, she was peripatetic and familiar with all the regional teams and central casework. Avril Hamilton took out her notes and sat down. Hart knew of her through his studies, the granddaughter of an immigrant after the hurricane of '44 and off the HMT Empire Windrush. Hart mulled over the passenger liner once called the MV Monte Rosa, a much nicer name, and renamed as a prize of war, and wondered why the word Empire often gets omitted when mentioned by the press.

Hart liked what he saw so far. The casually dressed

man about his age was obviously known to all but him. He introduced himself as a government employee, a catch-all phrase that Hart understood meant he either worked at the Kremlin, Thames House or the ziggurat at Vauxhall Cross. He smiled around. Lucas Guess. He sat down, relaxed. He had no notes or no evidence of anything with him. He then stood, took his jacket off and slung it over the back of the chair and sat down again, stretching his long legs.

Good name, Hart conjectured. He was more concerned at his presence.

When the room was quiet, which was in seconds, Avril spoke. "The purpose of our meeting today is threefold. When I've explained the agenda, please let me know if other issues need raising. Now is the time to do it, not in court."

That sounded good and bad. Hart shuffled on his chair. Guess looked half asleep. He reminded him of someone.

"Let me be clear. We have an exceedingly complex case pending here, that is the Crown versus Penny. Our main objective is to discern whether it is in the public's interest to proceed. The forum is open. Please aim to be succinct."

Everyone nodded.

"Of equal importance is the thorny issue of self-defence. I'm sure I don't have to brief you on the complexities of such. The Leeds police force have been exceptional, scrupulous in their casework. You have all read Lucy Freeman's reports."

Hart was among some of the best legal brains in the country. It felt good, edgy yet good.

Avril allowed herself an aside, giving the panel time to think. "I've never met DI Freeman. Freeman is in charge and very much in control. Her casework is a model of good practice, more than enough for us to go on. You've all digested it?"

Another round of nodding and, to Hart's surprise no interruptions. The authority in that quiet voice alternating to stress key words and make pauses was duly noted by Hart. The volume stayed fairly static. Her next statement rung in his ears. It confirmed his own conclusions.

"It shouldn't be last, but it shouldn't be first either, but the rule of law and culpability are central issues here. The defendant does not deny his role. I want no pleas of manslaughter, though murder could be the charge. If we decide he has acted lawfully then there is no case. Did the defendant do what was necessary? The dead woman's past is not important at this moment." She eyed Hart as she spoke. "Any questions? Any additions to our agenda?"

Guess moved as if to say something, then clammed up. His turn would come. In Hart's opinion he looked as if he had another agenda or, more precisely, he wondered what the hell he was doing there and in what capacity.

Avril concluded her opening. "Unless you need time out to think about the agenda, we can begin." She placed her notes down and stared at Hart.

Freeman was talking to Penny. He had no idea his fate was in the hands of Hart and the legal elites at the Old Bailey. She was making conversation for the sake of it, nerves jangling. "You seem to have settled in nicely, Ronnie?"

He smiled. Freeman, who was usually so deadpan, seemed

animated, concerned. And she used his first name. He checked himself. "I don't know who offered bail. I don't want it. I wish I was home. One other thing: I've been writing stuff." Stuff was a useful word, covering so many avenues and it omitted the details. "Being here has helped me. The food is okay and the bed comfortable enough."

Freeman hoped it wasn't a police canteen recipe book. "Any news of Alice?"

"No. Dove thinks she has slipped out of the country. I tend to agree. The obvious place is Ireland as a stepping-stone to foreign parts, Europe. Remember the map in Wright's car? Ireland, the west coast. We women can change our appearance far easier than men, though Charlie Peace was able to fool us for long enough."

"Did you catch him?"

"We did. In 1878, on attempted murder of a police officer John Robinson who he shot but failed to kill. He was at first sentenced to deportation, then other evidence came in. His retrial took place here at Leeds assizes. Peace was hanged in February the following year."

"PC Robinson, you say?"

"Yes, a hero. He was awarded £25 and given a watch for his troubles. It's more complicated. You can look it up…" She tailed off. She realised his fate was in the balance. The story of Peace wasn't appropriate. She wanted to talk. She wanted justice too – for Penny, for Hart – for without justice there is no peace. She read that somewhere.

"Richard."

Hart straightened up in his seat when he heard his first name. He wasn't prepared to give out yet. "I would prefer to hear the case for the prosecution and their misgivings first. I assume that is what we're here for?"

Avril eyed Nesbitt who was eager to ask Hart a few questions. Her look implied Hart was correct. Procedurally the defence usually follows. Avril smiled and turned to Nesbitt.

She didn't say touché, she merely implied it. Nesbitt was forthright, then cautious, which Hart read as a sign of the problems with the case, or should he say issues?

Nesbitt spoke. "We have a solid case for prosecution. A man trained and out for revenge, perhaps? A man whose so-called defence involved the use of a knife and implies training, skill if you want to see it as that; a man who has little respect for the law, that we can find out."

Avril fixed her gaze on Nesbitt. "Perhaps."

Hart wondered what Nesbitt was doing. Abduction or merely taking the listener to the extreme, overstating his convictions? His statement fell between the factual and theoretical.

Nesbitt winced at Avril's reply, denoting possibility.

Avril spoke again. "And your misgivings? I know you have them."

"Ah, the misgivings. Avril, there is a lot missing here, a lot unsaid. I feel at times I'm looking at morsels only of the whole meal, and that is a dog's dinner. If we go to court, I fear unspoken aspects will rise to the surface, and thus we are wasting time and money. I can't fathom out what these aspects are, though I feel the inadmissible is at work. There is hearsay and it is prejudicial to the case, to the late victim and the defendant. I would ask those in the know to share that information within these walls. "And," he emphasised, "we keep it within these walls." He eyed Hart sternly.

The case was fraught with problems in Hart's analysis, inference, anecdote and analogy, not to mention character references, or assassinations. Nesbitt was holding back. Circumstance might be important. He was also fishing. Nesbitt confirmed such in his next statement.

"There is the digital evidence on the victim, which is not related directly to this case. Or is it? Is it authentic? No witnesses, no need for forensic, he did it. On first appearance he is guilty, but we all know the problem with *prima facie* evidence, don't we?" He glared at Lucas.

Hart was warming to the man Guess. He still couldn't fathom out why he was there. Clearly there was some history between the prosecutor and Guess. Nesbitt was beginning to bore him.

Avril interjected. "I don't have to reiterate to you the five rules. We can tick four boxes; the aspect of evidence being complete is the flaw. The background too. I trust that today we might fill those gaps. The exculpatory will cause more doubt. This man Penny has a knack of finding trouble, and the news, and that colours the case badly."

Hope-Langdon jumped in. Her bell-like voice appealed to Hart and her caution wise. "Roger is right, though it is the exculpatory that weighs heavily on Penny, the 'ex' is a media nightmare. His reputation will not help, or it might, and by that, I mean it might help or hinder prosecution and defence, though I suspect it will weigh in favour of the latter. The public love a rogue." She smiled slyly. "As for your recipe, Roger, you offered only tasters yourself."

Nobody said hear, hear though it showed on all the faces bar one – Nesbitt's.

Hope-Langdon continued. "Guiding a jury through this is a task that problematises testimony. What should they base their decision on? How to get them to ignore clever opening and closing statements is one dilemma. Fat chance. I'm there to be their guide, their judge. As Roger said, we are up against it. That shouldn't deter us from the right path in law." And then modifying it, "If there is a correct path in this case?" It sounded to Hart as if she was seeking reasons to avoid a case. He couldn't be sure. Roger Nesbitt responded.

"Barbara. I'd hate to be on a jury in this case. True, Freeman has muffled the press. Her excellent control of things will not prevent them having a field day in court. I recall the Tableaux Case." He looked at Hart with what Hart deemed an apology of sorts. (Or a wind-up.)

Hart kept schtum.

"He also featured heavily in press reports in the Loftus cases, neither of which came to court."

Hart mused, Penny and gap-filling, the nightmare that is Penny.

Avril peered around. Hart remained still. Lucas's mouth remained tightly shut. Hart could certainly fill in the many chinks in both cases, on the victim, as Nesbitt called Maureen, and the defendant, the cryptic Penny. He didn't have proof of the poet's link to Jim. A prosecution lawyer could blacken Penny easily, but probative values were more important here.

Penny killed Mo, that was a given. A plea for the relevancy of other evidence is pending. He was learning fast, and though eager to throw in a bombshell or two, he held back. There were plenty of facts to negate the plot, not the evidence.

"I suggest a short recess for refreshments." Avril had ordered tea, coffee and biscuits. Lucas Guess apart, all helped themselves. Hart had a clear strategy in mind now and was hoping to begin proceedings after the break. He was about to make things problematic. It was not to be. His step two was yet to come.

Lucas's phone had obviously vibrated in his pocket. He apologised and left the room. On his return he sat down and waited for tea break to finish.

Avril spoke again. "That should keep us all going. We hope to curtail the proceedings in an hour, maximum. Please be succinct."

Hart leaned forward to speak as Lucas Guess began. "Sorry, Richard, I have another significant issue waiting. I will need to return to my office. I trust, Chair, you will allow me to say my piece. If that is not the case, I will need to make another call. It is important you hear what I have to say, as my comments may resolve the grumbling issues you have raised so far. It may also help to make clearer some of the ambiguities. I trust it will not exacerbate them. It is a peculiar fact that the word itself, ambiguity, has more than one meaning."

Another silent gestural hear, hear from all but one. Nesbitt raised his eyebrows in disapproval.

"My statement is governed by issues arising from *our* somewhat antiquated Official Secrets Act." He emphasised the word our as if to cast no doubt on the current proceedings. They all understood the gist, and comprehended the failure to keep pace with the new social media and cyber world – Edward Snowden's iPhone case…

No hear, hear this time.

"On top of this, everything I say, we have concrete evidence for." The room felt tense though Hart breathed easily. Who, he wondered was, 'we'? He was enjoying the cut and thrust. The feeling was that Lucas was going to upset the flow of things. What happened to the recently proposed Espionage Act and its obvious leaning towards surveillance and attack on the freedom of the press? Hart wondered.

Guess didn't waste words. "Maureen Wright and her associate Alice are known to us as hired assassins. In this case hired by someone we prefer to keep anonymous, an ex-government agent who hired Wright and partner to kill Penny."

Hart wondered why he didn't name, and shame. It became clearer as he spoke.

"The man in question was linked to 'government' rather than employed by 'us' and did dirty work; the sort of man I have no time for. That is not the point here. He hired the two women to kill a child. He is no longer with us."

Hart wondered where this came from. The Max case was still open.

Nesbitt was trying to butt in. Lucas silenced him first with an assertive hand gesture. Then he spoke. "Roger, the case will bring these things out, admissible or inadmissible. We cannot take part. We would never release anything to the press, but they will get hold of it. And it will no doubt be half-cock. The Loftus case, other unresolved issues. The act prevents us. Under oath we would have to tell."

Rogers was red-faced. "Are you saying you'd leak it to the media?"

"Did I say that, Roger? Come now, someone will."

Barbara Hope-Langdon was trying not to smile. Avril remained quiet. Hart discerned a mischievous look. The process enthralled Hart. The same people who caused him a dilemma in Loftus were creating an even bigger one for the law and for justice – in Nesbitt's opinion at least. Lucas directed his next statement at Nesbitt, though it was for all.

"The information is official! If the present learned panel wishes to see that information it will be bound by the same legislation. The 2017 review suggested the US Espionage Act took into consideration current leakages. The spin-offs affect us too. Shit happens, my friends! We live in an age of information overload and surveillance. Penny is both considered toxic as he is newsworthy. The press will be in there like the proverbial…" He paused.

To Hart, the expression dog's dick came to mind; others in the room probably had their own take. A communal nod indicated their understanding of his incomplete statement. Hart wondered if he knew Penny. It did sound like it. Best not to ask.

"One final thing: Penny appears an extremely honest, though misjudged, man. He will appeal to certain jurors, and not to others. His articles, be they scurrilous, created debate and raised awareness of his subject. The man himself appears to fluctuate between his academic world and its linguistic pretentiousness, then draw his words from the back street or borrow from crime fiction, a hard-bitten noir. In court, each persona could achieve much or nothing. His writings often have a moral message. If I were to offer a parallel, its similar to the recent deconstruction of our colonial past. It begins with extremes and gradually finds a path that will balance the picture. It has to start somewhere. He will hold up well in court. Killing is wrong. Yet he rid the world of someone who was a hired assassin and a torturer."

He stood to leave as he spoke. "Sorry, Avril. I have to go. I will be back in touch after an hour. It will have to be a video call." As he rose, he wished everyone goodbye and good luck, then he turned to Hart. "Good to meet you, Richard. Do look me up if you want anything." That was emphatic. It stated where his vote lay. Roger's anger was subsiding or cloaked. He waved a feeble goodbye.

It was Hart's turn. Step three.

Hart looked at the remainder of the panel. He began. "As you know I was involved as a detective in both cases Roger and Lucas referred to." He decided to use first names, though preferred Nesbitt. "Both had holes in them. One remains unresolved, the murder and torture of Max, a young man. We know who authorised the act; we haven't proved who committed it. Lucas has access to other information we don't. In a sense he has explained why access was denied."

Nesbitt was in again. "A name?"

"Jim Trout."

He told the story of the hiker who veered off the path into a wood near Loftus to make a toilet stop and found Jim's body. "His wife Liz met her death too. Most unfortunate in her case. We now have partial evidence to prove he farmed the job out, the killing of Max. Whether he suggested torture is doubtful. That was down to Maureen and Alice, though it does appear it was the deceased that delighted in inflicting pain. Trout contracted the killers. We now have written proof. This is evident from Lance Peirce's emails."

Barbara looked astonished. "And Mr Peirce?"

"Tortured and dismembered. Peirce, a computer whizz, intended to leak their plans to Penny. He died later in hospital. The two perpetrators are extremely intelligent. One of them is still out there. They were highly trained, ex- military. Penny was very lucky."

Avril posed the next question, one they all wanted to ask. "What made you support Penny?"

Hart barely disguised a grin. "Penny is fundamentally a forthright man but muddled in his pursuit of his aims. He taught me a lesson." He chose at this point not to elaborate. "He feels remorse and guilt. He refused bail and help. He needed a shock, and I was it. We share a trauma. Shall I say empathy is at work."

Avril cocked her head and said, "That's a story for the future over a glass of something."

Hart got back to business. "The real issue here is that a case against Penny will founder, more to do with the man. I'm not blowing my trumpet here. It will create havoc in the press, or more correctly the press will create havoc with it. Furthermore, it will rebound in police and legal circles. He killed a woman, a woman armed with a knife and a gun. She was military-trained; by sheer luck he prevailed. You have my paperwork. You have his statements." Hart chose to clam up at that point, leaving them all thinking he had more up his sleeve. He had. He sat back and focused on each in turn.

Avril spoke. "You've been helpful, Richard. Why do I get the impression you're holding something back?"

"Avril," (he nearly said ma'am), "if this case goes to court it won't be a travesty of justice – it will be a farce. By that, I mean it will deal with the improbable, the ludicrous, not in the sense of buffoonery or silliness. I mean no disrespect. You have read Lance Peirce's statements?" He looked around. "I am holding back. I believe that nothing will change the direction of this case. No disrespect, nor offence."

"None taken. Yes, we are all familiar with Peirce's emails. Is he reliable?" Avril eyed the three remaining members of the panel. "We have a tough decision to make, one I believe Lucas has forced on us. It isn't a *fait accompli*. I wish he were working for us. By that I don't mean he is working against us. His comments and the gist of this morning's talk are not to go outside these walls. Richard has offered a wider picture, one that raises the issue of the contradictions between transparency and so-called confidentiality. If he chooses to hold information back that is his problem…

"We have a name to add to one of the frustrating gaps in this case: Jim Trout."

Hart realised Lucas had left that to him. He knew Jim's name, and more.

Avril summed up. "A case would not be in the public interest. I will call Lucas to ask his final opinion before we depart."

Barbara asked if they could adjourn for ten minutes.

"Of course. Please discuss anything, either together here or in private." She indicated a small side room. Roger and Barbara left the room. Nesbitt glared at Hart over his shoulder. Hart managed not to smile.

Avril spoke. "You were very brave to take this case on, Richard."

"Or foolish."

"No, not at all. You have valuable insights into the psyche of Dr Penny. He does have an appeal that the public might latch on to, an anarchic self that can be a magnet. And, bearing in mind the personal outcome of the Tableaux Case, I can understand your empathy with the man, and admire it."

While barely hiding his pride, he added to that. "A magnet for the press and for trouble. In his favour, he is a team player, his close friends are loyal to the core and not to be meddled with."

Her face told him she knew of Dove and Periwinkle. She moved her head as if to say, indeed. Barbara and Roger returned, the latter looking unconvinced. It was his job. Avril linked her fingers loosely and waited.

Hart was laying bets that Roger would take the chair. He surmised that Nesbitt didn't like the role Guess or he had played. Lucas had thrown it all in the air then exited stage left. The prosecutor's apparent disgruntled state probably wasn't so much a product of the fact he was convinced to go ahead and prosecute, it was more to do with the fact it was out of his hands. Hart had him sussed. Lucas had laid the groundwork for him.

Nesbitt spoke. "I'd prosecute whatever. However, my learned friend here," he looked sideways at Barbara who barely resisted a wink at Hart, "is convinced that nothing good will come out if it if we proceed, and we will lose."

"Not just the decision, our credibility." Barbara added to his pain.

He was annoyed. Hart couldn't understand why he brought fixed ideas to a panel like this unless Avril planted him as the thorn. Avril looked across, unfolding her fingers as she did. She gestured towards Hart.

"Richard, do you have anything to say before I bring Barbara back in?"

"One thing only, the one thing that we have left out: the defendant's abilities! Penny is versatile to say the least. In the past I've been the victim of his innate and educated self, not just simply outwitted due to my own failures to share information and to have set ideas on the law. He has taught me a lesson. In his own strange way he has a knack of highlighting one's flaws critically which one has to rectify. I'm working on it. He is, or was, a great teacher."

Barbara nodded her approval. Roger was sulking. Hart would most likely outwit him in a legal battle. Best not to say anything, say nowt as the defendant would if necessary.

Hart summed up. "You know my feelings This case should never go to court and that is not for Penny's sake." Hart added more for good measure. "His academic career is over; he writes, he has a puckish nature that isn't vengeful, he may unsettle the proud and cocksure. And he is publishing." He didn't get to say "trust me" as Avril interrupted for Nesbitt's sake.

Roger started to protest. Avril stopped him there. "We need to decide. I'm going to phone Lucas in my office. I'll not be long." She swept out the room, leaving a vacuum plus Roger's remorse at not getting things his own way. Hart wanted to go to court at that moment simply to wipe the floor with the arrogant shit. However, the guillotine was about to come down on the meeting.

Careful he warned himself, *hubris. This is your first big case.* He had learnt there is such a thing as failure.

Avril focused on Roger before she left the room. "Well?"

His reply was what Hart expected. "I'm not sure a case is worthwhile, Avril. Barbara here has convinced me."

Hart wondered about setting someone else up, never taking responsibility for one's actions. Roger was powerless, and his response was to turn his gaze to Barbara. His glimpse at Hart warned of future clashes. Roger was a spiteful man.

Hart responded. "I don't bear grudges. Neither does my client, a thing in his favour, which is in any situation a bonus, never mind a courtroom and a murder trial. I believe Roger's opinion (*or is it Barbara's opinion?*) to be rational, practical, pragmatic, if you wish, and just."

Nesbitt wanted a final word. "I am fully prepared to go to court. I also envisage the case dismissed after the prosecution statements, thrown out in the half-time submission; Penny charged but not convicted, a waste of resources. On the face of things, the key evidence is solid, he killed her, but in other ways fragile. Too many ifs and buts. Moreover, the evidence that could be brought before court would definitely not present a fair trial!"

Barbara made a last-ditch effort to smooth things over, and at the same time, put people in their place. Roger snorted and Barbara intervened. "Your case is sound, Richard. Whether Penny's retaliation was disproportionate might be questioned. Plainy, he was in imminent danger." She stopped the conversation there with a waving left hand. She turned to Hart.

"We look forward to seeing you in court another time, Richard. We have nothing to gain by this case. It is self-defence. Despite the violent and bloody conclusion, Penny defended himself against a killer. His 'instinctual' act saved his life. That another lost theirs is sad."

Avril returned and summed up, adding to Roger's remorse. "Lucas opposes a court case. He also gave me further information which I'm reluctant to impart, though it does imply the case with Jim Trout and the victim will refract on errors in certain governmental departments." She eyed Hart as if to say we are now in the same boat.

"His department, I expect," Roger said haughtily.

"No, closer to yours I'm afraid." That shut him up.

"Enough is enough. As a representative of the Crown Prosecution Service, I propose we drop the case. Penny should go free and have some help. Can you arrange that, Richard? Furthermore, we understand he is in protective custody which says a lot. Lucy Freeman is an outstanding law officer. Is he safe?"

"With Lucy, yes." Hart allowed himself a quick grin.

Roger excused himself without a goodbye. The door slammed.

Avril beamed. "He'll get over it. Because his 'chums' are in power up the top, he wants it all his own way." She held out a hand to Hart who shook it. He was in seventh heaven. This was where he belonged. His whole body reacted. He wanted to embrace someone. Instead, he embraced the fact he had arrived, perhaps at the beginning of a long journey, but one he desired.

Barbara too shook his hand and said, "Well done. See you around, no doubt."

Hart left, floating out of the room. He needed to call Lucy. She would be on tenterhooks. Saida had texted. Dove and Periwinkle would be next, though he sensed the presence of the latter in the meeting. A strange chap…

As the door closed behind him, others opened. Barbara and Avril nodded their consent and appraisal of him. "He will make a difference, Avril. This is a man who has pounded the beat and risen through the ranks. His record evidences a stickler for the law." She smiled. "At the same time, he is prepared, and more than able to support the mischievous Doctor Death." They laughed and parted with a hug and, in one case, a deep sense of relief.

Step three (or was it four?) Hart was in the Magpie and Stump nursing a pint of real ale. One only — not enough to break the law.

Lucy Freeman was in her office when Hart called. She stopped pacing and grabbed the phone.

"Three pieces of news, DI Freeman. "First, and most important, you can throw Penny out of his cell and send him home. Job done."

Freeman yelped a loud yippee. "I will. Not, you understand, because we want rid of him."

"Secondly, the Crown Prosecution Service and QC spoke highly of your policing and management of the case. There are aspects which I cannot disclose. I hope you understand?"

"I do, boss."

"Thirdly, I'm leaving the force to start a post in law. I was at home today. As you know I don't have the stomach for the work, though I have done my best. You're the best, Lucy."

Freeman wasn't surprised, though her own feelings were mixed. She admired his understanding of the law and his work ethic. His qualifications were up and above of anyone she knew in the force. "You'll be missed, Richard."

"Thanks. Tell Penny I still have some questions for him. You might ask him if he knows a Lucas Guess."

"Guess?" (She did later and that's exactly what Penny said.)

"Yup, that's the one. He's attached to government. My guess is MI5." Hart rang off. He was about to have another stab at who authorised Jim's demise, then in a change of mind decided never to say any more about it.

Freeman dropped Penny at the car park where it all began.

He was lugging his laptop; loads of paperwork and the few clothes he had managed with. He resisted saying 'I'll miss the company.' There was still the threat. Keeping him in the cells would stretch the law and her staff.

"If there's any sign of Alice, get on the hot line immediately!" She handed him a phone.

The lights were on in the living room. He opened the door and shouted, "It's me," and walked in. Tammy was sitting with Silver on her knee, stroking his ears. Silver was so pleased he forgot to bite him. He jumped down and rubbed up against his legs.

"Are you hungry?" Tammy had cooked and left the food to go cold. They shared it heated up. He opened a bottle of wine. It felt good. The wine went down too fast.

Tammy spoke as they were sipping their wine. "I'll stay the night if it's okay and look around tomorrow. Maybe you want to be on you own? I'm so pleased for you, Ronnie."

The phone rang. It was an unrecognised number. He mooched about picking it up, then let it ring out. He then broke a rule and called the number back. "Ronnie here," he said tentatively. "Sorry. I didn't get to the phone in time!"

"Or was it uncertainty?" the voice said.

"Truth is, I don't pick up calls that are unknown. I might call back if they leave an answer message."

It was Saida. The soft tones of the voice, her gentle manner flew in the face of the tough police officer. He hoped she was not on police work. He owed them a lot, but enough was enough. He knew Jarret and Murphy's families and all their issues. He knew too that Freeman was exceptional. He'd had enough, not so much of the police themselves, but the law and its representative bodies, and of academia. "Saida, how on earth are you?"

"Just put the evening paper down. You are still attracting adverse publicity. It's only to say you're off, or under, the radar. Never mind. How are you? Freeman has done an amazing job of keeping this out of the papers till now."

"What are you up to? Where are you? How's Periwinkle?"

"One question at a time, Penny. Where do I start? Firstly, I called to say congratulations. There are two other reasons."

Penny felt his heart sink.

"The prime reason is I've had an interview for a new post."

"Well. Did you get it?" He had a hundred questions he wanted to ask and his impatience was revealed in his abrupt tone.

"I'm getting the terms and all the legal bits and bobs sorted tomorrow. The answer is yes, and it's outside the force." He'd hardly recovered when Saida confirmed that she was not in the force anymore. "It's a long story which began towards the end of our stay in Loftus. I'm teaching. Periwinkle and I are seeing more of each other, which is nice." He wondered if change was a result of the always shifting northern weather. She didn't say what she was teaching, or who, or where. She paused.

"Gosh," was all he could say initially. "I'm so pleased for you. I thought you were going to question me, arrest me, or read me my rights."

"I am in a way, Ronnie-boy," she said with humour and a gruff impression of Dove that wasn't half bad. "Just joking."

"Excuse me a moment. Can you hold?" He went back in

the living room. Tammy was gathering her things. He waved a hand.

"What?"

"You're staying here until you can get somewhere to stay. We'll manage."

"Is that an order?"

"No, it a request. The company will be nice, and your intellect. We would miss you!" She was going to argue. Penny wouldn't have it. "Your room is yours until you find somewhere to go. My aim is to keep you here."

"House arrest?" She spoke as she disappeared up the stairs. "I need to ring my mum. Oh," she pointed at Silver, "he is she!" At that, she went upstairs.

He questioned his patriarchal self and the notion of gender reveal. He turned back to the phone. "Saida, you still there? Good. So, the cavalry are on the way. I'm pleased about your new post. I know you will be as successful in teaching as with the law. Where is it?"

"I'm teaching law – Hendon. Following in Hart's footsteps and training new constables with a view to a full-time posting in the south."

"All change." So much to take in after his monastic life in the hole.

"We'll be meeting soon at Lucy and Asma's. Let's talk then. You must be tired. Sleep tight."

He could hear Tammy upstairs chattering to her mam. He was determined not to let her go. The house was alive. He reached down to stroke Silver who reminded him of his neglect by nipping his hand gently. He picked her up and put her on his knee. She snuggled in and purred quietly. All change it was. At that moment his energy drained. He dozed with Silver. He called Hart. Hart was sound asleep and never picked up.

A knock on the door caused him to lift the cat onto the floor. A police officer. "Sorry, Mr Penny. We have to take you back in."

He decided not to argue. "I'll just let my friend know."

"Sorry. We have instructions to bring you in straight away."

Tammy shouted down, "Who is it?" No reply. She rushed down the stairs. He was gone. Silver miaowed.

Penny was on his way back to the hole. Someone had blundered. Despite Lucas's intervention, a court case seemed inevitable. Hart was to get his day in court. Back in the cell he knew well, he pondered Hart's actions. Lucas was wrong. The CPS had erred. He couldn't remember the name of the barrister Hart mentioned, the prosecute-and-be-damned school of justice. He was in the dock. Hart had celebrated too early. All the outcomes seemed favourable, then fragmented, flowing, then shattered, like dreams.

Open justice, the very term made Hart wince. It wasn't that he didn't believe in it, more to do with the provision of information. His reluctance to share must change. His new role as a defence lawyer placed him on 'the other side.' His successes as a police officer were down in part to his theoretical grasp of law. Confrontation by lawyers had little effect on him. It was his turn, decision time. He took a breath. He thought deeply about what he had shared with his client. Was it sufficient?

He looked at the crowded courtroom. Open justice. It was here and he believed in it. The friendly media, or frenzied media, as he termed them, had printed their headlines. The one-liners made him want to laugh or to shiver. Groan-worthy puns abounded. They related back to the twins and their sculptures. Mysteriously acquired information on Loftus and the discovery of a body in the woods crept in. Leaks everywhere and no plumber. *Have a Hart* made him groan. Toxicity was key. One would think contact with Penny would contaminate or cause severe harm. The readers loved him. The papers aligned him with the plague in a Stephen King novel, the punters found a new anti-hero. Hart himself could confirm that exposure to the man could certainly damage your health.

They dug up other dirt which made his client as popular as the premier with certain factions of the masses. Not good. Captions such as *Toxic Avenger* and *Doctor Death* coloured the case. Leakages from old colleagues both begrimed and muddied the water and painted a picture of a man full of contradictions. That was true. How the jury were to remain unbiased was anybody's guess. Hart aimed to represent him fairly. Lucy Freeman spoke with Penny and he volunteered to go with it. Lambs and slaughter came to mind.

For Freeman, the case was problematic. During his briefing to Penny, Hart had said that he, the defendant, must prove he was in 'imminent danger.' A warning followed. "No silly jokes, please." If he could only persuade Penny to follow his legal advice and say nothing. Penny's attitude frustrated the boundaries of his patience. Slim chance he would keep silent. The case wasn't crowd-funded as Penny had jested. The view of Hart was that some of the crowd were with him, and many weren't. He was a copper. Public trust in the police was at an all-time low.

Hart was concerned about the therapist Jeanine's statement. Her personal declaration of the facts of Penny's trauma were spiced with accusations of misogyny and were damning. That it was a woman he had killed was going to be an issue. If Jeanine's unbiased affidavit was to be believed, Penny helped make misogyny a hate crime all on his own. The Fawcett Society was quoted.

Worse still, recent police cases of misogyny were cited. Hart felt defeated. Despicable treatment towards women was a feature of the Press along with Crown gossip. He didn't give a shit whether good prince whoever was victimised, but he did care about hate and the victims of press hacking. He could add hate speech and hate crime to that growing list. Partisan newspapers were, in his eyes, as guilty as the greatest hate machine of all, social media.

Smart, the prosecution barrister hinted at calling Jeanine as a witness. Hart made a note about context. Piss and wind was Dove's take.

The jury had already had more reshuffles than the last Parliament. Hart felt some sympathy for the court clerk. How many U-turns might follow? U-turns can sometimes be beneficial, best not to knock them.

The court clerk asked, "Do any of you recognise the

defendant?" She might as well have asked who reads the tabloids. Gradually the jury was whittled down to page three and the popular press plus one or two 'intellectual' readers. Penny reminded Hart that Thatcher once appeared on page three courtesy of Rupert Murdoch. Anything can happen. Hart refrained from comment. Was she fully clothed?

A guy appeared. Penny was instructed to call him m' lord. He swore them in. They were to contact no one during trial. The court clerk then asked Penny, "Are you ready for trial?"

Hart had prepared him for this. He wasn't prepared for his answer.

"I've never been off it!"

The clerk took that to mean yes.

Forensics, police, medical examiners, Freeman and Dove were listed as witnesses for the defence. No Periwinkle. The sight of Freeman in the courtroom was a calming influence. Hart took his place as solicitor advocate. A woman sat beside him.

Someone shouted from the gallery to Penny to 'give 'em hell'. The judge threatened to clear the court. Penny wondered if it was the cliché that caused it. Then there was silence. Hart understood that other old chestnut, deathly hush. It was the moment before the coffin went into the flames. He saw Dove in the public gallery next to Tammy who looked concerned. Dove showed no signs of any duress whatsoever. He stroked his well-trimmed beard at one point as if contemplating then looked straight ahead.

The case was also attracting police 'interest'. Penny took that to mean they expected a perverse verdict and would fight for it, maybe even against it. Who knows? The press and media were waving their UK press cards. Inside the court they were taking their ever-so-accurate notes. Police interest in the case meant representatives of local and national police bodies were present. Their public statements implied they were keeping an open mind rather than believing at this stage that the accusations were credible and true. Credible it was. Hart hoped the media would find a scapegoat elsewhere. He thought of the media and Press as an attack dog and transgressor.

Hart however wished they direct their ministerial codes closer to home. His career as a police officer had been in jeopardy as a result of the press. What next? Trial by error? Was he guilty of demonising the demons?

The court clerk read the charges. It was as the charge sheet: murder. In the light of any substantial evidence and the absence of Alice Byron, a lack of agreement for a plea for murder was originally overruled then reinstated. Evidence of a premeditated crime would be difficult to ascertain. Hart felt the uncomfortable presence of Nesbitt. He was nowhere to be seen.

Why the prosecution asked for a charge of murder was unknown; the prosecution did imply that there were elements of premeditation. Penny had planned it, in his own way, though his planning ability was in question. They would come to that. Causation, the prosecution team had argued, was evident. Hart allowed it. He had a theory. He chose not to enlighten Penny. One theory was enough. Indeed, Hart declined to brief Penny. He explained that it meant a lack of rehearsal and that would work for them best. He didn't want to sound too contrived. Some hope. He sounded glib.

Penny took his place in the dock. The prosecution had first say, the evidence against the defence. The pathologist's report came alive in barrister Smart's presentation of the facts, animated even; the killing of this woman in her prime danced a jig for the jury. Penny admitted to killing her. The description of the tussle followed. Hart took notes.

"You were aware of the fact your blow with the rock had incapacitated the victim?" Smart's smug half-smile annoyed Penny.

"On the contrary, the *victim*," Penny couldn't avoid making his inverted commas which irked Smart, so he did it again, "the *victim* was very much alive, and having lost the knife due to the blow, produced a gun from behind her back."

"And at that moment were you aware of your tactical response?"

Hart made a note as he weighed up the import of tactical. He deliberated. He wondered if spontaneous was a wiser substitute; tactical, deliberate. Spontaneous may imply a negative too. Smart knew his stuff.

"Can you explain, please? Tactical implies an aim. My only aim at that moment was to survive."

"The defendant is being coy, I suspect?"

"If you meant to ask if I was trained to use a knife in hand-to-hand combat then the answer is a negative."

"But your colleagues are?"

"I don't know my colleagues' skills in this way apart from martial arts. It wasn't them that faced a known killer. Had it been so the outcome would have been much clearer."

The QC had that wiped from the record.

"Now I will ask the question in another way to the

defendant." Smart smiled tightly as he spoke. "Were you in any way trained in self-defence? Martial arts?"

Penny felt that he was the only one to take the stand, barring affidavits from 'reliable witnesses'. He was the only person questioned. Criminal law meant that between probabilities and reasonable doubt was a yawning chasm. Hart wasn't even going to call Periwinkle. The reasons became clearer with hindsight.

Penny answered. "I learned some jujitsu in the Boys' Brigade." That raised a snigger. "I bumped up my skills recently with the help of a friend after Maureen and her partner threatened me."

"So, you were highly trained?"

"Boys' Brigade was fun."

"Your honour, the defendant is prevaricating."

"Could you answer the question, please? Just a yes or a no."

"Yes, I was prevaricating. No! I am not highly trained. I did a ten-day course in self-defence. I barely scratched the surface." Before Smart could reply with some smart-ass remark about scratches on the surface, Penny said, "I received only a top-up from a friend, who is highly trained. I am not."

"You know how to wield a knife?"

"No. I learnt how to defend myself, and to use my hands and feet if necessary. Knives were never included."

"How about a pistol?"

Penny looked stymied. "I do know how to shoot."

"Is that usual for a university lecturer?"

"Not yet, the day may come. The fact is I am not a university lecturer; I'm a writer!" He drew himself up and spoke with some dignity. Hart saw Dove give him a smile. Hart stared at the ground. A snicker from the gallery told Hart that Penny saw the whole thing as a piece of theatre and was making a rather good job of winding up Smart. As for Smart, he was getting angrier by the minute. Playing to the gallery came to mind. The judge threatened once more.

"If there is any more catcalls or interruptions from the gallery this court is cleared." She turned to Penny. "Can you answer the question?"

"I have, I can shoot. Is it relevant?"

Smart shifted tack immediately. "When you killed the victim did you deploy any of the skills of the infantryman that you have accrued in your training?"

"No. It was all so sudden. I acted out of instinct and fear."

"The instincts of a teacher-cum-writer of fiction, no doubt?"

"That is closer to the truth. But irrelevant to this case. That is fact"

Smart detracted and took another direction. "Toxicology indicated she was free of chemicals, drugs, and alcohol."

"And so was I," Penny added.

Smart decided to lay it on. "She died, not from the rock to the face but rather a well-placed knife through the aorta. Already incapacitated by a previous blow, the defendant finished the victim."

Penny spoke regardless of protocol. "The rock would've silenced a normal person; not so this well-trained sociopath." He denied himself a retort about knives, butter and spreading it thick. *Save it for later.*

A caution followed; another deletion from the record

took place. Smart was addressing the jury as Penny wondered how to answer. Smart turned back. "Did he set out to kill this woman out of some notion of revenge?"

It didn't sound like a question. Hart signalled to him to stay shtum. Hart also looked to the judge to weigh up her sense of the slanted and selected language. It was so distorted and so false, it fell into the well of opinion, dragged down by bias.

The judge didn't look over-bothered, yet he detected a sense of disdain. Was she allowing Smart to dig a hole? In the light of her lack of reaction, he decided to play it straight. No fancy stuff. If he was to counter Smart's circus, he would do it from the hip.

Thanks to Hart, Penny had amassed a new vocabulary during his briefings. He so wanted to share it; verify, validate, authenticate, substantiate, confirm and corroborate were his favourites. He needn't have bothered writing them down, he was going to hear them *ad nauseam,* and that speedily removed his doubts about their individual meanings.

Smart continued. "It is the contention of the prosecution that the defendant understood fully his actions. If not meditated, they were rehearsed. I shall corroborate such when I call the witnesses."

There were no witnesses. Penny thought. Naively, he'd never heard of bad character evidence. Hart had gone for the straight and narrow, allowing Penny's past and character to be admissible. It was a gateway they began to regret.

Smart continued. "I will demonstrate that the defendant used excessive, even gratuitous, force, and that was, I contend, while the victim was unconscious!" He eyed the jury.

Penny startled. The judge intervened to remind the jury

there was no evidence the victim was unconscious. She faced Smart. He decided to up the trickery. Hart brought to mind a recent paper he'd read, *Lies, Damned Lies, and Alternative Facts,* written by an American author who had personal experience. It was relevant in its subject matter, and in the here and now. Be bold and imaginative when lying.

Penny eyed Hart. Hart looked confident. Smart wouldn't let up. "The defendant is deemed to be in good health and of sound mind." That was straightforward enough, the implications weren't.

In the gallery, Dove grimaced. He was expecting the prosecution to use whatever he could. He did. No straightforward circus this one, a circus of horrors. Same tent, same morbid crowd watching and waiting.

Smart mentioned twice that the victim had no family, or none was extant, and that her partner was unavailable for questioning. There was no mention of the fact that her partner was hiding out from the law.

The neurologist confirmed the damage to the face, and that it was not the cause of death and could not have caused death, rather, he surmised, stupefaction, unconsciousness. The knife did, but it wasn't always the case. Others have survived such a wound. A martial arts expert confirmed Penny must be a whizz at the 'sport'.

Cecil T Smart from London seemed pompous to Penny. It was apparent after a few comments that being in the North and Leeds was a source of personal scorn. The wastelands… His suit smacked of southern money and his perfume expensive, a woody scent, with hints of amber and jasmine, probably Mugler, Hart thought. Its top notes pervaded the gallery. Smart kept it in his briefcase. As a new apostle of simple soap and no 'pomjom'. Hart found it made him gag – the perfume, that is.

Smart was definitely out to nail Penny. He gave the forensic evidence, the medical examiner's evidence, which seemed pointless. He cited Penny's academic "cleverness." The words rolled off Smart's tongue and were double-edged. They crept in like an unwanted visitor, a cockroach, and sowed the seeds of doubt around Penny's degree of responsibility and self-control.

He recounted some of the lecturing stories and other misdemeanours, no doubt supplied by Dean Treachery and friends. The jury and the gathered crowd found them highly amusing, the deception behind the lecturing stories and other misdemeanours. The van rental lecture was impossible to dampen down. He was trying to establish Penny never took anything seriously. The crowd were virtually pissing themselves, quietly in this case, as they didn't want to miss out.

The prosecutor read the statements. Some were reckless. There were hints about his role in the Tableaux Case; mention of the University fraud; incidents in Loftus heaped up the image of a man who was, if not the cause of serious trouble, was a common denominator to it. "The defendant is devious, sly, and unable to accept responsibility."

The judge had difficulty in silencing the crowd and, in Hart's opinion, herself. Her teeth firmly nipping her bottom lip, she ordered silence. "Please continue."

Smart was grinning. He was saving something nasty. Hart could see Penny was having some problems with the character assassination. The issues were the lack of context.

Hart was convinced that understanding wasn't so simple. The jury might supply their own context for these ambient events. That might work either way. Their own processes of identification were in his favour. Smart laid it on thicker: Penny's divorce, his relationships, and his past record for political "agitation" as a man of the Left. Penny hoped *Guardian* readers on the jury outweighed *The Telegraph*.

Hart was taking notes and looking at the judge. The judge called for a recession.

Dove called Periwinkle. "Your presence here would be useful."

"Not going to happen. You know why. How is it going?"

"The prosecution is daunting, but I do sense the jury are not convinced. I don't know. Penny is holding up. Hart has to do his bit yet."

Periwinkle's voice faded away as he said hello. Dove heard him utter a few words as he turned to speak to someone else. As his voice faded, Dove snorted angrily. Periwinkle was unphased.

"Dove, we can do more from here than there."

"Whose we?" He added, "For fuck's sake," under his breath. He heard a phone ringing.

"Speak later." Periwinkle hung up.

Dove went back into the court and joined Tammy. She looked bereft. Dove said, "Chin up," and sat.

The court reassembled. A host of oft repeated expressions

ran through Dove's mind: *Don't volunteer explanations of your questions; May the record reflect…; Members of the jury, you are instructed to disregard the question…; the witness will resume the stand.*

Dove summed up. So far, the witnesses, both absent and present, had been fuckwits. Then there was Periwinkle, or then there wasn't.

Opening statements sounded as if they were evidence. Smart had a way of slanting evidence that came from years of bad-mouthing plaintiffs, bad character evidence if you like. The word 'intent' crept in regularly, and the 'fact' that Penny's academic self was questionable. The burden of proof seemed to lay at Penny's door, not with the prosecution. Penny was a man who demonstrated a lack of responsibility. The story of his arrest for offensive language against an 'officer of the law' as a twenty-something-year-old; the university fraud case was dredged up. A few minor infringements added to the stew. Misconduct was repeated, the word reprehensible crept in. Penny began to feel he was back at the grammar school.

Penny answered yes to the offensive language. He was about to explain how he put the police officer in the dock then questioned him. Instead, he said with some pride, "The fine was under £5. The 1828 Obscenities Act and my impure thoughts cost me dearly." He wasn't sure it was 1828, but it all appeared so archaic. He told a policeman to fuck off.

That gave the court clerk something to laugh about later.

As for the mention of fraud, Penny let it go. The prosecutor didn't pose it as a question, more part of the picture of a man who had escaped justice until now. Smart was doing well. The judge asked him to demonstrate where this was leading.

"I shall come to that, your honour." The judge was tiring. She also saw another side to the accused's profile, one that will sell books. Was Penny thinking the same?

Smart continued. "The medical examiner's report states clearly that the victim was on the ground having been battered with a rock then, helpless, the defendant knifed her in the abdomen." Smart showed the pictures of the wound. They were horrific. He chose not to mention the knife, a very negative Exhibit A, which was Mo's. The knife and the gun were there in the court, the former a sleek-looking thing with a label, tactical and deadly, a military-style knife, or a survival MoD blade. It was in fact an old Fairbairn-Sykes commando knife, solid brass, a stiletto with a seven-inch blade. The bonus was it was double-edged, like Courbet's palette knife, like Smart's tedious questions.

Smart had gained permission to show one picture of the victim. No relatives had complained, in fact, none appeared. This caused Hart to stir and make notes. Penny felt sorry for Maureen. She must have a brother, a sister, mam and dad.

Hart had briefed him to keep quiet. He sat in the dock and twiddled with an elastic band he found in front of him. It was difficult, but his own game of 'elastics' eased the temptation to shout twat at Smart.

The prosecution alluded to Penny's history and status as an academic "retired by the university." Hart took more notes. Smart was out to keep the murder accusation and

Penny was looking at fifteen years. Hart sniffed the spectre of spite – Nesbitt.

Looking more concerned with his elastic band twined around his fingers, Penny let the prosecution case fly past. He recalled phrases like necessary force, acting in good faith to protect himself, followed by bashing someone's brains out with a stone then plunging a knife into their lower body. The judge insisted on striking certain leading phrases from the records. However, they had led. The jury clearly were reaching saturation point. The amount of information would befuddle the brightest of them.

"I leave it to you to decide if the defendant's actions were necessary, and I'm sure you are capable of deciding." He eyed the jury. "Self-defence? Never! My contention is that the defendant intended to kill."

Contention? To Hart it should have been contentious. How was he to demonstrate a causal link, a motive? It didn't look good. Maureen was the victim, an innocent jogger with a gun and a knife. To Hart a song came to mind. The gun, as he recalled, was exceptionally light. Smart's description was an education. His summation was that it carried seventeen rounds, ideal for the jogger out to enjoy an early evening's exercise. How was he to deal with that?

"The pistol had no other prints barring Penny's." Smart looked around the court as he spoke.

Penny decided he would wear gloves if he ever got his hands on another gun and Smart. Is there such a thing as a Smart Gun? Hart said there is.

As far as Hart could discern, the angle appeared to be one of disproportionate force. Mo would've fought to the death. Military trained; a fact omitted. That it was her gun was obvious, a runner needs protection these days. The Great North Run could be a case in point.

Smart asked Penny a crucial question. "Could you have retreated? I'll put it more simply: could you have run away?"

Penny thought for a second. "No."

"What makes you so sure?"

"I wasn't sure she was alone. Running with one's back to a 'survival' knife, as you call it, seems foolhardy, especially in the hands of a trained combatant."

"You knew the victim?"

"Only by reputation, and reputation appears to be significant in your analysis." Penny decided to play Smart at his own game. "Are you aware of her past?" Hart held back a smile.

The jury eyed Smart, who looked concerned. If he left it, the jury would query it, or if left open it might hamper his case. If he answered, Maureen's past would be broadcast. A hush descended on the gallery; the media, police and the people leaned forward.

"That is your opinion only and would be hearsay," Smart replied, "and is not evidence. I suggest, m'lady, that the jury ignore the remark."

Penny spoke out of turn. "One doesn't carry two offensive weapons for show, Smart. It would be worth mentioning the so-called victim was handy with both. As for hearsay, we've heard quite a lot already. The oral evidence is flawed."

Smart appealed to the judge. Once again, she quietened the courtroom, after which she reproached Penny. The rules on disclosure are strict. Hart thought he detected a wry smile on her face. The defence was barred from revealing Maureen's role as a torturer and killer. Smart had used clever disclosures to reveal Penny as a troublemaker.

Not yet, Hart thought. *Two can play*. Furthest from his mind at this juncture was the real sentence Penny faced. He wanted justice for Penny, for Max, to close a book, closure for Lance, others and some unknown children in Afghanistan. It seemed farcical. The burden of proof weighed heavily on Penny. Hart's intention was to pass it back to Smart. He wondered who the plaintiff was in this case. No court case is cheap. Who was behind this?

"I doubt the accused showed any remorse." Smart eyed the jury.

It wasn't a question. Penny answered. "With hindsight, and with sadness, I feel I had grounds to respond in the way I did. At no time did I think about it in advance. It hasn't left my mind since."

"And what grounds would that be?"

"Self-defence, but over and above that, survival; survival against a well-armed and ex-forces trained killer."

The prosecution complained again; the judge ruled it as inadmissible.

"I would like to call a witness for questioning before I ask one or two more questions of the defendant. That," he glared at Penny, "is admissible."

The judge scanned the courtroom and, with no expression at all, called for an adjournment. "The court will reconvene at 15:00 hours."

Smart looked befuddled, Penny surprised. Dove looked at his watch. He and Tammy rose to go. Penny looked around.

Where was Periwinkle? Hart folded his papers and smiled. Hart was more confident.

Penny began to plan for his lengthy spell in HM Prison, or somewhere for the criminally insane. Where was Periwinkle? Where was Guess? Had they submitted statements?

The court was only back in session an hour when the judge called for a further recession. Smart had asked so many questions, Penny had asked him to separate them out. He addressed the judge with a polite yet assertive analysis. "Your honour, I hear two questions posed as one. If I answer the first it will be a no. If I answer the second, it will be a yes. It could be misleading." At that moment, the judge called for a recess and demanded she spoke to Smart and Hart, who had not really objected to anything. He didn't need to.

She was blunt. She said it wasn't the shortest murder trial on record as many only took eight and a half minutes when the old Bailey was first in session, but one of the shortest in Leeds assizes. It was in danger of being the longest. It was a waste of money. "This case is dismissed."

Smart didn't argue. She offered no explanations, then insisted on having a word aside with him in chambers.

As Hart ushered Penny out, avoiding the press, he spotted a lithe figure flitting away towards the rail station. He wasn't sure totally, but it looked like Lucas Guess.

Chapter 27

Hart started. A book was open on his knee: *In Your Defence*. He felt the past lifting, his anxiety, his future consolidated. It took him a moment to grasp reality. Past memories faded, policing, the awful deaths remained, though not as a nightmare.

Fugue state or not, he had his moment in court. Being a defence lawyer might be fun. Defending Penny was best in dreams, safer. Smart, his opposition, a sign of his ability.

Lucas Guess was to haunt him like Periwinkle. He doubted he would find anything on them. He would try. As Penny had often reminded him referring to his school reports, try implied failure. He rang Penny. Penny was out walking. "Talk later, nothing spoiling."

Chapter 28

The group that celebrated the CPS dismissal of the case went back to Lucy and Asma's. Saida arrived with Periwinkle who was sporting a stunner of a waistcoat: double breasted dogtooth patterned, crowned with his beret. Dove and Hart followed. They had already sunk a couple of beers. Olivia and her partner in crime, as Penny called Murphy, couldn't make it. Murphy's kids were playing up, or as he said had had a total meltdown. Olivia had promised to have a meal with them later and "a glass with Penny."

Dove and Hart were on form. Hart's good-humoured speech nailed Penny and his machinations. His dream helped. Who speaks through a dream? What spirits move in the night? His dream was lucid. Throughout he knew he was dreaming a parable. The parable of Smart? He didn't need a Joseph to interpret. His clever reference to schoolchildren's essays ending in 'Then I woke up' was funny, though it meant more to him than to the others.

All present applauded. He finished by saying everything was guesswork. He glimpsed at Penny as he said it. Two other people in the room raised their eyebrows. Neither of them was Lucy. Periwinkle turned away.

Dove followed with a small and leading toast. He was after information from Penny. "It's a double whammy, folks, as Ronnie has another book written, a novella, another Penny dreadful!" It also served the purpose of avoiding a postmortem. They clapped.

Saida said, "What is it? Your story?

"It's a legal case, or should I say the case is central to the plot. *The Death of Chatterton.* I've submitted it to my agent. In Meanwood I travelled back in time to Victorian Britain and Ireland to research." (Laughter.) "I had the research ready and wrote it up in a police cell, which should indeed sell. It kept me from having the mulligrubs (a word he stole from Periwinkle). The rest would be a spoiler." In response to the groans, he gave away a snippet of unimportant information. "The original research was done in the British Library!"

Lucy and Asma prodded him for more. He teased them and said, "Signed copies are available for a friends' rate."

The book was to lead to more issues. How could a case that took place in the 1860s cause havoc in the 2020s?

Chapter 29

In the morgue in Sheffield Lance's mother identified her son. She hadn't seen Lance for two or three years. She thought back to the day the two men had knocked on her door, Dove and Penny. She never mentioned them to the police. She read about the latter. Penny was there with him when he died. Her son did have a friend. As a boy, he was a loner. She felt she had failed to do anything to resolve it. She attempted to find him a friend. Lance had nobody to play with, her bright young son. There was no conflict at home, though his dad was absent. He didn't seem shy. Her intervention strategies fell by the wayside. Lance sought refuge in his first computer. In that world he stayed, his social skills never improved. At school, his isolation was perceived as a lack of skills. He didn't suffer anxiety. His chronic loneliness stayed. He was wary of commitment. Finding fault in others reached a peak with Penny, a man whom he misunderstood. Penny, she thought, must also have his fears.

She was on her own. Lance, despite his silliness, was all she had. The death he suffered was horrid. She wondered about the likes of such who could commit a crime of this nature. She couldn't read the newspapers which piled up on the living room floor. The few belongings he had went to charity. She kept one thing, a small gift she bought him as a child and was surprised he kept it, a lucky charm, which wasn't lucky at all. She placed it on the shelf with the other memories and bric-a-brac – a small plastic mouse.

Never did he write home. Never did he mention a girlfriend, boyfriend, partner, lover, or colleague. She wanted to ring Penny. Was he Lance's friend? She started to call and disconnected. A key word.

On a hill in Ireland a rifle focused on a handsome stag. The distance was about seven hundred metres. Amy Smith AKA Alice Byron hummed a Suede song as she squeezed the trigger. She brushed her blonde spiked hair back and smiled. The target, a fine-looking stag, went down in one. Its knees buckled; slowly it sank to the ground. She watched as a dark patch discoursed the grass, red on green. She smiled as the beautiful beast died. "Haven't lost it, have I?" As she was about to wrap up for the day a man appeared and stared down at the stag. She focused the rifle again. A head shot. It looked like a ranger.

She replaced the rifle in its bag and walked to the car with poetry in mind. Her time would come. She looked back at the stag and recited, "'Where is tomorrow? In another world...'" She faltered in her recitation of Young's words on life, death and immortality, turned and watched the ranger as he scanned the horizon. Alice decided not to prejudice the hit.

She walked away.

"Change at Limerick Junction for the train to Ennis. That's not in Limerick, mind you!" The man at the ticket office smiled blithely as he handed Penny the three tickets.

"Thanks. I'll bear it in mind." With time on his hands, Penny wandered Dublin's crowded Heuston Station. He was about to accompany two real detectives, one private, one 'public' on a case. His notebooks were in his bag.

Dove and Freeman didn't listen to Penny's impromptu lecture on the original Corinthian columns or the railway station name change, or of the man who was a leader of the rebellion in 1916 and worked in the ticket office. The concourse was teeming, and he felt okay.

They, his fellow detectives, were busy. Lucy went off to buy a newspaper and Dove a bag of humbugs. Neither of them were sure about the wisdom of Penny's presence. Freeman was on leave. Freeman was on a mission.

Alice had stopped a police officer in County Clare to ask directions, then she was seen in a shop in Galway. The hunt was on. The second sighting was by a ranger. Freeman may have been on leave, but this was her case. Dove volunteered. He too had a desire to meet Alice again. Freeman didn't argue.

Penny had insisted that his presence on the trip might entice the killer out. That was what worried them. Dove tried to justify it by convincing himself Penny was safer close by. Freeman, short-staffed and ordered from above to move on, decided to take time out. Penny was the only one to have seen Alice close up, though Dove had several sightings. His accurate memory of her height, her gait and build were something to go on. He too wanted to be there. Freeman felt better with Dove around. Freeman's hands were tied legally, however, there was always 'appropriate action'. Her take was that when she decided to act, she was back on duty. Not quite legal. She pictured a postcard with a message: You'll never guess who I met on holiday.

On the train Penny nattered to a man opposite about Limerick. He'd heard stories. The man informed him that Limerick was not a place to hang out. "Stab city," he warned. Penny changed the subject to the weather. Lucy read her newspaper. Dove stared from the window, sucking on a sweet. The shop had run out of humbugs, the sweets he bought were highly coloured and Penny's tongue was bright red, Lucy's blue. He muttered to Lucy about her getting the unlucky dip. She wasn't impressed.

At Limerick Junction the train terminated. About twenty or so passengers dismounted. The guard told them to wait in the waiting room. Twenty minutes passed. Then the guard/ticket man reappeared and said, "Back on the train." To comments unrepeatable with swear words in between, they all got back on the same train which took off for Ennis. "Un-fickin-fathomable."

Intel informed them that Alice had been lodging in County Clare. They surmised that she'd moved on as sport and security beckoned. She was seen in Coole Park, Galway, near to Gort, probably armed and definitely dangerous. A police caution warned 'Do not apprehend.'

Freeman was intent on reinstating cross-border policing, very cross in her case.

The sun shone, the turlough side which in summer was carpeted by common Vetch, Yellow Trefoil and Meadowsweet, was now dying back. Alice was oblivious to the colours singing, and intent on tracking a potential victim, a contract not yet signed. She took time out to see the Autograph Tree and recited Yeats's poem *The Wild Swans at Coole*. Yellow Brimstone butterflies and orange and cream Fritillary flitted past. Alice thought she could get to like butterflies. She thought of Yeats: '*The bell-beat of the wild swans' wings above my head…*'.

It was good to be back in business. She eyed the only remaining section of a once proud house – a wall, a place once pivotal to the Irish literary revival. Its dereliction and dismantling testified to the gross wilfulness of the State at the time.

The contract was to arrive by email. A little preliminary reconnaissance felt right. She watched the intended prey as he poked around in the water remaining in the lough, unaware of any presence. She had followed him as he hiked through what is known as The Seven Woods of Coole and onto the turlough side. Some were natural woodland cover, others looked planted, and there was clearly more than seven. Such is the power of Yeats's poem. He followed no straight path as he walked. He stopped to look at trees or a plant by the side of the pathway. He was a loner. He walked, he spent hours in the fresh air and countryside which was to be his grave. She didn't give a shit what he had done. He was a dead man. Her senses heightened as she tracked his meandering passage through the woods and onto the waterside. On the way, three Scots Pines caught her attention, a gateway through a wood, proud and tall. In the walled garden, a Catalpa. Its heart-shaped leaves would soon begin to fall, the flowers already gone. Two deer sat under a tree.

She watched him. He inspected pools around Coole Lough. Was he looking for newts, sticklebacks and minnows? He appeared like a happy schoolboy, missing only the obligatory jam jar with a string handle. She watched as he studied a strip of Shoreweed above water level with its tiny greenish flowers, its tufts running alongside the receding water and the mats of bright green spike rush. The water was subsiding into the limestone. Soon the turlough would be empty and sheep and cattle grazing. The small creatures that amazed him began to make her curious – newts and lizards, spiders – as did the range of flora. Soon, the trees would be in their 'autumn beauty' as per Yeats's poem of Coole.

Suddenly, her quarry turned and veered away. Random, thoughtless, totally immersed in his task. Alice had read him wrongly. She felt safe. Brexit had served her well and the police force on one side had no jurisdiction on the other.

Chapter 30

No sea mist today, a sparkling ocean and, as he pointed seaward, Penny remarked that America was west across the water, over three thousand miles from Eugene's Bar in Ennistymon to McSorley's Old Ale House E 7th Street, New York. Both were quirky and connected, from a variety of memorabilia and coloured glass to sawdust, and in McSorley's a pot-bellied stove. Both have Irish bartenders! "Two of the greatest ale houses on the planet, from a good pint of Guinness to two types of ale and fish chowder." Penny was prepared to argue the case. Dove seemed interested, Freeman on edge.

"I was joking about the unlucky dip earlier," Penny apologised. That didn't work. Freeman's rigid posture told him so. The taxi to Lisdoonvarna helped or, more appropriately, the driver. Like the *Ancient Mariner* he told the tale of Limerick, stab city, and in a laboured way talked of the investments and aims to upgrade the city from stab to fab! Fab city. Penny and Dove waited. The story was too pat. The hook came inevitably.

"Last night three people were 'fabbed' to death."

Freeman heard the laughter. She realised she'd missed out. Her mind was on Alice Byron, now Amy Smith. She wanted this arrest, she wanted her alive, off duty or on. She also wanted to hurt her. The feeling troubled her. She questioned herself. Was she the best person for the job? That didn't matter. She was on holiday. Killing Alice would be a pleasure. The thought made her fret. She wanted Alice dead.

Digging around in the water, Matty Browne watched the woman and her movements. He admired her agility; assessed her ability to track him. He wondered what her purpose was. His few years in the forces told him she was unwelcome news. Her body language spoke of one instructed, of military precision, a hunter stalking a kill. Matty wasn't ready to die. His own training had been different. He was hiding from his past. Thoughts of his time in Angola as a soldier of misfortune arose. The right-wing military tag came up, or alternatively the accusation of vile jingoism caused him to ponder. He would never shake it off, it was the ape on Sinbad's back.

As a young man, in his early twenties, he made the front page of the papers. He regretted that too. A comrade-in-arms had a wet gangrenous leg. He was going to die. A medic was available. No surgeon followed. Matty still had the horrors when he recalled sawing the man's leg off at speed, the smell of rotting flesh and fluid. It saved his comrade's life. Then the medic took over. Matty walked away, burying his rifle. That too made the papers. He recalled a snippet of the news: *Soldier disappears with rifle. Hero turned villain.* He aimed to bury his past with his rifle. After that, both sides were after him.

He had bought the near-derelict cottage in Galway on

his return. In military fashion he made modifications to the place. Some years later he retired to Ireland after making a living as a schoolteacher. He spent his time wandering the disappearing lakes before they vanished altogether. In between he kept fit. That had stayed with him. He kept himself to himself, though folk evidenced he was a pleasant soul, well liked in the village when he went in for groceries.

Who wanted rid? There was one way to find out. It felt odd. His muscle memory was on red alert, his body still fit. Was it prepared for battle? Moreover, was he mentally prepared? Forty years of forgetting, forty years of hiding a past, one tainted by the atrocities of Luanda. He was indeed a soldier of misfortune. He had walked away to survive. He took his mother's Irish surname, Browne. At another point he considered using his first name Robin then he plumped on the name Matthew. Currently he was Matty Browne. Robin Simpson was dead.

Alice followed him from a distance as he shouldered his pack, noticed his gaiters and his patterned anorak as he strode towards the woods. He was a big man, and his thatch of white hair stood out like a halo in the bright sunlight. She noticed a limp as his left leg appeared to drag slightly. The result of a stroke?

Tracking a person through social media had nothing on the skills and excitement of combat tracking. She recalled the running, the adrenalin rush, her companions following their best friends, the tracker dogs, the sense of purpose and the ultimate aim to track down and kill. Alice had read about the combat trackers in Vietnam who were so good there was often a bounty placed on their heads. While she was going over it, dreaming of the great visual trackers, the enemy vanished. Tracker dogs were not required by the experts. Right now, one would be handy.

She circled back to where she had been, seeing no signs of the quarry. The signs remaining should tell the tracker everything about the quarry. Where was he? There were no signs of disturbance, nor of Matty Browne. That was a sign in itself.

The adrenalin coursed. She was about to confront a trained man. No, this was an ex-schoolteacher, retired, a man who lived in a hovel miles from nowhere, painted red and green with huge rocks around the periphery and creeping plants. He must have sat down to rest, probably opened his flask and having a sandwich. She waited. Not a peep, not a sound, nothing. She felt the gun under her vest and moved on.

Matty was no longer limping. His reconnaissance confirmed his suspicions. What the hell did she want? She was adept, which was for sure. She wasn't doing it for fun or misguided love. He chose to stay put and watched her, then made for his jeep. Work to do.

While Alice was combing the path already taken, he drove away.

In the woods she laughed inwardly. Coincidence? She couldn't wait to see the file on this man. A challenge.

Chapter 31

Freeman checked in at a B&B near to Gort. The price was reasonable. Gort was an 'underrated place to live'. Penny suggested they divide their labour.

Dove and he booked in at a residence named Craggy Island near to the skeletal remains of a castle in between Doolin and Lisdoonvarna. Penny and Dove fancied sneaking away for a pint of the black stuff. Pleasure first, then down to business was Dove's take. McGann's, McDermotts and O'Connor's bars were all really good according to the B&B owner. They debated it along the coast road and settled for O'Connor's.

At the bar, a man addressed all and sundry. It turned out he was a supervisor on the council. He was toying with his mobile. "The feckers," he said, loudly addressing the bar. Ears pricked up. He waved the mobile in the air. "I sent a crew of eleven out to a job this morning!" He paused for effect. "The feckers have just called in and asked for eleven shovels."

Dove and Penny listened. They had little choice. The supervisor continued his open address to the pub.

"I thought about it. The buggers didn't need a shovel for the job. So, I asked them what the feck they needed them for."

Dove leaned forward to catch the next bit. The gaffer held for a moment, then broke out into a grin. "Bloody Hogan and McMahon himself on the phone. I should've known. A couple of jokers." He held. The pub waited. "I'll ring their bloody necks when they get back to the depot." Another timed break followed. "And do you know what Hogan said?" He paused and supped his pint. Then he delivered the punchline. "He said we've got nothing to lean on!" He pocketed the phone.

The man next to Penny could hardly swallow his pint. When he did, he eyed the two strangers and said, "Welcome to Doolin." Then he said, "Moloney," and held out a hand.

Chapter 32

Information had leaked through the system to Freeman's office via Constable Murphy in Leeds. His brother sent him a local Irish paper, *The Tribune*. Gleaning through, he spotted a small article about a shooter leaving dead deer for the kites. Random killings of fauna might not be coincidence. The deer population was massive; culling was inevitable. Leaving the bodies was unusual. A shooter was killing them at will. Two short paragraphs detailing several dead and rotting carcasses.

Murphy mentioned it to Jarrett, Jarrett to Freeman. Freeman made a couple of calls. She was directed to Colm, a ranger. A tenuous link.

Freeman's chat with Colm was informative. He had reported wildlife killings. The local press put a snippet in the paper, mainly to expose the perpetrator. Kids had been ruled out. The sniper was using a high-powered rifle. The policy was to cull; these graceful creatures had a negative impact in the countryside, crops and wildlife. That was the official line.

Freeman informed the ranger of similar policies in England, with an estimated population of six million deer, the damage to cereal crops, decline in bird numbers in woodland areas and road accidents. "The RSPCA estimate around twenty people are killed every year."

Colm concurred. "Likewise, the poaching has always been rife, but the usual scenario would be to collect the corpse when all is clear. Someone is doing this for sport. I don't like it."

Colm was more concerned with biodiversity, illegal hedge or turf cutting, and bird traps. In an interview he'd mentioned the random killing of fauna. "Wildlife criminals kill to eat or sell," he told Freeman. "Turf cutters and poachers are the biggest problem, and deer the target. Killing them for food is one thing, leaving their bodies on the ground is another. What I'm saying here is that someone is doing this for the hell of it!"

Freeman asked him to say more.

"I've found three carcasses so far, a stag and two badgers. It was thought to be kids at first, bloody hooligans. The shooter has put a rifle bullet clean through the skull. The bullets are from a Russian rifle. They cost a lot of money. Probably a Havoc." Colm was angry. "The fecker could have done this from quite a distance. Kids aren't that accurate. They are good at it, if that isn't a bad choice of words. Perhaps tutored is better. The kids about these parts can't afford a weapon like that."

Freeman listened as he quoted the statistics of wildlife crime. Her eyebrows signalled the recognition of the enormity of it. He side-tracked onto the importance of snails as an indicator. "Not of wildlife killing, you understand, as an indicator of the long-term stability of natural habitats." In the course of the conversations, snails took on a completely different vibe. Snails, she thought, are unappreciated. They may have been guilty of eating her lettuces; they were innocents abroad. One of her colleagues was nicknamed 'The Snail'.

She promised to treat him differently. And she saw another use for such intel. It could be deployed to disarm Penny. He would scurry off to research it.

"Any other animal killings reported? Domestic pets, for example?"

Colm sounded aghast. He thought for a moment. "Bugger me, there haves been a few reports of cats gone missing, none found dead as yet, that is in the village. I could check elsewhere."

Bingo, thought Freeman. She looked grim. She filled him in on as much background as she could, or was able to, and with it a caveat. You might inform the others in the business and locals to report any strangers."

Colm wasn't convinced. Lucy tried again. "Contact me with any sightings whatsoever."

Colm gave in. "Will do." He had made a brew, as he called it, which had gone cold. While he supped his tea regardless, he listened to Freeman. He made a concise list of six others to contact who he would ask to keep a lookout, people who wandered – botanists, zoologists and dabblers who simply liked mucking about in the mud. One of them he starred, the man who had found the stag. The last on the list didn't have a phone number. Matty Browne. He read it out. Freeman made notes and thanked him.

"He's the original quiet man, if you'll forgive the reference. Lives in a wee place on his own, full of books, no television, no phone. I suspect he doesn't read a newspaper. He's out in all weathers. Matty knows the land like a local. Had the pleasure of his company once or twice. Yes, a quiet man. I'll email the list, with more detail." Colm was a man who multitasked. He didn't waste time. He did it then. He included a map.

Lucy thanked him. "You've been an immense help, Colm." It was time to divvy up the labour, talk to a few locals. "Keep in touch, please."

"I will. We don't want the likes of them hanging around."

"Any help appreciated, but information rather than interference. Nice to talk with you, Colm. Keep up the good work."

She highlighted one name.

Alice wasn't hanging around. She was watching. The contract would arrive the next day. Then, only then, she would decide on how to remove this man, the man who had either by design or accident slipped away from her. She needed to know which it was before she killed him. She was also curious to find out about his past. Such is the curse of the academic mind.

She thought of Penny and of misrepresentation. He was always going to be in the thick of it. She read a critique of his book. The writer must have trawled through, and with some malice and triumph found an odd sentence. What a strange world academe was. There's always some small-minded eejit out there looking for something to criticise, often misunderstanding text. Do they go through the whole and feel victorious when they find a strange sentence or something they deem pretentious? 'Got you' syndrome? Sad and spiteful. Alice cleaned her rifle. Maybe she was better off out of it. One day at a time…

Chapter 33

Dove and Penny were supping their third Guinness in McGann's. They considered Freeman's list. Penny wanted to interview Lorcan, a ranger, and Matty Browne, the man with no phone or television. He was insistent on talking to the man. He wanted to discuss life without television. He referred to Dove and Periwinkle's switching off, overconsumption, and playing sports instead of watching. His television had gone. His landline had gone (Penny had given up the landline a year earlier). After several months he recalled hearing a phone ring a few doors down and reaching for a landline. Television was the assassin of time, he told folk incessantly. He doubted they would test out his theory.

They decided to use one car. Dove opted to drive to Gort, to pick Freeman up and drop her off. Three of the list lived within walking distance of each other. Freeman opted to walk about. She arranged to meet later. A text would do. Dove, who appeared well informed on watering holes, drove to Gort the long way via O'Loclainn's Irish Whiskey bar, a haven for malt lovers s. Over seventy whiskies, and only time for one.

Freeman took over the driving. Outside the bar, the old metal advertising sign for Player's Navy Cut Cigarette; inside a bar 'stacked with gems'. Dove was singing, "'Stand and deliver, for I am the bold deceiver'." Penny joined in.

Penny decided he wanted to see the art college at Ballyvaughan. He took time to view Newton Castle. Freeman let it go with a sideways remark about a lack of urgency, 'like certain football teams'. Penny let that go. To counter their indulgence, as well as let them know who was boss, she pulled over at Hazel Mountain Chocolate and went in. The vegan truffle collection took her fancy. She returned clutching a box. Asma would love them.

The journey was interrupted by visits to filling stations with a picture of Alice no one recognised. The filling station pump at Ballyvaughan was so slow it prompted Freeman to make a comment about Ireland and the pace of life. Then she stopped at the local post office to send a card to Asma.

Otherwise, the journey was fine – Corkscrew Hill, the road to Fanore and the view of Galway Bay. At Kinvara Dove's rasping baritone cut through the silence, parodying an old Irish melody. The one whiskey clearly had done its job.

They all wanted to see Coole Park. Freeman had work to do. She was quick to remind them that they did too. Penny stared out of the window across to the Martello Tower at Rossaveal. The turn-off to Athenry, which they passed on the left, sparked yet another song.

Penny and Dove had two calls to make. They started with Lorcan. Penny looked up his name; it meant 'little fierce one'. He was anything but. A large and gently spoken man, Lorcan's knowledge of the countryside was extraordinary. He spoke of the problems of the turloughs, especially Rahasane, the largest turlough, where sheep and cattle graze in the summer.

It was above the southern basin the ranger found several

dead deer. His accurate memory detailed the find. He gave an impromptu history of the wildlife rangers in Ireland, followed by a lecture on snails. Penny made notes about the Kildare Town Bypass case and a rare snail and the boglands. Determined to research the symbolism of snails, he wrote a reminder in his notebook. He was enjoying this bit. Snails found a place in his heart alongside leeches. "What do the poachers normally do?" he asked Lorcan.

"To answer your question differently, it could be that poachers shot the deer overnight and it was discovered before they returned during the early morning to collect it."

"Why do that?" Penny queried.

Lorcan confirmed the logic of it all. "They return without weapons to 'find' a dead deer."

"Ah, got it…"

"Africans have their elephants we have deer and snails!"

Penny imagined a snail the size of an elephant. They could've stayed all day. Dove felt envious of the lifestyle, the wild landscapes, and the proximity of the vast Atlantic Ocean. Penny was still talking about snails and mumbling something about microcosmic spirals when Dove looked at his watch.

"We need to talk with Matty Browne."

"Imagine carrying your house with you." Penny was still thinking of snails. Lorcan had warned them Browne wasn't a talkative man, not unfriendly, more reclusive.

"Matty the hermit, nice fella. You'll need a crowbar to open his mouth. Mind you, if anybody spots anything it'll be Matty. Eyes like a hawk and the senses of a cat. For a retired schoolteacher he's a contradiction… Unless the schools over there require such skills."

Penny confirmed that some did. On a lighter note about

his own teaching experience, he remarked that he didn't learn jujitsu for nothing. They shook hands and parted, with Lorcan promising to keep him posted, especially if anything came up.

The drive to Matty's place was difficult, the roads narrowed, the ruts and roughness alleviated by the display of the bordering Montbretia and Fuchsia and in between the crimson autumn leaves of the dying Purple Loosestrife. It was a chance visit. There was no way of contacting the man apart from a letter. And from what Lorcan said it was their best shot. Just go.

At night, Penny recollected that the headlights caught the montbretia and illuminated the roadside. It was late in the year, but still flowering. Rain beckoned and set in; the rainy season was due, though at times it was difficult to distinguish from the rest of the year. Penny had helped a friend with a large plot in Doolin some time ago. The overstated comparison with the trenches in the Somme were a regular feature of the chatter. Each day they slithered in the clart while fencing off the land to offer some protection for the young plants against the wind.

The final road to Browne's was a dirt road with gravel here and there. The surrounds of the cottage were unkempt, a glorious wilderness, with large boulders draped in hanging plants, fern and lichen. Old woodland bordered the surrounds. A vintage Land Rover jeep stood to the side of the traditional full-gabled cottage. The lurid red and green façade signified a break from the whitewash and the pretty thatched versions depicted on postcards sent home. Before Penny could enlighten Dove with his knowledge of 'cottage-ology', Dove shushed him. Penny was counting the windows.

"Quiet," Dove ordered. He paused beside the car and looked around. Dove shook his head and marched towards the front door and rapped loudly. The presence of the jeep suggested the man was at home. They were visible. Dove looked uncomfortable. Dove pointed towards the overhead wires. Electricity it had, and a well. No holy well or raggedy bush – this was his water supply. Dove indicated speaker cables that ran off into the trees. He eyed them and screwed his face up.

They waited ten minutes. Dove took a piece of paper from his little red notebook and scribbled on it, sticking it under the Land Rover's windscreen wipers. He put a phone number, regardless of the fact the man had no telephone (that they knew of). Then they got in the car to drive off.

A tap on the window made Penny jump. Dove gave his 'result' look and grinned. The man who tapped was over six-foot, white hair, not unwelcoming, but unsmiling. They got out. He eyed Dove, then Penny. Dove held out a hand and said, "Dove." Signalling to his left, "This is Penny. Ronnie Penny."

The man never spoke. He did shake hands. He scrutinised Dove, head to toe, then glimpsed again at Penny.

"May we talk?" Dove cocked his head and gestured openly with his hands.

Finally, the man answered. "Yes." He turned and walked indoors, and they followed.

Alice had planned to watch the place that day. A night shoot and a trek across the edge of Rahasane back to the rented worn thatched cottage was her schedule. It had brought about some frustration. The broadband was slow, the satellite inadequate – or was it snail mail? Nothing came through that morning. She decided to go and survey the hit anyhow. She might get a better signal on her mobile along the way.

She liked the metallic taste of the well water, she liked the place, but people were nosy. Shame, but it was inevitable a further move was necessary.

Freeman struck lucky. She had one more witness to visit. Anne, a local country guide, welcomed her in. Freeman felt at home in the place, she liked the renovations which kept its features without vandalising its character. A small desk and laptop stood out among the wildlife prints, bric-a-brac and odds and sods. Her own experience of such bits and bobs was a browse of popular vintage and craft suppliers' websites. In her life outside of work function ruled over form.

She stared at a small figurative painting – *Bring Home the Peat* – an oil on canvas. Around the room several in the same ilk hung. She stopped as she saw an anomaly, a poster of a cubist-like abstract, a seated female nude. Anne was courteous.

"Go ahead, browse my gallery. I wished I owned the real things."

Freeman looked at the artist's name on the nude. "Mainie Jellett," she spoke out loud. The colour, the rhythms and female form were quite attractive. She liked its Cubist manner. Anne declared it was a personal favourite.

"Yes, a woman. A central figure too in Irish culture and a pupil of Gleizes. One of the first abstract painters in Ireland!"

Freeman aimed to remember the name. She might ask Ronnie if he knew of her. That and snails…

"Check out Evie Sydney Hone, early Irish Cubist, and her amazing stained glasswork. There are others too. However, that's not what you're here for." Freeman found Anne's throaty brogue, her twang, endearing. Anne confirmed it was part Connemara, part Culchie, but she could alter it to suit whoever she spoke with. Time to get to the point.

"What can you tell me about this hunter, the one who leaves the carcasses to rot?"

"To date I've found two carcasses, quite late in the day, which implies it wasn't poachers. The deer we found were shot from a distance by an expert shooter and left to rot. There have been one or two sightings of a woman, a stranger, who flits away as soon as spotted." She pointed at a map. "She was seen near to Gort, and close to the lough." She tapped the map.

"Did someone who lives nearby see her?"

"No, it was incomers, visiting the estate. They swear there was a woman who was, as they put it, 'stalking a man who was looking in the puddles of the turlough like a child watching newts, leeches and sticklebacks'. They chatted to folk in the hotel, the Lady Gregory. They were American. In McCarthy's they met a ranger."

"Lorcan?"

"Yes. How did you know?"

Freeman didn't answer. "Any idea who was being watched?"

"Could only be Matthew, Matty as we call him, the quiet man, as locals dubbed him, a harmless soul, ex-schoolteacher I believe."

Freeman had heard enough. She was about to excuse herself when Anne offered tea, some soup and fresh baked bread. It was worth waiting for, though there was a distinct taste of something in the tea, sulphur, the water straight from the well. The soda bread was gorgeous, Anne's grannie's recipe, crusty bread with a leek and potato soup. Lucy wondered what the body count was elsewhere.

She left feeling smug and full. She tried ringing Dove. No signal. The weather was shifting and thick dark clouds gathering.

Matty's hearth was in the middle, as Penny expected. A log fire was going. Penny looked around. Books, more books, maps, and a large ginger cat called Rufus. When he sat down, the cat headed straight for him and onto his knee. Rufus settled in after pawing his legs for a minute.

Dove stated their purpose. "We're looking for a woman," then added to his statement before the stock response came back, "This is a particular woman. She is, as the police say, armed and dangerous."

Matty looked at Penny who was stroking Rufus's ears. Dove assumed he was trying to work out their relationship. Matty aimed his next sentence at Dove. "You a military man?"

"Ex-navy. You?"

Browne clammed up. To Penny that meant a yes, or alternatively a pacifist. He decided to butt in.

"Mr Browne, this woman is lethal, I can testify to that. If you have seen her, then it is important you let us know." (He was pleased at leaving out 'crucial.') He added, "Your background isn't important, your future is." He decided to engage the man in general conversation. He intrigued him, with his absence of a phone and television. There was an old wireless in the corner, a beautiful piece of furniture in a dark wooden cabinet, a valve radio. It was lit up too, a sign it was working. He thought of the sad-looking wireless in Peter and Annabelle's kitchen. No music. If it hadn't been for Rufus stretched out in his lap, he would've crossed the room to examine it, try it.

Dove noticed it too and the wires running from it to the wall. On top, and wired in, was an old cassette player. Penny's curiosity got the better of him. He placed Rufus gently on the floor. Crossing the room, he studied the machine. "Gosh, a Dragon Slayer circa 1984!" He also browsed the cassettes before returning to his seat, followed by Rufus who planted himself back on Penny's knee.

Browne spoke in a more relaxed tone. "Tandberg, left by the previous owners. They both work well. The family, who had been residents for several generations, left a supply of valves for the wireless. The Slayer is a relic from the 1980s. I've connected it to a part of my woodland and hung small speakers. When I first moved to Ireland I wanted to listen to music in the woods." He laughed. "The woodland has its own orchestra. I do test it out every now and then."

"Wow." Penny was impressed. Penny was wandering the woods listening to Tom Waits.

Browne continued. "I once had the pleasure of walking in a sultan's estate. He had speakers installed everywhere so he was able to listen to classical music as he walked in the garden. I liked the idea and wanted to follow suit."

"The late Sultan Qaboos." Penny recalled the sultan's

estate at Seeb and the tiny zoo. He then mentioned Radio Luxembourg. He couldn't make out the stations on the old wireless, but guessed Luxembourg was there, and Athlone if in name only. Penny, like Dove, saw in the man a military background. He never quite confirmed he was with the military. He was in Oman. No other reason to be there when he was a young man. Could've been an oil worker.

Browne continued the conversation in a more relaxed vein, surprised at this man's familiarity. "Marconi connected to here at Clifden and via Derrygimlagh Bog onto America." Browne pointed out the window.

Dove was becoming impatient. "Mr Browne, if you have seen this woman, it is important we know her whereabouts." He couldn't really give a description.

"I have. I was examining flora in the crevices of the turlough at the estate, Coole that is, and there was a woman tracking me. I gave her the slip."

Dove was convinced he was military on meeting him; his bearing, his manner, his speech spoke of the forces. There was a thin line between acculturation and institutionalisation. He recalled his own culture shock upon leaving. He asked a pointed question. "Tracking you? In what way? You gave Alice the slip?"

"Alice?" Browne's language had given him away and his remark a clue to his background. Why was he hiding it?

Dove cut through all the shit. "Mr Browne, Matty, Matt or Matthew, whatever you're called, it would be better if you gave us a straight answer. The woman, Alice is an assassin and ex-military. She also has a penchant for torture. If she is following you, tracking you, as you put it, she means business. Furthermore, it will be contractual, paid business. You must have someone out there who wants rid of you." He pointed out the window.

Dove paraphrased the history of the so-called poets. He included a short history of their role, Hart, Freeman, Raed, Periwinkle and Penny. Browne listened. Penny didn't interrupt. Dove then rose from his seat as if to go.

Penny considered it a bit harsh. Dove's elementary psychology did the trick. Penny couldn't think of an alternative but blue streak psychology came to mind. Browne offered to help.

Matty Browne was back searching in the crevices of his mind, the untamed landscapes of Angola, from which he escaped for a short while into another feral landscape of altered consciousness, drugs, politics, and finally rehab, teacher training, and a job. Wild landscapes stayed with him and Ireland nodded during his years at the chalkface. He bought the derelict cottage. Fuelled by paranoia, his first years of ownership were spent doing essential repairs along with what he considered to be security measures.

His past reared up before him as Dove spoke, his loss and displacement, and his piecing together of his life. There was something about these men that told him they had been there too, in differing circumstances. A pub conversation at the age of twenty-one with fellow squaddies, the modern press gang, the drink he couldn't hold. The money that sounded fantastic, the cause lost on him. He signed up for Angola.

"What branch were you in, Dove?"

"SBS."

"And you, Penny?"

"I swung from a few branches as a kid. Ended up teaching art history. That was my speciality."

"Was?"

"I was retired for reasons that may become clearer to you if we ever get to know each other." He looked sternly at Browne.

"We are here to help, as well as nail Alice Byron," Dove chimed in. "I can recognise an ex-squaddie when I see one. I also understand the need for retreat. Your ability to give the woman the slip, expertise in the field, is useful though Alice isn't going to go away." He was standing up as he spoke and signalled that they were leaving. He handed a small box to Browne. Penny side-tracked as he pointed at the wall, a large poster print.

"*Sacred Mirrors* series." Browne wasn't prepared for the lecture. "Sophia by Alex Gray. Not my field, though I would place it late '80s." It told him a lot about Browne's escape, his search for the spiritual. The poor condition of the poster indicated he'd held onto the picture since 1989, or whatever it was. "An acrylic with a gnostic poem, *The Thunder, Perfect Mind* attached. 'For I am knowledge and ignorance!' The former is best deployed to understand the latter. That is, to be aware of one's shortcomings." Browne looked perturbed. He didn't need any more therapy or advice.

Dove brought things back to earth. "If you want to share the burden, give me a call." He pointed to the box. "The phone will last three months whereupon you will have to make a choice to contact the world or put it back in the box." Penny assumed he meant both the world and the mobile phone. The meaning was clear. "It's already up and running, the phone that is. If you have any weapons hereabouts, make sure they are primed."

They made for the door. Browne followed them, the box in his hand which he opened as they walked, his mind in a whirl. He trusted this man, Dove. He wasn't bullshitting him.

Matty was closing on sixty-eight. The thought of re-entering the battlefield was a prospect he never wanted to face. Another side of him tingled. He thought of his rifle stowed in a tunnel below the small rooms, his shelter. As a result of his early paranoia, he had equipped his place to repel attackers, his tunnel digging, his defences, his escape routes all kept in shape. He had shaken all that off, and joked to himself about it, yet the work might now come in handy. He had maintained the defences, evidence that his old self remained.

He looked at the phone and the instructions. There were two numbers in the directory, one for the man Dove and one for the police officer he had mentioned, Freeman. As they walked to the car, he relented. "I'll keep you posted." He waved the phone as if to confirm his promise.

Penny acknowledged him with an affirmative nod. They got in the car. Browne waved them off. As they drove, the skies emptied in a torrent of rain battering the windscreen. As they pulled out from the dirt gravel road a car passed them and turned in. The rain obscured the view of the single driver.

Dove drove for a couple of minutes then with a loud, "Fuckin' hell," pulled over. He grabbed his mobile and dialled. It rang and rang. Matty assumed they were testing the phone. He answered.

"I do know how to use the bloody phone. I wasn't

expecting a call so soon."

"Matty, I don't know if you're expecting visitors but a car is heading your way, a grey Audi."

"No, I'm not. I will be all right. Check back by phone tomorrow." He was surprised. The signal was clear, the reception fine.

He could hear by Dove's tone he wasn't sure. "Freeman is waiting for us in Gort in the wet." He turned the car around, then decided against going back. He spun the car round again and drove to Gort. "We will pick Feeman up, then call again. I have a feeling our victim Matty Browne isn't going to lie down and die. I can't wait to see what Periwinkle produces on Browne. I'll contact him later."

Freeman took refuge in a lone bus shelter. The rain poured. She hadn't seen a bus all day.

Dove phoned Periwinkle. "Need you to do a search for someone. Calls himself Browne, Matthew Browne. Age, late sixties, and ex-military. There is a problem. I don't think that is his birth name! It's a bit of a chew, I guess. He may have legally changed his name. He's definitely hiding something in his past, a military issue, something he's ashamed of." He looked at Penny. "His book collection resembles the shelves in Foyles on Marxism. He has a library that would shame the Kremlin… not our Kremlin, the one that comes with Mad Putin (Ras-Putin), philosophy, history, and they have markers in them, books that had been well thumbed, definitely not for show."

Penny cut in. "Gramsci's *Prison Notebooks*, Trotsky's *On*

Art and Literature, Lenin's Last Struggle, Althusser, Poulantzas, Mandel, you name it he's got it all. On the side was an open copy of a work on the Paris Commune."

Dove rang off and turned to Penny. "I saw *Das Kapital* on the shelves. That takes some reading. As for reading, I think we've given Periwinkle a tough task to resolve."

Not so, as they were to discover. His past well documented. Robin Simpson's or Browne's files had never closed. He had other pseudonyms too. His history could have inspired Penny to write a biography, a genre he avoided. Making sense of this life, giving it order, were not part of his remit. Balance wasn't his thing. It probably wasn't Browne's either. The scales might be in his favour, however. Matty Browne, he concluded, might be weighing the odds as they spoke. Would he do a runner? Dove didn't think so.

Matty Browne was preparing for war.

"The schoolteacher has a past," Dove said, then glimpsing at Penny, "We all have!" Penny assumed he was referring to him and to Periwinkle rather than humankind. At that moment Freeman came running from the shelter. As she did the rain stopped. The sky cleared.

Chapter 34

Alice Byron was convinced she had seen Penny's comrade Dove, though the rain blurred the view somewhat. That meant her quarry was on the alert. She couldn't be sure. Caution was best.

She parked up as the rain ceased. Hitching her heavy backpack on her shoulders, she headed down through the woods in a circuitous route. The man had no phone, no company and lived a hermit's life in the wilds. He could be dead for days before anyone discovered him. What had he done? Who had he upset?

Her innate sense of curiosity, the engine that stimulated her kicked in. In the woods, the trees passed on their philosophy to the poet. She thought of the Autograph Tree holding the spirits of Yeats, O'Casey and Shaw, a huge copper beech, a tree with shallow roots.

Alice stopped. She put down the pack. This would be her last job. The money was good, and Spain beckoned. Who wanted this strange man dead? What had he done?

She picked the pack up, slung it over her shoulders and advanced towards the cottage.

Chapter 35

Matty Browne camouflaged his jeep in the woods. In the shade of a huge sideboard, he lifted two of the natural limestone flags and descended into his cave. Rufus slipped in beside him. It felt safe. He threw a light switch, carefully replaced the flagstones from below. He felt pleased as they slotted in perfectly.

Rufus loved the passages. He occasionally trapped a mouse. He had one in his mouth. Rufus took pleasure in cruelly toying with it. Captured, released, chased, captured, the poor beast was terrified. Matty removed the mouse. To Rufus's dismay he put it through a small grille in a wall where it could survive. Rufus looked pissed off. He was unaware of the significance of his game. Or was he?

At the end of several tunnels were escape routes into the wood. He admired his artisanship. Testing it out, he put his weight on the sturdy supports built into the limestone and clay. Whoever this woman was, he wasn't going to let her have it easy. He unlocked a padlocked door towards the end of the main tunnel into a small workshop. There was plenty of water, emergency rations for three or four days. Browne opened an old chest and removed his rifle from an oilcloth. He thought of the past. He felt the barrel, the stock, its beautiful wooden handle; he thought of the Cypriot mercenaries and others he fought alongside, before he buried his other rifle in the Angola soil and disappeared.

Underneath that Angolan soil was oil, till over slate, limestone. From 1955, the country produced oil, by 1975 it was locked in civil war, a war that led to strained relations elsewhere.

He was lucky. For many it was a one-way trip. He didn't need the hatred, he hated himself for it. He went AWOL. Someone, he guessed, had sussed where he was and who he was. They had dug him out from the records. Among the awful ones – *les affreux* in the Congo, in Nigeria, or Rhodesia, the human vermin of Africa as they were known, plied their trade. Among the racists, the crazies, and the big money, someone had survived to suss him out. He had an idea who it might be, the very man who recruited him, a member of the extreme New Right in England, or new extremists, those calling for the death of members of the armed forces. To him, England appeared a broken and Right-Wing society. Traditional values were disappearing as fast as the high street shops. It was a society in disagreement, one given permission from above to vent their spleen on others: women, blacks, Muslims. If he had his way, he'd rewild the playing fields of Eton. Out there, someone wanted him dead.

He thought about the Portuguese withdrawal, a drunken night with squaddies, and a plane to Africa. His semi-automatic rifle was left interred. He felt some regret that he had submitted to his inner fears and instability to purchase another, an L1A1. The weapon was still unused. Was he capable? He shouldered it, checked the aperture rear sight, the tilting breechblock, then wrapped it up and put it back in the box, closing the lid firmly. The day of realisation came back. He slumped down on the ground. His walk away from the coastal lowland of Angola, avoiding the more populous high plateau, was fraught. He got away. He was fortunate. Many weren't. Was there an alternative to violence? Ghosts abounded.

Chapter 36

Alice Byron waited half an hour. The car with the Irish plates didn't return. If it were Dove, he would've followed. Surely the sight of a car heading towards a single gravel road would have raised his curiosity? Not entirely convinced it was Dove, she shouldered her pack, her rifle, and moved slowly towards the cottage. On a whim she decided to follow the pathway through the wood. In the clearing there was no sign of Browne's jeep.

The door was open. That was silly. Or was it? He was miles from anywhere. Casual burglary was doubtful. Assassination, she mused, more probable.

She circled. The back garden was a curious landscape. Browne's rustic retreat defied analysis. It did offer an idea: this man looked at life differently. He was an outsider in one of the many rural peripheries. He chose to be here. What was he hiding from? The difficulty of access to the cottage was a bonus for the resident. That was something she might take on board herself when her final move took place. The huge stones everywhere meant there wasn't much garden at the back, merely moss and lichen-clad chunks of stone. In between grew bracken and various grasses. What was this landscape saying to her? Maybe a wilding experiment? Maybe a warning? Daylight might be the best time to strike.

Alice's senses said leave it. The half open door beckoned. She entered. It was dim. The remnants of a fire glowed in the hearth. The smell of pine lingered. Alice wondered if there was any wood that smelled bad while burning. Pine burns fast, a 1930s poem on firewood told her so, and Ash green or brown slowly. She gripped her knife. She congratulated herself. It was *The Firewood Poem* by Lady Congreve.

The cottage appeared empty, yet she sensed a presence. Her mind switched to red alert.

Below her and in the dark, seeing was no problem for Rufus. All the lights were out. The only flicker was cat's eyes as Rufus watched with Matty, who was recalibrating, becoming a former self by meditating, a process he knew as unrecognising himself (a process an academic would call unpacking). Browne sensed in Penny a vibe, an unsettling portrait, a stranger; not completely educated but untamed – like his garden. He pondered the aptness of his analogy. What he saw was a contradiction, a portrait. He knew nothing of Penny's reputation. If he had, it would've meant nothing to him.

Rufus miaowed. No sound carried from the tunnels. The doors were wired, so Matty now knew whoever it was, was in the house. He thought of texting Dove, then left it. The mobile phone was going to be handy. It may not work down below, so he needed to test it.

Alice surveyed the books, the maps, and edged along the shelves, no poetry except a collection of Robert Burns. A noise interrupted her browsing. A small noise. She was back undercover in the woods in no time and heading towards her car. The click of the door movement told Matty the intruder was gone. He hung back.

Chapter 37

Lucas Guess chose to drink fizzy water. His lunch guests did the same. The club was private, the food was good, basic pub grub in a secluded booth which offered them the privacy they desired. He thought Uncle Peri a very lucky man. Saida was a match for him in more ways than one can imagine. Saida and he could have gossiped for ever, sharing information, social and otherwise, bonding. Periwinkle sat back. It was Saida that stopped the chit chat. "I suspect you want to get down to business?"

He removed a yellowed tome of a file from his briefcase and laid it down on the table. "Where do I begin?"

Periwinkle spoke apologetically. He appeared taken aback. "Sorry to break the thread of the conversation. Don't tell me that huge file is on our man Browne?" He wasn't expecting anything.

"So, he is called Browne?"

"He is now. His dossier reveals what lies behind the mask that is Browne. I'll precis for you the threads that run through. We've kept tabs on Browne – real name Robin Matthew Simpson, but Browne since the 1980s – before I was born." He laughed and then put down his fork. "Going through the years, the typing, the Tipex years, and then the processed word requires differing mindsets to read. Browne has been with us a long time. He came to our attention at the age of twenty-one as a mercenary in Angola, where he amputated a comrade's gangrenous leg and saved his life. That's by-the-by. Yet, it says a lot about the man. He underwent a change of heart. Disgusted with the racism and hatred for the so-called Left, he walked away, vanished. He changed his name. Our next data on him was with the anti-Nazi league, an activist, a pacifist, though one more than capable of defending himself. The SWP were central. He was out on the streets leafletting, marching and involved in several skirmishes in Lewisham, London area, and the south coast while he studied to be a teacher. It all turned nasty. Michael Foot labelled the ANL as red fascists."

Lucas tapped the file with a forefinger. "That was enough for Browne. He stepped aside and concentrated on his teaching. We still keep a watch, though as a man in his late sixties, retired and reclusive, we doubt he will ever be involved again." Lucas paused. Periwinkle signalled him to continue.

"After 1981, intermittent appearances, rock against racism, and some pamphlets. Nothing radical apparently. What has he done?"

Periwinkle did the gap-filling. "Alice Byron, who has also changed her name, is in Ireland. If Freeman, Dove and Penny are correct, he is the target for her next hit. She is back in business. Matthew is the mark in this case."

"Penny is there with Freeman?"

"Yes, he's what he described as the lure. He has changed since his case. Maureen's death signalled a shift. He's safe with

Dove, safer than on his own anywhere."

"Is Dove safe with him?"

Saida laughed. "Good point. Who is?"

Guess saw some kindred spirit in Browne and Penny. "I think Browne and he would get on well. I must try to find out what the hit is over – his early branding as a Right-Wing fascist, his later branding as a red fascist? Angola? I hope it's not linked to the current black activism. It's a pity as Browne will respond, not in a kneejerk way, more likely as a professional soldier, highly organised and competent. He had an exemplary record as a British squaddie until he bought out. Hunted by both sides, Browne escaped Angola on his own. Few did. I know from our most recent checks he keeps extremely fit, battle fit. He's a one off." He closed the file as he spoke. Periwinkle signalled he didn't need any more.

Lucas eyed his watch. "Another perishing meeting. Great to see you, Uncle Peri, and lovely to meet you, Saida. One further point: Browne had a first-class record as a teacher, no politics, nothing! He tutored young kids. I hope he doesn't foul up. I hope he survives." He paid the bill and left.

Saida and Periwinkle spent the rest of the afternoon in the British Museum. Before that he left a lengthy message for Dove. Lucas, he assumed, was going to follow it up in his own way.

Chapter 38

At the end of a short tunnel Matty Browne took out a huge key. He unlocked a padlock from a small iron-barred cell and checked the six by four-foot space. The grille extended over the wall. The padlock was unreachable from anyone in the pit, as he called it. No pendulum, no inquisition. An enclosed space for a prisoner.

Inside this claustrophobic space he looked up at the inclined wall. He surveyed his handiwork, his spadework. He tried to climb the wall. No way. The trapdoor up top was a thin wooden cover with a scattering of gravel atop. That part was working. The switch threw the trap and anyone outside the front door could find themselves in a pit. The drop was about thirteen feet, not a lot, but the walls were sloped, lined and completely unscalable. The landing was comfortable.

As a secondary precaution he'd constructed a stronger lid. *Bring it on.* A moment of sadness washed over him. He locked the cell and went upstairs to read a while. Rufus was staring out of the window as if expecting someone. Matty looked at the bookshelves. Things were out of order. He pictured Luanda, the slaughter, the Right, the Left, the MPLA, the massacres, the National Front for the Liberation of

Angola and Unita, and the influx of Cuban troops to support the MPLA. He had studied. His sympathies moved to the Left, questioning his own gathering knowledge of the MPLA's killing. Back home in the 1980s the Left shot itself in the foot. The rifle was best locked away. There was no way he could use it, not even to threaten someone. There must be other ways…

He took some comfort in the fact that his paranoia had paid off. His traps and his tunnels might come in handy. Caging someone with a rifle might be an issue. He wondered what Dove would think of it, and the academic guy Penny who clocked his book and cassettes collection, particularly his New Left books which he hadn't touched in years. They reminded him of another self, just as the rifle did, his past, the long darkness that is history.

How to resolve the contract? He decided to hand over to Freeman, whoever she was. She might also uncover who was behind it. He wanted to live out his retirement without a return to Angola. He wasn't going to let Alice whatever ruin it. Did Rufus look at him as if in agreement? Hard to tell. Funny things, cats.

Freeman, Dove and Penny were back in County Clare. All three were walking the road from the B&B to Doolin Pier. It was a glorious evening. For Dove, a pint of Guinness beckoned – O'Connor's bar. In fact, they thought they might do all three: McGann's, McDermott's and Gus O' Connor's. They could see across to the ocean, the waves frothing in a green sea, the remnants of the earlier rainfall flooding off the cliffs in rainbow torrents, and not a soul in sight. Dove smiled lovingly at the Atlantic Ocean. As they strolled, he passed on Periwinkle's information on Browne.

Penny was most excited. He gasped when he heard his first name was Robin. As they spoke, a text came from Matty: *'Had a visitor. A woman entered the house and looked around.'*

Dove and Penny immediately wondered where the hell he was when a visitor was in his house. Dove forwarded it to Lucy. Penny's novel sense of reading was already on the case (or was it too many novels in this case?) "He probably has a secret tunnel under the house." Dove laughed. "If not, he was watching from the woods."

Penny's face coloured in a blush of embarrassment at his naivety.

Matty was sitting in his living room deliberating his next move. Should he defend? Should he attack? His take was one picked up from an American soldier that the best defence is a good offense. He began to sort out suitable attire. The greyscale gear, he called it. Unless Alice was colour blind and had an enhanced greyscale vision, he would be invisible. He knew the woods intimately.

Over the next two days Alice scouted around. He watched. He left the door wide open and on day two as a result noticed something very peculiar. She approached. She was about to enter when Rufus appeared. Caught unawares for a second or two Alice unshouldered her rifle, a recent Russian model. After a momentary face-off Rufus skedaddled indoors. That wasn't so peculiar.

It was her initial reaction that caught Matty's attention, one of fear. It showed on her face. It showed in her body language. Ailurophobia he thought was rare. Something about Rufus's sudden appearance scared her shitless. Her hands were shaking when she shouldered the rifle. She didn't go in after him. Matty had an army colleague savaged by two cats as a child and suffered afterwards. He had called his condition 'felinophobia'. She's scared. Could it be Rufus?

As a child Matty watched a local dog worry two neighbourhood cats. He spotted one on the garden wall. Young Robin watched as a second cat waited behind the wall. As the dog barked and growled and jumped at the cat, the other cat leaped onto the wall and over. Spitting and clawing, they attached themselves to the dog's side. They tore at it mercilessly as it ran down the road screeching in pain. Don't fuck with cats.

Byron didn't like Rufus. Was it mutual? Rufus wouldn't harm a fly. He did try to catch them, but never, ever succeeded.

Chapter 39

Alice finally received her instructions. There was no indication of what Browne had done. She would look forward to killing him and his ginger cat. It was a straight kill. She was to receive a note which she was to leave by the body if possible: *Angola*. That did arouse her curiosity. She thought about killing the cat first. She had no curiosity about its past, she just hated it. It wasn't curiosity that would kill the fucking ginger thing. No poems, postcards, no warnings, the cat and the man together. And definitely no torture. That was Mo's area of expertise.

She decided to spend another three days of reconnaissance, then choose her moment and her spot. Or, if a moment arose, take the shot. She was enjoying the hunt, the stalking. The man was confusing, not random like Penny. Sometimes she thought he was watching her but saw no trace. She so wanted it to last. Did he know she was there?

His sudden disappearances signified a game. The notion occurred that her quarry was unhinged, reclusive, and eccentric. He didn't seem aware of her. Was he? She decided to assume he was and work it from there.

A site in the woods looked good, one with a clear view. Her handgun would finish the job if she had to go in. Best from a distance. The three days were a lesson in camouflage and the craft of hiding. Browne would appear and disappear into the grey zones. He would go behind the big stones and melt away. She lost him several times. The notion arose that she was being led up the garden with no path.

To Matty, she was the Borg Queen, one single mind. Resistance is futile. He was human and therefore unpredictable. He read that somewhere about *Star Trek*. In the dark he assessed his trapdoor, from indoors and outdoors. It worked a treat. Rufus's finely honed senses knew something was going on. He started prowling around and became quite excited. He prowled the tunnels. He strutted ahead or beside Browne. He watched as Matty operated his trapdoor. The simple pulley beat all electronic devices for Matty. His jeep now stood outside to signify his presence indoors.

Alice drove back, and prepared herself for one more day's tracking, then the hit.

Chapter 40

Dove, Freeman and Penny were discussing their next moves. For Freeman, the course of action was to go in and lift her. If she put up a fight, take her down, but not kill her. Freeman was quite happy to do it herself. She needed to see the location and the environs. If Alice was rooting around, that would be difficult.

Dove wasn't armed, neither was Penny. Penny left it to the professionals, though he had lots of games theories from warzone, intricate games play.

Matty Browne had different ideas. He didn't want to kill his opponent or maim her, though he was capable of such. He wanted a prisoner. Several times he could've taken her out. Alternatively, he considered she could have taken the shot and disposed of him. She didn't come across as a procrastinator. His conclusion? She enjoyed the hunt.

He just wanted to be alone, left to wander. This was upsetting. He was, however, recalibrating at speed and his old, or young self, a self he had masked and hidden, was coming to the surface. He must involve the law, and he must be careful. No mistakes. He slept below in the small secure room off the tunnels. She could burn the house down and he would survive. Something told him that would spoil the game for her, unless of course she could watch. He slept well. Rufus spent the night prowling around outside with an air of expectancy.

Freeman was happy for Dove to talk with Browne, yet decided it was best she met him. Time was at a premium. She suggested that they went before light, hid the car, and went to Browne's through the woods. The chances of Alice being there at night was a consideration. They would have to move carefully and separately.

Dove spoke with Browne. He hinted that he would be sleeping out of sight. Could he text when they were in the woods? Browne tested the mobile. As luck would have it, it was operative below ground. He informed Dove that, "she has a Russian rifle, and from my own surveillance of her, is carrying a knife and a pistol. She does have some skills, so beware."

Dove was aware. He said thanks.

On the third and final day of her reconnaissance, she felt he was tracking her. It felt uncomfortable. He had completely vanished. The damn man had left the cottage, walked into the woods and vanished into thin air. When she circled and relocated elsewhere in the wood, she felt his continuing presence at the back of her. She made several detours. When she worked her way back, he appeared in a front window.

The day before, he had walked around the back by the big stones and similarly had disappeared to reappear to her left at the front near the well. She did see him as he entered the cottage one day but didn't see him surface in the woods and watch her.

Was he armed?

At that very moment she was in his sights, staring at the cabin door. Yet he wasn't sure he could take the shot. He went back in and rang Dove. "We need to talk. Can you bring Freeman with you?" He thought for a second. "And Penny, of course."

Why he said of course Dove couldn't suss, but Penny it was. "Yes. Is now a suitable time?" They turned around and headed back as he spoke.

"It is. But bear in mind she is watching, and your presence may alter things. I have an idea, call it a plan. It may contravene what DI Freeman considers policing, but—" He stopped dead.

Dove assumed control and finished the sentence. Best not to hear what Browne had in mind. Best not to even think about what Freeman had in mind. "It might just do that; alter things, I mean."

Penny's presence really would change the game. "Penny was her last hit. Failed." Dove wasn't aware he was part of the earlier package.

"That explains something… or nothing. I'm not sure. See you soon."

"Okay, we're on the way."

Freeman checked her Glock 19. Dove and Penny looked at her with 'what about us?' faces. "I have a baton, CS/Pava spray. Take your pick. The Glock came from South Yorkshire. Quite happy to go with whatever. My wish is hand-to-hand combat."

"I wonder if Browne has any weapons." Dove looked at Lucy.

Freeman didn't answer. Best not to know.

They had set off early hours, Penny and Dove leaving the B&B in the dead of night. Both had been looking forward to that one-off treat, the big Irish breakfast, and the white pudding, 'a heart attack on a plate', as Dove described it.

They drove to Galway in denial, dreaming of big breakfasts, then left the car in a side lane about a mile from the dirt road and walked. Browne told them to check a particular spot in the trees where Alice parked up out of sight. To date she had used one spot only. Dove and Freeman skirted and found no car. Freeman erred on the side of caution. "She isn't a fool. Let's work several metres apart and if there's any siting at all, signal, then work our way towards each other quickly and quietly."

The next day was to be the kill. Initially, Alice couldn't sleep. She would make the hit in the morning. Browne was a dead man. She settled into a wild shelter, a well-constructed dome of twigs, and waited. As the night darkened and the moon shifted, she dozed, happy at the prospective shoot.

Chapter 41

In London, Guess was busy. He rang Periwinkle late. "Hi. Can you tell me if Dove and Penny are carrying?"

This was Lucas asking, family. Before Periwinkle could answer, he spoke again. "I'm sending a man over tonight, one of the best! The police officer will have a Sig or a Glock and the usual extendable baton and such. Not much against a Russian rifle and pistols. We know from the bullets extracted from a stag the type of rifle."

Periwinkle listened. "Lucas, I'd like to go too."

"Be ready in fifteen minutes. Pick you up."

Periwinkle allowed an inward smile. Lucas knew him well, easily anticipating Periwinkle's next move. Periwinkle was ready and waiting outside the flat in London. Saida was still asleep. *Back soon* read the note … Ireland signals.

Lucas was driving, a smart black car, and in the back seat was a man. Periwinkle said hello and clammed up. The man replied similarly while staring out of the window. They drove for twenty minutes or so then turned into a field. A hangar, an airplane, a government agent and 'Uncle Peri' to the rescue.

Finally, Guess spoke. "I don't underestimate Dove. I realise Penny too has certain attributes that count in his favour.

Freeman is well versed in martial arts and can fire a gun. By the way, this is Johnson. Johnson, Periwinkle. "

Periwinkle didn't ask his first name. Why should he? He was to find out that Johnson was his first name. The plane was already rolling across the field, a landing arranged in Galway. Closed to commercial traffic, the flying club had given permission to land. Carnmore East it was. They were in the air before Periwinkle could say Johnson.

There was a cache of weapons. Johnson took a knife, a pistol and a rifle, plus night vision goggles. They wasted no time. Johnson never spoke. Periwinkle looked at the weapons. He picked a knife. Johnson eyed him curiously. Periwinkle sat back and appeared to doze throughout the seventy-five-minute flight. They arrived in Galway at just after 23:00. It was a bright night. Landing was comfortable and the plane taxied toward a hangar.

The pilot addressed Johnson. "My instructions are to wait here, and to bring back whoever turns up. Any idea how many? Or is it top secret?" The sarcasm was evident.

"Joe," Johnson smiled wistfully, "you can get your head down. I'd say a day or so, and five, six passengers to fetch back… if all goes well." He picked up the rifle and walked towards a car parked up beside the field. The driver was British, and his sat nav tuned in ready. They set off, Johnson in the front, Periwinkle in the back. Johnson wasn't sure why Guess wanted Periwinkle along. He speculated, then left it.

The driver spoke. "Twenty minutes or less at this time of night."

Periwinkle leaned back and made himself comfortable. Johnson eyed him in the mirror. Periwinkle had a beret on and appeared sound asleep.

Johnson needed to be careful. Working with a stranger was one thing, trust had no purchase in the here and now and had been replaced by group sanctions. He chose caution. Something about the man's attitude caused slight concern.

Matty Browne did one last reconnoitre of the woods around his house and made some adjustments. He checked a cable connection to a small speaker hung from a tree nearby. It was quite well-hidden, then another two at a measured distance. Nighttime would cloak it further. His electrical knowledge was fine, his lack of products in the house more an aspect of his retreat. He listened to the radio and loved music, music of any kind. This wild wood was his sultan's garden. Oak, Ash, Hazel, Birch and, near to the house in a space, a beautiful Rowan. No palms, just native trees.

He tinkered with the connections and decided they were good to go. He also checked the trap again. As a further precaution he wired up a couple of trips with bells on the periphery. Then he went inside and made a pot of tea. His mobile beeped. A strange number. He laughed. They were all strange. "Yep?"

"Lucy Freeman here, Matthew. We are on the way. We intend to leave the car undercover and cut through to the back of your place. There will be Dove, Penny and myself."

"It's a longer hike, Freeman, but safer. I sense our predator is out there."

"I estimate an hour or so. See you then."

Freeman was keen to meet Matty Browne. Penny and Dove had no concept of what was to happen. Dove was happy to improvise. Penny had stopped theorising. The events of the last few months had altered him. His humour came back in fits and starts, a flurry of irony or satire, then a relapse. He had one thing on his mind: the capture and arrest of Alice Byron, alive. He guessed she was awake to their presence, and that same sense that Periwinkle demonstrated, that perception of the proximity of the enemy, buzzed. He had to assume she knew they were there hiding in the wood.

Johnson, Lucas's best man, was still mulling over his dilemma on Periwinkle. Had the man recognised him? His first glance indicated that he had then closed his eyes and dozed. He eyed Periwinkle again. *Looks harmless.*

Before dozing off, Periwinkle texted Dove to fill him in on the details, his whereabouts and a short note about Johnson.

Dove texted back: *We're on the way to Browne's. Watch carefully back and front.*

Periwinkle remained, for all to see, asleep. When the car stopped, Johnson began to wonder if the tall gangly-looking man was really asleep. This wasn't the time for empirical testing. They had a job to do.

"Everybody out." Johnson was already opening the boot and kitting out. "You stay here," he ordered the driver. The driver with no name looked relieved and settled back in the car. "Keep your phone on for messages." At that, Johnson turned to Periwinkle and said, "Ready?" He glimpsed again at the beanpole figure in black. Best not to underestimate him. He looked at ease.

Periwinkle nodded himself awake and took the sheathed knife from the boot, fastening it to his belt. They slipped into the wood. Memories shaped and activated by the woodland put both men on their guard, neither trusting the other. Johnson oozed confidence. Periwinkle weighed the man up. His gait spoke of a natural fitness. Johnson led the way. In the distance a dim light signified the location. They headed for it, veering here and there. Johnson started as Periwinkle overtook him and stopped and turned.

Touching his lips with his left forefinger, he signalled silence. He held up his hand. Then moving to his right ear, he indicated a sound ahead to the right and pointed towards its origins. Johnson understood that this was not the sound of the night. Someone was moving very cautiously in among the trees. He crouched down. Periwinkle did the same, staying put. A pencil light beam criss-crossed the woodland. They both laid down, barely breathing. The light moved again and then cut.

Browne's acute senses saw the light flicker, too. He prepared himself for battle. He moved away from the window to a peep hole and stared out, near the door, his trapdoor switch at hand. He moved quickly across the room. He switched the cassette radio on. A slight initial hum followed, a sound that told him the old tape machine he'd salvaged all those years back was operational.

In the wood Johnson's ears pricked up. He looked inquisitively at Periwinkle. Periwinkle had detected the low frequency hum. Johnson wondered if the other man's senses were well-honed. Was it beginner's luck?

Alice had a clear view of the front. The distance she gauged was around three hundred metres. She held her rifle. She wasn't satisfied that the noise she heard was an animal, it was too cautious. She lay low, too. Alice prided herself on being one of the four per cent who could hear a global hum. Odd sound in the woods. There it goes again.

The movement behind her had stopped. She estimated the distance at less than one hundred metres. It wasn't Browne in the woods as his shadow passed the window briefly and back again toward the door. Then she heard scratching. It wasn't fingernails on a blackboard, though equally annoying, a sound she associated with a beast of prey, a cat. Bugger the theories on the human ear, this sounded like an animal scratching. It made her skin creep. Then it was gone.

Dove, Penny and Freeman had fanned out further. Some blundering about occurred when Penny tripped over a stone. They stayed still for a minute or so, then moved on. Their instructions were to tap on the back window on arrival. Cover was plentiful. The huge stones at the back were adequate. Tap three times. Penny wanted to do that. He wanted to hum a pop song even if it was silly, both the idea and the song. He did anyway under his breath.

There was an opening before the large stones where they

would be visible to anyone on the south side. Dove hesitated; Freeman drew her pistol. Penny indicated that the stones formed a pattern and offered cover if they were prepared to dodge about. Were they deposited there by nature or by Mr Browne?

He moved off, and once behind the first stone, Lucy followed. Dove came last like a cat. Penny still hadn't achieved that alacrity, that ability to move in that way. Freeman had, and when he made to head for the next stone she'd already gone. This time they moved swifter. They covered the ground to the back window in seconds. Penny rapped three times. They waited.

Dove was having second thoughts about the safety of the place. He preferred the open, his memory of Alice's abilities clearer and his experience of them a rankling sore. A whisper said, "To your left and down."

Dove saw a small opening between the bushes, enough for a human to get through, even one of his stocky build. He dropped down and, without hesitation, crawled through. Penny followed as Freeman sat by with her pistol in hand. They were in a small room, the size of a decent cupboard. Browne stood across from them at a door, smiling. Penny whispered to Lucy to follow. She slipped through easily and all three shook hands with Matty. Freeman figured this man was full of surprises. She figured right. *Alice in Wonderland* came to mind, *White Rabbit*. Alice, she reminded herself, was out there. This was no psychedelic experience.

They entered the living space; the curtains drawn, a single light burning. There was a strange humming noise that Penny couldn't place. As he moved his head around to trace the source, Browne pointed to the cassette radio. The Dragon Slayer – St George Redux.

Dove introduced Freeman and did the talking. "You have a plan, Matty?"

Matty's face lit up. It recalled Penny's puckishness. "Yes. I want her out in the open, out of the woods and in the clearing." He indicated the front door.

Dove had faith in this man. He replied, "We've also got two men in the woods lying low. I have contact with one of them if a signal is okay."

"It will be. She must be quite a dodgy lass, this Alice?"

"Don't underestimate her. She's frightened of nothing."

"We shall see." Matty Browne gave them a knowing smile, his top teeth over his bottom lip. "Everyone's scared of something."

Freeman spoke. "I want her alive, if possible."

Dove texted Periwinkle. Johnson and he were prone on the woodland floor. Periwinkle turned away and read the text. Johnson edged closer; Periwinkle shifted. Periwinkle assessed what his friend Dove would do with Johnson. *Kill him. He's up to no good.* Periwinkle knew exactly what it was.

In the house, Freeman questioned Browne. "How do you propose to get her out in the open?"

"I hope to startle her. If your comrades can help flush her out into the clearing, the rest is going to have to be a joint effort. If we can disarm her, at least of firearms, that would be a bonus point. Rufus will do the rest."

Dove looked at Penny as if to say, 'we've got a nutter on our hands.' Freeman said, "Rufus?"

Matty looked across the room. In the old armchair Freeman saw a huge ginger cat. He stretched and then settled. His time would come. Freeman looked at Dove and Penny with an 'oh dear,' gesture. Penny was thinking about Silver. And Tammy.

"We can certainly offer to create hell when she is in the clearing." Dove looked sideways at Penny as he spoke. "Penny is a specialist in these matters." Penny didn't know whether to thank him or not. He acknowledged it with a nonchalant shrug.

Browne issued more suggestions, orders. "Get your men to push her this way, if they can. I'm going to sit by the window." He took Freeman's arm. "If she comes within a yard of the front door pull this lever."

Freeman considered. She didn't think sitting by the front window was a good ploy. She had no other ideas. They were indeed improvising. Penny's look said to trust this man. She did. She wanted to get her hands on Alice. Penny wanted that too. Freeman had said to Dove that if it comes to a fight, she's mine. She didn't want to be holding a bloody lever.

Dove simply waved his hands in a motion that implied 'we shall see'. He wasn't sure what Browne's next move would be.

Alice listened. The wood had gone quiet. The hum hadn't returned; the scratching noise gone. Relief that she wouldn't have to face a big cat like the man Trout, caused a shiver. She trembled, then adjusted the sights.

For a second, she thought she saw a figure beyond the window. As she did, Browne moved over to his cassette player. He began to twist the knobs. No distortion on the high, no hiss on the low, well, no electrical fizz. Browne patted the machine fondly. "Go to work." He switched on a cassette.

Johnson laid his firearm next to him. Periwinkle leaned and whispered in his ear, "Chicken of the Woods, Johnson!" He indicated to his left. Johnson turned to see in the half-light some fan-shaped sulphur-yellow fungi bracketing a pine. When he turned back, he was staring down the barrel of his own gun. Periwinkle took his rifle, leaving him with the knife only, a weapon with which he had proven he was good with. Periwinkle had second thoughts. He indicated Johnson's belt with the rifle. Johnson removed the knife from a holster at his waist and dropped it on the ground. Periwinkle kicked it aside.

Johnson didn't appear ruffled, more bewildered. Periwinkle ordered Johnson to lie down face up. His hand gestures were plain enough. Johnson obliged.

It was then they heard the sound of a cat, not a big cat this time, an eery miaowing, followed by scratching. It seemed to echo throughout the trees and bounce around in the night. Then it stopped.

Alice heard it too and froze. She couldn't discern its whereabouts. It was all around and up in the trees. She heard movement behind her, the same direction as previously. She began to move toward the house on her belly, rifle by her side. The noise started again, a loud caterwauling, even closer than before, accompanied by more movement from behind. She crawled faster and, despite the coolness of the wood, she began to sweat, then shiver, her whole body turning to ice.

Johnson took advantage of the noise and spoke. "What are you doing, man?"

Periwinkle made as if to hit him with the butt of the rifle, then stopped. "Johnson," he said, "if you want to die in this wood the same way Jim Trout did, that's fine, a shame, but fine."

Johnson had underestimated this beanpole of a man. Periwinkle's voice was unemotional. Johnson was in no doubt he would fulfil his promise – or was it a threat?

"Johnson, we're here to help capture a killer. If you have something to resolve with me, do it after. Right now, we have a job to do. Trout had it coming, to use the filmic phrase." Before Johnson could respond, he handed him the rifle, keeping the knife and pistol. The caterwauling stopped. Periwinkle took charge. His assumption was that his nephew would've told him if he was party to Trout's killing. Unless… That didn't bear thinking about. If Guess wasn't aware of Johnson's role in Trout's demise, that made Johnson a maverick at best, a mercenary at worse.

"Right, let's move. Our purpose is to flush her out, toward

the front door."

The sounds of the cat died away slowly in a whine. Alice could still hear it. She was now at the edge of the wood, the trees thinning out. In front was a jeep. The cat's miaows and whines bounced around her head. She tried to clear it. It permeated her whole body, top down.

Johnson moved first. He proceeded very slowly and crouched. Periwinkle followed without a sound. They spotted a shelter through the trees, a wild shelter, well-constructed. They separated, then circled around at a distance.

The cat started again. Periwinkle located the sound and beamed. This man Browne was a weirdo, according to Lucas. He had filled in enough of his history to know he was no mug. The cat thing was aimed at rattling the hunter. It had definitely shaken a memory for Johnson who couldn't work out how Periwinkle had so easily disarmed him. Yes, he would resolve it later. Periwinkle was the other man in the wood that night. *Damn.*

Alice was visible to Browne now and in some consternation. She was shuffling about, and her body movements indicated discomfort. He couldn't yet see the others.

Johnson and Periwinkle also had the cottage in sight. A shadow appeared at the window. Browne? Johnson thought it suicide.

Alice shouldered the rifle. The cat noise died down. It was deathly quiet in the wake of the sounds, sounds that reverberated from a loudspeaker, though Alice and her phobia had blanked that out in her fear. Her brain wouldn't process the fact. Stark fear and hatred for the feline species distracted her. The time added moments to Browne's life.

She focused on the window. Hissing, growling and yowling followed. Alice covered her neck with her scarf.

Penny and Freeman were out the back and working their way around, Dove inside and positioned by the door. Freeman insisted she was not going to be a bystander. Penny had demanded he accompany her. Dove chose not to argue. Freeman had opted out of the door switch. This was her case. At some point he would have to go out. Browne hadn't had time to explain anything about his bloody lever. "Just pull it when I say."

Rufus had disappeared. In the house, the screeching of the cat was barely audible. Outside it crept up on one and was chilling to the bone. Johnson whispered, "Creepy." A cat cry, like a baby, followed. The fight was on. Alice was in the clearing.

Johnson and Periwinkle stood up; the woman focused on her target though dithering. The seconds ticked away. Freeman had reached the corner of the cottage. Any move she made now she would have to do in the open leaving her exposed and vulnerable. On the other corner Penny was thinking the very same. He was trying to fathom a way to resolve that. Nothing came.

Chapter 42

Lucas Guess stayed up late. His partner was sound out. He wondered how Uncle Peri was doing. He estimated they would be in action right now. Johnson, he thought, had accepted the job rather too easily.

It was then he put two and two together. He began to wonder if it was his best man who took Jim Trout out. It had to be. Too late to contact Periwinkle. He did, anyhow. Had someone 'upstairs' authorised it? It was unusual for him, but a list of ifs and buts followed. What if his uncle recognised Johnson?

The issue was Johnson. Would he recognise his witness? Had he seen him? If anyone could take Alice Byron down, it was a team consisting of him and his uncle. He was fretting over his decision. Had he been party to the original hit he would've found an alternative. He shook it off. Too late. Both were professionals. They would work together.

Johnson saved Penny's life. Periwinkle had witnessed it.

At that moment, Penny was hovering at the corner of the

left side of the building, Freeman the right. Penny had ideas of his own that bordered on the crazy. So did Browne. Rufus was watching out of sight. Dove kept his focus on Browne's bloody lever just inside the door. Evidently it operated to open a trapdoor.

Guess sent a message, then poured a large gin and tonic, ice and lemon. He sat back and waited. Periwinkle had sent a one-word message, one that was not common parlance for him. It read: *Sorted.* Lucas grinned, put his gin down and raised his thumbs. Poor Johnson, a lesson learned. He hoped he let him live.

He wasn't the only one sitting up that night. Hart was on tenterhooks for Freeman and the lads. This was dangerous shit. In Otley, Tammy sat trying to read. She missed Penny. He hadn't called for two days. Silver mooched about, making the atmosphere even tenser. She decided to call him even though it was night-time. She toyed with the phone. He must be asleep by now, more likely supping Guinness with Dove. She put the phone down.

Guess poured another large gin and put his feet up on the coffee table.

Then, to quote Dove, all hell broke loose. Penny was on the corner in shadow, Freeman on the other peering round but still out of sight, her gun tucked away.

Alice focused on the shadow of Browne, who moved. The horrid cat-wailing started again. Rufus, pissed off with the competing unidentifiable cat, retreated into the gloom. Browne moved back to the window seat and picked up his book.

Penny's phone rang, his Agatha Christie chime, loud in the still of the night. Dove moved to the door, but Browne leaped up and yelled, "No, wait."

Alice, taken completely by surprise, swung the rifle to the left and fired, then in the same movement took a second shot at the window which shattered, spraying glass all over Matty.

Periwinkle nodded to Johnson and indicated forward. They both moved at pace. Penny appeared from the side of the building, then disappeared. Johnson fired a shot in the air as Freeman ran forward.

Alice refocused on the window. There were at least two men coming up behind, one on the side of the building, and it looked like fucking Penny. Was it Dove behind? No. Where was he?

Time to move, and fast. She headed across open ground and aimed inside, firing at the window with the pistol. Freeman came in from the side and Alice saw her too late. Freeman shoulder-charged her. The rifle fell. Alice swung the pistol around and fired. Freeman hit the deck. Penny feared Freeman dead, but she then leaped up and moved in as Alice turned her attention to Penny.

Periwinkle had broken from the woods at speed. Johnson too. Inside, Browne indicated to Dove to stay at his post. Alice reached the door, then everything changed. Freeman kicked her side on, her right leg parallel to the ground. The pistol fell. The body-blow connected with Alice's solar plexus. Alice was winded. Alice turned and saw Penny running toward her.

He was feeling foolish and wanted to make amends. How on earth had he forgotten his phone? Who would call at this time?

Freeman kicked Alice again with the ball of the foot high in the chest, then elbowed her. Alice staggered to the doorway and corrected, ready to counter. She withdrew her knife. The third kick was definitely illegal – as Dove remarked later – firmly in the lower back to the kidney. Freeman moved in again. Alice still came forward. The knife missed Freeman's body by a fraction.

The training took over. Alice took a step back to adopt a warlike stance. She was quite prepared to take on all comers, and one or two she might kill. The cat miaowed loudly. She turned. Alice heard someone shout, "Now!" and her world went black.

Freeman leaped backwards as the ground opened up before her and she fell heavily. Penny managed to skid to a halt as he too connected with Alice. Alice felt herself falling, sliding and then she hit the ground in a heap. She still held the knife out and tried to focus in the dark. Freeman stared at the pit before her and felt some relief she hadn't gone down there with Alice. Penny stood, his toes on the edge. For a second or so he wobbled, then stepped back.

Dove saw her disappear as he pulled the lever. True to form Dove said, "Fucking hell!" Browne acknowledged him with a sideways shake of the head and a wink, then got up from the chair, splinters of glass everywhere. Matty Browne was either mad or very lucky, or both. Yes, he and Penny had a lot in common.

Alice felt around the walls, measured the space, and looked at the bars into a dark tunnel. One wall was shiny and inclined. She tried to climb. It was impossible, then a huge bang blocked out the stars.

Periwinkle and Johnson saw her disappear and neither said, "Fuck me." Periwinkle simply smiled, and Johnson said, "Cool."

Browne ushered them indoors. Freeman spoke first. "I have to admit that when I got to the corner of the house, I hadn't a clue what to do next. If Penny's phone hadn't gone off, I would have had to charge her."

Dove laughed. He too shook his head. Not in the same manner as Matty Browne – more in disbelief, well, not really, this was Penny. He introduced Browne to Periwinkle, then he in turn introduced Johnson. "This is Johnson, he is interested in fungi."

Johnson grimaced. Browne looked confused.

"Where is she?" Freeman was keen to sew it all up.

Matty looked mysterious. "Remember what I said? She's being watched."

Periwinkle was more curious about the cat sounds. Johnson was still stewing over his amateurism. He wondered who the hell Periwinkle was.

"First comrades, a wee toast to a successful operation." Matty Browne took a bottle of old whiskey from the shelves and spread six glasses on the table. Dove, who had warmed to the man, felt a closer bond. Periwinkle signalled a no.

"This bottle has been waiting many years. I haven't really

drank since the night I was 'recruited.' Long story. Are you sure, Mr Periwinkle?" 'Mr' Periwinkle was sure. The rest tasted the whiskey, which Dove said was class.

Penny looked at his phone – Tammy. He texted: *Love you. Speak tomorrow.* He realised he meant today but decided against his better judgement not to correct it. He missed her. That was it. Tammy had saved the day.

Periwinkle excused himself and went outside. He texted Lucas: *Job done. Alice secured.* Lucas sent a thumbs up, drained his glass and went to bed. Freeman texted Hart with the same. He would let Saida know. Saida was already up and travelling north to keep Asma company.

Below the cottage Alice was shivering convulsively. It wasn't so cold. Another reason was at work.

Johnson joined Periwinkle outside and looked at him apologetically. He had some explaining to do. Periwinkle did the talking. "You need to talk to Lucas."

Johnson nodded. "Sorry."

Periwinkle went back inside, leaving Johnson to resolve his dilemma. Dove was nattering to Matty about his bizarre, yet highly effective, 'security' measures. Matty was topping up Dove's glass. They could have talked for hours had Freeman not suggested they make a move. Dove, Periwinkle and Penny particularly wanted a kip. Dove spoke for all.

"You can show Freeman Alice's cell." Dove wanted to see it also. Lucy and Dove followed Matty over to the sideboard. He lifted the flagstones. He switched a light on. They descended.

Penny's curiosity alleviated his tiredness. He followed in the labyrinth. None of them expected the sight that greeted them. They followed Matty along a tunnel and took a turning. Other tunnels ran off. At the end was the cell. In the far corner sat Alice in a foetal position, her body rocking, her face a mask of fear. Outside sat Rufus enjoying the moment. He watched her, moving toward the bars every so often as if to demonstrate his power, her fear. She shrunk back. He kept a safe distance all the same.

"How did you know?" Penny had to ask.

"The day she entered my cottage she ran into Rufus. It was apparent she suffered a serious phobia. Rufus, in his cat world, recognised her hatred, and fear too. He's a smart geezer."

"Gosh, Silver would get on with him." He missed her also.

Browne didn't ask who Silver was. He was quiet again. Many things had risen to the surface that day. He was recalibrating once more, with differing aims in mind. Yes, he was going to continue trawling his beloved countryside, search the disappearing karst lakes. Yes, he was still going to keep himself to himself, but not all the time. He handed Dove the mobile.

Dove passed it back. "It's still useable. You can continue to use it as long as you pay. Contact a few friends."

"I will."

The issue of poet's contract would need sorting. This time they had a live witness and would be able to track back. Alice appeared in an almost catatonic state as Freeman cuffed her. Freeman frogmarched her down to the road. Mute since the scene in the woods, she rocked back and forth in the car. Johnson called the driver who drove part way down the dirt road. Freeman asked Browne if he would be available for court, or at least to make a full statement. He nodded a yes but didn't look happy.

No one spoke of Alice. Penny surmised that there was nothing to say. Alice was now in her own world, one that had closed in when she fell down the hole. Freeman read her rights. Dove, aware of cross-border policing restrictions, knew it was bullshit. But, if it made Freeman happy, so be it. Should she have contacted a garda?

Johnson did begin to say something then clammed up. He was sizing up Dove. Simultaneously, he was beginning to feel some relief he hadn't removed his friend and ally Periwinkle – if it had been possible. It could well have been the other way round. He would tell all to Lucas and take the flak. Upstairs, someone had bypassed his boss. Lucas was going to be pissed.

Penny jumped in feet first. "You can stay at mine, Matty, when you come over."

Then they left. Browne didn't agree to anything. He simply waved goodbye from the roadside. As they drove away, daylight came. Browne turned away without waving, closing the door behind him. As Penny turned to look back, the lights in the cottage dimmed.

The return journey to the airport was slow and traffic busy. Periwinkle and Freeman travelled in the front car with their driver. Alice, cuffed and bound, stayed in total silence next to Johnson in the back. Johnson was nursing his pistol on his lap.

Penny sat next to Johnson. He said nothing to Johnson, the man who smiled at him on the stairs. Instead, he looked at Johnson in the mirror, then at Periwinkle questioningly, and Periwinkle's look told him, 'not now'.

Penny did ask Johnson how his memory was and if he could fly a B212 helicopter. Johnson didn't know what the hell he was on about. Neither did anyone else. He didn't answer. He was in for a rough ride back in London. Penny's memory of that day in London was clear. His two and two together resulted in a skewed odd number.

Freeman had left to collect her belongings and was back in no time. She decided she would definitely like to visit Eire again with Asma, a holiday on the west coast. Johnson briefed the pilot that there was to be six passengers. Dove and Penny said, "Four," together. They had some unfinished business waiting in Doolin. Periwinkle needed to get back, and he was happy to escort Alice with Johnson. He would escort them both back. Johnson would have to face Lucas Guess.

He studied Alice, not as tall as Maureen, but lithe, tattooed, with spiky hair and fair skin. Alice hadn't spoken since the scene in the clearance. Browne's cat thing was, as Penny put it, genius. Had it tippled her over the edge? He wasn't sure. Four of her potential hits were present at the end, all of them failed. That too must have had some effect.

Though her mind told her the cat noises were a record, sheer terror had taken over, the phobia so strong she couldn't close down on it. Rufus had finished her. The large ginger cat kept peeking in at her then strutting around outside the bars. His arrogance and posturing must have been hateful to her.

He was in his element.

She appeared to be in some sort of state of withdrawal, dissociated, a non-being. Penny made mental lists. His theories and guesswork were but that. He thought of stupor, catatonia, hebephrenia. Following that and an Internet search (to cancel out the lot and to contradict them), a supremely manipulative brain at work which was capable of vile torture, one lacking in any empathy. Beware. If it was the latter, then they hadn't heard the last of her.

He rang Tammy. He left a voicemail. "I'm coming back tomorrow, clear the decks for action. You did a fantastic job!"

Tammy picked up his message and her notes. No longer mystified by Penny's errant nature, she shook her head. She pocketed her USB stick and headed for lecture theatre three. It felt nice walking in the same corridors as Penny had. As she looked out at the car park, it did as he had said: burn like Brueghel's tower in the evening. They would take that walk along the old railway line, the one the politician's promise to look at reopening prior to every election. She hoped.

Chapter 43

McGann's was throbbing. There was a fiddle player on his own, playing jigs and reels. Gradually others would join in as he shouted out, "It's a polka, it's a jig," or waltz, or whatever. A uilleann piper took over, did a few tunes, then had to leave for another gig. A Scandinavian flautist joined in, adding what Penny discerned as Jazz Fusion. He tapped his foot to the improvisations. She had dropped in for the session. Dove was more comfortable with the sea shanties and folk tunes. Penny picked up the hooks and choruses and did his best.

An old man with a worn cloth cap took his penny whistle out of his tweed jacket pocket and did a tribute to Micho Russell. The virtuosity stunned Penny. Dove's loud whistling drowned out parts of *John in the Fog* and *The Boy in the Gap* but no one gave a damn. Penny was high, though the thoughts of Alice's capture whirled around in his head and took his attention away from the music. He wasn't sure even if Freeman had authority in Eire. In fact, she didn't. By now they would be in England.

Others got up and sang or played as the Guinness flowed. They ate in the pub – bacon loin and cabbage washed down with the black stuff. The landlord and landlady of the B&B

joined them for a 'couple' and the night rolled on. At the close of the night, the B&B couple bought a dram, and they toasted, "Slainte!"

The walk home was unsteady. The couple enquired how they got on in Gort. Penny said they loved it and the turlough was fascinating. "The whole of the coast is beautiful, captivating. I'd like to come back for a holiday." They were too addled to suss his glib reply. Then he said the wildlife is fascinating too… He was about to lecture them on snails then decided against it. He hoped too many questions didn't come their way. He changed the subject to music. That took them along the coast road singing and then they cut inland back to the B&B.

They were catching a coach to Dublin the next day and flying back to Leeds. Shannon was an option flying to Manchester, but Dove fancied a coach trip. Back in Blighty, as he called it, he aimed to settle the paperwork with Freeman, then rejoin Periwinkle in London. Both men wanted the lowdown on Johnson. Dove had sussed who he was by Periwinkle's sidelong glance and throat cutting gesture. Periwinkle's earlier text primed him. The full story would come later. For now, they both needed to get back to life.

Penny had a lot on his mind. He was mulling over his future when his phone rang. He didn't recognise the number and, about to ignore it, he chose to answer.

"Dr Penny, Lucas Guess."

"Hiya, Lucas, how's things?"

"Exactly what I was going to ask you. I hear you bagged the torturer's accomplice. It sounded like a good team effort. I know from my files Browne has a reputation for the bizarre.

I hear cats, or should I say catcalls and real cats, played a significant role. Don't want to detract from your efforts and your phone trick!"

Penny laughed. "It wasn't a trick, Lucas. It was a fuck-up. A cat and a Dragon Slayer did it all. We were bystanders."

"Whatever it was, it worked. Uncle Peri also solved an internal issue for me, to boot. Johnson is going to get his wrists slapped. He is too valuable a man to lose, even if he did work a contract for a ne'er-do-well upstairs."

"Ah, the Jim Trout case. Will Freeman be able to claim that one?"

"No. That's my main reason for calling. The case is cold, for us, closed. I want it kept that way."

"Fine, I'm quite happy to never hear his name again, Trout that is, not Johnson. As for your colleague, it doesn't pay to underestimate 'Uncle Peri'."

"Cool. Uncle Ninja… good luck. As I said before, if you need me, you know how to find me." He rang off.

What would he need Lucas for?

Chapter 44

Was Alice unfit for trial? There was some debate about her mental state. Consent to go to trial was immediate. Her killing to order indicated a thought process fit to plead. Her work was strategically planned and executed. That indicated premeditation. She had never spoken from that day in the pit. The judge entered a plea of not guilty. The case became complex. The judge's understanding of her crimes, and her payment for such, implied a rationale, despite her lack of empathy. The definition of criminal insanity was not clear, her culpability obvious. Alice Byron was very capable of rational thinking.

Throughout she remained silent. She stared around the courtroom not recognising anyone. Hart attended. He witnessed her vacant stare as did the others. They all thought she was looking for a verdict of insanity. Matty Browne spoke eloquently about mercenaries. He also detailed the events of that night. He couldn't wait to get back to his crested newts. He didn't stay over. He wished Penny good luck and said to visit if he came over. As he left, he winked. "Rufus is looking after the place on his own at the moment. I'm sure he'll manage."

"Hope he's got some decent music to listen to." They shook hands and parted.

Alice was heading to HM Prison Bronzefield on a restricted status basis then, pending further psychiatric tests, Rampton. There was no plea, no written testimony from her, nor any sign of interaction or understanding of what was going on around her. Dr Penny had his own ideas on her condition.

He wondered what Dove or Periwinkle would have done in that situation. She was either very brave or mad. When she looked at him that night as he charged from the side of the house, he still had his phone in his hand. It was that very moment of disbelief and a final miaow that allowed Freeman to get close.

He thought of Lance and what could've been; he thought of Maureen and finally Alice Byron, ex-squaddie, assassin, torturer and her fragmented self, and finally her phobia which she must have carried with her all her adult life. What brought in on? He tried to imagine.

Tammy interrupted his meandering. "Fancy a walk?" Before he could say anything: "There's a lovely walk down the old railway line. I hear there are some interesting holly hedges to view."

He had his coat on. They set off. As they slipped off the road up a few steps onto the old line, he reached out and took her hand. Neither were quiet, a condition Penny found alien. They babbled nothings. On their return Freeman was waiting outside. She handed him a large box.

"For you." Without explanation, she turned and left.

Indoors he opened the box. On top a note: *Please*

pass these books to Dr Penny. No signature. He started to go through, Tammy looking on. It was a treasure trove of valuable books, scholarly in the main, Edith Stein's thesis from 1916, with notes from the sender. Stein was murdered in the gas chambers of Birkenau in 1942. Notes clearly testified to the fact the reader had studied her work. There were other gems too. At the bottom wrapped up was a small parcel. Penny unwrapped it. A well-worn, well-thumbed children's book. Tammy laughed. "I read it when I was a kid." *Charlotte's Web.* Penny studied the story of Wilbur the pig and a barn spider, Charlotte. He looked at the lovely illustrations. Who will keep Alice company? He read a passage about swinging on a rope and loved the rhythm.

At the bottom, unwrapped, *The Little Prince.* He opened it. Inside the cover, a message from loving parents to an only child:

To Alice.
Happy Birthday.
Love you lots,
Mum and Dad

What did it teach Alice?

Freeman had an inkling Alice was faking, though her trauma had been apparent. Matty Browne with his crazy speakers in the trees and his big ginger cat had achieved what the British police force and the army failed to do. They had nailed a killer.

Browne, despite his initial reluctance to communicate, had proven to be a most amicable man, if not reserved. Johnson seemed okay too, though he too didn't have much to say. Johnson's sideways glances at Periwinkle suggested some pressure. In court he was excellent, eloquent, detailed in his description of the events, so much so the judge had more or less congratulated him. She wasn't sure who he worked for. When he said he was a civil servant, Freeman shrugged it off.

Lucas Guess was absent. He supplied the court with 'information' on the side. A medical examiner, an 'expert in the field', mentioned global aphasia several times, and stated the fact that Alice showed no signs of a stroke, though severe trauma might cause such a condition. He needed to do more tests.

The hogwash about the differing areas of the brain didn't fool Penny. He'd read *Livewired*. Wernicke's area, Broca's area, and the rest were there to fool the punters. Freeman's opinion was that Alice never played by the rules. No apparent signs of brain damage… A most interesting case. The specialist from Ashworth pissed Penny off so much, he said very loudly, "Isn't that where Dr Jimmy Saville worked?"

The judge looked sympathetic though warned him. She too was probably wondering about aphasia and if the so-called expert could put a meaningful sentence together. Perhaps working in those places did it to you? She asked him to put it in lay terms and he found that even more difficult. Penny and co realised he didn't have a clue.

Dove leaned over to Penny and whispered in his ear. "Should try showing her pictures of cats and tortured children."

Whatever, the ripple that ran through the courtroom that day signified disbelief. Alice was going to get a ticket out of mainstream prison so somebody could finish their doctoral thesis on aphasia. On the quiet, she was volunteering for it.

Freeman wished she'd shot her. Penny wished Freeman had shot her. Johnson wanted to kill her for varied reasons. Dove wanted to watch. Periwinkle, on the other hand, said something about graveyard poets: '*Some mute inglorious Milton here may rest*'. Or better still, '*Pressed by the Moon, mute arbitress of tides*'.

"Charlotte Smith," Penny announced.

Penny watched Alice. She didn't show any recognition, no emotion – not expected. This was a manipulative brainy person social media had taken to heart. Dove announced online they should spend a weekend with her at Bronzefield. They could dress her as Ophelia; show people around perhaps. Better to keep her locked away and in a secure prison.

The court case wasn't a farce. The judge was astute, sensitive to all the issues. Her insistence was Bronzefield where they might do their Boston (or whatever) aphasia tests. She had no doubt that Alice would manoeuvre a move due to her 'condition,' but she wasn't going to give in easily. Evidence from Lance's computer provided enough. Lance had left the world one good thing. His detailed log of their interactions was in a sense hearsay evidence but joined up the dots. Though the laptop may have ended up on a road, the content was saved.

His mum declined to attend.

Alice was guilty. Of that there was no doubt. To a few

in the courtroom she was not insane. She had planned these killings. She was scholarly. She was able to hold a job down too. Her army records read well, up to a point, then there were the suspected atrocities, and though not proven, her drumming out indicated their suspicion of her cruelty to humans and animals alike. The judge, who had studied everything and had consulted with Hart's new friends at the CPS, finished with a comment that nearly brought the house down and, according to Penny caused a momentary flinch from the accused. It was fairly abstract. To the crew who brought her in, it was apt.

"The cruelty this woman has shown to man and beast is despicable. We hope this woman never sees the light of day again. Alice Byron seems to live in the dark and that may suit her, sadly alongside cats, a species she has no time for."

The press (a few only) made hay of it. (Penny preferred catnips.) The 'cat lady' was locked away. After Bronzefield she was heading for Rampton.

Chapter 45

Asma and Lucy Freeman did the cooking. Everyone was on first name terms. Tammy volunteered to help. Asma shooed her from the kitchen. The food was fabulous. (Dove said that before Penny could.) Penny wasn't as abstemious as the previous meal, though he was on his best behaviour for a short while. That was a relative thing.

They decided not to mention that night. Tammy, however, raised the issue of her phone call which Penny had detracted from. Lucy took her aside. Tammy was also mute for a short while when Lucy explained that the call had actually created the diversion required. She snuggled up to Penny who was being incredibly silly, then realised he might think she approved of his behaviour. Penny refused to leave the stage.

She moved and sat with Saida and Periwinkle. The dress code was 'come as you are'. The wardrobes that night would've rattled Alexander McQueen. Murphy was there with his wife, Siobhan. He called home twice to check the babysitter was 'still alive.' Siobhan wore a simple black dress. Murphy sported a suit with a much-admired Nehru-retro style collar. Olivia Jarrett looked like a different person in jeans and a black top, and a simple jet choker.

Hart looked splendid in a pair of non-pressed jeans, and T-shirt, though still Paul Smith. Saida was in traditional costume, which sent Penny back in time. When he looked at her, she said, "no prayer mat." Once again, he had to explain the story… whoops. Periwinkle's waistcoat was Penny's favourite, his doeskin. Dove nearly came in uniform but decided at the last minute his corduroys and casual shirt enough. His stories captured the atmosphere, tales of comradeship.

Lucas had declined, but volunteered Johnson. Freeman was fine with that. He too had some delightful stories to tell. His outfit was out of their wage packet or pension. He spent some time nattering to Periwinkle who looked extremely pleased.

All in all, a brilliant night. Then the phone rang.

Hart looked around the room and reflected. Maureen, Alice – Wright and Byron – had affected them all (infected, he thought initially). They had impacted on so many lives, and they had done so without remorse.

Some of their deeds he would never know about, but there was those he was aware of in Loftus, relatives of the dead, some still carrying the scars, the families, Lance's mum. He thought of Jack the ex-matelot and Dove's mate, dead, Liz and young Max, also dead. He looked at Johnson and wondered what he was thinking. Jim Trout? Johnson looked back. Yes, he was deep in thought. Hart now knew the truth.

Hart thought everyone seemed to be looking at him. Yet

it was Freeman's phone that rang. It was 11:30.

It was as if their own lives had become fragments. The corpus of folk gathered in that room were holding one another together, bound by two people who had shown little care in their lives, had killed for pleasure and for gain. Hart looked around and thought that the full breadth of their crimes will never be uncovered. There wasn't enough time or the money to pursue them. Other folk – the victims' friends and relatives – will report in and join the leftovers of the assassins' pleasure and trade and would need support.

These people gathered were friends too. They had found each other in a time of trouble for them all, Penny with his trauma, and he with his realisation he was in the wrong trade. In another sense, though difficult to use the word positive, first the twins Peter and Annabelle, then Maureen and Alice, had brought them together. His life had changed. What was fragmentary and disunited and an illusion was taking shape. The anxiety was lifting. Pandemics came and went, knife crime and murder escalated. As for the former, the news headline warning of a 'Twindemic' of flu and Covid caused Hart to shudder, after which he forced a smile. He lifted his glass and managed to say, "To friends!" He looked at each in turn and then toasted, "There is enough friendship and talent in this room to beat the greatest odds!" He thought to himself it sounded quaint, silly, but glasses were raised and put down as everyone cheered as he spoke again. "And to a cat named Rufus!" More cheers followed. He looked at his unpressed jeans and smiled.

Then the room was silent. He glimpsed at Penny and tried to smile. Penny was looking at Tammy. Dove and Periwinkle too stared at each other as if to say where do we go from here? Saida held Periwinkle's hand and stared down. She had moved on. Hart had moved on. Murphy and Jarrett had also been there, but in a sense were beginning their lives. Murphy, the man whose intelligence sent them to Ireland; Jarrett whose support for Penny while in the cells had carried him through. The word stalwarts came to mind.

Asma had come from the kitchen and held Lucy's arm as she picked up the phone. Freeman cuddled Asma and then put the phone down. "It's only work. It can wait until tomorrow."

Penny eyed his phone and signalled that a taxi was waiting. He and Tammy insisted they saw themselves out. The hugs were warm, and a cab beeped outside.

Freeman decided to wave goodbye. At the back window she saw Tammy get into a cab, Penny into another, one turning into the Otley road, the other towards Headingley.

She never waved.

Acknowledgements

Many thanks to The Literary Consultancy and Jonathan McAloon for reading early drafts. Jonathan's help was a key moment for me.

Thanks also to Bev O'Connor at 'Craggy Isle' near Doolin and that beautiful trip to Coole Park in Galway. An inspiration!

Above all, I'm grateful to the whole team at Cranthorpe Millner for their support and hard work correcting my errors.